More praise for devorah major's

An Open Weave

—⁓—

"With the publication of *An Open Weave*, devorah major, an African-American first-time novelist, presents a voice well worth celebration . . . passages of intoxicating language . . . a fine book, showing more than a hint of brilliance to come."

—*Seattle Weekly*

"Vivid, concise descriptions of revelatory moments distinguish major's first novel . . . Some of these stories are gems."

—*Publishers Weekly*

"Highly recommended."

—*Library Journal*

"There is much metaphor here and a lot of magic, the ordinary easily made extraordinary. major's poetic writing style is engaging and enriches the tale."

—*Quarterly Black Book Review*

An Open Weave

Weave

devorah major

BERKLEY BOOKS, NEW YORK

AN OPEN WEAVE

A Berkley Book / published by arrangement with
Seal Press

PRINTING HISTORY
Seal Press edition / September 1995
Berkley edition / February 1997

The Putnam Berkley World Wide Web site address is
http://www.berkley.com/berkley

ISBN: 0-425-15665-6

BERKLEY®
Berkley Books are published by The Berkley Publishing Group,
200 Madison Avenue, New York, New York 10016.
BERKLEY and the "B" design
are trademarks belonging to Berkley Publishing Corporation.

PRINTED IN THE UNITED STATES OF AMERICA

10 9 8 7 6 5 4 3 2 1

Acknowledgments

—m—

THANK YOU TO EACH OF my parents who read the first manuscripts and asked the questions I needed to hear. Thank you to my agent, Janell Walden Agyeman, who has shown so much confidence in my work. Thanks also to my editors, Holly Morris and Faith Conlon, who worked with me to make the work stronger. And thank you to my children, Yroko and Iwa, who despite missed meals, distracted conversations, and canceled outings because I was chasing a deadline, remained excited about their "mama's book."

An Open Weave

[signature]

Birthday

—∿—

THE FIVE OF THEM SAT around that small hilltop house fussing, and fussing at each other's fussing. They let the coffee grow cold, then made fresh coffee, and then left that untouched, too. A birthday cake was resting on the heavy oak table near the center of the house's main room. It was late and they all knew that they were going to have to start the dinner pretty soon, with or without the birthday girl, Imani. Off to one side of the room, Ernestine Moore was, despite her house full of people, lying down on the plush double bed she shared with her daughter Iree. Her loose grey hair was braided into short squared-off plaits and her sightless eyes were pointed towards the loom. Her loom was empty, no cloth hanging from its harnesses, no thread winding through the shuttles. Next to the loom was a basket full of dark, blood-red yarn, which she was going to use to make a winter cape for Imani. Everyone always said that Ernie's folks must have been from some sort of

1

Masai tribe because she was so long and thin, but that evening, she looked shriveled and showed all of her seventy and then some years.

"She got to do this one without me," Ernie had resolutely said before she lay down, turning her head away from the four adults clustered around the table.

The house had only one other room besides the main room and bathroom. That was Imani's room, which sat off to the south side and was always full of sun. There was little furniture, except for an oversized chest with a round mirror above it that Imani usually kept covered with one of Ernestine's woven cloths, and a thin, smooth mattress lying in the corner. The main room contained everything else the family needed. At one end was the bed, at the other was an overstuffed dark green sofa, a table with a radio sitting on it, and a small fireplace. Ernestine's loom sat near the center of the house, across from the door. From there Ernie could sit and listen in to folks on the couch, or be close to whoever was sitting at the big shiny oak table. The table was almost never empty. Family or friends, someone was sure to be visiting the house and leaning over the table, eating, talking, doing school work or playing dominoes. The table was built to last generations and large enough to sit eight people comfortably, and twelve with a bit of squeeze. On the west wall of the room there was one of those serious cooking stoves. It had big gas burners that could provide a stew-pot boiling flame just as easily as it could produce a whisper of candle fire for simmering a slow bubbling soup.

The conversation had stopped suddenly moments before as each person avoided another's eyes, and tried to believe that everything was normal. Al sat, in his usual board-stiff manner, at one end of the table. Zelma, his wife, was standing in back of him resting one hand on his shoulder. Zelma was always one to keep a conversation going. Whatever the situation she always had a short joke, laughing memory, or long story handy. Her held tongue made the house eerie with its quiet.

Zelma, Al, Ernestine and Jeremiah had been family friends so long that most people in the town believed they were sisters and brothers by blood. Over twenty-five years had passed since Jeremiah had introduced Zelma to Al. Inside the Moore house only Al still called her Zelma; everyone else called her Zulie. Iree never liked the name Zelma, so she just renamed her one day, and like everything in that house, from the smell, to the songs they sang, it stuck to Zelma's skin and her heart. Al had that chocolate "good black don't crack" skin. He'd been able to hold back the years more than any of the others. Although he rarely took time to compliment himself, he was proud of the way he had resisted wrinkles and grey. Zelma, on the other hand, had a round full face crowned by a soft halo of silver kinked hair that contrasted with her finely lined walnut skin.

Ernestine's youngest brother Jeremiah was

lounging in the overstuffed sofa, looking and acting all salt and pepper, cantankerous as ever. His
given name was Jeremiah, but his family and closest friends called him Mico most of the time. Jeremiah had retired a few years before from a formal
job as school custodian, and had become the
neighborhood's fix-it man. He had been taking
apart and putting together appliances and machines since he was a child. Now he ran an infor-
mal business out of his home. Al was always
threatening to hang a sign outside Jeremiah's
home proclaiming Mico's Fix-It Shack. But everybody knew that Jeremiah's habit of barking one
moment and purring the next would chase away
any but the most committed of customers. Jeremiah fixed things because he liked to always be
doing something. He rarely sat still, claiming that
he could only think clearly with some kind of tool
in his hand. Now only his empty hands, clenching
into fists and then reopening, showed how worried
he was about his grandniece Imani.

Imani's mother Iree was pacing up and down
the room, pausing to perch on a chair before
standing back up and pacing again. She had dark
brown eyes that sat out from her head kind of
bulblike and made you want to turn away when
she aimed them at you. Few found her pretty; she
was too thin, like Ernestine, her adopted mama,
was at that age. Every few minutes she went to the
door and said, more to herself than to anyone else,

"It's so warm and nice, just perfect for today. I guess I'll walk around outside for a little."

Most of the time she didn't go anywhere, she just stood in the doorway and looked out. Not that there was much to see outside. The land was mostly flat, and mostly dry, resting between the desert and the ocean. Ernestine and Iree's home was on top of one the town's few long sloping hills. A scattering of one-story wooden and stucco houses spotted the hillside. While most had yards, few people planted trees or lawns in front of the houses. The land was too grey and dry, and most people didn't feel it was worth the effort.

The porch of the Moore house had nine wide, deep stairs leading to the carved front door. A flat wooden bannister sat on either side of the stairway. Despite Ernestine's insistence that the entire house be white, Jeremiah changed the bannister color each year, from bright yellow, to dusty red, to its current burnt umber. When Imani was small, she and her best friend Amanda used to spend hours setting up fantasy worlds on those steps. Ernestine would have Iree carry a chair out to the cramped porch landing, even though it blocked off part of the front door, so she could "keep an ear on Imani." She didn't like the idea of Imani exploring her hometown any sooner than absolutely necessary. Ernestine was sure that the town, while safe, would not welcome Imani or appreciate her talents.

The town of Buttonhole had never been able to

grow into a proper city. It started off as a settling place for black men who had moved farther and farther West after the Civil War, some as cowboys and others as retired soldiers. Later they had brought their wives, built houses and took up farming or continued on as ranchhands at nearby homesteads. More than a few of them had owned their own homes, but in recent years the young people had begun to sell off the land and move to Los Angeles or San Diego where there was "more action." Over the years the community had grown very slowly; on the southern perimeter a close-knit Mexican community took root and a solid group of whites gradually moved into the core of the city. While Buttonhole had nothing that made it particularly attractive, it was close enough to large cities to be a good place to live for those who preferred to have some solitude, but not isolation. Most people kept to themselves; they knew but could easily ignore their neighbors.

The road was still empty; no sign of Imani in the growing darkness. Lights were beginning to flicker on in the nearby scattered houses. Iree came back in and settled on the bed next to Ernestine. She began to rub her mother's feet as she looked hard into the woman's smoke-grey, sightless eyes. Ernestine was and wasn't Iree's mother. Iree was the daughter of Ernie's best friend Sibyl, who died when Iree was about four years old. Sibyl had an aneurism that had burst inside her brain and bled her to death. Iree was there when it happened.

Some say that having to show her mother through the door to the next journey was what made her so strange, what marked her. When it happened, Ernie didn't think twice about what to do with young Iree. She had been helping to raise somebody's children, whether her mama's, her brother Jeremiah's, or even Zelma's, since she was thirteen years old. So Ernie just naturally took Iree in with no authority but her own when Sibyl passed on.

It was a good thing she did, too, because something had happened during the birthing of Iree that gave her a strange kind of epilepsy. Iree would pass out anywhere and sometimes stayed in a coma for three or four days. It didn't show up in a major way until after Sibyl died, but from that day on she'd get to falling out and foaming at the mouth and then just lying still like the dead for days on end. It frightened most people, but Ernie always acted like it was ordinary, as normal as some people having hay fever every summer or getting the flu every winter.

Iree got up from the bed and moved to the couch where she sat rigidly, balanced on its edge. Imani had been gone since she left for school early that morning, as the sun broke onto her seventeenth birthday. Now, as the moon rose pale and puny from the dark, clear, northern sky and the night wore on, one by one, each elder began to tell stories about Imani, hoping to reach out and bring her home safely.

Iree began, speaking softly, telling how Imani

was so reliable, sure to be there to meet her at the bottom of a long hill, or to open the front door before Iree's feet even touched the bottom of the stoop, bursting on her mother, smothering her with laughter and chatter and hugs. Al joined in, repeating for what seemed to be the hundred thousandth time about how he'd been spooked by Imani's eyes from the first day he'd seen them stare back at him, too clear and probing for any nine-day-old baby, and how it was just like her to disappear like this on her birthday. Jeremiah retold his story about the first domino game that Imani won, beating his friend Jonah in three rounds when she was only seven years old. And finally Zelma started in on the story of the night Imani was born, seventeen long years before:

"Yes, I remember helping her come in, kind of holding the door open for her, if you will. It was an accident, my being here that night, one of those pre-arranged accidents of fate that makes you climb a longer and steeper hill than you thought you were ready for, and sometimes ends up taking you clear across the planet."

Al caught her hand as she moved around the table, fixing everyone's plate. She kissed him on the forehead and went on with her story. "Yeah, that was some night. Back then, I hadn't stopped straightening my hair yet, spent hours keeping it just so. I kept it straightened and pulled back in a bun most times. Anyway, that's how I wore it the night when Imani was born. There I was, sitting with Ernestine and Iree and always-got-one-or-two-feet-in-his-mouth-Jeremiah-Mico-Jefferson, when suddenly Iree gave out this shudder and whistled a long thin stream of air. It was then that I realized that while we were sitting pushing around domino tiles, Iree had been measuring her breaths and was getting ready to push out that baby, close to two months early!

"Remember, Ernie? You were tying off the ends of that baby blanket you had finished weaving the day before. That yellow blanket with the soft white roses at the ends and the yellow and white tassels. And Mico, Mico you was teasing as usual, laughing and pulling on your beer."

"Yeah, Zulie, I remember. Mico had just played bogus . . ."

Mico cut in laughing, "That's not how I remember it."

Ernestine drew in her breath. "Well you and me don't usually agree on memories, do we?"

Zelma smiled broadly. "It was just like now, Ernie. You fussing at Mico, and Iree and I laughing at the two of you. At least it seemed to me that we were both laughing. But now, remembering back, I can see Iree just tight smiling and holding her laughter, blowing it out softly like a bell. So it was and wasn't a surprise when it all started happening. But then, that's how things always are here. Somehow, more than anywhere else, you always seem to know what's going to happen in this house right the instant before it happens. So it made sense to me when I realized what was happening right then and there, and I knew, like I know when to pull a corn bread out the oven, or pick a blackberry right before the juice bursts, I knew there wasn't going to be any doctor. No, just us three bringing a baby, who was in way too much of a hurry to come into this world.

"It was all right somehow. I mean I knew it would work out. Of course, Al, every time he thinks about that night, he calls out some more thanks to God for that little baby not dying. Don't you, sweetie?" Zulie sat down next to Al, who just shook his head in response.

Ernie chuckled. "Al, if you'd figure out how to match your faith to your book learning you might just get it. There wasn't no way my Imani was going to die, nor Iree neither. And you know why, because one and one is going to be two no matter how many books you have or haven't read. When it turns into three, why it just ain't one and one no more, no matter how you count it."

Al got up from the table with his plate and moved to the couch, tired of once again being the butt of their jokes. Zulie followed him and resumed her story:

"Anyway, there we were relaxing around the table and then suddenly Iree let out this whistle and Ernie raised up off the loom bench and said, 'It's time, Zulie, help me make the bed right.'

"Well, I pulled back the bed covers and put up some pillows so Iree could lean back. I was terrified for the first few minutes that she would have one of her epileptic fits, until I realized that's why I was there. Not to be Ernie's eyes, Mico could do that, but to keep Iree in the room. There she was with the baby pressing through her wide-hip middle and I was supposed to hold on to her mind, make it ride with mine, not let it pull away and dive into another time, a different world. I was never so scared before or since as that moment when I realized my task. And then Mico, you just came up behind me where I was standing holding on to a corner of the bedspread with my mouth all slack, and you put your hand on my back real soft and whispered, 'Glad you're here, Zulie.'

"That was all, then you started rearranging the bassinet which you'd just fixed up and painted. Well, I didn't know exactly what to do, so I just sat down on the bed and grabbed Iree and started to chattering about my first time with Garvey. I told her, 'Garvey didn't want to take his place on this side of the mountain at all. If he coulda stayed inside me for another few years I swear I do believe he would have.'

"Iree started smiling and I felt her hands trembling. She looked at me real hard and was moving her mouth but nothing was coming out. I felt her pains coming right up from my inside and I almost jumped out of my skin. I mean suddenly, all of gravity was just pressing out from between my legs, and my back was sore, and the wave was about to knock me over. I just started to breathe and never stopped talking. Yeah, I was going on about Garvey and saying anything just to keep the words going like water out the tap. I told her:

" 'Yes, girl, he didn't want to rush out like yours there. I think we got us a girl baby, what you say Ree, I can tell, got us a girl. Now you just breathe here with me, you just don't let go of my hands, and let's just swallow us some air and feed it to that baby.'

"Iree, she didn't take her eyes off of me, and as her breath released I felt the pain roll off of me too. Then I heard Ernie close at my ear saying, 'Don't take it all through you, Zulie, she'll give it to you to carry and leave. You gotta hold her *here*, not sail with her.'

"I raised my voice then; I was so scared. I swear I wanted to pee so hard you'd a thought the baby was pressing on my pelvis. Now, I had already had my five babies, and I was too old to have another one, even by proxy. So I just grabbed all of my me I could find, and raised my voice up: 'Ree, Ree, you got to feel the opening to let the baby out. You got to feel it. See the hole getting wider and just pulling back. Now I'm getting up . . .'

"By then I was screaming at her. My voice was so high and thin I swear I thought Iree was holding my throat closed. I yelled, 'You're walking with me across this room, and you gonna tell me what you see inside this room and not go nowhere else!' "

Iree smiled in spite of herself and reached out,

pulling Zelma closer to her. "Zulie, you were acting crazy, yelling in that silly voice. Where did you think I was gonna go?"

"That's just what you said then, girl," Zulie answered. "Then you started wanting to know all kind of details about Garvey, why he didn't want to get born, which wasn't what I had said at all. I didn't say he didn't want to get born, I just said he wasn't in no big hurry. Boy ain't never hurried, won't hurry, can't hurry, can't even spell hurry. Just when I was trying to explain this to you again, I felt another contraction coming.

"This time I only got a piece of the contraction. But Iree you pulled my face close to you and your eyes split way back to my brain and for a minute I could of sworn that we were in a cool breeze outside the house, but the house was gone, and all that was there was some dry grass and a big oak tree. We were both outside. I was the same, but when I looked at you, Iree, you were different, almost transparent. I mean, I could see that baby pressed sideways, pushing the wrong way to get out. Even though I didn't see any walls I kept talking like we were still inside. I called to Ernie, praying she'd answer me, 'Ernie, tell Iree we walking in here. And tell her she's got to get that baby to turn itself right.'

"Then soon as the words came out my mouth there was Ernie turning those smoke eyes at me and saying like she could read all the way through Iree, 'Which way was the head facing, Zulie?'

"I don't know how I knew, but I knew for sure that the baby's head was kind of twisted to the right, and not only that but that the cord was over its face and would probably catch and choke the baby when it was pushing time."

Al cleared his throat. "Lucky, that's what you three were, damned lucky."

Zulie ignored him and kept on with her story. "Then Ernie got me to help Iree sit down. She slipped off all of Iree's clothes and then had her to lie flat on the bed. Then she started to rub her back and had me to hold Iree's shoulders still while she, calm as could be, started rubbing Iree's too-small womb and running her long fingers up and down the length of Iree's belly.

"Now this all took, seemed like hours, but since there was nothing happening but the baby coming too early, and Mico putting wood on the fire, well, time didn't have a hold on us. Iree and me were just breathing with the contractions and she was trying to pull me in with her and take her pains for her, and I was trying to chatter on about having babies, and Ernie was just running lines across the belly and humming the same words over and over, 'Come on, pretty girl, swim around. Come on, pretty girl, swim around. You gonna rush into this world, you better come in straight. Come on, pretty girl, swim around.'

"I was going on, trying to keep Iree occupied while Ernestine did her work. I remember Ernie just easing away from the bed and me watching

Iree's belly until I saw that the baby had adjusted and the head was dropping straight down into Iree's groin. I know what you're thinking, Al, but I'm willing to swear I saw it, on any book or statue you choose to believe to be so holy that it can't hold lies.

"The pains were coming harder and longer, deeper. I held her hands tight like I used to do Garvey when I took him downtown, crowded store shopping. I breathed her in and held her till she snatched back her hands."

Iree cut in, "Zulie, you almost broke my fingers. I couldn't of gone anywhere. I didn't leave the room all night, you were the one who was flying."

Zulie drew in her breath. "I know what happened, Iree. I was there. I spent the rest of the night with you, we walked and sat and lay together. I felt every contraction just before it started to swell, and you sent me bouncing around the house, rolling down the hill, but you stayed in your now time. When it came time for Imani to come out, why Iree you rose up off the bed where you'd been laying, naked as you please, and walked outside into the night. I grabbed one of Ernie's cloths from a hook on the wall and ran after you. I threw it over your shoulders as you moved down the porch stairs. Mico, you came out after us laughing to cover your worry."

Jeremiah sighed. "Iree, if the truth be told you are one crazy child, that's all I got to say. Iree, you know you got alla my heart, but you are one crazy child."

Ernie spoke up, "Hush old man. You never didn't understand nothing. Iree ain't no kind of crazy, Mico, just different, special is all. Anyway it was fine to bring a baby out in the night air. There was too much light and smoke in the house anyway."

Zulie got up and walked over to Ernestine. "Well I thought it was crazy, too. I'm not gonna lie. We watched Iree kneel underneath that old oak tree and start to digging a hole with her bare hands pursing her mouth and whistling each time her hands filled with soil. I went to stop her digging and bring her back inside, but Ernie, you held me on the porch. Then you walked down the steps and laid a sheet out on the ground, next to that hole.

"Iree walked onto the sheet silent as could be. Then Mico went and propped her up on one side and I walked down and took the other side. She squatted against us and pushed and blew and blew and pushed and didn't make even a whine until all of a sudden this scream swirled up from her middle, and her mouth dropped open, and she arched back her head and howled until the leaves on the trees shook, and my ears liked to fill with the blood of her cry. And then this tiny screaming baby slid into Ernie's waiting hands. Iree had that baby, less than five pounds, pale and curly-haired and open-eyed.

"Imani, why she hardly took a moment to cry a welcome to her new world before she settled on Iree and started to suckle her breast. Then when the baby was all the way situated, and the cord was cut, Iree just wrapped that baby in her mama's shawl and scooped up the afterbirth with her free hand and pushed it into the hole she had dug. Then she walked back into the house and fell asleep while little Imani just cuddled up close to her mama and looked all around. It seemed like she already had a house full of stories to tell."

Zulie paused. "Yes, that was one long and scary, wonderful night."

Everyone was quiet. Al had moved back to the table. Mico picked up his fork and began to eat. Ernestine got up from the bed and sat down at one end of the table, feeling for her dish and stirring the food around her plate. They all sat without speaking, remembering that tiny baby you could almost hold in one hand. They tried to eat calmly, and pretended not to be watching the door, waiting for it to open so they could each hold and scold Imani, finally knowing that everything was all right.

Daughters

———✹———

THE TWO GIRLS WALKED EASILY next to the shore-
line, shoulders grazing from time to time. Imani,
often just a step ahead, would stop, bend down
and dip her hand into the foam every few waves
before continuing on. Her ankles were covered
with wet salt after each swell, and she, like the
tide, was alternately laughing and frowning. Her
words were tiny bells against the deep breaths of
the ocean.

"Here," she opened her arms and spun around
Amanda, "this is all yours."

Amanda reached out and touched Imani's
shoulder. Amanda's eyes had once again filled
with tears and her face showed red blotches
against the opal sheen of her skin.

"Imani, you're always giving away stuff as if
you own it," Amanda spat out.

"I do!" laughed Imani, running to the edge of
the warm foamy waves glistening in the autumn
moonlight. "My mother gave it to me, and hers

gave it to her, and since your mother isn't back yet, why I thought I'd just give it to you myself, 'specially since you're always talking about everything you don't have."

"Yet." Amanda smiled a bit.

"Yet," Imani agreed as they resumed their walk down the shore, squeezing the warm soft mud sand up between their toes, feeling the tickles as the water and sand slid out in the last pull of wave. Imani was tall, slim and chocolate, her hair a crown of short tight dreadlocks. Amanda, on the other hand, was wide and short, her hips rounded like her face, and her hair becoming a loose halo of kinks flattened in front by a wide headband. They walked for what seemed like hours, not saying anything except when Imani pointed out a particularly bright star or when Amanda located an unbroken shell caught in the spray of light that travelled from moon through water. She would pick up one shell, show or give it to Imani, then a few steps later, pick up another and place it in her pocket or return it to the land. Sometimes she traded off, casting one away to pocket the latest.

"Mandy? Why do you do that? I mean why not just wait till you find the perfect one and save that one?"

"If you don't like how I pick out shells, pick your own out. Otherwise leave me be, I'm not bothering anybody."

The air was full of Mandy's salt, and her fear

rustled around her like the soft cotton of her loose flowered blouse.

"Imani, I'm pregnant."

Imani breathed in.

"You know that's the two hundredth time you've said that. . . . So now what?"

Earlier that day Imani had seen Mandy and Jerome leaning on the Kiss 'n' Tell wall. That's what everyone called the side of the high school which was girded by an eight-foot concrete wall and shaded by a string of thick oaks. Even though several trees had been felled, and a mural painted to brighten up the wall and discourage its use as gossip and fondling corner, it remained the most popular school-grounds meeting place for every kind of best friend and secret telling. The wall was where Geraldine had told Jeannette about her first time doing it, and Geraldine had told Amanda, and so then, of course, Imani knew. The wall was where Farika told Sonny about being afraid for her mother who had lupus, the disease that seemed to make the body hate itself, and although it would not, it seemed, kill her mother, it made her mother want to die. It was where Amanda first met Jerome, who was hanging out to see if Sonny had finally asked Farika to go with him. He had, and Farika had said yes.

That afternoon when Imani saw Jerome hovering around Amanda, she knew something was wrong. Amanda wasn't moving her lips, just looking at Jerome, and Jerome returned her gaze unflinchingly, but with full eyes as if he were about to cry. Imani had decided to walk to the front of the school and sit on the wide steps. She had been waiting there for over an hour when Amanda walked up silently and stood red-eyed in front of her.

"Imani, come over to Mrs. Meecham's with me."

Mrs. Meecham owned a variety store on the far side of the city. She had hired Amanda as a clerk because she didn't need to be paid too much and was humble enough; a quiet girl with concentrated manners and good work habits. Mrs. Meecham held tight to her beliefs and was rarely troubled by conflicting fact. When she was told that chain drugstores would put her out of business, she clenched her teeth, spat on the floor and swore she'd hold on to her dying day. And hold on she did. Mrs. Meecham smoked cigarettes, drank warm beer and knew almost every customer by name. She also kept a back room, really an over-sized closet, with a single bed that she provided for Amanda ever since she understood that the girl needed a place to run away to and find refuge.

The girls left the school and rode the bus to Mrs. Meecham's Variety Plus without a word. They walked down the narrow alleyway to the clean stark storeroom with one small window set high, next to the ceiling, a crawl space for sunlight. Amanda worked two hours while Imani sat on the cot eating a crisp pickle and paging through an old fashion magazine. Amanda came back for a break and sat on the bed next to Imani, listening to her critiques of each model's make-up or hairstyle. Just then Mrs. Meecham burst in the room.

"Amanda Bresely, where did you put the rose water? Serena wants a bottle. I know it came in yesterday, I just don't understand . . ."

She paused, noticing Amanda's swollen eyes and hunched back.

"Are you sick, child? Did that boy hurt you? I told you to—"

Imani jumped up and took Mrs. Meecham's hand. "Come on, I saw the rose water when we came in," she said, ignoring the fact that she hadn't walked through the store that day. She led Mrs. Meecham down the center aisle, watching the elderly woman's eyes scan the shelves without seeing and finally was able to call out, "There, you just passed it. See? Right next to the hair spray. I guess the perfume shelf was too full."

"Thank you, Imani. You always can find things in this store faster than me. You have got at least two sets of eyes."

"You're welcome. I guess I'll get back to Amanda. She's not feeling well," Imani sang out and ran towards the back of the store as Mrs. Meecham rang up the customer's order. Imani ducked back into the storeroom and grabbed Amanda, pulling her off of the bed.

"Let's go eat some beans and rice at Rene's and then go to the beach."

"Imani, I'm pregnant."

Imani already knew. She had known for a while. In fact, she had waited for the last couple of weeks to be told. She had seen a new cast over Amanda's face and had been waiting to offer help. Still, she pretended it was news.

"Oh."

"You mean, oh finally you're telling me . . ."

"No. I mean oh no, and oh my, and I mean oh, what now . . ."

"What do you think?"

"I think we should go eat and then walk on the beach."

"Imani, I'm pregnant." This time Mandy was pleading for an answer as her tears started to fall again. "I don't want to have a baby I don't want, like my mama had me. But I don't want to not have it. I don't know what I want. I want it to be last month and everything was easier."

"I'm hungry and so are you. Let's go eat."

They didn't talk through dinner except for Imani offering stories about the fellow diners' lives.

"She's out with him, but has another one at home. Oooh, and he doesn't even know. That child wants some ice cream for sure. . . . Look at that boy, he's hella-fine. I think he might want to talk to me . . ."

"Imani, shush, even if you're right it's none of your business. Always looking in people's heads."

"Well you're not such good company and I might want to talk to him. But it'll wait."

"Imani, I'm . . ."

"I know, you're pregnant. Come on. It's not going to just go away. Let's walk some."

They reached the beach just as the sun was setting. Imani had not even thought to phone her Auntie Zulie or Uncle Mico so they could bring a message to her home. Her mother would worry, but she would know from deep inside that Imani would be home soon enough. Besides it wasn't her fault that Gramma Ernie refused to get a phone. Imani knew everyone was probably waiting for her, but that was too bad. Mandy was her best friend, and Mandy needed her *right then*, without having to worry about curfew or adults with a whole lot of questions and "why did you"s and not one bit of comfort or solution. Yes, it was her birthday. As far as Imani was concerned that meant *she* was supposed to choose how she wanted to spend her day.

"So what's Jerome say?"

"He says it's my decision. Like we made it together, but I have to decide what to do with it. He says, whatever I want. Imani, I don't know what I want. I want, Imani, for the second time since she left, I really want my mama."

Imani wrapped her arms around her friend's broad shoulders and Mandy cried full out, heaving moans coming from her throat, trapped in years of trying to forget she even had a mother. The girls stood there for what seemed like hours, Amanda crying and Imani stroking her head and saying nothing.

"Let's go find her," Imani finally said, as Mandy's cries subsided. "Let's just go find her. You know we can. We'll sleep in the storeroom tonight and pool together your little money and my little money and get on a bus and look for her. Didn't you say she had people in Seaside? Let's go."

Amanda didn't take chances. In fact, letting Imani and Jerome get close to her were two of the most courageous acts in her young quiet life. She didn't go anywhere. She didn't protest. She didn't get riled. She just moved forward like a slow tractor pulling logs. She pushed her future like a tight clod of earth out of the road. But now she had no reason not to go, and no reason not to stay. And Imani was prodding her once again, urging her forward. Imani was refusing to leave her alone and quiet, insisting instead on chatter and activity.

Amanda sighed. "She gave me away."

Imani stood up. "So it's settled. The bus couldn't be more than twenty dollars round trip."

Just then Amanda saw a sand dollar, perfectly round, still purple, breathing in the air, looking for the saltwater. She picked it up and tossed it back into the receding tide.

"Mandy, it was going to die anyway."

"You don't know that. If you don't like what I do with sand dollars, pick up your own sand dollars."

The girls laughed. Imani hugged Amanda and

grabbed her by the hand. "Race you to the middle of the curve and back again, ready, set . . ." and then just before *go*, like she always did, Imani reached a foot out and Amanda stretched an inch farther. They ran to the end and met each other at the curve and stopped, winded and laughing.

"Imani, I'll be vomiting all over the bus and you'll be telling your god-awful stories about all the other riders and the bus driver, and all that we'll have to eat is greasy burgers . . ."

"So, it'll be an adventure . . ."

"Yeah, I know, but I guess what I want is for her to come here. Anyway, I know where she is. She does write once a year on my birthday. She mails it to the post office. You know, Ray Mac-Intire works there. From time to time he finds me and then gives however many cards he saved up, and some cash, twenty or twenty-five dollars, every year. She always puts her return address on the envelope, but I never write. It's probably not real anyway."

She heaved a sigh of resignation. "No, Imani, I don't want to go looking, but I don't want to go home or to Mrs. Meecham's either. And I don't want to go visit your house. Everybody at your place will see and be pushing and pulling, and I have to hide from everybody at mine, and Mrs. Meecham's . . ."

"Mrs. Meecham's a pain. It's still early, let's go to a movie and think about it."

"Imani, I'm . . ."

Imani looked at her friend and screamed past her cheeks and into the wind, "PREGNANT."

Amanda shook her head and smiled, mimicking under her breath, "So now what?"

The girls turned and began to walk back to the road to wait for the bus that would take them into the town's center.

An Open Weave

—m—

ERNESTINE AND IREE HAD MOVED to that house, where they all waited for Imani's return, a few months before Imani was born. Ernestine's son, Ezekiel, had driven them to the house and declared it the perfect place to have a child. When Ernestine had questioned him about who the owner was he said, "You are, now. I'm working the final closing of a deal with Bartell today. I'll bring you the deed and the bill of sale. Everything will be notarized so you won't have any problems. You'll just need to register it at the courthouse yourselves."

A month later Ezekiel came to visit Iree, who was full and pregnant. He brought a smoothed and polished barrel bassinet that he had made. He teased Iree and she started smiling for the first time since they had settled in and unpacked. He gave Iree and Ernestine an address and told them to mail a house payment there every month for the next five years. After that, he told them, the house would be theirs. The three of them ate dinner on the porch steps, laughing and telling stories. As the moon set, Iree and Ernestine went to bed. Ezekiel chose to sleep on the porch, enjoying a burst of early autumn heat.

The next morning Ezekiel rose early and went inside. His mother was already up, sitting at the loom and sailing her yarn-filled shuttle back and forth.

"Mama, I'm going out to get the house papers." He rubbed her shoulders for a few moments and then bent over and kissed her cheek. That was the last time Ernestine ever saw her son.

Since that time, in the months and years that passed without word from Ezekiel, Ernestine had not produced a weaving of substance, something that was more than a breath and a sleeping between the patterns. It seemed that her whole life flowed in and over the warp, as if she were a part of the wool, here and there a strand breaking, threatening to unravel the whole, while other strands were tied up short with a shell pierced by sea water, or a tree pod still smelling of its mother, musty and sweet, remembering moss, or glass beads with their markings worn thin by salt and flesh rubbings, a cloth of many woven strands. A cloth of too many memories.

Ernestine sat at her loom, her long fingers flattening the yarn, smoothing the row: sailing across, pulling taut, sailing back, pulling again, changing the harness, adjusting the tension. Open, pull, sail, pull, loose, taut, open, pull, sail, pull. The loom clicked and clacked at each change as lint settled softly across her feet, a cloud of colors rustling against the dark wooden floor.

"How come these spaces with no direction?" she hummed, sweat collecting on her brow. Imani, who was just five, sat near the corner, her hands loosely clasped around sunbeams.

"Gramma, please, need a jar," she sang lightly in a voice that knew more yeses than nos. Not losing a beat the woman tipped her head toward the kitchen. Sail, pull, clack, sail, smooth, shoosh, taut, loose.

"Can't go myself, Gramma," Imani pleaded. "I'll lose the sunbeam. It's real special."

"Nuther one come child, get your own jar."

"Can't reach anyhow. Need a REAL BIG one!"

The old woman laughed, and rose up from her loom, stretching her spider limbs and moving gently toward the child. Kissing her brow she breathed, "Y' can't trap sunbeams, child."

"I can try!"

Ernestine moved to the kitchen shelves, quickly returning with an oversized jelly jar, sparkling and cold. Then she sat, and once more began the click and hum of the loom as the cloth grew thick and the shuttle swam like a lover between the threads, first caressing, then stern. As she began to beat the cloth too insistently, Ernestine pulled back and eased the tension.

"See Gramma? I got a jar full, hot and heavy.

devorah major

Feel this jar. See how much it weighs now. Fulla sunbeams, hot and heavy."

"Won't last past sunset, child."

"Course they will, Gramma. I caught them and they can't go nowhere till I set them free. Only you got tired eyes and can't feel things so much."

"Mind your manners, child." But her grandmother smiled and returned to her song.

"Gramma? How come you never really finish your cloth? Just weave and weave? We got cloth all over the walls, but ain't none of it finished, just cut off in funny style ways."

"Nuthin' to finish, Imani. Nuthin' never finished. Only things stop sometimes and then start up again. Nuthin' never finished."

Ernestine's cloths hung from the walls, were pallets on the floor, were draped as screens and curtains from the ceiling, each cloth loose at the bottom, rough and tattered. Rose patterns were cut off before they were completed, torn from the loom as they were about to blossom, then stretched haphazardly across a table or over a shelf.

"Nuthin' to finish, child."

The loom began to creak again as Ernestine threw the shuttle across its middle, rushing against a deadline that would never arrive.

"Mother," Iree finally spoke up. She had been watching Ernestine and Imani, and as always, had kept silent. Iree had a way about her that most people found unsettling. Despite her almost con-

32

stant movement and presence in the house, visitors would forget she was there. She became a comfortable chair most folks passed up for the more substantial couch or frivolous settee; a pleasant painting that had faded into the wall and was rarely noted. Then, of course, when they noticed her they would jump, startled at her presence, and in word or look accuse her of being a ghost.

"What did you say?" they would ask her, knowing full well Iree hadn't said a word. Iree was pretty enough, smart enough, but remarkable only for her haunting way, the way she made people too aware of each other, while making herself nearly invisible.

"Mother," Iree repeated in a voice full of frustration. "They're gonna put us out soon. We've got to find that deed and register this house."

"We got us a place, Ezekiel said we own it, we own it. Ezekiel said he went to get the papers, then he did it. Ezekiel said there's a deed, there's a deed."

"Yes, yes, but then where are these mystical papers?"

"Well I guess he's got to come back and tell us, daughter."

"Mama, he's not coming back. He's dead."

"Ain't no dead, daughter."

"Oh, Mother. Nuthin' finished, no tomorrow, no dead."

Iree paused from the packing she had been do-

Let the Screams out answers in..." FAITH

ing and looked up weary and sad. Her tears hung like shadows across the room.

The old woman bent over her weaving, wheezing, moisture falling on the cloth, melting into the softly woven tapestry.

"This is a hard one, daughter. I need your faith. I keep telling you there's no need to pack. I tell you we're staying here. Something we was supposed to do we didn't do. I need your faith to figure what it is."

"For someone who always berates church goers, you talk about faith too much. We need more than that sometimes."

"Child, what's church got to do with faith? Did you check the candles this morning, daughter? Did you open your heart, daughter, and let the screams out and the answer in?"

Iree sighed and looked at the seemingly endless supply of yarn, wax and trinkets around the house. She eyed the cloth-covered walls. There was a panoply of shades of white, some flat, others somber, still others alive and full of reflections. Some of the cloths were woven in soft yellows and bronzes, matched to Imani's golden skin. Each color was a call to an ancestor, a prayer to an orisha, a calling for guidance and protection.

Iree had tried to believe in this fortress Ernestine had built. She tried to believe in the candles, the beads, the smooth triangular black stone, and the cloths made of color, but Iree knew that Ezekiel was dead. She had witnessed his death, two days

34

after he disappeared, during one of her seizures.
She had seen his head bashed in by drunk, frightened and angry men, who thought him dangerous
although he made no threats.

Iree had seen it all clearly. She had been out
getting a few last things before the baby came. She
had bought some pins and diapers and mineral oil,
and some scented oil for Ernestine. On the way
home she took a shortcut and passed the Tipped
Jug bar. A sudden wave of dizziness came over
her, and she sat down on the ground in the empty
lot next to the bar, leaning against a telephone
pole. She felt fear crawl up her back and she
whimpered as it took her. Her head fell back and
her mouth foamed and after a few moments she
passed out.

When she came to, the bartender from the
Tipped Jug was pouring water on her face and
trying to lift her up and move her inside. She recognized his face. She closed her eyes and the vision
replayed in her mind. She saw Ezekiel in the bar,
how he threw back his head and slapped Bartell
on the back, holding a drink in one hand. She saw
him demand that Bartell acknowledge their business deal. She saw the drunken men gather around
Ezekiel, calling him a liar; they didn't want to hear
what he said. She saw the bartender send them out
onto the lot. She saw them as they surrounded
Ezekiel and beat him. She saw his eye socket crack
and fold inward, his lips growing and then bursting into maroon rivers flowing down his chin, his

ribs cracking one by one. She saw how he fell to the ground and lay still on the dirt. How the men carried him away.

As the water from the bartender's glass streamed down Iree's face, she trembled uncontrollably and pulled away from him in terror, despite his assurances that he was only trying to help. She looked down at her hand and realized she held a chip of tooth and a torn piece of a shirt that she knew to be Ezekiel's. Iree stood up and slowly walked away. When she got home she took Ezekiel's few remains and laid them in the closet altar, next to the white candle that never seemed to quite run out of wax. Then she lay down in the doorway and slept.

Her mother had told Iree that Ezekiel would save them all. He was supposed to somehow shore up a family splintered and stunted, and put them back on the righteous trail. It was his destiny, Ernestine said, the prophecy painted in the birthmark that lay across his third toe, spreading like a fragile purple wing over the sole of his strangely unlined foot.

Poor Ezekiel, brought up on too much faith and too little reality, Iree thought. She shook her head and resumed packing the books and magazines scattered between the drawers of trinkets that would eventually find their way to Ernestine's cloths.

"No death, daughter, only passing. Ezekiel come back. Seems he wasn't meant to lead quite like I thought. But he'll be back." The old woman started to hum again, measuring her breath against the shift of the loom.

Iree opened the closet door and stared at their altar, her eyes crossing each candle and picture. Beads were carefully draped across the woven white cloth. Generations, faded in sepia tones, smiled at her in crisp formality, offering faint comfort and broken pieces of advice from the rolling corners of their photographs. How does one pack a temple into coffee cans and cardboard? Iree thought. Especially a temple in which one no longer believes.

Her hands fluttered across the items and she sank, tired and frustrated to the floor. She began to rock, building a wind around her, rocking, rocking in circles until her belly ached, as the sound of the loom's crossings guided her rhythm. Across the room, Imani lay down in the sunlight, tired of her play, and fell into a fitful sleep as her mother swayed and arched, dutifully rocking to a private song.

It took Iree, as it always did, whether she called it or not. Sometimes Iree went months without it coming. Then suddenly the rocking would begin and she would know no hours or minutes. Over the years she had learned to feel it coming and was able to reach shelter most of the time. Still, people called her crazy and "rockin' gal" and laughed as it swept through her, leaving her dazed and alone. Iree had even learned to like it, at least when it took her to certain times; when she found herself swimming in gentle rivers or dancing in quiet ceremonies, like the time when she found herself bathed in fresh goat milk and wrapped in a blue cloth that went from morning sky to summer dusk, glistening at her hips. Then there were the worst times when it split her into pieces. Last week the rocking had begun while she was at the playground with Imani. She had tried to still herself and quiet the rocking, but she felt her hip split underneath her and cried out from the crippling pain. Before her eyes spirits she knew as long dead rose from the neatly mowed grass and taunted her. A woman bloodied from a fifty-year-old rape screamed against her eardrum. A cat reached out its claws as it hung in front of her, strangled with the tied ends of a child's suspender straps. The playground became icy and full of wet cement, as sweating workmen yelled at her to move out the way. Then a crane reached over to knock down the climbing structure where Imani stood poised to leap into the waiting sandbox. Iree leapt up and caught her falling daughter. Suddenly the rocking stopped. Iree stood her laughing child up and brushed off her skirt. "Time to go, Imani. Mama's tired." The two of them had walked home, buying their traditional chocolate chip cookie and lemonade on the way, and trying to remember the words to Imani's newest favorite song. Iree had wondered how much longer she could hang on.

This time Iree did not try to fight it or push it

forward. She rocked until the room around her disappeared. Suddenly Ezekiel stood in front of her, clean and unbruised and smiling.

"Hey gal, long time crossing," he said fondly and grabbed her hand. "I don't know when I can come back again, so listen close now. Uncle Jeremiah's got to dig out the deed to this place. When the sheriff comes, you just show him my shirt and remind him a bet is a bet. Tell him his wife knows the truth. Say it just like that. Tell him you know you and Ernestine own the house. It's yours now, yours and your child's and Mama's. And tell him that Jeremiah is at the courthouse registering the deed. Don't let him touch the shirt. Tell him you found the tree branch, too. He'll not bother you again. And unpack all that stuff. You worry too much. I told you you'd always be taken care of. Your child seems real sweet. I see her, you know. And tell Mama that I'm still loving her every day, every day and every night. Tell her I'm still looking out. Don't forget. I got to go now, Iree."

Ezekiel let out a joy-filled whistle and began to fade. Iree saw the gap between his teeth, and his tongue jutting out as he started to whistle one of those long pretty tunes he used to make up every time the weather changed.

Iree opened her eyes and looked around her. Ernestine was stretching out lengths of yarn across the floor. The dishes were unpacked and the years of woven cloth lay in piles heaped against the walls. The altar was reassembled, including the white candle which was burnt to its nub and would soon be out. A photo of Ezekiel had been moved to the front of the candle. Iree saw that her mother had restored the house and was preparing to stay. She rubbed her thighs with her palms and spoke quietly to Ernestine,

"Mother, Ezekiel came back. He said he told Jeremiah where to find the deed that was hidden during a bet. He . . ."

"Yes, Iree, I know."

"But Ezekiel's . . ."

"Nuthin' never finished, daughter. Come on, you have to bathe. I got a sweet milk bath run and I know Jeremiah's gonna bring the truck round in the next little while."

"If you know, why do you make me travel so?"

"Child, I can't see. I can only push and pull. I don't even know what your smile looks like anymore, Iree. You know that. Ol' tired eyes with the rickety cane. Help me to the doorway, Iree, and I'll get me some sun while you wash."

Imani woke from her nap to the sound of their voices and walked over to her mother and kissed her cheek. "Mama, are you feeling better? I am. I had a good nap." Iree smiled as Imani wrapped her arms around her waist and turned to Ernestine. "I'll help you to the porch, Gramma."

As they moved towards the door, Imani asked for the hundredth time, "Gramma, how come you know how to weave all these colors when you can't even see?" and the old woman answered for the hundredth time, "Imani, how come you know how to catch sunbeams and never get burned?"

"That's silly, Gramma. Ain't nobody ever got burned catchin' a sunbeam."

"Well if that's so, it's only because most people don't ever try and them that do don't hardly ever succeed. So let's us go sit in front and wait for Jeremiah to come and visit."

The old woman and the child laughed, enjoying their private joke as Iree slid into the cool fresh bath.

Dominoes

—⨍⨍⨍—

THE LAST TIME IMANI HAD been to the beach at night had been ten years before. She had been with her mother who wanted to walk near the water after winning round after round of dominoes. Her mother had loved to wade in that ocean's cool water. As she and Amanda boarded the bus back to the town's center, Imani remembered that night, sitting outside her Uncle Mico's house while the adults played dominoes.

"Hem," Mico wheezed from the steps as Jonah threw down a bone. "Just like he always plays it. Fours and fives and throw'd the rest away." He spat on the sandy ground, into the still of the humid evening, and nodded to seven-year-old Imani, who was hopping up and down the two steps which led to his front door. Iree's turn was next. She sat at the flimsy card table with Mico's friends, Al, straight-backed and tight-mouthed as ever, Jo-

nah, full of curses and off-color jokes, and Malachi, calm and soft-voiced.

"Always think he gonna pull the most that way,
but numbers is always got their power. It's threes
and sixes make the balance."

Black dotted, a warm smooth tile clapped onto
the fragile card table. "A sweet christine," smiled
Iree. She tucked her tongue between the gap in her
front teeth, and marked a circle and line to indicate fifteen on the score sheet.

"Now y'see, she played a two, three, threes and
sixes that's the ticket. Y' got t' feel 'em out of the
pile. Your mama always could pull 'em in, even at
your age."

Imani laughed as she continued to hopscotch on
the two porch steps, up, down, up, down. "Fives.
Five, ten, fifteen, twenty. Fives, Uncle Mico! All
the rest don't matter, just who-ha talk!"

"Li'l girl, who you ha-in'?" he scowled at her,
but a quiver in his lips let out a crack of a smile.
"Imani, you just like your mama, though you are
quicker to get there. Sure, you score with fives, but
it's how you put them together makes the count."

Imani shrugged as she skipped to the sounds of
the tiles, clackety clack clack, her thoughts jumping in the darkening sky.

Jonah leaned back in his chair, gargling a laugh
caught in his bone-thin frame. "Twin motor cities
with a spare on the back for a clean domino!"

They scored the round, crediting Jonah's
twenty-five and adding another twenty as Mala-

chi, dark and full-chested, ambled away from the table towards Jeremiah. "Come on, Mico, take my chair. I see you over there trying to school little miss in your professional," he stretched the word and laughed, "av-o-ca-tion. Mr. Cool Breeze is tired."

"Mr. Hot Wind," Jeremiah gruffed out, pulling on a tall can of beer. "Naw, it's too thick for me. You all need to take a break and let the table cool down."

Mico turned to Iree, who sat in silence, her eyes sunk in deep shadows.

"Where you been, niece? Ever since you three came back from Georgia, that old spider of a sister of mine always says you ain't in, or ain't well, as if I don't know you. It's been too long since you climbed down that hill to visit me. You still feeding that old mutt that hang round your place?"

Iree showed her teeth, her lips pulled back against the buzz of mosquitoes and firefly light. "Of course I am. And you know where I've been, in the house ailing. I had one of my spells while we were gone and it took me a time to get well enough to be around people again."

"Child, you strong as a horse!" Mico teased, knowing where to find the crack in her reserve. Silence hung in the steel blue evening.

Imani broke in, "Well, I can tell you where I been, and all by myself too. I'm in the second grade, and you know how good I can read, Uncle Mico, and now I can walk to school all by myself down that long hill, and a whole nuther seven blocks, and when I . . ."

"I believe I was talkin' to your mama," the old man rasped out, chuckling in the back of his throat.

Iree turned and looked her uncle full in the eyes, trembling in the heat. She began to mutter, more to herself than to the men around the table, "When we first got there it was so nice. I mean all the family had everybody so warm and all. Everybody seemed to have something right, and then too something wrong with them, and people didn't treat me so strange. You'd a thought I was blood to them the way they carried on. Well, I still didn't want to go out too much there, not knowing my way around and all. So I didn't go out for a real long while until the last week. It was a real warm Tuesday, and everybody that had a job was off at work. Mama made me take her, us really, to the beach. We rode a little jitney bus that came about one every hour or so, to about five blocks from the beach edge. Then we walked through the dunes. Imani had been crying all day to go swimming, and Mama told me she was starting to forget colors and needed the salt on her eyes and tongue to make her remember, so we had to go. It started off so . . ." she paused and smiled, "so peaceful like. It was hot, but the breeze on the water made it real comfortable."

That had been the day when Iree finally learned to let her body slip off like a soft hand-sewn quilt, instead of in ragged convulsions. She had been able to let it fall of a piece, and then let herself rise through the center. After that she felt more in control, and her mother wove with less fervor, did not beat her through each journey. For months before that day in Georgia she had stayed inside the house, leaving only for groceries, to cash their checks, and once to do the recertifying: she, as crazy; her mother, as blind; and her daughter, walking a perilous wire with the state, as dependent. Going to Georgia was like going half-way around the world, and going to the beach in a strange place was even harder. It had taken all of her courage, and much pushing and cajoling from Ernestine to get her to take that trip.

Iree continued dreamily, "The water let me breathe through my skin. Imani was singing and splashing, being her mermaid self, and Mama was unravelling a real old cloth, rewinding the strands to use again, when suddenly I could feel the sand all the way at the bottom, where the edge of the ocean used to be."

Imani stopped her skipping and moved to her mother's chair; she sat at her feet and rested her head in Iree's cotton-skirted lap. Mico turned on the porch light as everyone settled and Iree, not noticing or caring, continued her tale: "It was like velvet and mountain tears, all smooth and liquid. First it was almost echoing with the quiet of the waves, but then I heard them just at my back. It was a moaning. Their bones scratched and then their song, dark honey and shadows, their song caught my womb and pulled.

"So many different tongues, singing their way home, singing sunshine they've almost forgotten. They were reds, yellows, purples and blacks just shimmering around me, touching my cheek and pulling my hair; their fingers passing through my chest and coming out bloody. I was cold and hot at the same time. They called me by my name and asked me to point them east.

"They never lifted their feet, just pulled them through the sand, making it ripple and fold. And the fish, they hovered in rings around their heads and ankles, like a halo, or a shackle, or a prayer. And Uncle Mico, you should have seen their skin. It was still oily, pushing aside the salt. They were bathed in coconut milk and palm oil and you could smell it sour and sweet on the water. Some of them were still bleeding from the lashes across their backs and ruts cut into their necks and chins from the shackles that had finally rusted and fallen off, turned to sparkles in the sand. When they bled, when they bled, lord, it was in fountains until all the nearby seaweed became a red-black with their blood." She snapped her fingers against the table rim and paused in her remembering.

"Girl, enough of your crazy talk! I came here to play some tiles!" Al spoke up nervously. When the stories began, Al would reassure himself that even if Iree was always so gracious and could play a mean game of dominoes and was one of Jeremiah and Ernestine's few remaining living kin, everyone knew she was an addled-brain epileptic. He didn't understand most of Iree's crazy talk, but that time he felt his own death in it and cringed.

"They jumped those ships hundred of years ago," Iree chanted on without acknowledging Al, "and some were even carrying babies suckling on their tits and you could almost see the cloth and baskets they'd carried on top of their heads, they were so straightbacked. They were still trying to find a way back after all these years . . . just pacing the sands, seeking an African sun, and bleeding.

"After a while, I was walking with them, dragging my feet along the sand towards the east, feeling the heat of sunrise. And then I was getting turned around and walking back towards the shore."

Iree rose from her chair and began to stamp her heels into the dirt, moving in a swaying pattern around the men's chairs. Her bare feet hugged the earth as she led each turn with her left shoulder, dipping down on the three and six count.

"Just like this." She began to chant, "The sand moving like a flowing shawl with us just walking, walking, remembering, walking."

Now Jonah spoke up. "Well, they shoulda just died like they was supposed to. When you jump off a ship in the ocean you die girl, that's it. You die, and you get ate, and that smooth velvet you was talking about was they dissolved bones or more likely the sun touching your brain while you was sleeping on the beach. So why not just quit your chatter."

Jonah had had his hands spiked and beaten by cotton barbs in his childhood, and knew a full serving of the pain his ancestors had suffered. He neither needed or desired any more reminders.

"Yeah, Jonah, you sure are right, at least that's what you'd a thought," Iree smiled. "Yeah, you'd a thought that for sure." She paused and then started to hum the song as she remembered it. "Even now if I went to the water, I'd just have to catch a handful of seawater and I'd hear them, singing like golden molasses." She began to hum again, cupping the air as she danced.

"Mama," Imani chimed in. "Mama, I bet some of them actually got home. Ol' Isaiah told me that it's thousands of miles to Africa, so it must take more than a hundred years to walk back. He told me people used to live hundreds of years. I bet you just met some of the slow walkers, but some of the others, why they made it. I just know they did!"

Jeremiah eyed his grandniece. "Why you say that, little bird?"

"Well I figure," Imani replied seriously, "that some of them knew how to get back, and they're at the bottom of their own ocean, singing and maybe gardening pretty orange coral or growing sea horses or something. And the ones Mama was with, they had a harder time finding their directions, you know, like old Mr. Malachi here." She nodded at the salt-and-pepper-haired man who stood next to her uncle. "You know, Mr. Malachi, how when you and me was downtown and we was getting lost over and over again, and you kept saying about all the new buses and trains and all. Well I guess there's lots a new stuff in the ocean too, especially way at the bottom."

Jeremiah huffed out a laugh. "Well, little girl, you just might be right. Actually though," he lowered his voice as if telling a great secret, "Malachi never knew his way around in the first place. Yeah, maybe you're right, just like old Mack here, they're walking in circles, forgetting where the hell they were going to."

Al cut into the laughter, "Well I know they are dead. Dead and departed!"

"That's what Iree was saying," Malachi chortled. "Only they just keep on departing."

Iree sat back down. "I woke up shivering on the shore. Imani was pulling me from the shallow tide pool, and Mama had a towel wrapped around my shoulders. Evening was coming and I was glad to be back. And glad to come on home, so I can ruffle Al's feathers, and eat some of Zulie's most delicious fresh baked pie, and take alla y'all's money at dominoes."

She turned over the tiles as she spoke and began to shuffle them as she smiled and winked. Jonah let out a soft sigh of relief and Al gave a grudging smile. Mico walked over to Iree, leaned down and kissed her cheek. Iree put her hand against his rough-bearded face and said softly, "So that's why you ain't seen me, old man. I had a lot to think about and remember. I didn't want to forget this one."

Imani, tired of grown-up talk, and humming her mother's recent song, looked up at the rising moon and wondered if she tried real hard how high could she jump.

The tiles were sorted and Malachi slapped down the double six with conviction, as Iree, leaning from his left, put down a six/three and laughed in answer, "Fifteen."

Jeremiah smiled. "Yeah, girl, you can make them tiles just get up and walk to you. It's threes and sixes make the balance."

Clackety clack clack, the bones fell against the tables as threes and fives floated against the star-filled summer sky.

"Imani," Amanda said, clutching Imani's arm. "Imani! I think I'm going to throw up again."

"Imani!" Amanda was more insistent. "We need to get off the bus now."

"Hold on, Mandy. Just hold on. It's too far to walk. I'll open the window and you can lean out. You'll be fine."

Imani forced open the window and Amanda leaned across her and retched onto the side of the bus. Then she sank back in the seat. Imani pulled a crumpled napkin out of her pocket and passed it to Amanda. "Imani, this is not fun," Amanda said wearily, neatly folding the napkin and wiping her mouth with it.

Imani did not hear her. She was listening to the faint sound of the ocean waves fading behind them as the bus turned onto Buttonhole's main street.

Friends

—ᴍ—

"YOU KNOW SHE'S WITH AMANDA. Those two been thick as winter molasses from that first day," Zulie said as she walked around the table ladling second servings of chicken stew onto each plate.

"That's the truth," Iree whispered softly to Ernestine, who sat as matron and queen at the table's head.

"Yeah, seems that way," agreed Mico as he reached for another baking powder biscuit.

"Not to me," countered Al from the sofa, where he sat tuning into a boxing match on the radio. "Zelma, I recall talk of how it took two months for that Amanda to say five words stuck together to Imani."

"No, they were friends from the start, Al. Iree was ailing around that time. So, I came and took Imani to the playground to get her out of the house. We hit the gate and she ran off to *her* territory, the swings. There was this pale child sitting on Imani's favorite swing. Not rocking or turning, just daydreaming or something. Imani was trying to get her attention, but that little girl wouldn't pay her no mind. Well, there went Miss Imani, trying to look as grown-up as her three and a half feet of little girl can, saying: 'Do you talk?' I'm telling you, just like this—" Zulie put down the tureen of stew, straightened up, and placed her hands spread-fingered on the hips of her loose cotton skirt "—sassy as you please to this little freckled marinery child, sitting looking as sour as a green lemon in a vat of vinegar. Now I could tell they were probably about the same age, six or seven, maybe five, anyway about the same. So when the little girl didn't answer, Imani got louder, 'I said, do you talk?' But that Amanda, she hardly looked up at her, just kept dragging her feet in the sand.

"Now you all know Imani, she isn't too big on long sorrowful looks, so she grabbed Amanda by the wrist and pulled her out of the swing and shoved her face in Mandy's, and said real loud, 'If you not going to talk, stay quiet, but if you're not gonna swing, get up. Some of us like to have fun, you know. You can sit on the bench with the old people or something, but I want to swing and I don't see why I should wait.'

"And Mandy, she just disentangled herself real smooth, peeled off Imani's fingers, and answered, 'This is how I swing,' and plopped back in the swing. Just then this little toddler who was doing belly circles on his swing got bored and left the only other swing open. Imani grabbed it and started kicking up real high, laughing and singing. And then she yelled over to Mandy, 'So you can talk? I'm Imani. Who are you? Can you go this high?' And the child starts bucking in the middle and pumping her legs and swings so fast and hard that her braids stood on end. And sure as can be, that Mandy started to pumping too and before you know it they were matching each other pump for pump and laughing. Imani would sing and say, 'Watch how far up I can jump!' And she'd jump off the swing, duck as it swung back over her, and then run to the back and catch the chain before it swung forward again. Right behind her would be Mandy. They did that all afternoon. I don't think Mandy said more than three, four other words that first day, though. 'I'm Amanda,' and, 'Goodbye, Imani.'

"By the time I walked Imani home, she was non-stop talking about her new best friend. It was Amanda this and Amanda that. They couldn't a been more than, what you think Al, maybe five and six years old?"

"Woman," Al focused on his wife. "Now if I say she was older, you're going to tell me every damn thing we did in the year you think she might have been six to prove it was six, when hell, what's the difference if it's seven or eight or five. They were little girls. And Amanda, that child was always spooky. Remember that night Mico, when she came by your place with Imani? She must of been about thirteen, fourteen then, just started running away from one of those homes, as I recall."

"Al, how about a simple yeah?" Zulie retorted.

"Zelma, I don't know when it was and don't too much care. You all know she's gonna be back soon and all of this carrying on is just an excuse to bother us and not let us listen to the damn fight in peace. You know, we were watching a fight that night she showed up at your place, Mico. Remember?"

The table became quiet as everyone ate and chewed on their thoughts. Iree, as usual, picked around her plate, eating the edges in a haphazard circle. She'd start to rock and then Ernestine would reach over and still her motions.

Al had stopped listening to Zulie or to the radio. He was lost in thought reaching back to that night.

"Look at that man dance, he ought to change careers, 'cause he can't punch worth a damn. Bright Lights Biltmore needs some glasses," said Malachi, clapping Al on the back.

Jonah pulled out a wad of folded bills. "Biltmore gonna take him out in the ninth, got to wear him down. I'm asking again, where's your money?"

Malachi leaned towards Jonah. "In my pocket, man, till I need to buy something. Mico, where's that pretty grandniece of yours? I'm ready to see

Imani whip poor Jonah here some more at dominoes! Learn him a little about mother wit."

Jonah walked over and stuck his face close to Malachi. "Anybody ever tell you you're an asshole?"

"Yeah, you, every time I see you. But everybody got one and maybe you need two to get all the shit you be talking outta you."

Mico walked over and handed each of them a cold beer. "Damn. I invited you two over to watch the fight, not star in it."

"Well Mico, I've got twenty dollars says Biltmore is the man of the evening. Right here, on the table . . ."

"Jonah, I'm not opposed to betting, but I am against losin'. I think I'd take your money, but it's just too close to call . . ."

"There's the sport, man." Jonah smoothed the twenty on the low, scratched wooden coffee table, weighing it down with the corner of a beer can.

"All right, but make it ten and spot me, too . . ."

"You got to be joking. When I win I get my own ten back."

Jonah turned to Al. "Man, loan this man ten bucks, so I can get some pleasure out of whipping his ass."

Al snorted and looked at Mico, who shrugged his shoulders and declined. "Guess I really can't afford it this week, brother."

The men all laughed and the cigarette smoke

shook in the air. Just then they heard an insistent but soft, repeating thud at the door. Jeremiah walked with his usual slow, deliberate step towards the flaking, cream-colored door, and opened it wide to reveal Imani, breathless and chattering, and Amanda, standing like a shadow behind her.

Imani pulled Amanda into the room. The two girls stood for a few minutes before any of the other men actually acknowledged they were there, then Al stood up to get a good look at his goddaughter, who, he noticed for the first time, was actually more woman than child. Amanda stood with her swollen eyes and blotched cheeks, while Imani pushed and pulled Amanda with as much alternating disregard and love as she used to give her dolls.

"Her mom is fighting with her dad again. That's all," Imani haltingly lied, as a start of an explanation.

"It's really not important. I'm their foster child, not their child," Amanda cut in. She looked hard at Imani, asking for silence with her eyes, then she turned to Jeremiah. "Mr. Jefferson, I just need a place to stay for the night and I'm all right and Imani said to come here. Tomorrow, I'll go home."

Imani pleaded, "Uncle Mico, she can't go to my house because Mama's sick again and Mandy doesn't really have a lot of family or real friends and . . ."

Mico interrupted her, "Imani, I know I'm old-fashioned, but I'm a grown man and I live alone and I only have this one room with that one bed to sleep in. Child, it wouldn't be right."

"I'll stay too. We'll camp out on the floor. It'll be fine, Uncle Mico. I'm your niece and she's my sister, almost, so she's your niece too. It'll be fun." Imani jumped over to her uncle and rubbed her face up against his like she had done ever since she was a baby.

Al shook his head. "Imani, leave your uncle be. The last thing he needs is you girls jabbering all night and crowding up his place. Imani, I'll take you home. If your mama is sick that is where you should be anyway. Amanda, you can come home with me. Zelma'll fix you up. But be prepared, child, she's going to talk your ear off. In the morning Zelma or I will go talk to your foster parents for you."

Amanda knew Zelma well. She was always at Imani's house laughing with Imani's grandmother, Mrs. Ernestine Moore, or cooking something wonderful. Al was more of a stranger. He was always dropping his wife off or picking her up and rarely said a thing to Imani and Amanda. She was surprised by his offer, and scared to take him up on it, but she could tell from the look on Imani's face that it was settled. "Yes, sir," she answered, standing awkwardly in the middle of the floor.

"Good," Al answered with a smile. Al rarely showed his pleasure full out, but he had, for the most part, thoroughly enjoyed being a father. Whatever the troubles of work, and squabbles with Zelma, and fissures and knitting of his friendships, fathering always suited him. He liked growing children in much the same way that he liked nursing and pruning the orange trees which shaded his yard. Cropping back the weak branches each spring, then carefully clipping the bud ends, returning with fine clippers a third time, and with bare fingers a fourth, to knock off small green, and then larger, hard fruit, so that only the biggest and sweetest oranges were allowed to grow to maturity and bend down the thick, stable arms of the trees. All of his children but one had made it through storms and fires; they all stood on their own feet, though they called or came home frequently. Yes, he loved the work of planting and growing, and he loved the fruit that was produced from his labors.

Imani burst into the silence, "But don't you want to know why Mandy needs a place so bad?"

Al looked Imani cold and sharp in the eye. "We know why, child. We know why." Imani didn't realize that the men had seen what Amanda could not hide. A bruised arm and a swollen cheek, a blue half-moon rising under her eye. Her blouse was missing two buttons.

Each of them knew men they had called friend or boss or neighbor, men with whom they worked, or played pool, or watched football, who would find little to stop them in pressing a girl to give them a little something more than chores and a sweet smile for the roof over her head and the food in her mouth. They sat in bars as the jokes were made about this one being ripe for plucking and that one needing to have her cherry picked, and they took pride that they themselves had morals and wouldn't violate a woman-child, instead turning and shading their eyes as others did the damage. The four men shifted in their seats and said nothing for a few moments until Malachi cleared his throat, and speaking just a little too loud, cut the silence.

"Girl, sit down. We were watching the fight. Mico, now you know Al needs another beer. Imani, go see if can you find a soda for you and your friend. Now, lookee here, Castro is mad, look at him driving after Biltmore, dance the brother into the corner. Come on Castro, hit on the left, he's open, come on over the top. Yeah, do it, stay on him, stay on him . . ."

Jonah jumped in, "Bright Lights cover yourself, don't get tired, man, come on. Damn that hurt. Cover yourself, man, cover yourself."

Mico moved back towards the kitchen area. "Bright Lights is getting dim, man. Getting dim."

"Then where the hell's your money," Jonah yelled back at him.

Amanda stared at the television, watching the two fighters punch and sweat. She mumbled almost to herself, "I think the gold-trunks one is going to win."

"Why?" Al turned to her, surprised that the girl had even noticed the fight.

"He's thinking harder."

Malachi smiled. "Now you see, Jonah. Even this child can tell a showboat from a show-your-stuff."

Jonah bit back, "What I see is that you don't know more than this here, what are you, girl, fifteen, sixteen?"

"Fourteen . . ."

"Don't know more than a barely fourteen-year-old girl!"

Imani returned from the refrigerator with two glasses of soda. She pulled Amanda over to two chairs near the window and gave her one glass. Amanda pulled out an ice cube, sucked off the soda and then ran it around her mouth frowning. Imani whispered in her ear, "Al's all right. Don't worry. And Zulie's great. Everything will work out. You'll see. They're my godparents. You can have them as yours too."

"Imani, they're not yours to give away."

"Shows what you know." Imani smiled and reached up and wiped away the tear that was rolling down her friend's cheek.

Three rounds later the fight ended with a split decision for Castro. Jonah protested the judges' corruption and/or clear stupidity. Malachi carped relentlessly about Jonah's inability to lose with anything faintly resembling grace. Mico cursed himself for not borrowing the ten dollars from Al,

64

and reminded Al that the girls were waiting to go home.

The girls didn't say anything as Al stood up and told them to come with him. He packed them both into the front of his van and dropped Imani home, walking her to the door for a poked-head greeting to Ernestine and Iree. He knew he'd have to give a report to Zelma when he returned home. After hearing that Iree was back and resting comfortably, and seeing that Ernie was as sharp-tongued as ever, he walked down the front porch stairs smelling the fresh air. Then he turned the van around and drove down the street, surprised that without him uttering a word, Amanda started to whisper out her story.

"They always fight. This time it was about me. Mr. Marciano, that's my foster father, he drinks, and his wife, she cleans up after him, and then they both fight. They've always fought like this. Since before I came, probably even before I was born. She doesn't care as much as she makes out that he has sex with other women. Sometimes the women even call the house. She just says it's the wrong number and hangs up the phone. Then she starts cursing and carrying on, but it always seems like it's just for show. Like it's the neighbors she worries about. She doesn't like to listen to the neighbors gossip and click their tongues when she goes by.

"But when he got drunk tonight and came grabbing on me, that she wouldn't stand for. It surprised me because she usually doesn't pay that much attention to me. But she heard me yelling and heard the chair tip over and came running. I was hitting Mr. Marciano and so was she and he was punching the both of us. Then Imani showed up.

"I forgot it was Thursday, and every Thursday after dinner Imani and I go out together and get a pop at the store and sit on the curb and talk. Well, there she was, walking in the house like she lived there. She said she had rung the bell and nobody answered, so she just came in. I think she heard the yelling. Imani isn't one to wait if there is some mess to be seen or gotten into. The next thing I know she grabbed my hand and was pulling me out of there. He was screaming after me, saying, 'Get the hell outta my house, you little hussy.' Like it was my fault he wanted to feel me up. And his wife was yelling at him and telling me my things would be packed and to send someone to get them. Both of them yelling at me like it was my fault.

"I'm kind of sorry, because that house wasn't so bad. I mean, Mrs. Marciano was not so bad. She took me in. She fed me. She taught me how to cook and even sew some of my own clothes. She was so afraid he was going to have sex with me. She kept telling me I was going to have to go soon."

Al responded gruffly, "You shouldn't be talking about your foster parents like that, young lady."

Amanda stopped talking and they rode for a few blocks in silence. Then she reached over and touched Al lightly on the hand, "I mean, just so you know. I didn't do anything wrong."

Al didn't answer. He just pulled into his driveway and walked around the van to help Amanda out. She sat there dry-eyed, holding a sob in her throat. She avoided his outstretched hand and jumped out of the van. "I'll be all right," she said and followed Al inside the house.

Those were the last words Amanda said that night other than "Thank you," "Yes," and "Good night."

Al went to sleep restless, saddened by the child.

Zulie shook Al out of his memory. "Yes, they were five and six, Al. Because you remember Sherry had just lost the baby and before I went to get Imani I had stopped by to ease her through the first days of losing the baby . . ."

"Woman, I don't care."

"Yes, they met when Imani was six and Mandy was still five. Because Mandy wasn't more than a little over six when they had that fire, you know, when her own mother went and abandoned her. And by that time, Sherry'd already had Tommy, who was just a little baby."

"You know, Zelma, we should of taken her in that night."

"You mean after the fire? But Ray MacIntire took her. Besides, isn't Ray MacIntire supposed to be her real father? What call would we have to take her away from him?"

Al shook his head. "No, Zelma, years later, that time I brought her home after the Biltmore–Castro fight and she stayed for three or four days. We should of kept her then."

Zulie walked over to Al and rested her hands on his shoulders. She knew he had been hurt when he had offered a sanctuary to Amanda and she had adamantly turned it down, as if she didn't want to get any closer to them than she already was.

She kneaded her fingers into Al's thick shoulders. "We tried, you tried, as I remember. She wasn't ready to come. She wasn't ready, Al. Anyway social services found her a new home and from what Imani says, she's doing fine. She'll be in college in another year or two. She's taking care of herself."

"No, Zelmababy." Al reached up and took her hand. "We should of taken her in. We should of tried harder."

Ernie spoke up, "Zulie, how 'bout fixing some tea? Make it strong and dark and put some molasses in mine."

Iree quietly cleared her plate and walked towards the door while the others talked. Mico followed her with his eyes, wanting to find a way to cheer up his niece. Suddenly the noise and heat of the small house was stifling him. He got up and moved to Iree, where she stood, door held ajar to let in a cooling edge of the autumn's dark night.

Where Linden and Hickory Cross

---◦◦◦---

RAY MACINTIRE WAS STONE COLD sober the day the earthquake hit. He had watched in terrified amazement as the earth opened outside his door, refusing to suck him down, offering instead only a warning and a sigh. Then he slowly and calmly walked down the block.

He didn't pay attention to where he was walking. He started off towards Hickory, towards Lorraine's house, then decided to take the long route past the Moores' hilltop home. He rarely walked this way, although it was a part of his mail route. The Moores almost never got mail, other than their monthly bills. When they did it was usually a package of seeds or a magazine. He always rang the bell so he could get a peek inside the house. The household fascinated him as much as it frightened him. He had seen Iree, the strange woman with bulging eyes, going into one of her fits, and he had talked with her pretty but impudent daughter, Imani, who always seemed to know something she shouldn't have known. Ernestine Moore, the elderly woman who seemed to run the household, usually waved him away from the door. She was always weaving, if she wasn't making one of her healing teas. Ray's wife had sent him up the long hill to climb those stairs a few times, to get one of Ernestine's teas to soothe one child's colic, or to bring up the phlegm in a different one's chest. Ray always obliged his wife. He loved to look at all the colorful cloths draped on the walls and across the furniture. He never did understand how Ernestine could weave those patterns, being blind and all, but then no one in the town really understood the "Stairstep Ladies," as he always called the three-generation Moore family.

Ray MacIntire didn't know what was pulling him up that hill, or why he headed there instead of going straight to Lorraine's house. He pretended he had come to see if the members of this isolated family were all right, but he knew that wasn't the truth. If anyone could make it through, he was sure it would be old Mrs. Moore, her daughter and the girl. Though he would never admit this to anyone, Ray believed, as he believed in little else even faintly smelling of religion, in the power of the old woman's candles. He believed in the seriousness of Iree's drooling epileptic travels from which she brought back stories and nightmares that kept the entire neighborhood on edge.

And he believed in the sunlight beams which he swore, especially vehemently when in a happy falling drunk, poured out of seven-year-old Imani's eyes.

He climbed that hill, hoping to happen upon a blessing, perhaps a survival cup of tea. This time he knew he was climbing for himself, not for his wife or children. He was altogether sober, if not altogether clear. These woman could provide him with something he needed. He didn't know what, but he knew they had it.

Iree saw Ray MacIntire approaching as she squatted against the tall frame of the open doorway, her fingers intertwined, the skirt of her forest-green cotton dress draped around the knobs of her jutting knees. She surveyed the now-crooked slice of world in front of her, and listened for her mother's loom to start clacking again, and for the soft whisper spin of the wool as it fed from the spindle to boat. But it remained quiet until the sirens rang out and in seeming unison neighbors began to shout, and Mrs. Girney began to shriek out Bible messages, and the dogs resumed their troubled barking.

Ernestine sat on the weaving bench, her back to the loom, sucking in her cheeks and praying under her breath, dipping her head to the four directions. Imani's head poked around the corner as she burst out, "Now that's what I call gettin' all shaken up. I thought the whole hill was going to fall down. I thought . . ."

"Hush child." The grandmother's voice was irritated. "You didn't think nothing. You finally got quiet for half-a-minute and stopped acting so damn grown-up and know-it-all."

Iree let a shudder run from the edges of her toes through her knees swimming up her spine until her head jutted at just the moment that the house began to sway again, a bumpy stretch of road, a swerve and then smooth. She noticed Ray MacIntire nearing the stairs. Although he never had much color at all, he now seemed to have lost it completely, even the splashes of yellow and sky blue that sometimes would grace the lining of a vest or open-collared shirt. He had become a sloping sculpture of corrugated cardboard beiges and soiled concrete greys.

As Ray reached the first step he greeted Iree. Without waiting to hear a reply from her, he climbed up to the front door. Ernestine had been listening to the fall of the footsteps, and smelled a familiar sour odor. "What you want, Mr. MacIntire? Seems like this earthquake caught you standing up sober. Well that's a good sign, Mr. MacIntire. Always can use a good sign, however small it be." Ernestine listened for Ray, who stood without comment, waiting it seemed, to be invited into a home which had never before welcomed him. He opened his mouth to reply, but no words came out, only a long sigh. Just as Ernestine was about to turn him around and send him home Imani spoke up, "How come you here, Mr. Mac-Intire?"

Ray paused and ran his hand over his two-day stubble of flat brown quills. "I guess I just came to give thanks and say how glad I was that we all made it through. And, of course, to see if you need anything or needed something. . . ." His voice ran out but his lips kept moving.

Imani walked over to him, looking hard into his watery eyes. "You should be at your own home now. We've got things to do. Anyway, something's probably wrong at your house. I bet one a those big old red-and-gold-cover books from the top shelf come falling and hit Ray Junior right on his head."

Both the grandmother and Iree snapped their heads and lengthened their lips into twin pairs of sharp hems as Imani gulped, "I mean, probably something like that, 'cause I know you got lots of books 'cause . . ."

"And how have you come to know that since you've never been in my house?" Ray retorted.

Imani regained her bearings. She swooped onto the front porch, put her hands on her hips and sassed, "That wasn't the point anyway."

Iree grabbed Imani back and pulled her into her lap, chastising with her grip as she comforted with the smooth cheek she brushed against the child's face. She said in her usual soft velvet manner, "We're quite fine, Mr. MacIntire. Thank you for checking. We are blessed and have very little damage. Imani's a little dramatic, but you probably should go home and do tell your wife I asked after her. I guess your son is over that last bout of the flu by now. Don't listen to Imani, you know how she prattles on. She has such an imagination. I'm sure your children are fine."

Suddenly Ray felt his stomach drop in fear and he vomited all over the stairs. He turned around and ran back down the hill, rushing frantically towards his home.

Iree stood at the doorway and watched his twisted run. "Damn, Mr. Walk-bent-over-alla-the-time-don't-see-no-real-future-whiteman, you can sure move when you want to can't you?"

Ernestine laughed ruefully. "Imagine that Mr. MacIntire, wanting another blessing. Why he already got his to be standing up and all the way sober when it hit. I swear some folks just don't know when they got something and when they got a little bit of nuthin'."

Iree stared at the stairs. "Mama Moore, you should see the mess he left behind. And Imani, when are you going to learn to hold your tongue? You don't have to tell people everything you think you know."

"But Mama, I only see what they already saw. It's not like I'm telling the future or nuthin'."

"It is to them, darling, if they haven't let it in yet. Mama, you think we got enough water to wash off the stairs?"

"Yes, child. Our side of the hill's been spared

water, but I don't know if we'll have heat to cook with or keep warm for a few days. You're going to have to hold on, Iree, and not go nowhere. No fits, baby."

Iree looked into her mother's glazed eyes, thick with layers that had turned her once-sharp vision into a haze that barely acknowledged darkness and light.

"I'll try, Mama, I'll try."

"Now," Ernestine continued, "we'll just wait till Mico gets here and then, Iree, I want you and Imani to walk the blocks and see can you help anyone. Imani, you go get the ammonia out from under the sink and mix it with that water in the blue jar. Then throw it down the stairs. Iree, you hose down the rest. I think I need to do me some more weaving."

With that Ernestine stood up, smoothed out her brightly flowered skirt, and walked to the other side of the bench. Iree and Imani moved to the rhythm of the shuttle, cleaning the stairs and watching their neighbors congregate in the long street of cracked-open doorways. As Iree rewound the hose and prepared to climb back up the clean steps, Jeremiah drove up, tooting his truck's horn in a six-beat rhythm.

"Uncle Mico," cried out Iree and ran to hug him.

"Well, ain't this week a blessing. I get to see you two days in a row. I know you and spider lady and my sunshine girl are fine. I just thought

I'd come up and maybe beat you at some bones just so you wouldn't worry about me."

He smiled, hugging her longer than usual, trying to feed comfort into her long, thin limbs.

"I figure Ernie got you two going on an adventure so I'd better keep track of her and maybe fire up the barbecue for some earthquake supper. I'll have the tiles waiting for you and maybe some of your neighbors could come and play a hand. In fact, we could have a block party so you could finally meet your neighbors proper." He laughed as they climbed the stairs.

Ernestine was seven years older than her brother Jeremiah. Some grey around the temples, softening around his waistline, and deep-set laugh lines were the only signs that sixty-five years and he were closer bedfellows than the fifty or fifty-five years for which he was usually mistaken. Jeremiah took a special pride in being the youngest of his mother's children, and in having shown his favorite niece, Iree, the ways to negotiate the privilege of being the youngest in a household with the hardships of receiving everybody's leftovers. Ernestine, who throughout their years had flipped her relationship with Jeremiah from sister to mother and back to sister, loved her brother fiercely and harshly, relying on his insights and loudly insulting his habits.

Ernestine had heard the tail-end of the conversation as her brother and daughter crossed the threshold. "Only block party I'm interested in is the one that pushes that block you carry around your head offa your neck," she snapped. "Meet my neighbors proper. Hmmph. I know everybody around here and what color they heart is and if they know how to hold water in their mouths and keep they peace. And mostly I do unto others as they do unto me, which is to leave well enough alone.

"You certainly took your fine time driving that old wreck of a might-run-might-not-run truck to check on your sister. And what about your children and the grands? Where's Michael and Kamau, and how you going to hear from Egypt up here where there is no phone?"

Jeremiah walked to his sister and, holding her shoulders tight so she could not navigate the shuttle through the warp, kissed her on the top of her tightly braided head. "Stop weaving your webs and turn around. I'm glad to see you're all right too, although everybody knows if anybody will make it, it's you three. You know, you're so mean that even if the earth did swallow you up she'd spit you back out, full and evil as ever.

"Now, you and me are going back to my house for a few days and you gonna have to do like all the other spiders and pull some string out your belly 'cause I'm not taking no damn loom with me. Michael was picking Kamau up from school today and bringing him by so I'm sure they are together. Phones are down, but Egypt is cool, and she'll get

79

through when they come back up. Come on now, woman, this ain't no time to be making cloth."

The old woman straightened her back and laughed. "Since when do you know when the time is for me to work and when the time is for me to be still? I thought your specialty was nuts, bolts, and how to open another can of beer."

"Ever since I figured out those wasn't arms and legs you carry on you, but spider limbs."

"Hush your rudeness, man. If we're going, let's get going. Iree, take Imani down the hill and go check on the neighbors."

Iree and Imani walked carefully down the stairs, still wet from the hose, as another shiver went through the house.

When Ray reached his front steps he saw his wife leaning against the railing talking to their neighbor, Mr. Beverly. Ray Junior was sucking on a lime green popsicle. A square bandage sat over his left eyebrow. Little Jean, named for her grandmother on her father's side, was skipping rope.

Mr. Beverly rasped out of his rounded chest, "Quite a shake there, Ray. You just get back? Did you see anything?"

Nancy squinted her eyes at her husband, unconsciously sniffing to see how many drinks he had found in the last few minutes.

"Yes, Ray, what *did* you see?" she asked sarcastically.

"I'm sorry, Nancy. Everybody's all right?" He

came close, letting her know that he had remained sober.

"I guess I'd better start cleaning up those books, huh? Got much glass to sweep?"

Nancy looked at him and gestured towards the door helplessly.

"Let's leave it for a while. Wait until it's all stopped."

"So Ray, what did you see?" Mr. Beverly rasped again.

"I just climbed the hill and came back down. Everybody I saw looked fine. The houses weren't badly damaged. You know, just broken windows and crying children and such, but I didn't see any big problems."

"What about over by Hickory?" Nancy cut in, with ice between her teeth.

"Tell you the truth," Ray looked at his wife and let the words out slow and even to be sure his wife understood the situation, "I didn't even think to go over there."

"Really?" Nancy said, not believing him.

Just then, another siren broke through the air, wailing through the streets. Ray and Mr. Beverly turned together towards the town's center and found themselves facing a rising spiral of smoke. Mr. Beverly rocked back on his heels and snorted, "That seems to be coming from near Hickory, I'd say . . ."

Ray knew exactly where the fire started. He felt

his bowels tremble and immediately stepped in the direction of the smoke and sirens.

"Got to go, Nancy. Maybe I can be of some help."

"Ray, let the professionals handle it."

"I've got to go to the store anyway. I need to get there before the streets are cut off and get us some supplies. I'll be sure and bring back some water and batteries and snacks, too."

"Get a big jar of peanut butter and two loaves of bread," Nancy shrugged and turned away from him. She knew that several years ago Ray had had an affair with a woman who lived somewhere around Hickory. Although it had been years since he had been with her, and years since Nancy had worried about Ray wandering off, Nancy still remembered Ray's late evening walks, which she had watched from a crack in the drapes of her living room bay window. She remembered how she had once listened for his 3:00 A.M. returns as she lay in bed. First she would hear the door close, then the inevitable squeak as Ray stepped on the third square of linoleum near the corner of the kitchen table. After the squeak Ray would stand still for a few moments and then pull out the kitchen chair, somehow never able to pick it up or put it down without scraping the floor. He would sit down, stand up, hit that squeaky tile again, get a glass of water, sit back down, stand back up and then sit, over and over, sometimes until the sun rose. As soon as she heard him settle into the chair

Nancy would drift off into a solid sleep. When those late night walks ended he drank a little more, but still provided well, and every night he crawled into her arms. It was on such a night that Little Jean was conceived.

Ray turned back and gripped Nancy's arm. Then he gave Ray Junior a cursory hug and interrupted Little Jean's jump roping by thrusting his hand in to pull her pony tail. As was her habit, she ducked her head and hit his hand away, grinning broadly at being faster than her father. Then he strode down the block, being careful to walk neither too fast nor too slow, pacing himself so that no sense of urgency would show. He decided to stop first at J&J Best Food and Liquor and get a couple of gallons of water, some batteries, cookies for the children and cigarettes for Nancy, as well as the long overdue nip for himself. He remembered the bread and forgot the peanut butter.

Grocery bag tucked under one arm, he cut through Pinball Alley, over to Hickory until he came to the intersection with Linden. He saw that the corner house in the apartment complex was in flames, orange and blue fire licking at the gauze curtains. Next door to the blazing building was Lorraine's house. Lorraine, once his lover, now the mother to a child who, she continually insisted, was his six-year-old daughter; to which he always replied that he was sure they had stopped having sex for at least a year before the birth. At first

Lorraine pressed the issue, now she simply accepted his rare visits and his small gifts.

A soft-voiced, wide-hipped woman, Lorraine always seemed to live her life in response to others, being moved and moving wherever she was pushed. A comfortable job as receptionist, a home passed down from her mother, and her one unwanted child, who was as stubborn and independent as Lorraine was quiet and cruel, made up Lorraine's simple and regimented life.

There had been a time when Ray actually considered leaving his wife to live with Lorraine, but she was too quiet and too meticulous and too different. At first he had sought her as a refuge from his loud and raucous home, from the constant barrages from his wife, who always was pushing, pulling or twisting. But there was something about Lorraine that was too calm and ominous to let him stay long in her carefully laid-out home. He felt that she might gather the free will she never seemed to use and quietly cut his throat one night, acting on the bitterness of a life spent always being pushed by others.

Ray remembered how Lorraine cooked the same meals every Tuesday, every Sunday, every day: Monday was meat loaf, Wednesday lamb chops, Thursday spaghetti, Sunday the inevitable baked chicken. It never varied. Her house was spotless. Her furniture sat, covered in plastic. Lorraine had told him that nothing had been moved in the house since her mother had died, and, except for the bright-colored parrot which he had bought her, nothing had been added to the living room in over twenty years.

Lorraine never raised her voice. Even in sex she had been hauntingly quiet, accommodating his every whim, but offering no changes to the menu. When he got out of her bed to walk the three blocks home, she sighed but never held him back. When he stayed away for weeks at a time she cried, but never refused him entrance. Even when he denied fathering her chubby, red-haired daughter, she put up no fight, only stared at him and listlessly showed him the door, remarking almost as an afterthought, "Well, she's as much yours as mine. Some day it'll come to you. You might even find yourself keeping her."

As Ray came close to Lorraine's front door, he realized that the fire was almost out in the next door apartment building, but it raged at Lorraine's house. The fire seemed to have started at Lorraine's place and leapt from her living room window to the apartment house's north wall. He could see that the bottom floor of her house was caved in. The sidewalk in front was cracked in two, and the basement door was tipped like a collapsed playing card house, splintered with windows thrown open, and Lorraine's trinkets and framed family photographs peeking out of the crevices, like laundry pushing up a hamper's cover. The room's heavy red drapes and large philodendron leaned out the broken bay window.

Lorraine simply stood outside her burning home and stared. Firemen were pushing her across the walk while medics tried to encourage her to lie down. She meekly followed them, wordlessly turning her back to the house.

It was then that Ray spotted Iree and her daughter. Imani was desperately talking to her mother, gesturing at the northernmost house, Lorraine's home, pointing to the cracked basement door. Her eyes were big and tearful and she was trembling as she pointed to Lorraine. Ray once again felt the urge to vomit and ran to the corner to hear Imani's pleas.

"Mama, she's in there! She's trapped behind the door. Her mama tried to open it, but when she couldn't, she just walked out. Mama, she's crying, she's in there. Mama, she'll die!"

"Who will die?" Ray intruded, and Iree reeled around. Her tongue was loaded with salt as she tried to push him away. "Well, Mr. MacIntire, from the smell of your breath I see you've gotten you your old support system back in place. Why don't you look after Lorraine while I talk with Imani?"

"The girl knows something, just like she knew about the books in my house," Ray answered.

"Mr. MacIntire, you need to give that bottle a rest and look after your own and I'll look after mine," Iree said firmly, pushing Imani to a nearby stoop and blocking Ray's access to her.

Ray followed and grabbed Imani by the shoulders, pushing Iree out of the way. "What did you see, child? Tell me!"

"Mandy!" Imani screamed, no longer able to hold back her vision. "She was playing dress-up . . ."

Iree cuffed her child on the back of her head, trying to get her to stop spewing out truths she should have had no way of knowing. But it was too late, Ray heard and knew that the child was telling the truth, and that a child, who he knew was his own, was trapped in the burning building, and that her mother had walked away.

Ray ran to the nearest fireman and began pointing frantically to the basement. He ran back to Imani and pulled her over, yelling at her desperately.

"Tell me! Tell me exactly where she is," he screamed. "Tell me what you saw!"

"I didn't see nothing," Imani wept. She hid in her mother's arms, sputtering out her words.

In the next moment Ray, in what was to be one of the few acts of courage he was ever to demonstrate, and one of the many acts of foolishness he was to continually commit, walked past the barricades and pushed open the cleaved door to crawl into the basement. He ignored the screams of the police and firefighters and fought off their attempts to pull him back. He pushed past a firefighter who was moving inside, oxygen mask in hand. Thick smoke filled his lungs and stung his eyes, which were already brimming with tears, as he went past the shadows and piles of boxes, past the silver artificial Christmas tree, the boxed Thanksgiving harvest basket, the plastic Easter lilies, until he found the small back room and wedged the door open.

He saw Amanda sitting in a corner and called to her. She crawled across the floor to him, threw her arms around him and clung to his neck. Coughing and reeling he staggered out with her until he bumped into a firefighter who led them outside just as the top floor, having caught fire, began to fall onto the stacks of labelled boxes.

"She's yours now," he heard Lorraine whisper as he was led, blinded with smoke, to the ambulance's back door. She followed him and continued to speak into his ear, ignoring the firefighter who tried to pull her away.

"I'm done with this place, Ray. I was never meant to raise that child, you know that. She came because you wanted her, not me. I kept her till you were ready. Now I'm done."

With that, Lorraine tipped her head in quiet prayer, bent over Ray, and turned up her daughter's face. She kissed Amanda on each cheek, got up, and boarded a waiting bus which was to take those made homeless by the earthquake and fire to a Red Cross relief station. She never looked back. Amanda, who had quietly suffered an abusive silence for most of her six years, did not raise her head as her mother walked away.

Ray looked around and saw Imani and Iree at

the end of the alley. Imani was jumping across sidewalk cracks and pulling against her mother's hand. She saw Ray and grinned widely. Ray motioned away the medics, assuring them that he and Amanda were fine and picked up the bag he had abandoned. Holding the girl on one hip, and the supplies on the other, he prepared to walk home. For a moment he was full of possibilities. Yes, tomorrow he would begin to process the child as abandoned and offer to become a foster parent. He knew the child would be well-fed and clothed in his home, and that his wife would welcome the increased money and would let her stay, but offer no comfort or love. She already took care of two extra children during the day and they were going to start school in a few months. Nancy would make more money with this one, and this one was quiet. He knew Lorraine was gone for good. He was going to keep the child, at least until a good home could be found for her.

Tomorrow he would bring Amanda up to Ernestine and ask for a blessing in exchange for keeping quiet about Imani's spooky talent. He knew that the old woman would not trade a candle for his silence, but he had to ask anyway, if only to let her know that he knew, and that he was not going to forget.

Amanda's hair filled Ray's dry mouth. It tasted of soap and lavender oil. It smelled of her mother, and for a moment Ray felt better and stronger than he had in years. For a moment he felt totally alive. And when the earth let out a quiet tremble under his feet, and he heard the house in back of him collapsing, he too skipped across the cracks and grinned broadly.

Dish Water
—m—

WHILE WAITING FOR THE KETTLE to boil, Zulie wiped off the table and prepared to put out plates for the cake. She had made up her mind that Imani was going to arrive any minute to blow out her candles and cut the cake, and that was that. Iree was washing the dishes and Ernestine was standing next to her, drying each plate and stacking them next to the dish drainer. Iree reached out a soapy hand and touched the tightly woven cloth that hung on the wall above the sink. It was rust colored with small and large triangles running down the edges. The piece had served as a rug once, the only day it had ever been used.

Iree thought back on that day and drew in a breath, laughing softly.

"Mama, you remember the day we got this house?"

"Of course I do. You were carrying on about leaving that old shack of a place by the playground because it was the first real home you remembered.

You were grown and pregnant with Imani then, but you were afraid to leave that old place, like you thought you'd lose a hold of a piece of yourself coming way up here. I remember I tied a piece of yarn around that scraggly bush out front of that house, and got in the back of Mico's truck with you and told him to drive real slow. I'd just let that yarn unravel and when the ball would run out I'd tie a new piece on to the end and let that ball run out. That way you could follow the yarn back. Seems like we started with a yellow and moved into a pink and got all the way to a dark green before the line broke and pulled out of my hand. You started to howling at Jeremiah to stop the truck so we could connect the strand back up. He stopped and got out of the cab to see what we had been up to. When he looked back and saw that snarly trail of yarn, he carried on so you'd a thought we'd been leaving some kind of gold on the ground. He drove all the way back to that bush and made you wind up that yarn into a ball. You started crying. You wound and cried and wound and cried. Finally, we were back where we started. Mico broke off the twig it was wrapped on to and stuck it in the yarn ball and big as you were he picked you up and put you in the cab of the truck talking about how he wasn't having no foolishness about leaving a trail from a shack to a real house. He was so mad!"

"Yeah, I held that ball of yarn for about three days crying and turning it in my hands," Iree said.

"But I wasn't talking about the day we came here. I was talking about the day we got this place to be ours. Forever. Remember how we had stopped paying Bartell rent on it years before, and started sending the money to the bank, just like Ezekiel said, but Bartell kept acting like he owned it? He'd come up here from time to time talking about how Ezekiel stole it from him and how he was going to get it back. Then we started getting all those court papers which you kept ignoring because he had your name spelled all wrong so you insisted they weren't for you. Finally he got some kind of an order to put us off the property. I was so afraid. But, you didn't worry a bit. Just kept working on this cloth . . ." Iree reached up and fingered the weaving. "The yarn was so thick that it took you a long time each pull and I remember you beat the reed so hard it made wind around you."

"Had the nerve, always calling me Augustine instead of Ernestine. Far as I could see none of those papers was for me anyway. Augustine, hmmp."

Mico was sharing the couch and radio with Al. Without turning towards the women he cut into their conversation. "What are you two hens whispering about over there? Moon isn't all the way up and you two are already trying to cast spells."

Ernestine snapped at her brother, "Hush, we wasn't bothering you. You sitting over there pretending to be listening to that radio, but I hear you getting ready to fall off to sleep with those creak-ing and cracking old bones of yours."

"I ain't hardly going to sleep, old woman, but I am glad to hear you are concerned about my aching bones."

"I didn't say I was concerned. I said I was listening to you hard as you was listening to us. Furthermore, Mr. Stick-your-nose-where-it-doesn't-belong-Jeremiah Jefferson, we ain't witches and we don't cast spells."

"Yeah, and chickens don't lay eggs."

Iree started laughing in her clear bell chimes. "I can't believe you two, how many years you been fussing at each other?"

Ernie sat down at her loom and ran her hands across the empty harnesses. Iree followed her mother to the bench, humming her ocean song. A few minutes later Zulie brought a steaming cup of tea to everyone and took a seat at the table. Iree turned the thick mug in her hands, feeling the heat seep through and almost burn her palms. She let the steam soothe the last of the tired feeling out of her eyes.

"You remember that day, Mama? I had one of my fits and was just getting out of the bath that you had run for me. Everything was calm and then—"

Mico joined in, "And then Sheriff Koresh comes up—"

Ernestine rose up from the loom bench and

glared at her brother. "You weren't there, you
can't tell that part."

"I've heard it enough times to know it, spider
lady."

"Still, it ain't yours to tell. Yes, Iree, I remember
how that flabby, swelled-up-idea-of-a-supposed-
to-be-man come swaggering up and shouting like
we are all deaf, telling us we need to quit this
place. Now you quit smoking and you quit gam-
bling, but you don't quit a home."

Iree laughed. "That's what you told him too. I
heard him yelling and pulled a dress over me quick
as I could. Soon as I got out the door I heard you
telling him that he might want to quit his job if he
thought he was going to mess with you and your
family. You told him he might quit living if he
wanted to, but he sure wasn't going to quit you
and yours out of your home. I remember he
started sputtering about knowing you was old and
blind . . ."

"Sputtering and spitting. I swear he about
washed my face with his slime."

"Yes, then Imani started asking him if his other
men were deaf and was that why he was yelling
so, because he was hurting her ears and she wished
he would quiet down."

Ernie started laughing. "Then he turned so red
I swear I could feel the color burning on the edge
of my fingers when he tried to hand those pieces
of paper to me."

Iree stopped laughing and her voice turned

quiet. "I remember looking past Koresh and there was Ezekiel, standing clear as day at the foot of the oak tree pointing to its north side. It was so strange because I was here in this time and everybody was awake and here with me, but I saw him, clear as day, clear as day. He was standing and looking at you, Mama, and laughing. I walked right past Koresh. He couldn't get you to take the papers so he pushed them at my hand thinking I'd take them. They dropped to the ground and started blowing away. One of his men started to chase after them, but I just walked down those stairs and over to the tree and started digging where Ezekiel had pointed.

"Old Koresh, he decided he was through talking to you and followed me to the tree, talking about he was sorry but we don't own this land, and we had to go. Standing behind him at the back was that squirmy Bartell, who knew he had lost the place to Ezekiel. And it's not like he didn't have another twenty pieces of land to get rent from and gamble away. Anyway we had paid every month like Ezekiel had told us to, so we were sure that we had more than paid for this little piece of house that Bartell never did anything with but ignore. I mean he's still got houses nobody has lived in for years that he just keeps, letting them rot away.

"Well anyway, I remember digging with my hands and Koresh standing over me with one of his no-lip grins, sweating and apologizing, trying not to look at me because he's sure I'm crazy, and afraid some of it might rub off. So I looked up from the ground and said, 'You know this house is ours. Ezekiel won it and got the deed and the bill of sale."

"Bartell's eyes squinted real tight on me and then he looked over my shoulder where Ezekiel was standing and he hissed out, 'You Moores are crazy. You all need to be in an institution.' "

Ernestine pulled in her breath remembering. "The nerve of him."

"Yeah, Mama, but you remember little Imani piping in, 'Well at least we aren't murderers. I mean we didn't kill nobody.' I jumped up from the hole I had been making and put my hand over that child's mouth to shut her up. Then I heard Ezekiel telling me to get a shovel, so I whispered into Imani's ears to find a shovel and keep quiet. She walked right past Koresh over to Bartell and spit all over his shiny shoes. Then walking as tall and proper as she could be, she went to the shed at the back of the house and got the shovel. Well, Koresh took that moment to send his men to start clearing our furniture out of the house."

Ernestine set her mug down and moved back to her loom bench. "Yes, indeed, I knew that was coming. But while he was giving orders, I went inside and got that old gun that Ezekiel used for hunting and stood at the top of the stairs just pointing it wherever I heard voices and felt movement."

"Yeah, Mama, pointing it at me, at Koresh, at the road. Mama Ernestine, there was no telling what you would of hit if you had fired."

"Wouldn't hit nothing, child. Gun was empty."

Everyone started laughing again.

Mico's deep voice slid through the laughter, "That was when I came up the hill. I knew that was the morning that they were coming to serve those papers. I wasn't worried they'd get you out. I came to make sure you didn't damage them too much." He chuckled. "It was a sight, I can tell you. Imani was there all frowned up with her face covered with dirt, digging with her hands, while Iree, you were using your bare feet to push in that shovel and Ernie was waving the rifle this way and that, and the officers were looking ready to pee in their pants. I swear I never saw Koresh so glad to see me in his life. It was like he was sure I was the nigger savior in the flesh. He ran up to the truck with the papers in his hand and tried to give them to me, spouting on about how, 'This is Bartell's land and you all got to move.' He went on like he was reading some kind of a prepared speech about how you had been sent several court notices and never did produce a deed or bill of sale. He was talking so fast it was like pus pouring out his mouth. And that man had some dragon's breath, poking his head in the truck window and spattering spit everywhere. Now you know I didn't say a word in response, just opened the door and cracked him right between the legs. Of course, I apologized."

Ernestine chortled. "Mico, I don't think saying 'Sorry, I didn't know you had anything there' counts as an apology."

"Well, I meant it."

Iree pulled them back to the story. "There I was, talking to Ezekiel . . ."

"Talking to the tree as far as we could see."

"Well, Mama Ernie can't see, and Uncle Mico, you don't look, and Imani was so busy throwing dirt in the direction of the posse that she didn't notice. Anyway, Ezekiel was telling me who to call out. He told me to look at old pimply-faced Crenshaw and ask him did he get the stain out his pants from when he messed on himself when he saw the side of Ezekiel's head cave in. So I called out the question, and the man's eyes seemed to turn around in his socket. And Imani called out, 'No, Mama, he threw the pants out.' "

Mico added, "Yeah and that man took off running down the hill. Said you were too crazy for him, and he didn't want no part of this business."

"Running from hisself." Ernestine stretched out one foot making circles in the air, and then stretched out the other. Then she spread her fingers and shook blood into the tips. She picked up a hook and started to pull a shiny crimson strand of yarn through a nettle, beginning to rethread her loom.

Iree went on. "No, Mama, he was running from

Ezekiel. He saw him too. I know he did. And the way the sun was glinting on Ezekiel's head, one whole side turn all red and flat while he stood there. Blood started flowing all over again. I'm sure he saw it. Then the sheriff came and grabbed the shovel from me. I tried to hold on tight, but Ezekiel, he told me to let go and just as I did, I swear, Ezekiel, he just pushed on the end of it so it hit Koresh right in the eye. I swear it wasn't me, even though everybody thought it was me letting go so sudden. It was Ezekiel. That old man fell straight away on his behind and the shovel fell right on top of him. He got up, throwing the shovel back at me and shouting and cursing and spitting, but right then Imani found the box. Sweet as pie she walks up to me and hands it over saying, 'Mama, is this what we're looking for?'

"Well, I grabbed that child and hugged her all up and then looked in the box and saw the title, clear as can be. Bill of sale, deed, everything. I walked over to you, Uncle Mico, and asked you to take me to the courthouse because we had papers to register. Koresh was talking about, 'Let me see those papers.' But I heard Ezekiel calling, 'Don't let him touch them.' So I held them close to my chest and moved far as I could from him. Mama Ernie, you started to waving that gun again and Imani, she ran in the house to fetch some shoes for me.

"I walked back over to the tree and tried to give Ezekiel a hug but he was fading. Even his voice

100

was sounding more like the wind and less like him. *I'll find a way to get back if there's a need. Don't worry on it if you don't see me any more. Smile, Iree. Come on, y'got to smile for me.* I was crying and smiling at the same time, and I swear I felt his fingers run down my cheek before he faded away completely. Then I slipped on those mismatched shoes Imani had brought me—one slipper of yours, Mama, and one slip-on loafer of mine—and proud as could be walked over to the truck. Imani held the door for me like I was some kind of queen. Then she turned her head and stuck her tongue out at old Koresh and said, 'Yeah we something, we something.' I pulled her into the truck behind me and slammed the door, because Koresh hadn't said a word, he was just looking hard. Then Uncle Mico, you walked over to Koresh and started talking real deep and quiet."

"Sure did, girl, I told him that his business was done up here for the day. I also noted that you, Sis, were not the best aim in the world, but that you balanced that by being very quick on the trigger. Koresh said he'd escort us to the courthouse and see if the papers were in good order, and if not he would be back and you would be moved out. What a fool."

"Yeah, Uncle, and what a sight we were. Imani and I covered with dirt. Imani's braids coming a loose and all dusty, and me with my mismatched shoes and clutching this box of papers. But they were the real deal, and this house was ours."

Ernestine sighed. "I wanted to go down to the courthouse with you, but I decided to stay here. I sat in front of that door and held that shotgun for seemed like hours till you folks got back. In fact, I scared away Mary Louise who came for a tea for her son's croup, and Mr. MacIntire who came up on one of his sideways strolls, just to see what was happening. Yeah, that was quite a day. What made you think of that, daughter?"

Iree walked over to the sink and ran her fingers along the triangles on the cloth. "You finished this cloth that day after we came back. That was the first piece you had all the way finished in a long time. You made a big ceremony of each of us cutting it off the loom and had Imani help you to tie off the ends. Then you had me hem it so it would hold its shape. When we finally had it done it was late, but you had us all to go outside to have a picnic under that oak tree, remember? We spread the cloth as a rug to sit on, then you let Uncle Mico do his dance and pour some rum for Ezekiel. Then, remember Zulie, you and Al came up, as if we had called you, and we all ate one of Zulie's special stews and spent the night at the foot of that tree trying to bring Ezekiel back, but he never came. Before the moon set we buried that torn shirt and chip of tooth right where the box had been. I haven't seen Ezekiel since that day, except when he comes in dreams. But that morning he was clear as day. Clear as day."

"Hmmph." Ernestine swallowed, feeling her

heart fold over itself in the place that her son used to ease. "It's been a lot longer since I seen him. Iree, when is that daughter of ours coming home?" She dropped the threading hook and began to feel around the floor for it. Iree came over and picked it up and placed it back in Ernestine's hand. She began to rub the old woman's shoulders as Zulie started putting candles in the cake.

Buses

———∿∿∿———

THE TWO GIRLS RODE THE bus wordlessly. Amanda was concentrating on not vomiting again. Imani tried to interest Mandy in their fellow passengers. "Look at his hair. I can tell he's afraid to touch it. Look at it, all oil and pasted next to his neck. I bet it smells, too."

Mandy just looked out the window, so Imani settled down and let her friend drift into her own thoughts as they rode the bus into the small downtown area. Mandy thought she saw Jerome walking next to the playground. She recognized him by his easy gait, slow and sure. That's how he walked the first day she saw him. She had turned around and watched him walk down the hall after he had showed her to her classroom door, slow and easy as if the late bell had not already rung. It had been Mandy's fault they were late. She had kept him talking after the lunch bell had rung.

That day Amanda had been sitting by herself, which was how she spent most lunches, drawing intricate designs in her small, blank-paged book, shading in the spirals and making almond leaves unfold in the corners.

Jerome had stood far off and just watched her. Amanda never seemed to notice when people stared at her. You could get right on top of her before she would startle and freeze, like a deer, eyes caught by headlights in an evening's drive. Then she would usually gather up her things with deliberate order and speed, and move off, conceding the space to the newcomer.

Jerome stayed back and called out, "You're Amanda Bresley, right? I'm Jerome, Sonny's cousin. Have you seen him?"

Amanda was shocked. No one ever talked to her outside of class except Imani and Sheila. And, of course, Barry, who was unswervingly and hopelessly sweet on her. In fact, Charlotte, who was always saying something hip or cool in class, had had the whole class laughing the other day when Amanda offered a line for a song to the guest artist in class.

"Why, I didn't know you could talk?" Charlotte quipped, and then turned to the class. "She never talks, does she? Mr. Willie, you got some talent making this child talk. And it's a good line too."

Amanda, who studiously avoided all attention, squirmed uncomfortably as the class laughed in assent. Then the bell rang and saved her. Charlotte came over and shook her on the shoulder. "You ought to talk more you know," and then swung out the door, spouting off about the way Tommy G. was swaggering down the hallway.

Amanda sat frozen in her chair, her lips partly open, not moving until a student from the next class shook her and said, "This is my seat this period." Then she rushed out of the room wordlessly. So she was taken aback when Jerome spoke to her. Didn't he know that she didn't like to talk?

"Well?" Jerome persisted, getting nearer and looking at her pad. Amanda shut it sharply.

"No," she said and started to pack up.

"Hey, don't leave. I draw a little too, but I like to draw airplanes and helicopters." Without being asked, he sat down, opened a notebook, and began to show her page after page of doodles. "See, this is a hospital plane. It's like a helicopter for landing, but it can fly fast and carry people in from everywhere."

Sonny came by a few minutes later holding his girlfriend Farika's hand and acting like nothing special was happening. Jerome called out, "See you tomorrow at the game," letting Sonny know he saw what was up, and knew that the after-school plan of one-on-one basketball on the junior high school yard five blocks away was cancelled.

Amanda barely talked, just listened to Jerome and asked occasionally how many people the plane would seat, or how far it could go without stopping. When lunch was over Jerome walked Amanda back into the school.

"I knew your mom," he offered, as he held open the heavy central corridor door. "She used to come by my uncle's car wash every Thursday just before six and have her car washed. She was regular like a clock."

Amanda started walking faster and looking hard at the floor. Jerome found himself almost chasing her. "Hey, no offense. I didn't mean anything wrong. Actually she was kind of nice. Always said hello to me, not like some of the customers. Always gave me a nice tip when my uncle let me work on the car. She liked to joke with my uncle."

Amanda jerked to a stop. "My mother never joked with anyone."

Jerome laughed. "Well now see, there you are wrong. I mean it took a long time of him telling some of the sorriest jokes you'd want to hear, but she did laugh. You want to hear one?"

Amanda smiled. "A sorry joke? No I think I better get to class." With that she turned the hall corner and immediately opened a door.

Jerome yelled after her, "I did think she was nice."

Amanda turned to face him. "I really don't remember."

Imani shook Amanda's arm, breaking her reverie. "Wasn't that Jerome back there on the street? I could of sworn that was him. It seemed like his walk, you know . . ."

"I didn't notice," Amanda lied.

"Now, why you gonna lie like that? Just say 'So what' or something. It's not like I said let's jump off the bus."

Just then Imani saw her friend Rose getting out of a sleek silver car. She was leaning into the front seat of the car, talking to the driver. Her lips flashed out her words like BB pellets sliding through the cracked window.

"Mandy, look, there's Rose. Come on." And with that she pulled Amanda to her feet, yelling to the driver, "Stop please. It's my cousin from Omaha. Oh, you have to stop." Amanda rolled her eyes as the driver slowed the bus and let them off a half-block past the stop.

Mandy hopped off the bus after Imani, then pulled back on Imani's hand. "You know I don't know Rose."

"That's because she's been in Ohio," Imani laughed back.

"You mean Omaha," Amanda answered.

"No, I probably mean Oregon," Imani giggled and then called to Rose who was waving the car away. "Hey girl. Whas up? How you been?"

Amanda trailed behind. "No really, I don't re-member her."

"Of course you do. Think back. Everybody knows Rose. You remember she got suspended for telling off the principal. Real sassy. She graduated last June and they didn't want to let her walk off the stage."

"Oh yeah, I signed the petition."

Imani and Rose grabbed each other and gave each other a big hug, then stood back and laughed.

"Nice to see you, Crystal Ball. I see you didn't get no lighter."

"Yeah, Stiletto Tongue, and you haven't quieted down. You're still cursing people out."

"Yeah, fool date wanted to take something I don't sell and I don't give away for free."

"Doesn't that make you a virgin?" Imani teased.

"No, girl, that makes me a good trading partner. Life ain't nuthin' but a business."

"That's not true," Amanda said.

"So you still hanging tight with the walking tomb, huh? Actually, girl, you got kinda pretty. What's up with you two? Aren't you supposed to be home by now?"

Rose had been on her own since graduation, and was alternately proud and resentful of her ability to keep afloat while so many of her schoolmates stayed cloistered under their parents' roofs.

No one answered. Imani and Amanda and Rose stood quietly looking at one another. Then Rose put her hand on Amanda's shoulder. "Well, since my date ended so abruptly I'm going home. I live a couple of blocks away. Why don't you come on and have a soda with me. Watch some sorry late night movies?"

"That's the ticket," smiled Imani, knowing Amanda would gladly fall in behind. The three of them walked back to Rose's apartment, laughing about last June when Rose walked capped and gowned to get her diploma, proudly raising her fist and shouting, "They didn't want me to get it, but it's mine now!" Then as soon as she had what proved to be a blank certificate in her hand, she shook the principal's hand, leaned over to the microphone and said harshly, with her deep clear voice, "And you all are still some small-minded, uptight bigots trying to hold a nigga back."

The auditorium got quiet as the principal cleared her throat and said, "Miss Mason, there are no niggers at this school."

Rose had looked up then and saw Imani craning forward from the lower row of the choir. "Well then, like my friend always sings, we be Africans. The point is, this is mine. You didn't think I was going to get it, but I got it!"

The principal ignored her retort and immediately read off the next name, "Fred Murdock," just as the choir broke into an amen, and the young people in the school football stands broke out into whelps and the parents looked sternly from side to side as the wave subsided and the list went on.

"Yeah, girl, I swear Fred sure did think he was popular. You see the way he walked up there as if all that yelling was for him!"

They had stopped at the foot of a long flat building. Rose searched for her key as Amanda said, "Everyone said you ruined the graduation."

"Girl, what are you talking about? First of all, it was boring, bor-ing. Second of all, I kept a whole lot of people in this little oatmeal town full of entertaining conversation. They ought to be thanking me. The last graduation I remember them talking about was when that Irish guy painted his face green out of some kind of protest wanting Irish stew or something."

Imani folded over. "Girl, you know you lying."

Rose did not reply. She put the key in the door and undid the lock.

The Porch

ZULIE STOKED UP A FIRE in the small fireplace, and then joined Al on the couch. They sat quietly, watching the fire and sipping their tea. Iree and Mico had moved onto the front porch. Iree sat on the edge of the stairs, her feet only one step lower than her hips, making her knees point up as if she were squatting, elbows balanced on each thigh. Ernestine got up from the loom bench and poured more tea into two cups to bring to Iree and Mico. She stood in the doorway, stilled by their presence on the stair's edge, feeling the steam rise from the mugs. As Iree looked into Mico's watery blue-grey eyes straining out of his rust wrinkled, full-cheeked face, she sighed and shook her head. Her fingers began to tremble until her uncle took her hands and pressed them together, like a heavily bound prayer book whose pages he was trying to keep from fluttering and breaking in a sudden gust of wind.

Iree shook her head again, relaxed her hands

and sighed, "I just can't hold on any longer. I'm always racing to catch up, and then I try with all my might to be in the here and now, but instead I slip forward or backward and just get bruised. It slides around me all soft and edgy until something happens, like you shaking me. Uncle Mico, why can't I stay, like you or Mama? Even Imani lives in the here. But me, I'm always in the cracks. I just can't hold on any more."

Mico let go of Iree's hands, which had finally stopped trembling. He ran his thick-fingered palm across the smooth of her cheek and caught the tear that had sat still as she spoke. He breathed with Iree and held her face as gently as he had held her whole body when she was newborn, surprised at its lightness and honoring its warmth.

"What makes you think I'm always here, girl? And no, I'm not talking about ol' Ernie's talk about me and my brew."

Iree let out a corner of a grin and started breathing in her own time.

"It's just that when I go, I know I'm gone. On the other hand, when I get back, likely as not, I don't know where I've been. You just remember your travels, that's all."

"Mico, you don't get it at all. I don't control me. It controls me. Like the other night, I was sitting in a bath and the water was really a comfort around me for a while, but then I got drawn into the waves and the water just heaved around me. Mico, I could feel the earth beneath my toes and the air was dry and warm as an August evening. There wasn't any house or any road or any bathtub, just me, naked, and the dirt and the wild grass, and over there some wild berries. Even the shade tree hadn't planted itself yet. It was so many years ago, and the air, Mico, the air was like silver and it smelled sweet, and Mico, the dirt, the dirt was . . . making me know it . . ."

Iree stopped again and her hands flew out against the wind as if trying to catch the words that might be hidden there. Mico reached out and caught her hands, gently holding them still. She pulled them back to her own lap and continued, "So I'm walking around the crest of the hill right over there—" she pointed east of the large oak tree "—and then I get stuck and start sinking into the land. I'm going in deeper and deeper and before it swallows me I scream 'NO,' and pull myself back through the water, just like I'm drowning, to get back to the today. Uncle Mico, I almost drowned sitting in the damn bathtub."

Mico interrupted, "Did I ever tell you 'bout the time the river spoke to me? . . . Or was it the beer I had before walking to the river? Never mind which one, what's for sure is one of them was doing all the talking and I was doing all the listening and taking some of its advice. Which is probably another reason Ernie questions my judgement as much as she does. Anyway, there I was leaving old Malachi's garage and walking down by the river. Lord, I swear I started hearing it sing to me, so I went for a swim. Girl, I was halfway to the bottom before I realized I hadn't taken my shoes off." Jeremiah leaned back against the step, tilted his head back and laughed clear and long.

"Uncle Mico, you're just like the rest," Iree whined softly, but then let a tip of a smile through her lips. "Well, at least I know enough not to take advice from the river when you're full of beer, or is it advice from the beer when you're full of river?" Iree paused and shook her head.

Mico stroked her face. "So maybe you hear better than some of the rest of us. Iree, there was time you couldn't pull yourself out at all. Besides, Ernie says it's a gift that you haven't ever gotten all the way unwrapped. Haven't even got the ribbon untied."

"I think Ernie's wrong this time. I don't think it's a gift caught in a knot, I think if I can just hold on, Uncle Mico, if I can just hold on . . ."

"But Iree, there's nothing to hold on to . . ."

"Mico, I got to hold onto me . . ."

Ernestine spoke up, startling Iree, who had not noticed her presence. Mico, who had seen her from the corner of his eye, frowned.

"No, daughter, I don't think I'm wrong. Of course, Imani'd be agreeing with you talking about my tired eyes, wouldn't she?"

Ernestine brought the tea to Mico and Iree, then settled down close to her daughter. She continued, "Remember, daughter, when Imani was so little and so sick? Remember when I told you you had to stay here and mend your child? You held on, daughter, you've always been able to hold on."

Iree closed her eyes and let herself drift back in time. What she remembered most about that time was not about holding on, but about being able to let go. What she remembered most was the end of a five-day vigil when Imani finally began to recover and settle into a more peaceful sleep. Iree remembered holding her child's feet softly in the palms of her hands and rubbing the soles in full firm circles, the way Ernestine had taught her. She had lain Imani down in the big double bed that Iree shared with her mother. It was larger than the mattress in the child's small room, and easier for Ernestine to navigate around. Most importantly, however, it had access to a window or doorway on each side of the large room, which provided the benefit of a fresh breeze to cool Imani's feverish skin.

From the day she was born, Imani had kept Iree moving from task to task. She had come into the world early and small, and Iree, in constant fear of losing her, had never let Imani sleep alone for her first six months. Iree was sure it was the bodies of close family, the smells and heat, as well as the endless stories that Mico and Ernestine would laugh into the child's bright, deep brown eyes, that kept her baby breathing. The child was so quick, turning, crawling, jumping, climbing, and talking, all earlier than Iree expected, so that Iree was forced out of her stillness into a constant activity, only finding an exhausted calm each evening after she finally put the child to sleep.

But that five days was the first time that Iree had been afraid that Imani would not pull through. She had shivered with dread at the thought of taking her child down the hill and across town to the county hospital, where, as likely as not, some official-looking clerk in a non-descript skirt and shirt, and a little too much make-up, would take the girl away, questioning the ability of an epileptic mother and blind grand-mother to adequately care for such a lively child.

Iree had become accustomed to having her own, and her grandmother's, abilities questioned and scorned by social workers, who would smile their fake smiles and insist they were only trying to act on Iree and Ernestine's behalf. One time, these "officials" threatened to separate the two women and place them in what they called semi-institutionalized care unless they signed some papers stipulating increased health monitoring by a "qualified" impartial outside committee.

Semi-institutionalized care, of course, meant a half-way house where curfews were set, and where there were rules and regulations about when and how and why to eat, or bathe, or pee. But, the officials assured Iree and Ernestine, "You can, within these parameters, go into the city in the day time, with any one companion of your own choos-ing." Semi-institutionalized care meant few eating options, although a hot plate and small refrigerator were allowed, and strict rules about overnight visitors, none being the maximum number. It meant forced lodging with people who shared nothing beyond being something other than the agreed-upon norm in terms of working body parts, or clarity of mind, or years on the planet. The social workers insisted that Ernestine consider this decision carefully, reminding Ernestine repeatedly that she was blind and aging, and could not properly care for her daughter, a woman who could have a fit and strangle herself on her own tongue.

On hearing this, Ernestine banged her cane three times sharply against the flat, dusty pea-green linoleum floor. Then she stood up and said crisply:

"My daughter is not intending on killing herself. She is perfectly capable; she is just special. I have raised her from four years until now, and she used to be much worse then, right after her mother passed on. My eyes didn't work then, and my eyes don't work now. But you, Miss, you can't see a damn thing despite your thick eye glasses and even thicker attitude."

"There's no need to get excited," the worker had greyly replied. "We are here to help you even if you do not want our help. Many people do not want to know what is best for them. And you clearly need, indeed want, our assistance. Therefore, I suggest you sit down, let me finish this paperwork, and then you can take it to window seven."

Iree, sitting next to Ernestine, had not said a word. She sat and watched the woman's moving lips. When the writing stopped and the lips sat firmly one upon the other, and when Mama Ernestine's mouth clamped tight, pursed and angry, thick with words she was holding inside, Iree picked up the papers, led her mother towards and then past window seven, and took the bus to Mico's house.

Jeremiah had asked Iree, and only Iree, one question, "What you gonna do? Old spider legs here won't let me move up to your house, or let me move you two down to my house, so you've got to find an answer. What you gonna do?"

Iree spent the next few days considering her skills and listening to Ernestine's sharp-tongued guidance, as the older woman lashed words and then pressed solace into Iree's head. It was hard to devise steady work for Iree, whose mind emptied and re-filled with a fog of different times, within an infinitely layered world, a haze of changing expansions in which she kept one fingertip, one eye in the present, while the rest of her body convulsed and twisted on the ground, her tongue folding and creasing and swelling, visions dancing around her until she fell into a seemingly bottomless sleep.

But Iree took stock of what things others needed, and in time she found ways to earn her keep. She sold Ernestine's weaving at the flea market, she assisted at healings, and she helped neighbors dig and keep gardens full of flowers and vegetables. Working with dirt had always sustained her and kept her safe. Iree learned to work her jobs on different days, in different seasons, because she had not learned how to stay, really stay, very long at any one task, in any one place. But she learned to work so well that her presence was valued by others despite her haunting ways and the strange and frightening stories she sometimes told.

Despite her successful independence, Iree lived in fear of the social workers' ability to come snatch her or Imani away. That was why no ambulance had been called when Imani was born, and why the baby, despite known complications, was born at home. That was why the child had no immunizations. And that was why, during Imani's illness, Iree had kept her in the house for those five days, doing round-the-clock vigils to push away the fevers, to keep her daughter safe from the intruding world.

The fifth night, when Imani took her worst turn, had been the longest night Iree could remember, longer even than the night Imani was born. Imani had vomited relentlessly and every sheet and towel in the house had been soiled with her sweat, her bile-colored retching, and the dead skin she was sloughing off like a snake changing seasons. Iree spent the entire night immersed in the work of healing Imani. She bathed her daughter from head to toe, holding each finger between her hands, pulling the cloth gently through the fold between thumb and palm, then the curl of the smallest toe, the crease in her neck, the crevices around her belly button. She cradled Imani's head and ran the soft thick cloth around her eyelids, over her top lip, under her chin. Iree remained completely quiet as she washed the child down with witch hazel and water from the basin at her feet.

Ernestine spent the night washing the linens, brewing teas and soothing Iree. She sat next to Iree on the bed and felt Iree begin to tremble and breathe in short quick gulps, as the fear poured into Iree's lungs like thick hot tar and made her want to shake the walls of the house off, to go somewhere, anywhere. Ernestine placed her long muscled fingers around the roped muscles in Iree's shoulders and neck, and then she spoke firmly to her.

"No, child, it's not the time to run. We already made it through. This child will heal, she just needs to settle into the thought of it a little more, and you have to bring that thought to her. Almost everyone heals when they get ready. You know what a stubborn baby she is. She's holding onto this fever just like she holds onto her favorite blanket, or last week when she wouldn't give me back my wooden spoon, just gripped it tight until her fingers turned all the way purple black and told me, 'Dat's not the way,' sounding just like you when you were her age, repeating it over and over,

'Dat's not the way, dat's not the way.' Ernestine chuckled to herself.

"Iree, you just keep working her and she'll get well. Healing is not all the mystery everybody thinks it is. It comes from insides most of the time anyway. The teas and all just keep us busy and are reminders to the body. But folks take to healing different. Some are just resistant and don't want to accept the responsibility. They the ones who call up here and ask me could I bring some tea or make up a poultice. Really what they're saying is, 'Heal me, because I'm just too tired to do it myself.' So I go down, if I'm in a mood to, and chat, and they get better and smile, and pretend it was so easy for me making them wake up their insides and row the boat themselves. Of course, others come through real easy once you convince them of the notion that they can get better. It's true that sometimes I use this herb or that salve or these smokes. And you have to learn them, too. For some, herbs are the bridges and candles the splint that keeps the regrowing straight. You always need to give them something to do, something to occupy themselves with, so they can focus on the healing instead of the ailing. But Imani, she don't need no more than the bathing and rubbing to work this through.

"People are funny about what they think they need to heal them. Ol' Malachi got to have his garlic chain, and Zulie, she won't get well unless there's some soup around. Now me, I like to pretend and use it as an excuse to smoke a little one now and again you know. Keeps me smiling. But any way will do. There's just not all that magic to getting well as folks think. Your Uncle Mico just keeps that black stone where he can rub it smooth from time to time. Let him lose track of it for too long and he's sure to get ill. And Albert, well he likes to take him some regular medicine. If it ain't from the doctor, he won't look at it. Lord, he loves doctors. Now you, Iree, you just lazy and can't really get sick. I mean, you've never had the fevers or flus since you were five. Instead, you make your specialness an excuse for falling out, and spitting a lot, and sleeping away your todays, hiding in some other place."

At this, Iree rose straight up from the edge of the bed on which the two women were sitting, ready to shoot a pellet of saliva right in Ernie's neck, yet ashamed at her venom. Holding the anger like water in her mouth, she turned towards the door.

"I'll get some air for a minute, Mother Ernestine, and be right back."

Ernestine kept talking as if she had not felt the change. "Sit down. It's just a little longer and she'll be in a full sleep. This isn't about you, me, or your stories. Besides, I don't know what you're so huffy about. You know what I think about your spells. Hold on to the child's feet. Keep rubbing, she's almost there. You can hear it in her breath."

"Mama, I'm tired and need some air . . . Can't you rub for a while?"

"Child, you are lazy and need to learn this healing now. I'm not going to be here forever. Somebody's got to take over for me, and Imani's too young. So it's got to be you."

"I can't keep myself in one piece, how am I going to pull others together?"

"That's what I'm trying to tell you, child. It's nothing you have to give them, so much as what you have to make them feel. This child wants to come back, she just is learning how, so it's taking her a while, but really, I think she'd find her way with almost anyone long as they stayed close enough so she could feel their heat. But there are others who need more work. You might get someone who maybe wants to be healed and maybe don't, which means maybe you can, and maybe you can't, and you got to figure out just how much time you gonna give this one 'cause there's a line in back of you, and some of them are sure they want to get well. To those who can't make up their mind, just give them choices, give them a ritual to follow, no matter if it's teas, or steaming, or baths or whatever, and you tell them you'll be back when they're better and not before. Most'll come around. And those that don't, well. . . . There's always more to be healed than can be healed, and there's always gonna be a long line waiting on getting well until everyone figures how to get to their own personal power."

"If that's so why can't you see? I can't believe
you didn't have the will to keep your eyes working."

"Maybe I didn't know how then. Or maybe
some things aren't supposed to be healed. I don't
know that one myself, Iree. I even went to the regular doctors on that one and they didn't have any
answers either. Just said it happens sometimes, like
getting born with extra fingers, or one leg shorter
than the other, or with a wrinkle in your brain
that makes you have fits. You can't change the
plan."

Iree sat back down and wrapped her arms
around Ernestine's broad back while she laid her
head against the soft woven shawl thrown over the
old woman's shoulders. "It's just too much work
for me. I do all the time, Mama. I clean, I run
errands, I cook, I grow things. The beans you cut,
I grow them, and the greens you boil, I grow them
too. And Mama, I take care of you, string your
loom, roll your yarn, and then, I'm always going
here and there. Pushed and pulled, and I can't control it. You never help me, Mama, just call me
lazy, and crazy gal, like the rest. Why do I always
have to be so strong all the time, instead of me
like I am? Some people, they can heal themselves
and their family and even strangers, and others,
it's all they can do to heal themselves, and others,
Mama, it's all they can do to stay alive, even
though sick. It's not like you say. You want things
to be so clean and easy, but it's not like you say.

There's more than inside, there's outside. Mama, inside is hollow, like looking for the core of an onion, but outside goes on forever, rings and rings and rings of it."

"There's a difference between got to be, and is, child, and you just ain't learned it yet. It's not that you *got to be strong*; you are strong, that's all. I mean lazy in the spirit, child, not lazy in the body. You are what you are, and as soon as you admit it you won't have a problem, you'll have a solution. Besides, I don't call you crazy because you fall out and have fits, I call you crazy because you don't deal with it. Now, you sound like you need some more peppermint tea, I'd say."

"Mama, you can't just will somebody a power. Maybe I can hold Imani here, but that's all. And that's only because she's holding on to me every bit as tight as I'm holding on to her."

Without replying Ernestine moved to the stove where she lifted the kettle to feel the water level and then returned it to the burner, setting the heat on high. She opened the cabinets to her left and felt the second shelf where the jars were lined up, pulling out one jar, smelling it and putting it back, and then removing the round wide lid from a second one, smiling as the sweet scent filled her large flat nose.

"Yes, some tea would do us both good."

Iree picked up her child's feet and again grazed the top of each arch with her thumb, bringing the toes to her lips and kissing them. Imani opened her eyes and wiggled her toes, smiling a half-smile, and slid back into sleep.

Ernestine began to hum, and Iree settled back into her quiet, placing Imani's feet under the cover and stroking a hand gently across the child's forehead, which was, finally, although still feverish, much cooler. After some minutes Ernestine brought the tea, heavily laced with honey, over to Iree and they drank silently as the child settled into a true sleep and Iree let go, lying next to her child, the two of them sleeping close, without movement or sound, for the next twelve hours. It was the letting go that Iree remembered most about that healing.

As Iree shook herself out of the memory of that evening, she found her eyes holding Ernestine's, who stared with veiled grey pupils into her daughter's face, not seeing, and yet still knowing the shape of the frowns that sat on Iree's brow.

"Yes, Mama, I remember. But she was here, right here. I knew how wide the problem was. I could touch her."

"Iree, she needed your touch then. She was sick. This one is different. Maybe she needs something else now."

Mico stood up and moved down the steps.

"I think Ernie's right about one thing," Mico said, leaning on the railing and resting one foot on the last stair. "Whatever it is Imani needs from us, she probably already has it inside her. We have to believe that. Meanwhile, I think I'll go for a drive. Not looking for anything, old spider legs, just driving, maybe pick up some more beer. Why don't you come?"

Ernestine spat on to the ground. "Old man, you think I'm going to let you crash me into some wall while you telling stories and picking your hand up off the wheel."

"I'll tell you what, old woman, I'll let you hold the wheel, how's that?"

The two of them laughed. "You know what, Mico, that might be nice. It's been more than a minute since you and I rode together."

"That's only because you insist on bringing all kinds of navigators and directors, as if I don't know where I'm going, or how in the hell to get there."

"Now, if it was hell, I'd know you knew your way around. But I don't travel in those areas." Ernestine chuckled again and hugged Iree, and then started down to join Mico. Reaching back she touched her daughter's face and said, "Like as not, Imani's not coming home tonight, Iree. Go on inside and have some of the bread Zulie baked before she gets mad. You know how whenever she gets nervous she just starts cooking up all the food she can find and demanding everybody eat it."

Iree smiled, stepped down to hug Ernestine, and then hugged Mico. She clung to him for a moment and then turned and walked back up the stairs and inside the house.

Ernestine and her brother walked slowly towards the truck, she baiting and he replying, the two of them leaning close to each other in a seasoned, coarse love.

Girl Talk

ROSE OPENED THE DOOR INTO a small foyer that had three rooms radiating from its triangular corners. To one side was a bathroom, crowded with an oversized claw-foot bathtub, small wash basin, cracked and stained but looking grand on its polished pedestal, and a toilet with fashion magazines stacked at its side. The kitchen had a small table and a cramped stove, refrigerator and sink pressed together at one end. It was spotless, except for the bright yellow wallpaper daisies coated with a layer of oil that hinted of years of fried fish and fried potatoes. The living room-bedroom was the largest space. A sofa-bed sat on one end facing a small television, a small pile of clothes strewn across it. A huge fern that was in need of some water hung from the ceiling.

"Well, this is home. Let me move these. I can't believe I spent all that time deciding what to wear just to find out Old Buckteeth Bryant is a total creep." Rose chattered on as Imani immediately started picking up the strewn outfits and holding them up to herself. Amanda hung back in the foyer, peeking into each room. Rose laughed and beckoned her in.

"Come on, girl. I only bite my friends and my enemies, and right now you ain't neither. Sit down on the sofa while I get this stuff up. No, Imani, you can't have my green silk blouse. Pretty though. You remember Henry, he was a senior when I was a junior, real tall, should of played basketball but didn't. We got together for a minute after I graduated. He gave that to me." She paused. "He was real sweet for that minute there."

Amanda slid into the room and sat on one edge of the couch trying to take up as little room as possible. Rose saw her and laughed again.

"Girl, you are turning green. I told you relax, baby. Everything's everything. Come on. Take your shoes off." Then she looked more closely and realized that Amanda was about to vomit.

"Not on my sofa, girl, hold it now!"

Rose ran to the kitchen and was back in three leaps with a stew pot as Amanda began spewing out what was left of her dinner in hard retching coughs. Some of it sprayed on Rose's lamb's wool coat and some slid down the sides of the pot.

Rose just shook her head. "Damn, girl. Take it easy." She led Amanda to the bathroom where she continued to vomit and hold her sides for several minutes. Then Imani came in and washed off Amanda's face and offered water for her to rinse out her mouth. She took off Amanda's wet blouse and began to rinse off the vomit.

Rose went to get one of her own blouses, and nervously passed it in to Amanda. She didn't stop talking for an instant. "One thing I hate is vomit. You ain't been drinking. No, not with Imani. That child be shore enough crazy if she ever started to drink. You got a flu. Damn this stuff smell. You got some kind of a sickness."

Then she stopped and became still, noticing that Mandy had stopped vomiting and was sitting perched on the toilet seat cover in her bra and skirt. "Put on the fresh blouse, girl. I need to wipe off this coat. Took me too long to finish paying for it, to have it messed up by this."

Imani moved out of the bathroom and started to hang up the rest of Rose's clothes. Then she turned on the television and sat staring blankly at the picture. Although Imani could handle it, and often had to, she hated being around sickness. It frightened her and muddled her thinking. When she looked at people in their fevers or flu all she saw was a picture of leaves withering and fruit rotting. All she saw was pain. Even her mother's falling out gave her pause, only those times were easier because with her mother, she saw nothing, only a black slate wall. Now, watching Amanda walk back in the room, Imani turned away. She hated being helpless, but she didn't know what to do.

"So some dude noticed you got pretty, honey.

Come on sit back down on the sofa, I expect you're done for a while. No, don't crowd in the corner, take some space. Jeez. Girl, ain't you heard of condoms? I mean really," continued Rose.

Amanda snorted. "They don't always work."

Rose laughed. "Girl, ain't it the truth, I've had more than a few break inside me. So what you gonna do? This gonna be a fatherless child or you gonna cut it off at the pass? I've got some pennyroyal. They say if the baby ain't made up its mind to stay and you catch it early that'll make the baby let loose of that wall and come tumbling down."

Amanda looked at Rose for a minute before replying, "Actually you need cohosh too, and even then it can cause a lot of problems and not do the job."

Imani moved over next to Amanda. "I'm not sure that Gramma Ernie is going to be too thrilled that that's what you choose to remember of her teachings."

"I remember most of the teas and salves. Anyway, if she thought it was so bad she wouldn't keep the stuff in her house." Amanda's side ached more than she wanted Imani to know so she turned her eyes from her friend's face and saw that Rose was still talking.

"I used the pennyroyal once, but I didn't bother waiting to see if it would work. I couldn't take any chances. I mean I've had a couple of abortions. I don't like the idea, but I'm just now doing for myself half-decently. How am I going to care for a baby? Besides the fathers weren't worth a hoot. Not that I'm saying you should do that, I mean my sister had two children in high school for her still-ain't-got-a-regular-job sweetie, and then she still got that old man to marry her, and she's had another two by him and seems happy as a lark. I mean it can work out."

Amanda wasn't really listening to Rose's words, she just let them slide over her as she tried to keep from thinking of the ache in her side. Her mouth was dry and she wanted some more water, but was afraid to ask. Imani looked up and saw her frowns.

"I'll get you some water, Mandy. What you want to watch?"

Rose answered, "I already told you. Late night movies. I love them. Cowboys, stupid love stories, monsters. Only ones I don't like are the war movies. All men talking in flat voices, digging trenches and shooting. Real tired."

"There isn't such a thing as a fatherless baby. I mean everybody has a father." Amanda looked up from her lap, her eyes meeting Rose's.

Rose sniffed. "Imani doesn't, all she has is a mystery. You don't, all you have is a rumor. Now me, I do have one. That is, I grew up with one in the house, but I swear I don't know if he said ten kind words to me after the time I started having my period. Come to think of it, I don't know if he said ten kind words before. I mean he lived in the house we all lived in, at least he slept there and fixed things that were broken, but he didn't have much to do with us children. Mostly our job was to do what we were told and run to the store for him. Other than that it was grunts and criticism. He couldn't even teach me how to tie my shoe. So me, I'm as close to fatherless as you can get. In fact when these titties started sprouting," Rose cupped her hands around her ample breasts and looked down at them almost mournfully, "and my hips started rounding, I swear you'd a thought I was the biggest whore this side of the Rockies. I wasn't even thinking serious about sex then, but that's all I'd hear from him in terms of his fathering duty. He'd be telling me how fast I was, how I'd better be ready for the streets if I thought I was gonna be sixteen and pregnant in his house, and about how dumb I was having so many boys as friends. Yeah, he had a lot to say then.

"By the time I started having boyfriends, I mean real boyfriends, Imani, not hold-hands-and-tell-secrets-and-kiss-in-the-closet boyfriends, but the kind that put something good up the middle of your legs, that ended it. My father didn't have nothing to say but, 'Stop or go!' Now how you gonna stop something that good after you started? So he said he was through with me and meant it too. I mean he didn't exactly make me move out, but soon as I was able, I did, and he sure didn't call me back, or tell me if I needed him he was there. Fact he told me if I needed a man I'd better call on some them no-count dicks I was screwing around with, and that's what I've been doing ever since. I count on them however I need them, with they touch, with they money or with they skills. Naw, just because somebody put some sperm inside of you and make a baby that doesn't make him a father. I say we just fatherless babes sitting up in my cozy place getting ready to watch a stupid movie on a Friday night. Ain't we living the life."

Imani cut her eyes at Rose. "I've got a father, not a mystery. He doesn't live here, but I've got a father. I've got lots of fathers in fact. There's my Uncle Jeremiah and there's Al, and even Malachi comes through sometimes. I've got lots of fathers."

"Sorry to hip you, baby, but an adopted uncle or a family friend ain't no kind of daddy."

Imani started walking around the room. "Rose, you don't know anything about anything. I've got what I need and if you didn't get it that's no cause to start talking about our people. I've got what I need."

"I'm just pointing out to tight-lipped Amanda that it's not such a trip raising a baby without a father. We all been raised and we all are here and came out all right. I mean I got my place and it works. I'm just saying it's not so much to trip about."

Just then Amanda jumped up again and ran to the bathroom. Rose watched her and moved over to the phone. She picked it up and spoke softly and briefly into the mouthpiece. Then she hung up and walked over to Imani, who was standing near the bathroom doorway. "Listen, Imani, you're cool and all that but I can't take all this vomiting and all. I mean it obviously doesn't mess with you. I'm going over to my friend's house and I'll just leave you some keys. I mean you can stay as long as you like, the night or a few days. But, I've had it."

Rose put her coat back on and poked her head into the bathroom. "Amanda, I hope it all works out for you, how you want it. I told Imani that you can stay here a few days. You can open up the sofa-bed. It's already made." She walked over to her closet, reached in to a high shelf and brought out two blankets. She threw one to Amanda who was coming out of the bathroom. "Here get some covers on. You should have more than enough blankets now. Not much food here, but take what you want." Rose gave Imani the other blanket and put a house key in her hands. "You might want to think about taking this child to a doctor," she whispered, kissing her on the cheek. "Good to see you again, Fortune Teller. Don't be such a stranger." Then she left.

Amanda sat down pulling the blanket over her shoulders. "I didn't mean to push her out of her apartment. I'm surprised she let us stay just like that."

"That's Rose for you. Once I got caught out in the rain without a coat or umbrella and Rose saw me and let me have her umbrella because she was all outfitted, you know Rose, boots, coat, hat, all matching. Well, the reason I didn't have an umbrella was I had left it somewhere, and that's what I did with Rose's umbrella, too. When I told her two days later she just laughed and told me not to worry, but that she wouldn't be handing me any umbrellas again any time soon."

Amanda pulled her feet up to her chin and covered herself with the blanket. "I've got a father too, Imani. I mean I guess Ray MacIntire is my father. I mean that's what all the gossips say up on the hill. My mother never told me he was, but the only thing they ever argued about was me. She'd start saying that candy and pocket money wasn't enough and he'd get up and leave, usually without telling me good-bye. Then my mother would come and hold me real close, talking about she really didn't know how to be my mother. Ray was okay. I mean he made little jokes and stuff. When my mother would punish me he'd tell her to be gentler, but she never paid him any mind, just kept doing or saying whatever she was doing or saying. One time she held my hand right on the electric plate of the stove to show me what hot was since I didn't mind her about staying away from the stove. Ray yelled at her then, but she just answered calm as you please, 'Now she knows what hot is without any permanent damage. I gave her enough chances.' Ray, he picked me up and ran my hand under cold water, and my mother, she just sat at the kitchen table, stony face. She told him he could always take me. Right at that minute, I remember wishing that he would.

"It's not like I know him. I mean not really. But he does seem to keep track of me. Always knows where to find me and sometimes delivers letters to wherever I'm living. Birthday cards from my mother addressed to general delivery care of him. But I never see him. I mean he comes when I'm not home and tells whoever answers the door that he was a friend of my mother and she sent this or that for me. It's only happened four, five times. Just enough to keep people talking. But I guess he is my father. I mean why else take the trouble. But it's not like I look like him or he raised me or anything.

"I went and got my birth certificate once, just to see. Of course there was nothing on it to see. There was my mother's printing, all tight and neat as could be. But where it said father's last name, unknown was typed, and for father's first name, it said unknown again. So, maybe it's all just gossip anyhow.

"I know that my mother knew who my father was. I mean one of the things I remember about my mother is how ordered she was. You didn't just throw the socks in the sock drawer. The ones with the pink trim went in one place and the ones with the blue trim went in front of them and the whites were all the way at the front. Nothing was ever messy or part-way done. I mean I was always Amanda to her, no nickname, no sweetie or darling or anything you hear people calling other people. Always Amanda, or Amanda Rene or Amanda Rene Bresley, if there was trouble. I remember when I asked her to call me Mandy like you did. She looked at me as if I was crazy and answered, 'Your name is Amanda. I call you by your name, properly, as it should be.' That was it. She was so proper about everything, it's hard to believe she would have had Ray as my father, but for sure my father wasn't unknown.

"Still, somehow I think if my mother knew Ray was my father she would have put his name down. I mean why not? She didn't write the unknown or anything, just left it blank. I could tell because her printing was on the lines that had the name and address and there was her signature all close and perfect; the 'A' perfectly peaked. But the father's name part was typed. On every other detail—date, her name, my name—there was her printing, every letter upright and small, printed so perfectly. She already had a name for me. No baby girl Bresley, but Amanda Rene Bresley. That's how my mother was, everything planned, everything thought out, nothing by accident, except me, of course. And of course, she got rid of that accident, in her own way.

"You know the day I got that birth certificate I just stood there at the window and stared at it. I looked at the printing, and then the signature, and then the place for father where it was typed unknown. The person in back of me had to push me out of the way to get to the window. I guess I must have been standing with my mouth hanging open or something, thinking 'unknown, hmmm.' Anyway, I guess only a blood test will tell for sure and it's not so important to me. And I've had enough from foster dads now and again to not really care for the idea. I mean I'm about grown now anyway."

"He did try to keep you after the fire."

"Who?"

"Your father. Mr. Ray Unknown MacIntire."

"No he didn't. He didn't try at all. He took me home for a night, but I don't know why anyone would have noticed. I think the earthquake just shook him up and he didn't know what else to do at that moment. I remember that. It was so strange. He just picked me up and held me in his arms and talked to me the whole way to his house. Not talked really, but hummed a little song and kept telling me it was his daughter's favorite song and didn't I like it too.

"I didn't mind going with him. Like I said, I knew him and all, from him visiting my mother. He always brought me candy or a toy and sometimes money for my mother. And he did get me out of that basement. Yeah, I guess he is my father. Sometimes he actually did stop her from hitting me, when he visited, I mean. My mother was so hard. Everything had to be perfect. Don't talk too loud. Don't forget to put a glass in the sink. Don't leave a wrinkle on your bed. Don't dawdle when she tells you what to do, and never, never talk back. She didn't say much but she had a grip on the wrist."

Amanda started to rub her wrist and tears started falling down her cheeks. "It's not fair. It's just not fair."

Imani got up and moved to the sink. She refilled the glass with water and ice and walked back to Amanda. She handed it to Amanda and gently rubbed her back. "You know what Mico always says, 'Life ain't supposed to be fair, baby. It's supposed to be lived, not fair. And it's not supposed to be easy, at least not for colored folks.' That's what he always says."

"It's easy for you."

"With my mother always falling out and my grandmother running everybody and never quite enough of anything, except food and yarn, girl, you got to be kidding. No, I try and make it go my way as much as I can, but that doesn't make it easy. But you told me your father tried to keep you and the social services wouldn't let him. You said he tried."

"You were so sure he was my father, Imani. I didn't want you to think he didn't try, and to tell you the truth I think I had made myself believe that he wanted me, at least a little bit. He was so strange, after we got to his house he acted like he wasn't quite sure how or why I ended up in his arms that night. He had me in one arm and a bag of groceries in the other and hummed all the way.

I remember that bag was loaded with cookies. Later on, I sat on the steps with his children and his wife and we all ate cookie after cookie. Then when we went inside, after I was put on the couch for the night and covered with this scratchy blanket, he got into a fight with his wife, who wanted to know why he brought me home instead of giving me to the Red Cross or something. He told her a story about how there was so much excitement that no one noticed me run off and he just decided to take care of it himself, just for the night, of course. I didn't know why he was lying, and really I didn't care. He promised her he'd take me to the authorities the next morning.

"Of course, when the morning came he was passed out on the floor next to the couch. He was all stinking and had a half-empty bottle of some kind of drink by his head. That was when I noticed the room, all full of books. I means shelves and shelves of books. They were so neat that it looked like nobody must of read them. Just kept them on those shelves like pictures. I was sitting up on the couch, legs crossed with my feet on the cushions. If my mother had been there she would have hit them hard right on the bottoms, but she was gone. I was sitting there sucking my fingers like I always do, I mean, always did."

Imani laughed. "Girl, you mean *do*. Why are you suddenly so grown? You know I keep a stuffed bear on the bed and I still cuddle it sometimes. It's okay. I mean long as you don't get

caught sucking on your fingers by some dude.
Lord, he'll tell alla his friends and they'll tell your
friends and the teasing won't end."

"Jerome saw me once. He didn't tell anybody.
Just pulled them out of my mouth and kissed me.
He never even said a word. My mother, she would
pull them out and then use the corner of a dish
towel to wipe a layer of hot pepper sauce over
them."

Amanda looked at her fingers. "Look, they're
still a little wrinkled. Not grey like when I really
sucked hard. I mean after my mother left town and
all, they got all grey and wrinkly. I remember my
first foster mother used to keep feeding me to try
and keep me from sucking my fingers. As if I
sucked them out of hunger. That's probably how
I turned out so round, sucking the juice out of my
fingers."

She rubbed her fingers and turned her hands
back and forth as if looking for some telling scar
or special symbol. She began counting the freckles
she found on each finger's back. "Not one freckle
on these two fingers. Not one. I sucked them all
off." Amanda smiled and then slid back on the
couch, remembering that morning ten years before.

The couch at Ray and Nancy's house had been
long and red with white string crochet doilies on
the back and arms. The night she came she had
kept playing with them, and Ray's wife, without

a word, would take them out of her hands and place them back on the end. Mandy would pick one back up and start fingering it and Ray's wife would take it again, each time her hand a little firmer until finally the woman's nails bit into the child's palms, and the girl bit the inside of her lip so as not to cry out.

The next morning she woke up before anyone else, folded her legs up under her, and took the doily off the couch arm looking at the intricate flowers woven in its curls. Ray slept, snoring softly on the floor, his clothes wrinkled and a sour scent raising from his back. Amanda had needed to go to the toilet. She knew where it was from the night before, but she was afraid to move. So she just sat looking at the room around her, waiting for Ray to wake up and take her back to her mother. Just when her bladder was so hard and full that it had begun to leak out its water into her panties, Ray's wife walked in the room and over to the couch. She kicked her husband, snatched the doily from Amanda and pulled the child to her feet. Amanda tripped on Ray who groaned and turned over half awake looking at Amanda and his wife in a blur as if he didn't recognize either one of them.

Ray's wife took Amanda to the bathroom, handing her a towel and telling her to wash herself. Amanda went in and peed for what seemed to her to be forever. Then she sat still, embarrassed that she had waited so long and started to mess on herself. Finally she got up and carefully washed her hands and face. Then she put down the toilet seat and sat back down, afraid to go back into the living room. That's when Ray Junior burst into the bathroom yelling, "What's the matter with you, girl? Other people got to go too, y'know." Before Amanda could get all the way out the door she heard his pee hitting the sides of the toilet and him sighing in relief. She pulled the bathroom door shut behind her and stood there until Little Jean came down the hall.

"My mother said to come get you because it's time for you to go. So come on and good-bye."

Amanda walked down the narrow hall and turned into the living room. There was Ray sitting on the couch rubbing the stubble on his face. "Nancy, I said I'd take her down and I will. The only thing you have to do is relax and fix the child some breakfast."

The woman ignored him. She stuck a bag into Amanda's hands and pulled her along. Together the woman and child walked to the bus stop. They waited well over an hour for the bus. Amanda had sat on the curb, like her mother never would have allowed, and looked in the bag. There was a sandwich and two pieces of fruit. She ate the apple and then the banana and left the sandwich for later.

A short bus ride later Amanda found herself at the police station being taken in as an abandoned child. Ray's wife had said, "No, I don't know the mother. No, I don't know the father. She ran away from the block with the fire last night and my husband brought her home. No, I don't know the child's name. What I know is she is no part of me or mine, and her mother needs to be found. I am definitely *not* her mother."

With that the woman left. She didn't turn around and say good-bye. Amanda spent the next few days being shunted from office to office. For three days she wouldn't tell anyone her name. Everyone was strange and although they smiled, it was more like Halloween-mask grins than real I-care-about-you smiles. Amanda was sure her mother would come, or Ray, or maybe her friend Imani's grandmother. Somebody would come. But nobody came.

Finally Amanda started talking. By then her mother was gone. She was placed in her first foster home. That one was relatively clean, and not at all quiet with three other children. It was so different from what she was used to, different rules and less attention. Not that her own mother had ever played with Amanda, but she was always teaching her, always reminding her how to sit, or telling her what chore was to be done, or giving her a book to read quietly and be prepared for questions later. That first foster mother loved to cook. Everything was heavy and oily but there was lots of it. Lots of potatoes, lots of peas, lots of meat loaf. Amanda's own mother always fixed a plate with exact portions and that was what you ate, no more and no less. A bite of food was never to be left on the plate and seconds were never offered. Amanda didn't talk much at that first house, but she ate well and after some weeks passed, she smiled. Before three months had passed, she stopped looking out the window for hours on end, waiting for her mother to return.

Amanda turned over in the couch and pulled the blanket up to her chin whispering to herself, "Whatever I want, I should do, whatever I want. I want not to be pregnant. I want it to be last month and me having terrible cramps and complaining about them. Whatever I want . . ."

Imani didn't say a word, just sighed. She walked over to Amanda and felt her head and neck. "Mandy, you have a fever. Maybe we should go to the doctor."

"Imani, I'm just scared and tired. I'll be fine. Really, Imani. I'm supposed to be the one worrying."

"Today's my birthday, Mandy. I mean yesterday was. In the morning everybody was sleeping hard so I slipped out to be by myself and get to your house real early. I knew they'd have something planned for me in the evening and wouldn't worry as long as I got back before dark. I bet they're all still sitting around that big table fussing, especially Zulie. I'll never hear the end of it. Twenty years from now Zulie going to be saying, 'And child, that night we sat up waiting for you . . .' "

"I'm sorry, Imani. I'll make it up to you."

Amanda reached over to her friend and gave her a big hug.

Imani returned the hug and didn't say anything. Amanda stuck her face up close to Imani and started making funny faces. "Well happy birthday, girl. Happy I'm-vomiting-and-you're-hungry-birthday."

The two girls smiled and sat back down on the sofa. Imani spread the blanket over their legs. The room was quiet as the two young women nestled under their covers. Each of them awake and neither of them speaking. Imani dozed off feeling her mother's prayers sliding down the hill and cushioning her restless dreams.

Truck Stop

—m—

THE TRUCK STARTED UP WITH a cough and then slid into an even grumble as Mico pulled out of the unpaved carport and down the long sloping hill. Neither he nor Ernestine said anything for the first few minutes. "Mico," Ernie finally said breaking the silence. "Mico, where are we?"

"Just crossed Hickory, moving west on Linden towards the beach front."

"So we're near where Mandy's old house used to stand."

"Yes, every time I pass that place I wonder about Amanda's mother. I just can't imagine abandoning your child, especially to a man like Ray. That child's so fulla love, quiet though she is. And she's got a grit to her I really like. You know, Al told me . . ."

Mico took a quick left turn and rounded the park's edge, which showed the shadows of swings and a tall and curling slide in the park's corner playground. For a few minutes they drove wordlessly, with only the whine and hum of the truck breaking through the night. Then Mico started talking again, as if no time had passed in the conversation.

That's how Ernestine and Jeremiah had always done it. They would start a conversation on Wednesday and get distracted, and then, on Saturday, they would start in again right from where they left off without a line of catch-up or word to remind the other one of where they had left off.

"That woman just walked off and left her child in that man's arms and ain't never looked back. Now that's what I call a heathen."

"You know," Ernestine interrupted, "I met Lorraine right near here. On the bench just inside this park. Iree was with me at the time showing me how graceful Imani was, swinging on the monkey bars. She was saying how Imani looked like a baby spider stretching out a strand of web, flying it to a branch and then swinging her arms and swinging her legs until Iree could almost see a silken thread coming from her fingertips. What a weaving that would make, huh, Mico?" Ernestine paused and listened as the wind rustled the branches of the trees.

"Iree was whispering into my ear and she spread my arms and rocked them to the rhythm of Imani's movement. It was like a dance. Anyway it must of made Lorraine nervous because I noticed she moved away. She was not really quiet, more like she was uncomplaining and didn't have much else to say but complaints, so she mostly said nothing. I could feel how pale she was. She never wore colors. Everything was beige or tan, except sometimes there was a tiny surge of yellow.

"She and her daughter never much spoke to one another. I mean Imani was always running back and telling me what she just managed to do and how she looked, and sometimes yelling from the top of the slide, 'Gramma, I'm gonna do a belly slide and turn over to my back half-way down . . .' But Lorraine's child, of course I didn't know she was Lorraine then, that child never said anything to her mother.

"They would come and Lorraine would say, 'Stay as clean as you can. When we go, we go.' And that would be it for one, two hours. I wouldn't hear the rustle of a book or paper or anything. Sometimes the child would come get a snack, but no words except 'please' and 'thank you' were spoken.

"One time Imani ran back and asked if she could share some of her friend's fruit juice. I said yes, and heard Lorraine ask what Imani's name was and say how pleased she was to meet her, but never a word to me or to her child. Most times when it was time to go Lorraine would stand, adjust her clothes and call to Amanda, 'It is time to go, Amanda.' And most times the girl would reply, 'One more swing' or 'One more slide,' just as crisp as can be, not asking so much as reminding her mother of a pre-arranged bargain. Then either

Lorraine would sit back down, or else after a minute of quiet I'd hear a 'Yes, Mother, right now.'

"Anyway, that day I first had a conversation
with her, I heard her stand up and tell Mandy it's
time to go, and the girl says one more something,
and the mother says, 'Never mind, child,' and sits
back down. Then she moves real close to me and
puts her hand on my shoulder and starts talking
as if I can see. Now I know she knows I'm blind,
because one time I heard her telling her daughter
that I should be wearing glasses out of a consideration for seeing folks that might not want to
look in my eyes. Now ain't that something, out of
a consideration, hmmp. Anyway, Mico, she starts
saying, as if my eyes are as strong as hers,

" 'Will you look at that child of mine. After all
that, she still is as colored as can be, more than
me, even. Look at her, oh yeah she's got that sandy
hair and green eyes, but those lips and that behind.
And all her baby curls turned into sagebrush. It
wasn't that I wanted her to be white, in fact it
would have been a blessing if she had been brown.
All the way brown like your Imani. I wanted the
best for her. It's hard being so in-between, nobody
really wanting you and everybody telling you what
you want or what you should want. I want my
baby to be proud, but I don't know how to teach
her that. I think if she was just a little whiter or a
lot darker she'd have it easier. Look at that child,
she's lighter than me, but looks like a full-blooded,
nappy-haired African.

" 'You know, I think I never should have had that child. I was so lonely, but you know that child doesn't really fill me up. Ray did, almost, coming to dinner reliably, always bringing something. There's not a place for me here really, but maybe for Amanda. She is quiet and reliable, for her age. She can play by herself so well. But sometimes, she'll just start asking the wrong questions, or wriggling and pulling away when she should be still. She says Ray is not her daddy, says she knows because he told her so. What about what I tell her? One day I'm going to shake the truth into that child.'

"Then Mico, she squeezed real hard on my shoulder, her fingers kind of gripped me on my arm, and her nails dug into the skin and was about to draw blood. Mico, you know me. I just rose up and struck out without really thinking about it at all. I just caught her wrist and then the sharp edge of her jaw. Right there on that bench. Jeremiah, I'm telling you that woman gave me the heebie jeebies, and you know I really don't much get rattled.

"Well Lorraine immediately starts to apologizing. She took my hand and shook it real formal, apologizing again and this time offering her name, 'I'm Lorraine Bresley. I'm Amanda's mother. I think you and your daughter call her Mandy. They get along together very nicely. I didn't mean to hurt you. I never mean to hurt anyone. I know I can't give my daughter what she needs, a better way. I work and come home and take care of my child and there is never any trouble. But there is no place for me, not really. Oh some of the people in my church invite me over for Easter or Christmas. One even asked me out to dinner, but he only wanted to take the place of Ray and I don't need that anymore.

" 'And then on the other side of town, I just don't like the same kinds of things. Everybody leaves me be there, too. Except the man who owns the car wash, the dark brown one with the salt-and-pepper beard. Let me see, I believe he introduced himself as Malachi Saunders. A nice man. He always teases me about washing my car more than I need. I just like to keep it clean. I go every Thursday, five-thirty, right after work. If I'm late he keeps it open for me and washes it all by himself. I feel very welcome there, but it is a business welcome. And it's like that at Merle's Hairstyling Emporium. I mean she is always pleasant, but some of the others. . . . The car wash every Thursday, Merle's every Saturday at eleven. Those are my best days.'

"Now I'm about flabbergasted and don't know what to say to her. I need another loony around me as much as I need Iree falling into another one of her fits again. So, I tell her pleased to meet you, and let's talk again sometimes, and I gather up Imani so we can get ready to go home. Just as we're leaving, Lorraine comes back over to me. She is obviously holding Amanda's hand tightly because Amanda is whining about her hand hurting.

"Lorraine pulls upside to my head and says, 'When it's time for me to leave, you'll be one of the ones I'm leaving her to. You help her like you help your Imani. You'll be one of the ones.' Then she switches her attention to Amanda and I hear her cooing over the child and kissing her.

"Mico, I didn't say a word to her, just reached my hand out for Imani and started walking straight towards the bus stop."

Mico rocked with laughter over the steering wheel.

"I wish I'd a been there. I've never seen you scared of nobody, gal. I swear if the devil was to stand up in front of you, you'd spit him in the eye."

"The devil has stood up in front of me any number of times and I try my best to knock him down most every day when I go downtown. No, this woman was different, as if she was planning something that was real hurtful, and I was a part of it in some ways.

"You know, she didn't come to the park for a few weeks after that and then when she did, she always brought me a small sandwich and a piece of fruit. Always came at the same time and always spoke to me. She told me once it was her birthday and she couldn't think of anything special to do, but she thought she was supposed to do something.

"I decided to weave her a shawl. Seems like somebody should remember your anniversary of coming into this world, somebody besides yourself. Two weeks later I gave it to her, bright yellow crossed with orange diamonds on the ends. The child needed some color. She kissed me and surprised me when she brought out a present for me. It was a scarf all full of reds and purples and this shiny emerald green in a kind of dots and paisley spread. I mean my fingers were just buzzing running over the cloth. It made me laugh just to feel them dance. Mico, the scarf was silk and soft and alive. Lorraine, she just presses it in my hand and says,

" 'Amanda, Mandy—I know you like to call her that—Mandy said you could feel colors and like them rich and dark. This was my mother's. It's far too bright for me, but it is beautiful. I just wanted to thank you for being so understanding.'

"And then earlier than usual she called Amanda to leave and was gone. Now I don't know what I was supposed to be understanding. All she talked about was how she couldn't find a way to fit in, and how it was probably the town, and maybe a new start would make a difference, and then finally she had some friends here and what if it wasn't the place, but really was something in her, something she couldn't help, a born-with-it-sin; and I just let her run on and told her to wear more colors. That's all. I mean I never went to her house or she to mine. I only was with her twice after that, the first time was months later, when she bumped into me at the fabric store . . ."

"You, the blind one, you bumped into her!"

"Mico, when you gonna shut up and let me finish my story? That's why you ain't never got nuthin' or getting nuthin' cause you don't listen long enough to no one . . ."

"Old spider woman I've been listening to you for on about the last hour and the girl is only becoming more distasteful, leaving that sweet child like that."

"Let's go over to Malachi's place. Mico, move on from here."

Mico started up the truck and slowly pulled off, leisurely driving down the street, and then turning and going up the next block as if he wasn't going anywhere, but simply driving, easy and cool, feeling the autumn breeze. His hands gripped the steering wheel and his head was pulled forward as he looked in the shadows and doorways, knowing that Imani would not be found in any of them.

Ernestine reached over and grazed the stubble on his rounded cheek. "Blind or not, I was standing still and Lorraine bumped into me and started apologizing real formal like she always does. Then the woman starts running on again. I mean from no talk for months to suddenly being like lava coming out of a volcano. She started in saying things like:

" 'I don't know what to do. I'm raising this one all alone, no family, nothing, just me and I just don't know. I'm hurting her all the time and I don't know how to stop. I think I need to leave this town and I don't want to take her where we might not even be able to make it, and I can't send her to her uncle because he's only my father's child by his marriage after my mother died, and he doesn't really think of me as a sister and I don't know what to do. Sometimes, Mrs. Moore, if I didn't know I'd spend all eternity with my soul burning, I swear I'd just walk through the next door early and beg for mercy at Mary's feet.'

"Then she hands me a bolt of cloth that's real coppery and full of fire and tells me, 'I thought I'd make a skirt to go with the shawl. This material will travel well, don't you think?'

"I told her it seemed lovely and I was glad she was taking to wearing more colors. And then she leans over and whispers in my ear not to worry, because Amanda is a very resourceful child and will 'find her way home.' It was strange as can be, then next thing I know she kisses me on the cheek and is gone.

"Mico, I know she didn't mean to start that fire, but accident or not she did it. Not that she wanted to hurt Amanda, she loved her child, but after the earthquake, and the fire starting and all the confusion. She wanted to get Mandy out but it was too hard. She got turned around and scared.

"Imani told me all about it. Not that night of the earthquake, but days later she was kneeling in front of me and leaning on my leg and she asked, 'Gramma, why did Mrs. Bresley start the fire?' "

"Now you know Imani makes up just as many stories as she sees."

"No, Mico. This wasn't one of her fabrications. She was so sad. Mico, I had really never seen her like that before. She was like Iree is when she comes to me, worried and quiet and breathing hard. Mico, Imani said:

Gramma, Mandy's mother she just took all these boxes of papers from upstairs, some of them fell before the earthquake and she just left them lying there. She took up the papers and she was burning them one by one in the fireplace. Then she did the strangest thing and took off that tan button sweater she always wears to the park and put it on the fire and I think it stank, because her nose curled. Then the earthquake came and that old stinky sweater fell out from the fireplace and caught onto a nearby box and she didn't try and stop it, just looked around and grabbed that shawl you made her off the sofa and reached for the silly old parrot.

She just stood there looking at the fire spread. Then she remembered Mandy and went down to the basement. But when she got to the spare room, she couldn't get the door open. Lots of boxes had fallen and it was a mess. So, she just kneeled on the floor, Gramma, kissed it and crossed herself and crawled out the basement. Why, Gramma, why did she do that? Mandy is so sweet. She's my

*friend, she always believes my stories and she
doesn't call Mama crazy or nothing. Gramma,
why was she doing that with the fire?*

"I didn't know what to say, so I just rubbed her
head and rocked her and told her not to worry.
We'd all look after Amanda. And Mico, hard as
it's been, I truly believe Lorraine thought she was
doing what was best for the child. If the earthquake hadn't of come the fire would never have
gotten out of control. She was trying to close off
her past and open a way to something new. I'm
sure she didn't want to hurt Mandy. Iree said that
when she kissed that child good-bye she was trembling and so sad. You know, she needed to leave.
She wasn't doing right by Amanda. That earthquake and fire just shook up her insides and gave
her the courage to go and leave her instead."

Mico leaned his head out the truck window and
spat. "Courage to leave her child with the Mac-
Intires. Hmmp."

"I don't think she was doing it for spite or
meanness or craziness, I think she wanted to give
the child more of a future."

"With a man that doesn't even admit to fathering her? The way I hear tell, he didn't even keep
her one day."

"She thought he would give her opportunity.
That he would be shamed into doing right by her
in terms of opportunity. She thought the child
would be better off, here in this town with us, all
of us, but *she* had to go, Mico."

"That's all well and good, but the child wasn't left with us. Amanda was left with Mr. Mac-Intire."

"No, she was left with us, only we couldn't get her out of that foster care. The social service didn't see us fit to raise our own child. Malachi even tried to get her, and he was told that it wouldn't do for a man with no wife to raise a girl child, even though he already was raising his own son by himself and half raising his sister's child, Jerome, too."

Just then Mico turned the corner where Malachi's car wash was located. Malachi was blowing on his trumpet inside the whitewashed shack that was once garage and now was office and refuge. Mico stopped the truck and listened.

"I didn't know he started playing again. I thought he finally gave it up." Sour notes were mixed with the sweet as the horn vibrated in the evening chill. Ernestine tapped her brother's leg softly.

"Mico, let's not go in. Sounds like he's got his own troubles he's working out. Drive on home."

Mico didn't answer. He turned off the engine and then reached into the glove compartment and pulled out a barely touched pint of rum. He found a half-smoked cigar and slid out of the front seat. Ernestine settled back into the seat and shook her head. Mico held the rum up to the sky and then poured one swallow into the ground. He lit the cigar, pulled on it hard three times, and stood listening as Malachi searched for the voice to hold his feelings. After some minutes the music stopped. Mico walked around the truck, opened the door and took a hold of Ernestine's arm.

"Come on, spider woman, let's go visiting."

Then he yelled out from the curb, "Malachi, come on have a toast with me for Imani's birthday. We're celebrating."

"Why are you always so damned loud," Ernestine protested.

"Why are you always complaining about people being the way they are supposed to be, old woman?"

Before Ernie could answer, Malachi had the front door open and was inviting them in.

Midnight Run

—◇—

IT WAS CLOSE TO 1:00 A.M. Amanda was lying awake on the sofa-bed, which Imani had relinquished to her. She had been restless most of the evening, and had spent most of it up and down, running back and forth to the bathroom. Imani had offered to help, but Amanda would just shake her head. Finally Imani stopped offering. It was cold and there wasn't any food to speak of in the tiny kitchen. Imani had worked through her earlier plate of rice and beans and was hungry again by the time she fell asleep on the floor. She had gone to sleep dreaming of Zulie's fragrant stew and was just about to swallow a large spoonful when she found herself jolted awake and staring into Amanda's moon-shaped face.

"Imani," Amanda whispered into Imani's ear. "Imani, I'm going on a walk. Come with me."

Imani cleared her eyes and sat up. "Girl, you're crazy." She saw that Amanda was dressed and ready to go and was inviting Imani more out of courtesy than a need for companionship.

"I need to get some air."

Imani rolled back the blankets and reached over to a chair for her jeans. "Well, I tell you, I was just getting ready to chow down on one of Zulie's specialty meals in my dream before you stuck your face up in mine. So if we're going out, and I'm game to go, it's okay as long as we end up right on top of some food. I'm more hungry now than I was before I fell asleep."

Amanda sucked in some air and shrugged her shoulders. Imani laughed and jumped up. "Let me wash my face and we can go."

Amanda sat on the edge of the sofa-bed looking into her hands, which she held cupped, one on top of the other. When Imani came out of the bathroom she looked at Amanda and winced. They both knew something was wrong, but neither one of them wanted to talk about it.

The two girls began to walk. The streets were deserted. Amanda was not paying attention to where they were walking. The only sound was their footsteps on the pavement and the whoosh of the occasional truck or car that drove by, usually slowing down just a bit as it passed the girls so the driver could get a good look at the two young women walking in a town which was almost completely closed down by eleven o'clock, even on a Friday night. Imani knew that there was one diner which stayed open until 3:00 A.M.

Touching Amanda's shoulder at some corners and pulling her by the hand at others, she silently navigated them to the fluorescent-lit cafe, where they paused outside to view the menu. Imani emptied her pockets and surveyed her cash. Amanda slipped a couple of more dollars into Imani's hand.

Imani started reading items on the menu. "Carol's Red-Eye Special: eggs, juice, toast, sausage and coffee. Umm, with piles of jam and butter, and those good big-cut potatoes that I like to smother in ketchup and black pepper."

"Imani, stop drooling all over the menu. Let's go in. It doesn't seem like being in front of food or away from food makes a difference in how I feel. Anyway, I know how you like to eat maybe forty-two times a day. Imani, how come you eat so much and stay so thin and I don't eat at all and I am always heavier than you?"

Imani laughed. "You know I love to eat, all the time. And you know how love keeps you thin."

Amanda ran her hand over her belly. "Not me."

"I said love, not sex. Anyway that's why Zulie and I get along so well, my love of eating. My mother, she just picks at her food, unless it's after one of her spells, then she eats like Godzilla or something. But usually she just pushes it around the plate and takes a bite of this and a swallow of that. I'm always finishing her plate, but it doesn't stay on me. Zulie says that's because I can't keep still, but I can keep still, I just don't choose to be still. Why? There's plenty of time for that when

I'm old or dead. See, you are sitting still as the dead all the time, so the food it just rests up on you. And then too, food, you can take it or leave it. You're just not passionate about it like me."

"You mean like you getting all goo-goo-eyed looking at that menu?"

"Exactly!" said Imani as both girls laughed. They pulled open the plate-glass door and were met with the sharp smell of grease and stale cigarette smoke. They found a large booth and quickly sat down. Imani ordered without giving any consideration to the menu handed to her. In a few minutes she was digging into a plate piled with food. Mandy nibbled on saltine crackers and drank glass after glass of water.

"Y'know, Mandy, maybe you need to go to a doctor," Imani gulped with her mouth half-full.

"Y'know, Imani, maybe you ought to swallow your food before you speak," Amanda replied, trying to shift the conversation.

"Mandy, come on, you know something's . . ."

Before she finished her thought Amanda interrupted, "You should talk. You've never been to a doctor in your whole life and you're ready to send me. I know how sick I am, and if I get sicker, I'll go."

"You have to go anyway. Just to be sure."

"I am sure."

"Mandy," Imani almost whined. Amanda was intent on looking out the window at the shadows of houses. "Anyway, Mandy, I *have* been to the doctor."

"No you haven't."

"Yeah, remember?"

Amanda held up her empty glass and signalled to the waitress that she wanted more water. The waitress was losing patience at being called back every five minutes to refill Mandy's and Imani's water glasses, both of which Mandy drank. She walked briskly to the table and banged down a pitcher of ice water, shaking her head and mumbling under her breath, "All this work over a two-bit tip, if I'm lucky enough to even get that."

"Why would she think we wouldn't leave a tip? We have home training. Maybe it won't be a big tip, but it'll be what we have," Imani exclaimed, insulted. Then she turned her attention to Amanda and said very slowly and firmly, "Really, Mandy, I really think we should get you to a doctor. I know that mostly nobody in my family goes to the doctor. I mean if Gramma can't handle it with a little help from Mama, then it can't be handled. But remember, I did go to the hospital once, on my twelfth birthday, when I fell out of a tree and had to have my leg set.

"I was supposedly keeping out of trouble while they fixed me a cake when I slipped trying to swing from one branch to the other. I'd swung the distance plenty of times before, but this time my mind was in the wrong place and I fell and screamed out, loud and hard. Mama was out the door and down those steps in two seconds flat. She saw me and how I was lying, and went right down to a neighbor's to call Zulie. Meanwhile Gramma broke a skinny branch from the tree, pulled my leg straight, and made a splint with the branch and some torn up sheets. Mama heard me screaming as she ran back up the hill. When she saw what Gramma had done, she just shook her head and started mumbling under her breath. Then she went inside and got a blanket. When she came out, Gramma made a litter to carry me on into the house. We were a sight. The litter was this huge green and gold cloth Gramma had made a few years back. I was inside it, yelling navigation to my Gramma, who I hoped wouldn't pick that minute to miss a step. My mama had been braiding Gramma's hair so it was one side neat and straight bowl lines down the head, and the other side sticking straight out making this silver crown. Mama meanwhile had two different sizes of combs in her hair, and was frowned up so hard at me I thought that her lips would crack off.

"Every time they'd move me an inch, I'd howl. And every time I'd howl, Gramma, who had insisted on leading, would jolt back and start to put me down. Mama got so mad, she stopped and put down her end of the blanket. I had my legs and hips up in the air on Gramma's end, and my head on the ground on Mama's side, and they were bickering about who is going to lead. I couldn't believe it. Finally, I hear my mama breathe out,

'Mother Ernestine, please.' Mama almost never calls Gramma anything but Mama, so whenever she says Mother Ernestine, you know it's the end of a showdown. Gramma, she just eased down my feet and apologized to me for having to put me down, and for my mother's 'hard head and little-bit-of-sense attitude.' Then she walked over to my mother who handed her the two ends of the blanket on my head side. Mama told me to be strong, picked up her end and called to Gramma to pick up the other end. They lifted me high above the steps. Gramma started to humming one of her weaving songs and Mama joined in and they carried me inside and put me down without another word from either of them or another groan from me. I didn't dare, I just bit my lip and prayed myself inside.

"Finally, when I was settled in the house, Gramma brought me a cup of water, but Mama took it from her hands and just spread some water on my lips and wouldn't let me drink. Mama pulled a blanket up around my shoulders, making a tent over my injured leg. Gramma took the blanket off and opened the window. By the time Al burst in the door all frowned up and ready to wrestle anybody who stood in his way, they had both taken seats on either end of the couch and were alternating between offering me a hard candy, a soft pillow, a cool hand, contradicting each other and then backing away and letting each other do for me. I started to laughing, until it made my leg hurt more. Even though I was hurting, it made me smile to see Al, all puffed up and sweating and ready to challenge both my mother and grandmother, who were definitely armed and dangerous. He walked right over to my Gramma, and just put his hands on my Gramma's shoulders and looked into her milky-grey pupils that can't see a thing, and said as clear and cold as I've heard him talk:

" 'Old woman, I am taking this child to the hospital. Now you was a fool to move her, and a fool to try and pull the leg straight yourself. But just because you and Iree have to carry special problems in your lives, does not mean this child will be crippled. Now you take your hoodoo or whatever the hell you call your herbs and poultices and use them on any kind of croup or flu you want to. This is for real doctors.'

"After that he walked over to my mother and put his hands on her shoulders. 'Iree, I leave you be much as I can. Zulie says you can handle plenty of things, and it seems like you can. But, you know you can't be sure of this. I'm taking this child to the hospital. I'll do everything I can to see they don't come up bothering you or Ernie, but this child needs a doctor, now.'

"Then he scooped me up off the couch and carried me to his car. I was crying, Gramma was calling Al out of his name, Mama was starting to rock. It was all crazy. But I have to say, when the doctors x-rayed my leg, they said it was pulled real straight and that the branch and cloth Gramma had tied around it held the bone in place real well. They put an old heavy cast on, and it was a drag for what seemed like forever. But my leg did heal straight, and I can run and climb and dance good as ever. So I guess doctors aren't so bad, it just that we Moores have never had the doctor habit, still don't really. But when we have to go, we go. So Mandy, when we leave here, you and me, maybe we could just kind of slide by an emergency room. I mean it could be like a ritual, going to the hospital on my birthday every five or so years."

Amanda picked up a corner of Imani's toast and started chewing on it. "Imani, my leg isn't broken, your birthday was yesterday, and anyway everybody gets sick in the beginning. Let's go back to Rose's, Imani. I'm tired and I think I could really sleep now."

Imani stalled at the diner as long as she could because short as it was, the walk to Rose's seemed real long. Finally though, the diner began to close down, so they got up and headed back. Amanda was feeling better. The color had come back to her face and she was walking with a surer step. "You know it almost feels like when I got my first period." She sucked in a breath at the corner and then continued, "Remember, Imani, it was right after school."

Imani had started menstruating more than a

year before Amanda. Her first time was in the middle of summer in her twelfth year and she had had few opportunities to brag about her "entrance to womanhood," as she called it. When school began she made the rounds of all the girls and collected their first-time stories to put next to hers. This one who hurt so much that she couldn't walk for three days, and that one who bled through three pads in two hours, and the other one who only bled six drops. Her own onset was dull compared to all of their stories. A bit of cramps, a bit of blood, and a bit of special attention for one day. When it was close to Amanda's time, Imani knew. The very day it started she whispered into Amanda's ear before their phys-ed class, "You better start wearing pads, just in case." Amanda, who did not want to have an accident like Latrice, who bled right through her white pants and was the butt of several young men's jokes for most of the previous spring semester, had been sporadically wearing pads for the past three months. She had found out how uncomfortable they were and how they made her walk differently because she was so afraid they would come loose and fall out of her panties.

"It was terrible." Amanda shook her head recalling the afternoon. "There was Dorrine wanting to fight me because Jerry had passed some note to me during science. As if I cared. I hadn't even read it yet." Amanda stopped and leaned up against a utility pole. "Remember that, Imani? She wanted to fight me over some boy I had hardly looked at. And my back was hurting and my insides felt like they were going to fall out. I remember she pulled on my sweater . . ."

Imani put her hand on Amanda's shoulder. "Are you okay?"

Amanda ignored her, straightened up and started walking again. "I was in no mood to be messed with. I turned on her and balled up my fist and was ready for whatever was going to come down, and here you come walking between us talking about 'Come to the bathroom with me,' and start dragging me off. You know that's one fight I would have won. But anyway, I was glad to get to the bathroom because I realized I had to pee really bad. The next thing I know I'm sitting on a toilet and blood is starting to drip out of me. Of course that was the one day I wasn't wearing my just-in-case pad. But you just wadded up a bunch of toilet paper and told me how to fix it until I got home. By the time we got out of the bathroom Dorrine was over in a corner rubbing on Jerry and didn't even see us leave. You know when I got home and told my foster mother she didn't say a thing except, 'You'll be having to move soon.' Just like that. I was so sad that day. After waiting and waiting, it seemed like it was just mess and pain. Just like now."

The girls had reached Rose's building. They

climbed the steps and as soon as Imani opened the door and switched on the light, Amanda grasped her belly and ran into the bathroom. The rest of the night was very long for both girls. Amanda tossed and turned all night, refusing any help. Imani lay awake on the floor, thinking about how she had missed her birthday and how she really wanted to go home. She could see what was happening, and she knew that she needed to make Amanda at least go home with her, but she really didn't know how to do it.

Amanda wouldn't go anywhere until she had made up her own mind. Imani understood that, not wanting anybody else to make your mind up for you. When Jeremiah taught her how to play dominoes he always told her, "Make up your own mind, or it'll get made up for you," and that's what she always tried to do, make up her own mind. Jeremiah never told Imani what to play or when, he just made her see pictures in the dots on the tiles, like the two/one being Mrs. Marie with her tight whistle mouth and the double six being truck wheels, and she always made up her own mind. So Imani wasn't about to try and make Amanda go home until Amanda set her own mind in that direction. Imani knew that no one could make Amanda do anything she didn't want to do. Amanda didn't fight or anything to hold her point, she would just sit there, not moving or blinking or answering when someone called her out. Mandy and Imani had been to many places together, and even though Imani wanted to go home and knew that they should go now, she also knew that she couldn't hurry Amanda along. Instead she tried to hurry up the sun.

Skeins, Colors

—◊◊◊—

ERNESTINE AND MICO HAD WALKED straight back behind the draped curtain that separated the converted garage into rooms. Heat blasted from an electric heater humming in the corner. Although Malachi's official residence was a small cottage five blocks away, this low-ceiling room with its lumpy couch, single hot plate, small refrigerator and two ceiling-scraping philodendrons was where he spent most of his time. It was also home to a bright-colored parrot who often sang while Malachi played his trumpet, and who was sometimes allowed to fly freely throughout the shack. Malachi had renamed the parrot Matilda when it was given to him. He paid it little attention, but always fed it and kept its cage clean.

Out front was where customers paid their bills and sometimes waited until their car was cleaned, buying extras like air scent or waste paper bags, or gee-gaws to hang from their rearview mirrors. For years Malachi had refused to sell them, not liking to encourage hanging crucifixes or dice in the windows. Jerome had made him rethink his opposition to other people's bad habits, and now a rack of cartoon figures, neon miniature sunglasses, and sparkling pendants were offered alongside the small flashlights and magnetic key hiders.

As soon as he had seen Mico and Ernie in, Malachi had turned his back on his guests, then picked up his trumpet and began to play a muted, plaintive wail. Mico helped himself to a beer, then found a hot pot of coffee and poured a cup for Ernestine. The sound of Malachi's horn made her sway in the same way she did when pulling lengths of yarn into the tight firm balls that would later fill her shuttles. Usually she would hum and rock as Imani, or Zulie, or sometimes Amanda, would hold the yarn taut between their forearms. Not more than a week before, Ernie had spent an afternoon with Amanda, filling a wide straw basket full of rolls of neatly bound yarn. Malachi's melancholy music took her back to that afternoon.

Amanda had come seeking Imani for one of the girls' regular Saturday adventures. Finding Imani gone, she had elected to stay and hold yarn for Ernie. Amanda was in an unusually talkative mood and posed question after question in her quiet, precise voice.

"Were you always blind, Mrs. Moore?"

Ernestine pulled a steady line of dark red yarn

into a tight ball, letting its heat make creases on the thumb and forefinger of her left hand. She sat with her back pressed against the front rim of her loom, the bar resting just above the arch in her back. The loom was a golden brown, and with eight treadles it was a maze of wire and wood crossings that Amanda loved, repeating on almost every visit, "It's *so* lovely, even without the yarn." Amanda loved to watch cloth grow.

"No, darling, I wasn't always blind. But I've never been able to see as much as I needed to," Ernie had laughed dryly, and continued to pull the thick soft thread.

"I had a sickness since being a real little child, and every year I could see less and less until only a mouse-hole of light showed through. I learned to weave as a child. When the doctors said I was going to be blind, my grand insisted I learn a craft so that I would never starve. She wanted me to sew quilts like her, but all that little stitching and constant pricking of these fingers with those too-long-and-always-seeming-to-break needles was just tedious to me. Much as I loved to crawl up under those blankets winter times, I really wasn't about to make no career sewing them.

"My defiance started to cause a family row, and then my youngest brother, Jeremiah, told them they ought to let me make the cloth for the quilts since I was determined not to sew them. For some reason they listened to him. I never did understand that, except my mother just stopped, she had a way of doing that, becoming as still as a statue, and just her mouth chewing on her tongue and sucking it in and out, considering what had been said, or more likely letting it flow through her, so she could know for sure if she was hearing a lie, a truth or a true guidance. No one much listened to Jeremiah, what with him being not only so young, but also so contrary, always insisting, whether he knew how to or not, that he be allowed to do it his own way. Y'know he's still like that today.

"Anyway, Mama just stopped, cocked her head, and then said real quiet, 'That will do it. That will do it fine.'

"I think that was the moment I realized she was going to die soon. Suddenly, I put all her preparations together, the way she had Jeremiah going over to his friend Malachi's house and learning how to fix things, even though Jeremiah had only just made nine. It all made sense at that moment, the way Darlene was learning how to cut patterns with Mrs. Stevens, and the twins learning how to cook together, and why my grand was visiting for such an extended time. Before, I thought it was just raising, but I realized that in the last few months everything had been sped up, and Mama wasn't going to see me through. Of course, she worried about me, but she knew I'd be all right. That's what she always told me, *It might be harder than you want it to be, child, but you'll always make it through. You gonna live as long as you're supposed to be, which'll be a lot longer than my time.*

"I don't know where they found that first loom. It rested on a table and had a splintered top and the racket it made when you got to beating the cloth. My, but I loved that loom. I made a loose linen for the first cloth. Oh, it was lumps and knots, hard wavy edges and loops in the middle. But Mandy, I tell you, the sound of the shuttle-boat skimming between the yarn, and then the swoosh and click as I pulled the beater forward and dropped it back, and then the ringing when I changed the treadles, child, you would have thought I was a musician. Everybody thought it was the cloth I loved. It took me years to learn to love the thickness of the yarn, the tension the warp could hold, and the way I could build it, weft strand by weft strand into a full fabric. But the sound, and the way I could get to rock and sway and no one hit me across the back.

"You know, child, when I got blind, people was always hitting me across the back whenever I started rocking, like I was supposed to sit still and just stare through those heavy thick glasses I had then. No, baby, I ain't always been blind."

"How did you learn to see colors? I'd like to do that, see colors with fingers like you do."

"Well, first child, you better learn to hold a skein of yarn better than that before you can try something like learning colors in your fingertips."

Amanda had let her elbows dip to her knees and

both forearms had come closer together, making the skein she was holding come loose and flop. Ernestine liked Amanda to hold yarn for her because she usually had such natural concentration. She felt concerned with the child's inattention that Saturday. She knew Amanda talked when and where she wanted, but rarely on demand, and almost never much. As Amanda sat herself up and re-adjusted her skein, Ernestine continued her story:

"After my mama passed, I cared for most of my brothers and sisters, being the oldest, but my grand was the boss of the house. My dad was long dead. Some says he was lynched down South for seeing something he wasn't supposed to see; my grand said he drowned in the river carrying bootleg liquor across the state line. Mama always said the only important thing to know was that it wasn't natural, but it was his time to go. Nobody ever leaves unless it their time to go, that's what she always said. Of course, that's one of those always-been-true things that most folks just don't want to accept.

"Like I told you, I could still see when my first loom was brought in and my second one, too. I got that one from my husband, Mr. Moore. But this loom here was made special for me. This is wider and a little deeper than the others. I'm so tall and I like to stretch myself over the cloth. Jeremiah and my son Ezekiel made this one."

Ernestine leaned back, rubbing her spine in a

cat stretch against the back of the loom, and rested a ball of knobby hand-spun, cream-colored thread in her lap. Then she stretched her arm against the harness and stroked the smooth and shiny top edge.

"Making this loom was quite an adventure. Ezekiel went to the library and got out a few books and talked with Jeremiah, and I swear it just rose up around me in a couple of weeks. Now that was a happy time. You know, I didn't even see Ezekiel hisself more than a year or two. When he was born I laid him next to me on the pillow and just looked at him all over, one little ear at a time, one tiny brown eye, half of his fist and his long feet; the right was unlined and the left was so ticklish. Funny how only the left one was ticklish. My, how I loved to run the edge of my nail down that sole and listen to him giggle. A few years later, all I could see was a pinprick of light and ever since then just this shadow darkness. I'm comfortable with it now, but when I was young, I cursed God and everyone else. But now, we were talking about colors weren't we?

"I remember, just after Iree came to live with Ezekiel and me, and be my daughter, I decided to make her a special shawl. I was going to buy some yarn and was wanting a bright, bright gold. I also needed some fresh linen for the warp roller to keep the weft smooth when it rolled around. By then my eyes were pretty weak and I was starting to lean hard on everyone for help, especially Jeremiah. But that day he left me in the store by myself and I walked up and down this row and that, trying to pretend like I could see as good as everyone and bumping into salespeople, children, ladders; I was a mess, I'll tell you.

"I started reaching my hand out to the walls, filled floor-to-ceiling with bolts of cloth, just reaching out to keep myself steady and I noticed that the fabrics were not only smooth and prickly but also cool and lukewarm and sometimes it seemed like they'd like to burn off my fingertips. I touched this one bolt, the material was smooth and I expected it to be crisp, but instead it was so warm my eyes started to sweat and I just wanted to bury my hands in the fire. So the saleslady comes by and says, 'Isn't that lovely? You have the richest gold in the place. A woman last week bought it for an anniversary gown. Better buy as much as you need because they'll never match this dye lot again. Look at the way it glistens next to your brown skin.'

"Well, I was way past seeing a glistening, but I could feel the warm. Mandy, I spent the rest of the afternoon in there, going from corner to corner, catching the edge of a chill or some pinpricks, or some hot steam, and each time I'd ask what was the color and someone would tell me. By the time I got to the section where the white linen was, I swear I could feel the bleach and the way colors just avoided its light. Now I can feel colors in anything, skin, yarn, walls, and know what they are.

That is, of course, if they're an honest color. I keep working at it, but it still leaves me sometimes, I do mistakes. So I didn't really learn to do it so much as I found out that I already could do it. Everybody has something they can do. Something, that nowadays is considered special or magical or strange."

"Everyone in *your* family."

"No child, everyone. Now Zulie, she's got a knack of being just where she's needed when she's needed, no call necessary and on top of that she can make food appear out of a cup of nothing and a teaspoon of a little bit. And Malachi, he's got a way of finding the locks on people's hearts, and breaking them off without ever bruising the heart. I never understood why he never chose to live with another woman after his wife died. I mean, he always keeps steady company with one, but won't live with any. And then your mother Lorraine, it seemed to me she had a way of seeing people's fear, knowing it in her fingertips, only her way was to feed on it, and even though she didn't want to, to make it grow."

"I don't see that as special, making fear grow."

"It was in the seeing. Had she learned, she could of learned to turn it, child. Now you, I'm not sure what your knowing is. You certainly were a gift to me last month when Iree was ill."

"Anybody can nurse."

"I'm talking about healing, not nursing, child."

Just then Imani burst in the door.

"Mama fell out at Mrs. Meecham's. She started spitting and swallowing her tongue and just passed out in the middle aisle. A customer was there and helped us carry her into the back room, and Mrs. Meecham was going to call the ambulance, but I convinced her Uncle Mico would come and get her and that she really didn't need a doctor because she'd wake up in a few hours . . . and she said Mama couldn't stay there that long, so I told her I'd be back in an hour, and I went running to look for Uncle Mico, but he's not home, so I went by Malachi's but he wasn't there, but Jerome was, and he's outside with their station wagon, but we need an adult or Mrs. Meecham won't let us take her, and you know she'll call the social service and we've got to go right now!"

As the breath ran out of Imani's lungs she stopped, looking scared and helpless. Ernestine put down the ball of yarn, reached towards Amanda and carefully took the rounds of yarn from her forearms and laid them next to her on the bench. Then she stood up and smoothed out her skirts.

"Come on, Amanda, let's go fetch my daughter."

Amanda's eyes darted back and forth from Ernie to Imani. "Please, I'd rather stay here . . . Maybe start dinner and get the bed ready."

Imani moved close to Amanda and whispered into her ear, "Jerome's been looking for you. He says he needs to see you."

Amanda looked hard at her friend, pleading, "I don't need to see him right now."

Ernestine brushed past Amanda and placed her hand on Imani's shoulder. "What Jerome needs to do right now is help us get your mother home. That's all right, Amanda, you just stay here. I think that's a good idea. It might be dark before we get back. If Zulie comes ask her to show you how to make the tea we'll be needing. Let's go, Imani, you know Mrs. Meecham's like to change her mind if your mother wakes up and starts to wailing."

As granddaughter and grandmother walked out the door, Amanda moved to the loom bench and sat down. Ernestine recalled that the first thing she had noticed after she had returned with Iree and got her in the bed and finally slumped back down at her loom was that Amanda had finished rolling all of the loose yarn.

Malachi's trumpet pulled Ernestine back to the small garage. His tone had changed and was now blaring out the cracks in the wall, screaming for an answer as the night returned only more questions. Sweat was running from his brow, and his salt-and-pepper hair glistened at the edges of his small hand-sewn cap. His lips clutched the now-burning horn and blues reached down the street, into the alley and came back circling under the door jamb, making goose bumps between Ernie's shoulder blades. Mico had picked up a large metal spoon and was keeping time with one bare hand, punctuating Malachi's cries, the sound of steel ringing against the small wooden end table. Finally when Malachi could blow no harder, and the notes could get no higher, and the walls would have had to move further out to accommodate the blasts, he stopped and listened to Mico drumming on the edge of the table. Malachi started again, a series of short quick bursts, and then a long sweet breath before he turned and sank back against the window sill, his trumpet still buzzing as he rested it across his knees.

Mico stopped his drumming and leaned back his head with a hearty laugh. "Man, what kind of devils you chasin' out of here tonight, or what kind of angels are you tryin' to bring in? Damn, man, I always told you, you should of stuck with that horn instead of spending your time spitting and polishing everybody's wagons. You still got it. I tell you. I tell you. Ernie, ain't he something? I mean really!"

Ernestine had not really heard. She rolled her half-empty coffee cup between her palms. Malachi stood his trumpet on the floor and moved to her, touching her hands.

"Give that to me, I know what you'd like, a fresh cup of coffee with maybe a spot of whiskey in it to hold back the cold."

"As if you could hold back winter," Mico laughed. "Although with the way you was playing that horn tonight it is something to consider."

Malachi went to the faucet and ran some more

water into an electric kettle. He plugged it in the wall and sat next to Ernestine on the couch. He ran his fingers down her cheek like she used to do to him in greeting, and sighed.

"You know, maybe I should of gone ahead and tried to marry Lorraine, at least tried harder to keep her here. We'd been friends. I had talked to her every week for close to a year. She had stayed here and we'd been together a few times. There was something in her that pulled me up so tight, like nobody but Mustafa's mama had ever done before. But Ernie, she had so many problems, and you know, I really just couldn't. But maybe I could of helped her raise Amanda. I mean instead of letting that child just slide from place to place."

Ernestine reached up to feel Malachi's hand which rested on her shoulder. "Bend down and let me feel your beard, old man," and she reached up and felt the squared-off beard, rich with its silver-grey strands. "I see you gettin' quite grey, there, old man. Now you know, you were too old for that young woman. She ran off of herself, not you. And her daughter runs off of herself, too. You couldn't have and shouldn't have stopped either one of them."

Malachi walked back across the narrow room and picked up his trumpet. He pulled the shade on the window halfway up and cracked the window. He put a round flat mute in his horn and began to play again. This time the song was light and sweet, its notes trembling lightly along the walls. Malachi flowed back to the last night he saw Lorraine.

One week after the earthquake and fire, Lorraine had come by Malachi's shop to say good-bye. Over time she and Malachi had become really good friends. Malachi had encouraged the friendship, sending his son Mustafa and his nephew Jerome home most Thursday evenings so he could tend to her car by himself. After a while he spoke with her about more and more, enjoying the way she would flatly reply, then loosen and smile and give the real answer. "No, I really don't mind if the rain comes. I like the way the sky looks just before a storm. And the rain." And Malachi would answer, "I wouldn't mind a good long rain myself." Smiling and laughing, until she would agree to come in and have tea.

One night, when she was particularly quiet, he asked her what was wrong. Although Malachi liked her precisely because he could be with her and still be alone, at times he also begrudged her a certain depth of her aloneness. She would talk for a few minutes and then stop, becoming veiled and apart. That night she looked at him when he asked and sadly shook her head.

"My mother's house, my house, it has these closets. They are so big, not little coat closets, but ones that go far back and you can put a bureau in one corner and still have room for a cot and a little chair and lamp. The closet off my parents' room, my room now, even had a little tiny window up in the corner that one time of the year would let through a little triangle of sunshine on the ceiling and on a part of one wall. Some days it hit the glass just right and I could see the yellows and the reds on the edge of the white light, breaking into the shadow. I used to spend hours inside that closet. You could sit in there, read a book, stretch out on a cot. There was lots of light and the smells of all kinds of clothes . . . my mother loved sachets and she always put them in the pockets of her coats and the linings of her drawers.

"I used to spend a lot of hours there, by myself. Whenever my parents would go out and have to leave me alone I was sent there. There was no choice about it so I learned to enjoy what I could. Sometimes quiet is nice, sometimes.

"It wasn't really that they thought I was particularly full of sin. I always felt they loved me. They were protecting me from the world. They thought if I went out on my own I'd be swept up in some kind of tide of evil darkness. They were so afraid, and so sure that harm would come to me. They said they knew that I wasn't old enough, or they strong enough, to 'keep me on the right path,' as they put it.

"The thing is, they were so wrong. I mean I haven't found the world all that terrible. Not more than that, not more than those late afternoons and nights into the early mornings, alone in a closet, the air sweet and stale at the same time."

After that night Malachi began to take her on walks. On one of those walks she began to talk to him about leaving town. Malachi remembered how he thought of how much he would miss her. She never spoke of a possibility of staying, and had stopped speaking of her daughter, Amanda. They had never shared their children with each other, except in stories. Malachi stopped questioning her silences. He never talked about her staying, and never tried to ask for more of her time than she gave without question.

The last day he saw her, that Thursday after the fire, the back seat of Lorraine's car was full of boxes. A tall box was tilted on the front seat, and wedged in between the box and the glove compartment sat a covered bird cage, holding a frantically squawking parrot. Lorraine had been dressed unusually brightly. She wore a loose copper-colored skirt, a tan blouse open at the neck, and was wrapped in the beautiful bright yellow shawl that Ernie had made for her.

"I was hoping you'd tell me before you left."

"I am telling you."

"That's not what I meant."

"Well then, I did tell you."

Malachi looked at her and smiled. "Did I tell you that you're looking unusually lovely this evening? So bright I mean, and that shawl really sets your eyes off, shows how they're special. I . . . I understand, I mean your house is burnt and . . ."

"Malachi, that's not the problem, it's the opportunity."

"Lorraine, what's the matter with you? Where's Amanda?"

"Amanda's fine. She's staying here, with her father. Malachi, you didn't make me and I didn't make myself how I am. I'm trying to work with what I have, fix what doesn't work, move on. Amanda needs to be here. There's a place for her here. Malachi, I would do worse than lock my child in a closet."

"You're doing worse by leaving her."

"Then you take her, Malachi. You take her."

Malachi had stood there, hands open, shaking his head. Then he busied himself with finishing waxing a customer's car while Lorraine watched. Neither of them spoke to each other for close to an hour. Then Lorraine asked him to help her rearrange the back seat packages in her car so that she could see better. Together they emptied and repacked the car until the front passenger seat was empty and a small view space was cleared in the rear window. When they were done, Lorraine handed the bird cage to Malachi, who silently accepted the gift. He took Lorraine's arm and showed her inside where he offered some cold water and a seat. All Malachi could think of was wanting to touch her face, smooth it dry, and press out the fine frown lines that were wedged in between the corners of her mouth and her full cheeks.

Lorraine looked at his eyes and then laughed like a trill of piano keys, the notes falling around the shadows of the room.

"There are only a few things I've done that are not things that I've been told to do, or things that I thought I was told to do. Even having Amanda. I didn't ask for her. I didn't want her. I kept her because I was told to. I know I'm supposed to love her in a way that's particularly mother. But I like to be by myself. I keep my own company. Now I want it back, that aloneness."

"You can get trapped in it."

"No. I had it so long, it's how I'm most comfortable now. It's the only way I know myself. I got together with Ray just after my mother died. You know, he works at the post office branch I used then. He sold stamps and sorted mail into the boxes, and picked up the oversize packages and magazines that wouldn't fit in the mail slot. We started talking a little there. Then one day he came over to my house. He knew my address because I was always picking up packages. You know I love to shop by mail and get packages. It's like getting a surprise present. Well, he brought a book and some juice. He came three weeks later, same time, same day, and brought me that parrot. Then one week, he came in and decided to stay longer, and I just obliged him. Oh, he had all the words of love and desire, but mostly I complied because, why not, it seemed like something I was deciding to do anyway. At the time, I didn't really think about him being white. I mean in the summer he was darker than me. Anyway, he made me less alone and I thought I was supposed to want that, to be with others more. I liked it as long as it was only once in a while.

"But then I got pregnant and didn't know what to do, so I asked him. Ray got frightened. He told me it wasn't his. He reminded me that we had slacked off, and he came only every month or so, that I rarely went to the post office branch he worked in, that it seemed to be over. I told him I didn't want the child anyway. He said I had to keep it. I told him if I did, it would be his. He called me crazy and left. After that he didn't come until six months after the baby was born. He wanted to see the child, but he wouldn't ask. So he didn't see her for another six months, when he dropped in and she happened to be awake. When he did he was relieved. She didn't seem to look like him. After that he came by every so often, offering some treat for Amanda, but little money and no acknowledgment. I didn't mind. I was too full of Amanda to mind.

"But as Amanda grew older things went so awry. Amanda was so willful. At first she was loud, until I taught her that to stay with me she'd have to learn silence. Sometimes I wouldn't talk to her for days, just snatch her up and push her down. I'm getting better at being with people, being with you, being with her, but I need to go. I have to go. It's too hard. I want to be by myself."

"Lorraine, I think you should stay. I'll help you find a place. I really do care for you."

"I'm not staying, and I'm not taking Amanda. Keep your eye out for Amanda for me, and tell her I did what I thought was best. I let her be born, after all. Maybe it's crazy, but he is her father. I mean Malachi, you don't want her and I can't keep her and . . ."

Lorraine paused and then kissed him softly. "Remember me, Malachi, remember me as more than nothing. I want to live like you, alone and not alone, on my own terms."

"I live with my son."

"Seems to me that you care for Mustafa, but you live on your own, tied up in a funny kind of loneliness."

"Well, you don't really know."

"I came to say good-bye. Not to fight, Malachi."

They said nothing for a few moments. Then Malachi spoke softly, reaching out his hand behind Lorraine's head and rubbing her neck. "I like the way you look. I can see the whole world mixed up in your hips and eyes and lips. You got quite a woman hiding inside you."

"Malachi, you are the nicest man I have known, even if it's only a little time I've known you. I will miss you, but I must be going. I wish I knew how to stay here, but I have to see more than here. I have to be somewhere else."

"Somewhere where you'll know nobody."

"I'll meet people. I met you didn't I?"

"Will you at least write?"

"I'll try, Malachi, I'll try. I know I'll think about you. Don't show me out. Just play me another song before I go."

Malachi picked his horn up and tried to make her stay. He played her cool touch, he played her hips round and full pressing his, he played his lips pressing against her forehead, cheeks, fingers. Then he began to play the air that circled around her, and the moments and spaces between her words, and then the time that stretched between the first time they met and the last time they had kissed, and as he played Lorraine slipped out the door and drove away, leaving the bright-colored parrot, a small lace handkerchief, and the scent of coconut oil on his sofa.

He never turned to see her shut the door, and he did not look out the window to see if she had turned back one last time to wave. He knew she had not.

Ernestine and Mico watched Malachi bend over his brass horn, each feeling moved by the song which moved like mercury, but was nevertheless sad and forlorn.

Finally Mico stood up. "Man, we've got to be getting on. If you see Imani, please tell her to get her behind up the hill and stop worrying all of us."

Malachi put down his horn. "No, Ernestine, Lorraine didn't run away, she was trying to get to something, something she wanted for herself, but I don't know how she could of found it without a picture of it in her mind. And probably, she could of found it here, but she wanted to find it somewhere else. She never did like this place."

Ernestine stood up and moved toward Malachi. She reached out and felt his moist cheek.

"Old man, I enjoyed listening to your music. We'll be leaving now."

Jeremiah took Ernestine by the shoulder and turned her towards the door. "Well that was one crazy woman if you ask me."

"Ssh." Ernestine tried to stop his conversation.

"Ssh yourself, spider woman, that was a crazy broad, leaving her baby like that. But that Amanda is a different story, got a nice grit to her. A real special girl."

Malachi waved them good-bye with his horn and began to play again. Ernie and Mico heard the song sweeping into the night as they started up the engine and pulled down the street.

Circles

—◊—

ZULIE AND AL WERE SITTING close to each other on the porch steps talking softly when Ernestine and Jeremiah drove up. Al was holding Zulie's hands in his and stroking them softly.

As soon as Ernestine stepped out of the truck Zulie called out, "Now, I don't know what Iree and you two was talkin' about on this front step before you left but . . ."

Ernestine snapped back, "A little bit of nothing and a whole lot of none of your business."

"Well it must of been something," Zulie continued.

Ernestine puffed up like a mother hen settling on a nest of eggs and started clucking loudly, "Zulie, I know you're not trying to call me some kind of a liar in my own house on my own front steps."

Jeremiah reached his sister and cupped his hand under her elbow. "Calm down, spider lady. Can't you tell something's happened? What is it, Zulie? Did Iree take off on one of her journeys again?"

Al let out a long low breath. "Around the world and back again."

Ernestine reached out towards Zulie who offered her a hand, moving over so that Ernestine could sit next to her. "Ernie, I just never saw it come over Iree like that before. I mean never, and I've seen her go in and out and around plenty, oh, plenty of times. But this time, it caught me all offside. Al had just finished helping me clear up the table. He was peeking out the window and saw you two heading towards the truck, and then he made a little joke about you having a habit of navigating who ever happens to be driving."

Jeremiah moved to the bottom step and squatted down. "Yeah, well she tried you know, but we got a good understanding." He reached up and put his hand on his sister's face, which had become taut with worry.

Zulie continued, "So then Al moved to the counter and cut hisself another slice of bread and poured out some tea and settled back down on the couch and was looking for some music on the radio. I was about to sit down next to him when the door cracks open and there is Iree, standing by herself like some kind of statue in a museum, just standing and staring. She looked all right, real peaceful like, and not worried about Imani, or anything else far as I could tell. She was standing at the front door, and she called out to me, but it looked like her lips wasn't even moving, still she called out to me clear and set as can be, 'Zulie, I can smell that bread. I'd like a large slice fulla butter and honey.'

"Well, now you all know how I love to cook, and I will serve when it seems logical, but my middle name has never been at-your-service, especially for those who are grown and got working limbs and reasonably intelligent minds to keep themselves moving. In fact, that's one of the things that Al and I always fuss about, him wanting to be the king and always having me to bring him this and fix him that and fluff the pillow and straighten the blankets and all kinds of doing for, and doing around, even when we both are sitting still wanting to do nothing at the same time. I mean, if he got a taste for some water, it's 'Zelmababy,' one word like, 'Zelmababy, bring me a nice cool glass of water.' Or 'Zelmababy, do you know where I put those needle-nosed pliers? Why don't you go get them for me?'

"Of course nowadays Al understands me being on call like that is a once in a while, sometimes, and maybe and a little bit more than that. Besides Al always was one to help out when I really needed him to, knowing we both got to go up and down the same stairs."

Al and Zelma had met at Malachi's garage, when Malachi was having one of his jam sessions with his friends. They were playing that send-you-somewhere-else music, all fulla dips and squalls that is hard to keep a beat with. They started out just as solid and pretty as you please, but after a while it was just like some kind of outer space talk to Zelma, who wanted to dance and be right where she was, on this planet.

Zelma didn't know what to do with herself so out of habit she started straightening up a bit, and from out of nowhere, there was Al next to her, helping out and talking real soft about how she looked like the kind of woman who might take to some downhome blues. Next thing she knew, Zelma was in his car and on the way to Josie's Blue Black Inn. It had nice booths with black leatherette cushions and shiny blue tables, and a little stage tucked up in the corner that was crowded with about five musicians where maybe three could of sat comfortably. Al, who didn't really take to smiling too much or talking really, walked Zelma to the floor real solemn like. Then he surprised her out of her shoes when he started cutting up the floor all around her. They were spinning and rocking and grinding and the blues was all around them like a hot summer rain. That night they danced until the sun came up. Then, when he finally took her home, he noticed that the screen was broken on her door and insisted on fixing it, just like that, early in the morning. Later Zelma found out that that was how Al always was. If he saw something wasn't straight or tied up right, he'd take care of it right away or he couldn't sit peacefully. From that day on, Zelma and Al just slid their selves together.

Zulie started to gently rub Ernestine's shoulders

as she continued with her story. "Anyhows, I was about to tell Iree to fix her snack herself, and when she finished to come on over and wash up the rest of these dishes, when her mouth drops open, and the cup she's holding falls from her hands and shatters on the floor, and she stands there dumbfounded looking at the pieces. Then she lets out the longest, most curled-around, piercing scream I have ever heard.

"Now you know, I been seeing this child fall out, well, since before she was even a school girl, so it doesn't frighten me anymore, not like it did. But this time, this time, I swear if Al hadn't been there, I'm not sure what I'd a done.

"Iree started to rocking toward the floor, and the sound that was coming from her throat, high and shrill and long, it started to squeeze water out my eyes, not tears, mind you, but the water that clears away smoke or sharp onion juices. Well, I tell you my mouth was hanging open and I was breathing hard and running to catch her, but Al was already in back of her and had his arms and feet spread out to surround her. He wrapped hisself real loose around her and helped her slide to the floor, like he'd a done it million times before.

"Now, usually in these situations I'm there, knowing what to do, but this time it just left me and I was standing there lettin' flies just hover around my mouth. Al meanwhile was trying to slip off the sweater he's wearing with one of his hands, I mean he didn't call for me to help or nothing else. He saw me startled and scared, really, and said nothing and was just doing. Well, when I saw his arm get caught, I started to moving too. I helped him get the sweater all the way off, and then I ran to get a broom and try to sweep up the broken pieces of cup. I got up as much as I could, then I got a cushion from the sofa and grabbed a blanket.

"Iree, she was just a-writhing and suddenly she sat up and started to heaving and all that dinner came up and then she started to working on lunch and breakfast, too. I was racing now, getting towels and a bowl and cold water to wash off her face, and Al, he wasn't saying a word, just holding her so she wouldn't bump her head on the furniture. When it seemed like her stomach was empty, I slipped off her clothes and started to wash her right there on that floor. Now, we had tried to move her to a more comfortable location, but every time we lifted her up, just a little bit, she started to dry heaving and tossing and screeching so we'd just left her on that hard floor. I took off her clothes, holding down one arm and then the other till I could pull off her blouse and then unfasten her skirt, so I could wash her down.

"Al was so embarrassed, but he wouldn't open his mouth. He just kept guard around her and turned his head away, kind of feeling her and catching her when she tossed, trying not to see more than a kneecap or the corner of a shoulder. Not that he was ashamed so much as he figured that Iree would not want him to be seeing her all naked like that. Of course that was Al being his preacher self, because Iree, she's got no shame for her body. You know what I mean, she's not brazen or showy or nothing, just real natural and don't think twice about it. You remember how when she used to feed Imani, she had to be taught to cover her breasts, and she'd do it, but only to accommodate others. If it was just me or Ernie, or even you, Mico, well she'd just let that old full titty hang out, and had that little baby suckle long as she wanted to. But anyways, for Al's sake I was trying to keep a towel draped over her privates, but what with the twisting and curling, of course it would fall off, and of course it took me a little while to get her as clean and smelling good and fresh as I wanted. But I finally did it.

"After I got her all cleaned up and wrapped one of Ernie's skirt cloths around her waist and pulled an overshirt over her head, well she seemed to calm down. She was sitting up kind of leaning against Al. Then she started crying, holding my hand tight and begging me, 'Please, Zulie, don't let it take me. I won't come back. Zulie, hold me.'

"Now the water that started coming after that, they was tears, from my eyes, I mean. And I was kissing her hands, and I pushed Al away and took his place. I wrapped my arms around Iree's shoulders and was holding her and rocking her and telling her she ain't going nowhere except to the bed where she'll be more comfortable. This time she didn't fight with us. We walked her to the bed and then laid her down soft as can be. It seemed like she dozed off. So I turned to Al, and I tell him that we can relax now because she'll sleep probably for hours and we should just put some towels underneath her in case she messes or anything. Al, he just looks at me, like he's used to dealing with this kind of thing all the time, and says:

" 'Zelma, that woman is no more asleep than you or I. Crazy is what she is. The only thing I know is that we should be going to a phone and getting her an ambulance to get her to the hospital. Zelma, tomorrow I'm putting a phone up here and I don't care what you or Ernestine has to say about it. No one is going to be stuck up here in an emergency and not have a phone. What's the use of living in a city if you don't even have a phone?'

"Then he moved to the couch and started playing with the radio dial again. I mean he was just stony, turning the dial and then stopping, sometimes not even on a station, just with some static. Then he would rub his fingers over his chin and say, 'I'll be damned. I'll just be damned,' and start back to switching stations again. I got up to move towards Al and Iree's hand shot out and grabbed my wrist as I passed her, and she dug her nails deep into my skin until I was bleeding. I swear, I still have a little half-moon right on the inside mound from where her nails dug. Anyway, she grabs me and cries out real desperate, loud enough to burst my eardrums, as if she thinks I'm real far away, 'Zulie, Zulie, please!'

"I started stroking her head and pulling the hair back from the crown, just stroking her, soft and easy. She was trembling and sweating, like she had been taken with the flu or something. Her eyes were fixed on the floorboards where she had been laying. She said real quiet, 'Nuthin's ever died here on this hill. Nothing with blood that is. How's that possible, Zulie? I mean there's always a squirrel or a mole or a sparrow or something that dies and rots. The land's been here for thousands of years. How come nothing but plants and insects have ever died here? There's a creek near, too. I mean a fish or a tadpole could of died. That's what keeps things going, the dying and the rotting and the soil that's made from the dead meeting with earth. How did it happen, Zulie? This land, it's got a dry breath and it's hoarse. Zulie, how come nuthin' ever died here? Do you think it wants me? It can't want me, Zulie. Land doesn't take the living, it only takes the dead, right, Zulie?'

"Now, I didn't have the faintest what this child was going on about. I mean talking about animals rotting and dying, and then staring at the floorboards like they breathing or something. But I was following her gaze and I saw some little sparkles of broken glass, so I got up real quick like and went to get the broom. Iree, she just let me go this time, didn't do anything but watch. I start sweeping the floor slow, wide, steady and hard. I thought that maybe she sees more glass and that's why her eyes don't move off of the spot. Then, I looked over to Iree again and I see her lift her head and look at the door. Then she sat straight up in bed and started to whining and trembling again.

" 'Zulie, why's it going to tell me something like that, what do I care? I mean there's probably lots of places on earth where nuthin' has died.'

"Al sat up and turned around and looked at Iree. Then he looked at me, and then he walked over to her. 'You might be right or not about things dying on this land. But, I'm not up for one of your stories today. I don't care about no dead people talking to you. I don't care about no rivers talking to you, and I sure as hell don't care about no dirt talking to you.'

"And then he walked back over to the radio, rolled the dial through every station making a comment to himself like, 'Naw,' or, 'Don't you ever play any blues,' and then grumbling, 'Talking dirt, damn crazy gal.' Then he'd turn the station and start talking to hisself again. 'Probably if she didn't eat so damn much dirt, she wouldn't think it talked to her.' After he went around the dial, must of been two or three times, he found a station with a soft saxophone ballad rolling out into the night. With everything starting to getting calm, Al walked back over to Iree and started in again, 'Now you listen here. You just hold onto whatever it is you hold onto to stay here, and if that means

you have to tell your stories, I guess you can talk
'em soft to Zelma, but I don't care to hear them.'

"Just then Iree, she starts to whine louder and
she jumps out the bed and starts humming and
then she runs outside. Al and me, we run out the
door and off of the porch and try to grab her, but
then she starts to rocking and this growl comes
out the bottom of her belly, and we drop her arms
and just stand back. She kneeled down and started
putting dirt all over her face and arms. Her mouth
was foaming and she was swaying back and forth
on her knees, hitting herself with clods of dirt,
tossing and turning. It was like we couldn't, neither one of us, move. Then Al, he snapped to and
went over to the oak tree and pulled off a thick
twig about one inch around. He walked back and
put his arm under her chin, cradling her head
against his chest, and put the stick in her mouth,
trying to hold down the tongue she was about to
swallow. She bit the stick in two and bit the edge
of her tongue which was bleeding into the corners
of her mouth. Then Al reached up to my waist and
pulled off the apron I was still wearing. He took
the ties and stuffed them gentle into her mouth.

"Iree, she starts to calming down. I mean she
slid down and was laying on the ground real still.
Al pulled out the apron strings that he'd filled her
mouth with and I could see that they'd got blood
on the edges. He handed the apron to me, picked
that girl up, by his lonesome, and carried her into
the house. He put her on the bed like she was a

baby. Then he just starts to rubbing her hands and feet, one at a time, and starts talking to her about how her fingers are so long and her feet so slim. I was right behind Al. As soon as I got inside I filled a basin and got a pillowcase to use as a washcloth, 'cause all the towels were gone, and I started in to washing the child again.

"Al moved away and Iree, she reached out and took his hand, gave it a squeeze and then let it go. Al kissed her forehead and went back to sitting on the couch. This time, he put his head in his hands and I knew he was crying. Before you knew it, Iree was fast asleep and Al and me, we were just sitting next to one another. I had my arm around him, and he was holding onto my thigh, rubbing it back and forth and we tried to talk, but didn't seem to have too many words to spend. Al, he leaned his head up against my shoulder and said,

" 'Zelmababy, I swear, for a minute I thought that if Iree could of been sucked into that hillside she would have been. For a minute, I thought I saw a cloud of dirt just raising around her. I know it was just the soil in my eyes and her throwing dirt every which way, but for a minute there, Zelma, I was afraid we might really lose her. I'm not up for this stuff. You know how fond I am of this family, but Zelma, this is just too much.'

"I told him, 'Al, she's through it now. It's over. She'll sleep for a good while and wake up fine.'

" 'You think so, Zelmababy?'

" 'I told you . . .' and then I had to stop because I knew what he meant. Iree might not come back right this time. She's never been so long in the spell. In all the years I'd seen her fall out it just came over her, went through her, and was gone. It never stayed like this, but I didn't want Al to call no doctors so I said, 'Al, whatever she's gonna be, can't nobody do nuthin' about it, but her. Either she makes it back or she don't.'

" 'Zelma, that's what they got doctors for,' he said.

"So I tell Al that ain't so. I mean they got doctors for broken legs. They got doctors for cutting growths. They even got doctors for giving out shots, but they ain't got doctors for Iree. We just sat there quietly for several minutes. We didn't even hear Iree when she came to. We were just sitting there, holding on to each other and rocking a bit. I knew now there would just be a long night of sitting. Then I heard Iree, her voice just like a bell, ringing real soft, 'Zulie, it'll be okay. I pulled myself out of this one. Zulie, it's not me it wants. When it called out, I shouldn't of answered. It didn't call me, only I heard.' "

Zulie took a breath and then continued her story, "I swear I felt a cool air blow against my skin. I'd been sweating hard. The breeze lifted the damp shirt away from the small of my back. The doors and windows were closed. Even the curtain was still, yet I could feel this breeze. Even Al told me later that he felt it too. He said he felt the air move up and down his spine. Said he started to shiver when Iree brought both hands around his palm and began rubbing it real hard. But I just remember the cool and Iree smiling.

"And then Al starts to lecturing her, just as stern and upright as can be, talkin' about, 'You Moores are a strange family.'

"I couldn't believe him. I mean not more than a hour before I was wiping up green retching and now he's gonna lecture this child. But Iree she just cut him off saying:

" 'Dupree. I'm Dupree, Dupree and Adams, I just wear the spirit of Moore, the coat of Moore, but I'm Dupree by my daddy and Adams by my mama. Imani, she's Dupree, Adams, Foster and Brooks. Everybody thought it was Ezekiel all the time. He was the only one knew, besides me and Imani of course.' "

Ernestine interrupted Zulie's story. "I knew. I didn't want to believe her. I mean I wanted Imani to be part of Ezekiel, but Imani's little feet had so many lines. They were long and slender, not thick and big and flat like Ezekiel's. That is I knew it wasn't blood of mine, but I didn't know, for a good bit anyway, whose it was. I mean it's not like that Bilal Brooks came calling regular like, no count that he is. Iree told me he lived on the edge of town, but I can't say I remember him at all, although I'm real familiar with his cousin. The one time I met him I could tell by his voice that he was one of those all-syrup-and-no-meat kind of men.

Then too, I could tell from his quiet way why Iree took to him."

Iree never really knew exactly what it was that drew Bilal to her. He said he liked her legs and arms, said they never stopped. He said he could imagine being wrapped in her arms and legs forever. He made her feel like she was a whole woman with his words, like there wasn't a part of her brain always ready to burst and send her some place that she didn't want to go. He never talked about her spells. Iree made herself believe it was because he didn't care, but she slowly learned that it was just fear. It was as if Bilal was with Iree to exorcise some of his own ghosts.

The first time they made love she could tell that something was wrong, but she returned to his arms again and again, wanting to make it right, wanting to believe in the possibility. Bilal had said that he wanted to do right by Iree and be a family with her, he said everything perfect, for a while. But you can't love someone you are afraid of, someone who makes you tremble when you touch them. At first Iree was such a fool for his trembling, she thought it was excitement. Later she realized he was like a child daring to look under the bed at night, shaking in fear the whole time.

That first month she was late, Iree didn't pay it any mind at all. She didn't even tell him the only time he climbed that hill to visit her. After some brief words with Ernestine he pulled Iree off of the porch and over to the big oak tree for a private conversation. Bilal squatted under the tree while Iree stood leaning on it. She sat outside listening to Bilal make promises he never intended to keep. He promised to move her off the hill and in with him, not to marry her, of course, just to stay together. For a moment Iree thought that she could of gone anywhere with him. But she knew, deep in her heart, that he would never take her away from there. He was too afraid, afraid for Iree and afraid of Iree. Despite his words on that day, she knew that they were already starting to part. The garden was planted and everything was starting to sprout and blossom, including Iree.

Then Iree saw Ezekiel come up the walk, whistling to himself. He saw Iree and smiled, and he walked over and began to squeeze the back of her neck like he always liked to do. He spoke gruffly to Bilal, shook his hand and squatted across from him. They had crossed paths a few times over the summer when Ezekiel came home to visit. When Ezekiel began to ask what Bilal was doing there he said, "I'm going home, all the way home to Louisiana. I came to talk to Iree about it."

Ernestine continued softly, a tear hanging from the corner of her eyes. "You know, Ezekiel lied and said the baby was his, and Iree, she didn't say anything, she just went over and ran her hand down the side of his face and smiled, and then why we all just switched subjects like a train moving from one track to another at the crossing. I let myself believe what I wanted to believe, and my children, they just helped me along the way. I remember one time I was so mad at Iree. We had been fighting about moving. She was so sure we were going to lose this house. It was in the middle of one of those spats that Iree started talking about how she needed to get moved so Imani could settle in and I told her in no uncertain terms there wasn't none of my blood moving from this hill, and Iree said, 'I'm talking about me and my blood, not yours.'

"Seemed like winter fell all around us then. That's about the last time I remember crying. But Iree, why she didn't say a word, just unpacked the boxes she had been filling, knowing full well that she was going to pack them back the next day. She put everything away and then sat down next to me and took my hands. 'Mama, she's your baby, just like I'm your daughter. But she's not your blood. You know that. Ezekiel and me found each other after Imani was made, not before. When Bilal left me, Ezekiel filled the space. She's your baby, but she's not your blood.' I don't think I talked to Iree for a good two weeks after that."

Iree never did tell Bilal about the baby. He found out later, but not from her. After three years of waiting to see if Imani was going to turn out what he called normal, Bilal came to visit again, played with Imani and left. He was pleased because Imani was so pretty, took after his mama, he said. Once Imani took the bus to Louisiana where Bilal lived. He kept her for three days, had his wife fix her a mess of food, and then put her back on the bus with a new pair of shoes, a pretty dress, and fifty dollars in her pocket. He was more afraid of Imani than he was of Iree.

The four elders sat quietly. Then Mico spoke up, "So she asleep now?"

Al growled, "After all of that, she best be. For the next two or three days, I expect."

Ernestine pulled herself to her feet. "No, she'll be awake come morning. We all better get to bed ourselves. If Imani is not home early morning, I guess I'll have to start worrying."

Mico came up behind his sister. "Well you sure were doing a good imitation of that worrying stuff earlier tonight."

"Hush your mouth."

Al said, "You two go on in, we'll be inside directly."

Ernestine and Jeremiah went inside. Al looked at Zelma for a long time. Then he wrapped his arms around her and pulled her close as if he were afraid she might start having a fit. He ran his hands all over her face like he was trying to remember something special about it and kissed her on each cheek and then lightly on the lips, all without a word. Then they went into the house together.

Ernestine sat down on the edge of the bed, where Iree was still asleep. She unlaced her heavy shoes and pulled off her knee high stockings and stuffed them inside. Then she said to herself, more than to anyone else, "I don't remember when I've been this tired. I just don't remember. Even my bones just want to fold up into nothing. Even my bones." Then she turned her back to everyone and fell asleep. She didn't wash her face or hands or anything else; she just fell, like a rock falling out of the sky, into a hard, hard sleep.

Zulie moved to help her into some night clothes that might make her more comfortable, but Mico called her back with a whisper, "Leave her be, Zulie. She'll rest fine." He sat down next to Al and clapped him on the shoulder. "So, old man, my niece kept you busy." Al didn't answer, just shook his head. Mico didn't seem to care and just went on, "I'll stay with the ladies tonight. If you don't want to be bothered with the drive home, why don't you two stay in Imani's room? I'll take the couch."

Al didn't say a word, just took Zelma's hand and led her to the back room. He undressed as slowly and meticulously as ever, folding each piece of clothing and placing it neat as could be on the corner of the big oak dresser. Then he pulled aside a yellow blanket that was hanging over the mirror and just stared at himself in the mirror. Al reached out and touched the mirror reflection of his lips as if he expected something strange to happen, and then touched his own lips just as carefully.

"You know, Zelmababy, it seems like looking in a mirror should make you more sure that you are here, solid and real. But sometimes it just makes you wonder more. I mean if what you see is really you or not. Maybe Iree is not as solid as the rest of us, like she's got more air to her or something. Maybe gravity doesn't hold her the same and maybe mirrors don't reflect her the same. I don't know."

He sighed real hard and long. "I guess hanging around these Moores is making me think as crazy as the rest of you all."

Zelma smiled at that, thinking of how Al really did have his ways, although he'd be the last one to admit it. Every night when he undressed, he folded over his pants and pressed them with his hands, even work jeans. Zelma, she just slid out of her clothes and put them in the hamper if that's where they belonged, or laid them across a chair until morning. Al picked up Zelma's things from where she'd tossed them, at the foot of the bed, and folded and hand-pressed them, and laid them right next to his.

Zelma smiled at his fastidiousness and reached out her hand. "Come on, old man, and get in this bed with me. Crowd on up close."

Al sat down without fussing about Zelma's clothes-flinging habits, and pulled back the covers. "Little as that mattress is and big as you've gotten, I guess I'll have to crowd." Then he smiled and slid under next to her. He let her fold her arms around him, and whispered quiet as can be, "Imani will be back in the morning. Zelmababy, we're just old folks worrying too much, aren't we?"

"Yes," she answered, "Lord willing she'll wake us up come morning." Then they settled into that skinny mattress and stroked each other to sleep.

Offering

——m——

IMANI HAD KNOWN ALL ALONG that there was a problem. She had seen it, but didn't want to believe what she saw. There was something inside Amanda's eyes, almost silver, like ashes which still hold heat after the fire is gone. For all the stories Imani had read in people's eyes since she had been a child, she had never really seen a dying before. At least she had not seen and understood it as that. Occasionally she had caught a glimmer of color, a particular way someone would seem to catch their breath or hold their thoughts that made her think of death, but this was the first time that Imani understood that glow to be the letting go, and the moving on.

Imani had always been able to see memories and worries and spirits hovering around people. She had never questioned the waves of color she saw surrounding everyone. It took her years before she realized that everyone didn't see that which was as obvious to her as obsidian-colored hair or red-tinted lips. At first, as a child, she would draw it in pictures. After outlining the eyes, nose and mouth, after shaping the hair and cheeks, arms and legs, she would put waves or swirls or raindrops in the space surrounding them.

Her mother asked Imani about the swirls, which no one else ever mentioned. Iree had awakened that morning from an all-night spell. While Iree bathed, Imani had carefully drawn a picture to give to her mother. "Mama, I drew you a picture of Gramma and you and the tree." Iree looked at the picture for a few moments before speaking. In the picture Ernestine and Iree stood smiling on either side of a tree. The were drawn flatly, with thick, hard lines. Around Ernestine Imani had placed light and dark purple waves. Around her mother she had traced bright, bright yellow, and one line of maroon.

"Imani," Iree asked, "do you see Gramma and I like this? Do you see these colors?"

"Of course, how'd I know what color to draw them if I couldn't see them?" answered Imani gaily.

Iree pulled Imani close and held her tightly until Imani squirmed out of the embrace. "Imani," Iree said catching her hand, "Imani, everybody doesn't see people the same."

"I know that, Mama. Gramma doesn't see people at all, and you see people who . . ."

Iree had put her fingers across Imani's lips. "Go play, Imani. Go outside and let me take a nap."

Years passed before Imani knew what Iree had meant that morning. She often tried to push aside the shadows of colors that hovered around everyone she saw. Sometimes, she almost succeeded, but not that morning. Amanda was already up, bathed and dressed, when Imani cracked her eyes open and began to stretch her limbs sleepily. She heard Amanda swallow the end of a moan. Imani blinked her eyes wide open and caught a glint of what could have been a teardrop in the middle of Amanda's pupil. Imani closed her eyes again and held them shut tightly. She rationalized that she was not quite awake, that Amanda was just morning sick. She pulled up images of several young women who had been sick in their pregnancy the first few months. Then she opened her eyes and faced Amanda. Amanda's eyes were dry, but the glint remained. Imani hoped it would pass, like a cloud momentarily covering the sun, but she knew it would not.

Amanda shook Imani's shoulder. "Come on, it's time to go. Now, Imani. I'm sorry if you're still tired, but it's time to go."

She rushed Imani through a superficial morning bath and a quick cup of tea and a slice of toast. Imani insisted on eating something and insisted on writing Rose a thank you note. Amanda didn't protest, she just kept Imani moving quickly and lightly until they had the living room straightened out, covers folded, and the few dishes washed. Then she took a deep breath and squeezed Imani's hand. "Let's go, girl." They went out, Imani following Amanda's lead.

Until that day, Imani had always fought with Amanda over her stubbornness. Imani would cheerfully suggest to Amanda that she should try to be a little more go-along so she'd have more friends. Imani didn't like the way Amanda always seemed to hang back or go off by herself. But Amanda didn't care, she did things in her time and in her way, which was, more often than not, quiet and alone. She seemed to keep this fence of iron around her. Only rarely did Imani ever see Amanda waver, see that iron inside her turn molten and pour out of her like lava. Last night Imani had seen the resolve melt away, but one strand of steel remained, like a thread that sewed together Amanda's insides and helped her to keep on. It was this strand, this stubborn thread that made Amanda special. Imani had always known that Mandy was special. And this morning she saw it again and let Amanda lead her.

After the girls left Rose's apartment they walked to the playground, which was still empty. They sat next to each other on the swings. Mandy began spinning herself in circles sweeping the toes of her shoes in the sand. Imani pumped as high as she could until she felt like she almost reached the top of the trees.

"Come on, Mandy, come up here with me," she screamed as she reached the top, and then swooped downward.

Amanda ignored her, and kept drawing circles in the sand under her feet. Imani stopped her swing and rocked next to Amanda for a few minutes. Amanda said nothing. She wound herself around and around until the swing's links started creaking, then she let go with her feet and spun around while the chain spiral unraveled. Imani saw that there was nothing that she could do, so she started to pump again. "Mandy, how come people stop swinging when they get older? Does it stop being fun?" Amanda smiled and started to pump. Imani continued to pump hard, sweeping the sky, while Amanda swung gently below. Neither of them spoke. Imani was waiting for Amanda to say something, but Amanda was content to stay there quietly all day long, swinging, then twirling, then swinging some more.

The Moore household was just waking up. The morning had started quietly enough. Ernestine could feel Iree breathing softly next to her. She knew Iree was awake, and calm. The grey light flowed through the window, bringing in the chill of dawn. Iree opened her eyes slowly and looked around the room. Ernestine heard her chopped sigh and spoke softly to her,

"It's early for you to be awake, child. Sunrise and you have never been friends. Worrying about Imani?"

"No, Mama," Iree lied. "She's all right. I can feel it. Imani's working something out, I guess.

You know, it's probably time we got a phone. She would of called. I mean we have a radio for God's sake."

"We don't have a radio for *God's* sake. We have a radio for Imani's sake because that crazy uncle of yours bought it for her and would not take it back down the hill!"

"As if you don't turn it on and listen from time to time."

Ernestine smiled. "Well since it wasn't going, I guess I made use of it."

Mico spoke up from the far side of the room, "You'd make more use of a phone."

"I don't remember you being invited in on this conversation," Ernestine answered.

Mico snarled back, "I don't remember needing your permission to speak, spider lady."

Just then Al walked out of the bedroom. "Well you three are certainly up early. What's the party about? You heard from Imani?"

Iree walked over to Al and gave him a kiss on the cheek. "Thank you for last night."

Al pulled back to his regular stiffness, smiling awkwardly and softly mumbling about only doing what was right. "Well what about Imani? Are we going to look for her?"

Iree got up and gathered the teacups. "First we all better eat some breakfast. How about some grits and eggs and biscuits?"

Mico caught his niece's hand as she reached for his cup. "Wait for Zulie, she'll help."

"I know how to cook, Uncle Mico. I know how to cook." She moved over to the kitchen area and began to look for the utensils she needed. Nothing seemed to be in the right place. Everybody watched her opening and closing cabinet doors and drawers, usually coming up empty handed, but nobody moved.

Al walked over to the front door. "Think I'll let a breeze blow through if you don't mind." Al stood there, cracking open the door and looking down the empty road.

Zelma was the last one awake. She sat up trying to shake off the last bit of her sleep when she realized that it was fully light again, and Imani was still not home. Everybody was trying to relax into a confident attitude about Imani, reminding themselves and each other that Imani was more grown than they wanted her to be, and grown enough to handle whatever was keeping her gone. By the time Zelma came out of Imani's bedroom, breakfast was half cooked, actually half mis-cooked, and the men were coming up with a new strategy for looking for Imani. Ernie was sitting at her loom, threading in strands of red yarn and complaining to Iree who was busy burning some grits. Al and Mico were fussing at each other about when the proper time was to call in the authorities, with Al insisting ". . . the day before yesterday," and Mico grumbling ". . . just about never, and that ain't here yet." Zulie walked over to the stove to help Iree, picking a dishtowel up on the way to wipe up some of the mess from the boiled-over pot.

After about an hour at the park, without comment or warning, Amanda jumped out of the swing and started walking again. Imani called out, "Wait up, Mandy," as she leapt from her swing. Amanda slowed down, but didn't turn or answer. Imani walked with her, but it didn't seem like they were going in any one direction. Amanda circled the park, walked by the block where her mother's house had stood, then to the street where Malachi had his garage. After a few blocks Imani stopped asking Amanda where they were going. She just followed Amanda's lead. Imani was so busy hoping that Amanda would decide to go home that she didn't even realize that they were making a wide circle toward the hill the Moores lived on.

Amanda and Imani were both tired when they finally reached the bottom of the hill. Mandy kept stopping every few houses and holding her belly. Imani could see that Amanda wanted to cry, but was holding it in. It was as if she was using those tears as an inside river to smooth the bumps out of her walk. It was five blocks up and Amanda was getting weaker and weaker in her legs, but Imani could see the glint becoming sharper and sharper in her eyes. They had to walk slow and neither of them said much. Imani would put her hand on Amanda's shoulder and look into her eyes, but all she saw was the need to keep going faster. Sometimes Amanda would reach out and pull Imani back when Imani got more than a couple of steps in front. Imani would slow back down for a few yards, but then pick up the pace. After two blocks that way Amanda suggested that they sit down for a moment on the stoop of a nearby house. As soon as Amanda caught her breath she got back up and started walking, leaving Imani on the step. Imani gasped as she saw the back of Amanda's skirt darkening with a spreading pool of red. She jumped up and pulled Amanda back.

"Mandy, you need to sit down. You stay here. I'll go get help. We're real close. You just stay here." Imani started running. She looked back to be sure Amanda was all right and saw that Amanda hadn't sat down, she was still walking. She hadn't sped up or slowed down. She just kept on walking at her same pace. Imani ran the few steps back and took Amanda's hands in hers and tried to make her sit down. "Mandy, I'll get some help. You should stay here. I'm going for help."

Amanda stopped and looked at Imani and smiled as she gripped her side. "Well, go get some help, Imani. That's what I'm doing, going for help." Imani saw that Amanda was not going to sit down, that she was intent on climbing to the top of the hill, not taking a bus to the doctor and not waiting for Imani to get back. Imani took off again, and this time she didn't stop. She tripped and fell, but the scrapes on her hands and knees just made her run faster.

When Imani saw the front porch of her home she leapt up the stairs and burst through the door. There everybody was just like they had held onto her birthday for her. Al and Zulie, her mama and Gramma Ernestine, even Uncle Mico. For a moment she just froze, looking at them, then she caught herself and started raining Mandy out of her mouth. She started telling them about her last day in bits and pieces, and then it was pouring out in a pile of gibberish. At first nobody understood what Imani was saying. They were still getting used to her being home, but suddenly it clicked in, and then Al asked, "What's that about Amanda?"

"That's what I've been telling you! We were on the way, coming home, and then when we were walking she was holding herself and then I noticed the blood, and Mandy . . ." she almost screamed out the name.

As soon as Imani screamed out "blood and Mandy" in one breath, Al just lifted out of his chair and took off down the hill with Mico and Imani right behind him.

Ernestine, Iree, and Zulie hurried out the door and down the stairs. Iree's arms were outstretched, reaching for the daughter she had been about to embrace. Imani caught up with Al, then led the way. It had been years since Zulie had seen her husband run like that. There he was behind, next to, in front of, and then behind Imani, almost bumping into her, hurrying down the hill.

As Al, Mico and Imani neared Amanda they

saw that she was still walking, not crying, not complaining, and not talking, just walking. For a minute before they reached her it looked as if she was leaning on somebody, but as they got closer they saw that nobody was there. She had just stopped, adjusted herself, and started up again. When Al and Mico reached Amanda they told her that she should let them carry her. Amanda didn't respond, she just looked at both of them and put her arms around each of their shoulders, and kept her feet on the ground, moving forward, like she knew just what help she needed, and like she wasn't taking any more than that. Amanda wanted to get up that hill herself. She would lean, but she would not be carried.

Zulie turned to Iree and realized how happy Iree was to have seen that Imani was all right. She was just grinning ear to ear, like Amanda didn't matter at all. Zulie had never seen Iree act in such a way, as if she didn't care why Imani was covered with dirt and blood, or why she was crying. Ernestine leaned on Iree's shoulder and breathed softly into her ear, "What do you see, child? What do you see?"

Iree just shook her head back and forth, smiling gently. Then she said:

"I never saw most of them before, but I know they used to come here. Maybe to harvest acorns. You know that rock on the other side of the crest, Imani says they used it to pound the nuts into flour. She says her teacher told her that's what it

means when there are those smooth bowls inside
of a large sitting rock like that. Their clothes look
real sturdy though, do you think that's deerskin in
her dress?"

Iree kept on as if Ernestine could see to answer
her question. And all that Zulie could see was
some shadows which she knew to be Imani and
Mandy and Al and Mico, like a kind of haze at
the bottom of the hill. But there was Iree just as
calm as could be, looking and pointing.

"What you think they use to make that rattle
sound?" she continued. "It's like a procession,
Mama. Look at them, it's almost like a dance the
way they swoop down and then straighten up. I
love the way they just walk and sing. And look at
that little child just tripping around their legs. And
Mama, see, there's Ezekiel. You see him don't you,
Zulie?"

Zulie looked real hard down the road and she
saw a broad, thick shadow that seemed to swing
in that way Ezekiel used to move when he
stretched up a hill, never slow, never fast, just easy
like. But she was sure that it was just the way the
light was hitting Mico. Zulie turned to Iree. "Iree,
I am not in the habit of seeing no kind of spirits,
or ghosts, or haints, whatever you want to call it."

"Well use your eyes, Zulie. Use your eyes."

Zulie looked at Iree. She had never seen Iree like
this before. She wasn't foaming and having a fit,
and she wasn't telling a story. She was just craning
her neck and looking. Then she started walking

very slowly down the hill. Iree looked back at Ernie whose face was screwed up tight full of wrinkles and worry that couldn't be brushed off. Iree ran back to her mama and grabbed her hand, and Ernie snatched it back as if Iree was holding a hot iron. Then Iree pulled Ernestine off the porch towards the edge of the hill.

"Mama, Mama, why's he crying, Mama? Why's he crying? Look like he can't see us. He's just kinda being pulled along in the crowd. He can't see us. And look, there's my mama too, Miss Lillian Adams, walking so tall, just like I remember her. And look at those clothes, all those robes just flying in the breeze. You'd think they'd just float them up off the ground. Can't you see them, Zulie? All those blue feathers, I've never seen blues so rich and so shiny. And everybody but 'Zekiel is laughing, laughing like it's some kind of a celebration. No, no they aren't. They're all crying. Mama, it's not a . . . they. . . . Oh no, Mandy!"

All of a sudden Iree was running as hard as she could, calling out, screaming while she ran, "Not Mandy, no! You won't take Mandy. No, not her. Not Mandy!"

Zulie started to follow her and tried to grab her back. Ernestine shuffled up close and quick and grabbed a hold of Zulie's arm and squeezed it until Zulie cried out, "Ernestine Moore! Have you lost your mind? You're about to break my bones."

Ernestine answered in a voice which was half-whisper and half-hiss, "Stop worrying and hold

still by me." Ernestine only slightly released her
grip and her voice came out thin and tight, "They
know what to do. It'll all be all right." But Ernestine's spirit trembled as she admitted to herself
that something was very wrong.

The two women stood at the top of the hill, as
Iree almost vanished from sight. Then Ernestine
did something she almost never did anymore, she
demanded that Zulie tell her what she saw, exactly
what she saw, every detail, every color, even how
the trees swayed.

"Ernie, I really can't see much more than shadows. Iree is about two blocks away and I think
there's a tall man, built kinda like Ezekiel leading
them up, and Mico he's walking to the side and
kinda towards the front. No, no, there's no tall
man, that was Mico all the time, and Al, he's holding Mandy on one side, but she's walking, bent
over but walking. Imani she's on the other side,
and next to her is someone I don't recognize. No,
no that must be Iree catching up to them."

"What kind of blue do you see, woman?"

"What kind of blue? Ernie, I don't see no kinda
blue at all. I don't know what you are talking
about, what kinda blue."

"How many people do you see?"

"Five, like I said before. Seems like five, anyway. You know I need my glasses to see that far."
Zulie didn't want to see any more. Her hands had
started to sweat and she wiped them on her dress.
As soon as they dried, she wiped them again. It

seemed like too many people were coming up that hill so slowly, too slowly.

"Ernie, you hear that? That's the strangest thing, I think I hear Iree. Isn't that her singing clear and sweet?" Zulie couldn't understand the words but she knew Iree was just singing away, trying to clear the panic out of everybody. Then Zulie saw Imani at the back of the group, swaying and humming along with Iree. Her face was covered with tears.

"Ernie, they're crying. Al, why he's crying too. I tell you, it seems like a whole lot more than five people pulling up that hill, a whole lot more than five. They're all walking in the shadows, and Ernie, there *is* a dark blue, like the sun is setting instead of just finished rising. Ernie, there's a dark blue falling over the horizon. I mean it started off such a clear morning and most of the sky is still a slate grey, but there's this blue . . ."

Zulie bit her tongue and didn't say any more to Ernie for a time.

"Zulie, what do you see? What do you see?"

"Ernie, tell you the truth, I don't know. I mean I can't really tell nothing for sure, nothing at all."

Moments later the family reached the top of the hill. There stood Mico and Al still holding up Amanda, Iree was to one side, and Imani seemed to be dancing from the front to back of the group. Iree ran ahead and went inside the house and came back out with Imani's yellow and white baby blanket that had been resting on Imani's bedroom dresser. Then she went over to the oak tree, knelt in front of it, dropping the blanket next to her feet. She called for Al and Mico to bring Amanda to her.

Zulie pulled on Ernestine's shoulder. "Ernie, now anybody in their right mind knows they should be carrying Mandy inside but, Al and Mico, they're going over to that old oak with Iree."

Blood was running all down Mandy's legs and her blouse was covered with dirt and sweat. After Al and Mico let Mandy slide to a sitting position on the ground, Iree motioned them to move back. They did so without a word of protest. Iree had Mandy squat down, then she went and crouched at Mandy's back, holding her. Iree spread her own legs and arms and made a kind of birthing stool with her body. Imani just kept humming. Her voice was trembling with her self-made lullaby as she sat in front of Amanda and wrapped her arms around her friend. Amanda let her head fall soft against Imani's shoulder as they both cried.

Al came over to Zulie without a word and just stood there looking kind of glazed. He was not doing his usual yelling about doctors, or lecturing with I told you so's. He was just observing, and tears kept coming slow and thin out of the corners of his eyes. Then all of a sudden Amanda started to howling, and it was as if she was being torn apart.

Zulie gasped and whispered to Al, "Al, you

hear that child. I swear it sounds like hell is reaching out the ground and grabbing a piece of Mandy and pulling her down. I swear if I didn't know better, I'd think her insides was splitting open and spilling out."

From out of nowhere, the wind started up and leaves started to spinning around. Imani looked in her mama's eyes, and without a word lifted up Mandy's skirts and pulled down the child's panties. Al didn't say anything. He just took the dish towel that Zulie had been holding in her hand all the time and walked over to Iree and handed it to her. Iree motioned to Imani who took it and wiped off the blood that was all over Amanda's thighs. Iree spoke softly into Mandy's ear. "Let it go, child. It's not yours to keep. Let it go. It doesn't want you, just the seedling. It's dead to you already. Let it go, child. Another one come if you want. Let this one go."

Amanda's teeth were clenched and her lips were tight and she was just holding herself still, biting down on the inside of her lip till blood started to trickle out the corner of her mouth. Iree put her mouth next to Amanda's ear and started talking cold as can be, "Let it go. Come on, Mandy, pull yourself back." And then in the next few minutes, out slid some pieces that looked to Zulie like a little bit of ground meat. It didn't look like any kind of a baby at all. Just like pieces of a nothing.

Soon as those clots came out of Amanda, she passed out and fell over Imani's shoulders. Al didn't say a thing. He just motioned to Mico. They lifted Amanda off the ground and carried her inside the house. Ernie was already inside sitting next to the bed with a basin full a water that had some dried leaves steeping in it. She was holding a cup of tea in her hands. When Mico and Al laid Amanda on the bed, Ernestine started to shake her awake.

"Come on, girl. You can't let go. Drink this tea I made. Come on, open those lips."

Ernestine pried open Amanda's lips and poured some of the warm liquid down her throat. Amanda choked on the flow, coughing and sputtering while Ernestine kept pouring until Mico came and took the cup away. When he grabbed the cup Zulie saw that Ernie's hands were quivering as she reached towards the basin at her feet. She went over and pulled the washcloth firmly from Ernie, who let go without a fuss.

"It's not to wash her outside with, Zulie. It's for her insides," Ernestine continued calmly, glad to be relieved of the task. "Let the cloth get full of the liquid and put it up inside of her to stop the bleeding."

When Al heard that he snapped to and started calling out, "It's time for a doctor now."

Mico pulled him aside. "No, we not about that this morning. If they need a doctor, they'll let us know."

"Child be dead before they admit they can't handle it."

While the men continued to quarrel in the corner Zulie kept working on Amanda until the blood flow seemed to ease. Zulie washed Amanda's legs and went and got a fresh basin of water to clean her face and hands. It was then that Zulie noticed that Iree and Imani had not yet come in. She looked out the window and saw that they were still sitting under the tree, and that they were still humming. They were no longer crying, just humming and praying. Imani had her arm looped around her mother. Iree fingered Imani's old baby blanket like it was precious silk, then she brought it to her mouth and cut a tear in it with her teeth, pulling it into two pieces. She took one of those pieces and tore that in half until she got her a piece of cloth not bigger than two times the size of her hand. Then she scooped up all the blood and droppings from Amanda with the surrounding dirt and twigs, and put them in the cloth. She folded it into smaller and smaller triangles, three times. Then she put that tiny triangle in the other half of the blanket and folded it over. When it was a compact bundle, she broke off a piece of twig and made a clasp to hold the package shut. She moved over to the hole that she dug the night before, and she lay the bundle down, slowly and carefully, as if it were a fragile gift. Then she filled the hole and covered it up. She smoothed it flat, and then sprinkled over leaves and twigs until no one could tell that the soil had ever been disturbed.

Ernie got up from the bed and walked outside

and went and sat with her daughter and grand-daughter. The three of them just held on to each other and rocked.

Zulie turned away from the window and saw that Al was getting Mandy to drink some more of the tea. Zulie fully expected him to go out and start up the car to take her to the hospital. But instead he just handed her the empty cup and said, "I guess we'll be taking her home with us come nightfall. We'll have her checked out tomorrow, because she'll be ours then." That was all. Zulie stared at Al without blinking. It was as if some-thing had been settled in that last few minutes be-tween him picking up that cup and offering it to Amanda.

"Fine, Al. If that's what Mandy wants to do. Fine, Al. I mean, I guess we do have space for one last daughter," Zulie replied. Amanda smiled, but didn't answer.

A few minutes later Ernestine and Iree and Im-ani came in. Imani started gabbing away, nervous and jumpy, pretending everything was as normal as could be.

"Zulie, I am so hungry. Do you know the last time I ate? The last time I ate a real meal was the middle of the night. And it was at that diner you don't care for, Cookin' Carol's. Well they made me some awful hard eggs, and I know you've got something good left over from last night. Is this my cake? Oh Zulie, you made my favorite again! I guess I'll start breakfast with this."

Then she walked over to the counter and saw her cake was still full of candles and she picked up a knife and started singing, "Happy birthday to me . . ."

Zulie saw that she was crying, real soft like, so she came up next to her and took the knife out her hand, and lit up the candles and then Mico opened up the song again in his big strong voice. They all crowded around Imani and started singing with her, because she was theirs, and she was all the way seventeen, and she was home, safe. When they finished the song, and Imani cut the cake, she put the first slice aside for Amanda. She turned to her and said, "This one is yours, Mandy."

Mandy smiled weakly from the bed, and answered back, "No, you take that one. Cut me a bigger slice . . . twice that big."

And finally, after that long night, they all fell into a kind of laughter inside of their sadness, because it seemed like the one thing none of them could hold on to was time, and the one thing that none of them ever let go of all the way was family. And that was a good thing.

About the Author

devorah major is a poet and a fiction and essay writer. Her work has been published in several anthologies and magazines, including *The Single Mother's Companion* (Seal Press, 1994), *I Hear a Symphony*, *California Childhoods*, *River Styx*, *Black Scholar*, *Calalloo*, *Caprice* and *Zyzzyva*. She received a Pushcart recognition for her short story, "A Crowded Table," and is a California Arts Council Writing Fellow. She recently published a book of poetry, *street smarts*. She has finished a collection of love poems, *Love Makes Me Do Foolish Things*, and is at work on a novel, *Brown Glass Windows*. She has a daughter, Yroko, and a son, Iwa, who keep her creativity and energy flowing. She lives in San Francisco where she is a poetry teacher, performer and an editor. *An Open Weave* is her first novel.

New in hardcover

finding
makeba

a novel

ALEXS D. PATE

Putnam

Fodor's InFocus

FoL 3

SAVANNAH

1st Edition

Where to Eat and Stay
for All Budgets

Must-See Sights
and Local Secrets

Ratings You Can Trust

Fodor's Travel Publications New York, Toronto, London, Sydney, Auckland
www.fodors.com

FODOR'S IN FOCUS SAVANNAH

Series Editor: Douglas Stallings

Editor: Douglas Stallings

Editorial Production: Jennifer DePrima

Editorial Contributor: Eileen Robinson Smith

Maps & Illustrations: David Lindroth, Mark Stroud, Ed Jacobus, *cartographers*; Bob Blake and Rebecca Baer, *map editors*

Design: Fabrizio La Rocca, *creative director*; Guido Caroti, *art director*; Ann McBride, *designer*; Melanie Marin, *senior picture editor*

Cover Photo: ImageSource/age fotostock

Production/Manufacturing: Amanda Bullock

SPECIAL SALES

This book is available for special discounts for bulk purchases for sales promotions or premiums. Special editions, including personalized covers, excerpts of existing books, and corporate imprints, can be created in large quantities for special needs. For more information, write to Special Markets/Premium Sales, 1745 Broadway, MD 6-2, New York, New York, NY 10019, or e-mail specialmarkets@randomhouse.com.

AN IMPORTANT TIP & AN INVITATION

Although all prices, opening times, and other details in this book are based on information supplied to us at press time, changes occur all the time in the travel world, and Fodor's cannot accept responsibility for facts that become outdated or for inadvertent errors or omissions. **So always confirm information when it matters,** especially if you're making a detour to visit a specific place. Your experiences—positive and negative—matter to us. If we have missed or misstated something, **please write to us.** We follow up on all suggestions. Contact the Savannah editor at editors@fodors.com or c/o Fodor's at 1745 Broadway, New York, NY 10019.

Be a Fodor's Correspondent

Your opinion matters. It matters to us. It matters to your fellow Fodor's travelers, too. And we'd like to hear it. In fact, we *need* to hear it. When you share your experiences and opinions, you become an active member of the Fodor's community. Here's how you can help improve Fodor's for all of us.

Tell us when we're right. We rely on local writers to give you an insider's perspective. But our writers and staff editors also depend on you. Your positive feedback is a vote to renew our recommendations for the next edition.

Tell us when we're wrong. We update most of our guides every year. But things change. If any of our descriptions are inaccurate or inadequate, we'll incorporate your changes in the next edition and will correct factual errors at fodors.com *immediately*.

Tell us what to include. You probably have had fantastic travel experiences that aren't yet in Fodor's. Why not share them with a community of like-minded travelers? Share your discoveries and experiences with everyone directly at fodors. com. Your input may lead us to add a new listing or a higher recommendation.

Give us your opinion instantly at our feedback center at www. fodors.com/feedback. You may also e-mail editors@fodors.com with the subject line "Savannah Editor." Or send your nominations, comments, and complaints by mail to Savannah Editor, Fodor's, 1745 Broadway, New York, NY 10019.

Happy Traveling!

Tim Jarrell, Publisher

CONTENTS

About This Book 5

When to Go. 6

1 WELCOME TO SAVANNAH. . 7

History of Savannah 9

Savannah Today 10

African-American Heritage 11

If You Like … 12

2 EXPLORING SAVANNAH. . 15

Exploring Savannah. 17

3 WHERE TO EAT 39

Historic District 42

Elsewhere in Savannah. 55

Tybee Island 56

4 WHERE TO STAY 59

Historic District 61

Elsewhere in Savannah. 78

Tybee Island 79

5 NIGHTLIFE & THE ARTS . . 83

The Arts. 84

Nightlife. 87

6 SPORTS & THE
OUTDOORS 95

Sports & Activities. 96

Spas. .102

7 SHOPPING 105

Shopping Districts. 106

Specialty Shops. 108

8 HILTON HEAD & THE
LOWCOUNTRY. 115

Orientation & Planning. 116

Hilton Head Island 122

Beaufort. 158

Daufuskie Island 170

Edisto Island 172

TRAVEL SMART
SAVANNAH. 175

INDEX 186

ABOUT OUR WRITER 192

MAPS

Savannah Historic District. . 20–21

Greater Savannah 35

Where to Eat in
Savannah. 44–45

Tybee Island 57

Where to Stay in
Savannah. 64–65

Hilton Head & the
Lowcountry 117

Hilton Head Island 124

Where to Eat on Hilton
Head Island. 127

Where to Stay on Hilton
Head Island. 135

Beaufort. 159

ABOUT
THIS BOOK

Our Ratings

We wouldn't recommend a place that wasn't worth your time, but sometimes a place is so experiential that superlatives don't do it justice: you just have to be there to know. These sights, properties, and experiences get our highest rating, **Fodor's Choice,** indicated by orange stars throughout this book. Black stars highlight sights and properties we deem **Highly Recommended,** places that our writers, editors, and readers praise again and again for consistency and excellence.

Credit Cards

AE, D, DC, MC, V following restaurant and hotel listings indicate whether American Express, Discover, Diners Club, MasterCard, and Visa are accepted.

Restaurants

Unless we state otherwise, restaurants are open for lunch and dinner daily. We mention dress only when there's a specific requirement and reservations only when they're essential or not accepted.

Hotels

Unless we tell you otherwise, you can assume that the hotels have private bath, phone, TV, and air-conditioning. We always list facilities but not whether you'll be charged an extra fee to use them, so when pricing accommodations, find out what's included.

Many Listings

★	Fodor's Choice
★	Highly recommended
⊠	Physical address
✛	Directions
⌖	Mailing address
☎	Telephone
🖷	Fax
⊕	On the Web
✉	E-mail
🖃	Admission fee
☉	Open/closed times
Ⓜ	Metro stations
⊟	Credit cards

Hotels & Restaurants

🏨	Hotel
⇌	Number of rooms
♨	Facilities
⦿	Meal plans
✕	Restaurant
⌲	Reservations
⊠	Smoking
𝄞	BYOB
✕🏨	Hotel with restaurant that warrants a visit

Outdoors

🏌	Golf
⛺	Camping

Other

♨	Family-friendly
⇨	See also
⊠	Branch address
☞	Take note

WHEN TO GO

There really is no bad time to visit Savannah. Spring and fall are high season, when the temperatures are best and hotel rates and occupancy are at their highest. But there are myriad reasons why these seasons are most attractive. The blooming of cherry-blossoms is followed by a profusion of azaleas, dogwoods, and camellias in April and apple blossoms in May. Spring and fall temperatures are delightful during the day, and mild at night. Art shows, craft fairs, and music festivals tend to take place in summer. The CraftBrew Fest of regional artisanal beer makers is in late summer. During the fall, golfers are out in full force, and though it may be too cool to swim, beachcombing is a popular activity in Hilton Head. During the high season it's important to make your reservations as far in advance as possible for both hotels and restaurants.

When to Go
Spring and fall offer the best temperatures, pleasant by day and delightful by night. Summer, on the other hand, can be hot and humid, even hotter than in Charleston. Savannah can also be affected by tropical storms and hurricanes in the hurricane season from June through November, when afternoon thunderstorms are also likely. Because of the large number of conventions and meetings, hotels in town can book up year-round.

Most of the city's major arts festivals happen in September or October, though St. Patrick's Day is an important holiday in the region, when hotels book up far in advance and raise prices accordingly.

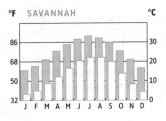

°F   SAVANNAH   °C

Welcome to Savannah

WORD OF MOUTH

"My very favorite pastime living [in Savannah] was just walking around the historic district. My daily running route was down Bull Street through all those squares and around Forsyth Park . . . I don't think there ever was a time I did it that I didn't notice something new that I hadn't noticed before."

—OO

By Eileen
Robinson
Smith

SINCE SAVANNAH IS SUCH A WARM, WELCOMING CITY,
you may find it especially easy to get acquainted with "The
Big Savanne," as it might have been called back in 1733.
Named after the surrounding grasslands, Savannah still
has its green belts in the shape of squares, now 24 strong.
Developers continue to recognize the value of not developing green spaces, and this keeps the inner city from looking like a typical American metropolis, laden with steel
and top-heavy with skyscrapers. The city also remains
connected with its namesake river; it is a commercially
active port with a pedestrian walkway along the riverfront,
where visitors can outpace the riverboats gliding through
the dark waters.

Savannah is also as photogenic as a pretty baby. You may
find yourself angling for the right shot of grand columned
porticos and verandas that bespeak of a wealthy antebellum
society. Countless stately old mansions are yours for the
clicking. Once run-down, the Victorian District will wow
you with its gingerbread fretwork and Italianate carpenter
styling. Brick-paved streets, such as Jones Street, are great
for close-up shots. Live oaks are draped in the gray of
Spanish moss—wearing it not unlike a mantilla—making
for atmospheric and other-worldly pictorials.

Tourists love that they can park their cars for their entire
stay and use their "shank's mare" (i.e., go it on foot). But
when the feet get sore, there are horse carriages or pedi-
cabs. Bicycles are a common mode of transportation for
students and travelers alike. As for accommodations, you
can have your choice of historic inns and affordable B&Bs
in the Victorian District. Many of the historic inns are very
atmospheric, with large rooms with antique four-poster
beds in the former mansions of the city's elite.

This city is a gift that keeps on giving. With strong European
influences, it is an enchantress with ethereal beauty. Savannah has eye-catching architectural history, and a haunting
mystery about her that wraps its arms around the hearts
of those who come from around the world to experience
it. Be prepared to feel passionate about Savannah. When
your innkeeper tells you to come back, he or she will mean
it. And, indeed, most visitors do heed that advice.

HISTORY OF SAVANNAH

1

Gen. James Oglethorpe, Savannah's founder, set sail for England in 1743, never to return. His last instructions, it's said, were, "Don't change a thing until I get back." That local joke holds more than a bit of truth. Savannah's elegant mansions, dripping Spanish moss, and sticky summer heat can make the city seem sleepy and stubbornly resistant to change. This is exactly why many folks like the place.

If ever superstition had you believe that 13 was an unlucky number, Georgia, the thirteenth colony, has proved that wrong. Savannah, Georgia's oldest city, began its modern history on February 12, 1733, when Oglethorpe and 120 colonists arrived at Yamacraw Bluff on the Savannah River to found the 13th and last of the British colonies. (A plaque now marks their original landing spot near today's City Hall.) The early years were grim, with a good many of the settlers having been "rescued" by Oglethorpe from England's debtors' prisons. Alas, the kind and sage founder believed that only hard work and temperance would reap prosperity and forbade the use of alcohol. (Modern-day Savannahians will tell you that's why, instead, many settlers found their way to South Carolina.)

As the river port grew, more settlers from England and Ireland arrived, joined by Scottish Highlanders, French Huguenots, Germans, Austrian Salzburgers, Sephardic and Ashkenazic Jews, Moravians, Italians, Swiss, Welsh, and Greeks. In 1793, Eli Whitney of Connecticut, who was tutoring on a plantation near Savannah, invented a mechanized means of "ginning" seeds from cotton bolls. Cotton soon became king, and Savannah, already a busy river port, flourished under its reign. Waterfront warehouses were filled with "white gold," and brokers trading in the Savannah Cotton Exchange set world prices. The white gold brought in hard currency; the city prospered.

Feared and hated throughout the South, Gen. William T. Sherman's army rampaged across Georgia during his infamous "March to the Sea" in 1864, setting fire to railroads, munitions factories, bridges, and just about anything else between them and the sea. Rather than see the city torched, Savannahians surrendered to the approaching Yankees. Sherman sent word to President Abraham Lincoln, saying that he had a Christmas present for him—Savannah. Sherman proceeded to live there in luxury for more than a year, taking over one of the city's finest mansions, the Green-Meldrim House, at the invitation of its British owner.

As the cotton market declined in the early 20th century, the city's economy collapsed. For decades, Savannah's historic buildings languished; many were razed or allowed to decay. Cobwebs replaced cotton in the dilapidated riverfront warehouses. The tide turned in the 1950s, when residents began a concerted effort—which continues to this day—to restore and preserve the city's architectural heritage.

SAVANNAH TODAY

After integration was enforced in Savannah in the 1960s, the white flight to suburbia began, with more neighborhoods and developments mushrooming in the 1970s. Only since the 1990s has that flight been reversed. Now, living downtown, especially for those without children, is the desirable—albeit expensive—thing to do.

The first years of the 21st century have been a busy time in Savannah, especially with regard to improvements in the tourism infrastructure. At this writing, the city is extending Savannah's River Walk more than 2,000 feet eastward from the Marriott and encouraging further changes that will make the area more upscale. On the riverfront next to the Hyatt Regency, The Bohemian, a Kessler boutique hotel, will surely aid these efforts.

Ellis Square will reopen in 2009 after a major beautification project. The parking garage there that was an eyesore was torn down, to be replaced by an underground multilevel parking facility. The square will have the requisite park benches and will be a new venue for concerts and cultural events.

Another new boutique hotel, AVIA Savannah, is expected to open in early 2009 near the old *Savannah Morning News* building on Bay Street. The old newspaper building itself will be a mixed-use development and will include retail on the bottom floors with 42 luxurious condominiums above, each with river views and high price tags.

The Savannah College of Art and Design (SCAD) was founded in 1978 and is now the largest art school in the nation, with 7,000 students. The SCAD kids and their creative institution have become woven into the tapestry of the city. SCAD has renovated or restored some 50 buildings in the Historic District and established several art galleries, one built in an old cafeteria. The school has stimulated the growth of local businesses, especially several coffeehouses, and has saved the downtown housing and rental market. One amazing rejuvenation turned an old carriage factory into the school's cutting-edge film and digital media center. Although the influx of edgy, artsy young people has taken some getting used to by Savannah's old guard (these young talents are often tattooed and pierced), the students become unlikely partners in preservation with the denizens of the Historic Savannah Foundation, who acknowledge and appreciate the enormous contribution that SCAD has made to save and transform historic buildings in the inner city.

AFRICAN-AMERICAN HERITAGE

In Savannah, after the Emancipation, General William T. Sherman read Special Field Order #15 at the Second African Baptist Church on January 18, 1865. This famous proclamation is the one that gave former slaves 40 acres and an army mule.

Savannah also played a major part in the Civil Rights movement of the 1960s. Martin Luther King Jr., prior to leading his famous march on Washington, D.C. in 1963, gave a speech here. The young minister took the pulpit in that same Savannah church where Sherman made his proclamation and exhorted them to follow him to the Lincoln Memorial, where he gave his most famous speech, "I Have a Dream."

Savannah has a large African-American population and has had since the plantation era, which was highly dependent on slave labor. The African slaves created a culture and a language that their descendants now call Gullah, which still survives on the sea islands and around the Lowcountry. Savannah is one of the most historically significant cities in the nation for African-American heritage. Savannah today is a far cry from what it was in the early 1960s. Many locally prominent businesses are owned by African-Americans, and members of Savannah's large black middle class hold noteworthy positions in government, from the Savannah Convention & Visitors Bureau on up to Mayor Otis S. Johnson. In the late 1960s, City Hall was a meeting place for local leaders involved in the Civil Rights movement, but before 1963, there were no African-American city employees other than custodians and messengers.

Several companies offer tours that relate the city's African-American heritage, and you can visit many individual historical sights that are important in the history of African-Americans in the United States.

IF YOU LIKE . . .

CONTEMPORARY SOUTHERN CUISINE

A new influx of young, talented chefs and entrepreneurs is expanding the offerings of the restaurant community. These cooks want to appeal to younger tourists as well as seasoned world travelers, foodies by their own admission who are coming to Savannah now that the word is out that the restaurant scene is not all about shrimp and grits. The best of these restaurants are finding ways to reinvent Lowcountry classics, using fresh, local ingredients like tasso ham and locally grown spinach and rice. Even standards like grits themselves are likely to be stone-ground in local mills.

You can find this newfangled brand of southern cuisine in contemporary restaurants like Cha Bella, Noble Fare, 45 Bistro, Bistro Savannah, and 700 Drayton. These chefs have updated their offerings, making their cuisine healthier and fresher, even as they keep some classic favorites. As in decades past, these cooks insist on using fresh wild shrimp from nearby waters, other seafood that can be sustainably fished, and free-range organic produce and meat.

STROLLING THE SQUARES

One of the true joys of Savannah is just walking through its squares and other green spaces, which were integral components of the city's original plan. General Oglethorpe, the city's founder, is given the credit for insisting on these vestiges of urban nature, which are mirrors of the many squares you can still see throughout Central London. Visitors learn from tour guides that in Savannah's early days in the 1700s, these communal greens were where settlers grazed their cattle, went for their water from the communal wells, and baked their bread in the communal ovens. As the only open spaces in the city center, the squares also housed the local fire towers.

These miniparks, 24 in all, are woven into the tapestry of daily life. They segue smoothly into the downtown

1

streets to slow motorists, who must remain ever mindful of walkers and joggers. Residents consider the squares extensions of their own living space, and so should you. Read the plaques on the monuments, and throw coins in the decorative fountains. On weekends, surely, you will witness a wedding. The most popular is Telfair Square. The Telfair Art Museum, its contemporary Jepson Center, and Christ Church are all neighbors there. Lafayette Square is particularly beautiful and shady, lined with two notable house museums—the Andrew Low House and the Flannery O'Connor Childhood Home—as well as the Hamilton-Turner Inn and St. John the Baptist Cathedral. Aristocratic homes front Monterey Square including the famous Mercer-Williams Home.

SHOPPING

Shopping in Savannah is as distinctive as everything else about the city. If you believe that shopping is the great American pastime, you can definitely redefine the term "Shop till you drop" here. Savannah's diverse population has created an eclectic selection of locally owned boutiques selling everything from antiques to contemporary home furnishings, from Bohemian-styled art objects to trendy, even funky, apparel and accessories. The unique stores here will appeal to the eccentric as well as the sophisticated. Quirky boutiques define the shopping experience. Gourmet foodstuffs and freshly made candies are good buys. One-of-a-kind jewelry is being created by SCAD students and grads. Art galleries are thriving by promoting local and regional artists.

Paris Market & Brocante is Savannah's version of the famous Paris flea markets, offering such finds as European-forged chandeliers and bunches of lavender. Copper Penny offers edgy designs and fashion-forward apparel and accessories. ShopSCAD is the outlet for the creative designs of SCAD students and grads: jewelry, fashions, furniture, and art. River Street Sweets makes the city's favorite praline and pecan candies. Grand Bohemian Gallery showcases the work of internationally and nationally acclaimed painters, sculptors, and jewelry designers. 37th @ Abercorn Antiques has 8,000 square feet of antique furnishings and collectibles from 50-plus dealers.

Exploring Savannah

WORD OF MOUTH

"[We enjoyed t]he museum trio: the Jepson Centre, the Telfair Museum (Ansel Adams photos and an exhibition of Kahlil Gibran paintings, respectively), and the exquisite Owen-Thomas House, available on a single ticket. We also admired the Davenport House, Savannah's original house museum, now restored to remedy inaccuracies of the 1960s restoration."

—tedgale

By Eileen
Robinson
Smith

SAVANNAH, GEORGIA'S OLDEST CITY, began its modern history on February 12, 1733, when Oglethorpe and 120 colonists arrived at Yamacraw Bluff on the Savannah River to found the 13th and last of the British colonies. (It was right where the City Hall is today, and a plaque marks the spot.) Yet the early years were grim, with a good many of the settlers "rescued" by Oglethorpe from England's debtors' prisons. Oglethorpe had a close friend, an author who had died in such a prison; once there, those impoverished had no way out. Alas, the kind and sage founder believed that hard work and temperance would reap prosperity and forbade the use of alcohol. (Modern-day Savannahians will tell you that's why, instead, many settlers found their way to South Carolina.)

As the river port grew, more settlers from England and Ireland arrived, joined by Scottish Highlanders, French Huguenots, Germans, Austrian Salzburgers, Sephardic and Ashkenazic Jews, Moravians, Italians, Swiss, Welsh, and Greeks. In 1793, Eli Whitney of Connecticut, who was tutoring on a plantation near Savannah, invented a mechanized means of "ginning" seeds from cotton bolls. Cotton soon became king, and Savannah, already a busy river port, flourished under its reign. Waterfront warehouses were filled with "white gold," and brokers trading in the Savannah Cotton Exchange set world prices. The white gold brought in hard currency; the city prospered.

Feared and hated throughout the South, at the height of the Civil War, Gen. William T. Sherman's army rampaged across Georgia in 1864, setting fire to railroads, munitions factories, bridges, and just about anything else between them and the sea. Rather than see the city torched, Savannahians surrendered to the approaching Yankees. He sent word to President Abraham Lincoln, saying that he had a Christmas present for him—Savannah. Sherman proceeded to live in luxury for more than a year, taking over one of the city's finest mansions, the Green-Meldrim House, at the invitation of its British owner.

As the cotton market declined in the early 20th century, the city's economy collapsed. For decades, Savannah's historic buildings languished; many were razed or allowed to decay. Cobwebs replaced cotton in the dilapidated riverfront warehouses. The tide turned in the 1950s, when residents began a concerted effort—which continues to this day—to restore and preserve the city's architectural heritage.

SAVANNAH BEST BETS

■ **Intriguing Architecture:** Close to half of the 2,500 buildings in Savannah have architectural or historical significance. The many building styles—Georgian, Gothic revival, Victorian, Italianate, Federal, and Romanesque— make strolling the tree-lined neighborhoods a delight. The 19th-century Telfairs's Owens-Thomas house is a particular highlight.

■ **Midnight in the Garden of Good and Evil:** John Berendt's famous 1994 book about a local murder and the city's eccentric characters still draws many travelers eager to see the places mentioned, including the Mercer-Williams House on Monterey Square, where Jim Williams once had his lucrative antique business.

■ **Famous Southern Restaurants:** Savannah's elegant, fine-dining restaurants, notably Elizabeth's on 37th and Olde Pink House, have well-deserved reputations. Gara-

baldi's has a beautiful interior and exquisite, contemporary Italian cuisine. And, of course, who hasn't heard of Paula Deen's restaurant, The Lady & Sons, from watching her show on the Food Network?

■ **Historic Inns and Bed & Breakfasts:** When most people dream of a trip to Savannah, they envision staying in a romantic old mansion fronting a prominent square, where they further picture themselves sipping wine on the veranda. It is an authentic and unique experience, and everyone should have it, at least once.

■ **Savannah by Night:** Savannah is known in the Southeast as a party town. If you can't have fun in the Big Savanne, then you simply may not have the capability to have fun anywhere. "To Go" cups make barhopping in this red-hot city a favorite evening activity. Ghost tours are another popular nocturnal must-do.

EXPLORING SAVANNAH

Savannah's real draw is the people you will meet as you visit the city. They give southern charm their own special twist. As John Berendt's wildly popular book *Midnight in the Garden of Good and Evil* amply demonstrates, eccentricities can flourish in this hothouse environment.

THE HISTORIC DISTRICT

Georgia's sage founder, Gen. James Oglethorpe, laid out the city on a perfect grid as logical as a geometry solution. The Historic District is neatly hemmed in by the Savannah River, Gaston Street, East Street, and Martin Luther King Jr. Boulevard. Streets are arrow-straight, public squares of varying sizes are tucked into the grid at precise intervals, and each block is sliced in half by narrow, sometimes unpaved streets. Bull Street, anchored on the north by City Hall and the south by Forsyth Park, charges down the center of the grid and maneuvers around the five public squares that stand in its way. The layout means the area is easy to explore and is best appreciated on foot. All the squares have some historical significance; many have elaborate fountains, monuments to heroes, and shady resting areas with park benches; all are bordered by beautiful homes and mansions that bespeak lovingly of another era.

Numbers in the margin correspond to numbers on the Savannah Historic District map.

MAIN ATTRACTIONS

28 **Andrew Low House.** This residence was built in 1848 for Andrew Low, a native of Scotland and one of Savannah's merchant princes. The home later belonged to his son William, who inherited his wealth and married his longtime sweetheart Juliette Gordon. They lived in a baronial estate in the United Kingdom for decades before divorcing. It was after her former husband's death that Juliette Gordon Low returned to this house and founded the Girl Scouts here on March 12, 1912. The house has 19th-century antiques, stunning silver, and some of the finest ornamental ironwork in Savannah. But it is the story and history of the family—even a bedroom named after the family friend and visitor, Gen. Robert E. Lee—that is fascinating and well told by the tour guides. ⊠*329 Abercorn St., Historic District* ☎*912/233–6854* ☜*$8* ⊗*Mon.–Wed., Fri., and Sat. 10–4:30, Sun. noon–4.*

21 **Chippewa Square.** Daniel Chester French's imposing bronze statue of Gen. James Edward Oglethorpe, founder of Savannah and Georgia, anchors the square. The bus-stop scenes of *Forrest Gump* were filmed on the north end of the square. Also note the **Savannah Theatre,** on Bull Street, which claims to be the oldest continuously operated theater site in North America. ⊠*Bull St. between Hull and Perry Sts., Historic District.*

❸ City Market. Although the 1870s City Market was razed years ago, city fathers are enacting a three-year plan to capture the authentic atmosphere and character of its bustling origins. Already a lively destination for art studios, open-air cafés, theme shops, and jazz clubs, this popular pedestrian-only area will become the ever more vibrant, youthful heart of Savannah's Historic District. You can rent a bike here or take a ride in a horse-drawn carriage. ✉*Between Franklin Sq. and Johnson Sq. on W. St. Julian St., Historic District* ☎*912/525–2489 for current events.*

❷❷ Colonial Park Cemetery. The park is the final resting place for
★ Savannahians who died between 1750 and 1853. You may want to stroll the shaded pathways and read some of the old tombstone inscriptions. Local legend tells that when Sherman's troops set up camp here, they moved some of the headstones around for fun. ✉*Oglethorpe and Abercorn Sts., Historic District.*

❶❽ Columbia Square. When Savannah was a walled city (1757–90), Bethesda Gate (one of six) was at this location. The square, which was laid out in 1799, was named "Columbia," the female personification of the U.S. Liberty Square, now lost to urban sprawl. It was the only other square named in honor of the United States and the concept of freedom that stoked the fires of the American Revolution. Davenport House and Kehoe House are on Columbia Square. ✉*Habersham St. between E. State and E. York Sts., Historic District.*

❹ Factors Walk. A network of iron crosswalks connects Bay Street with the multistory buildings that rise up from the river level, and iron stairways descend from Bay Street to Factors Walk. The area was originally the center of commerce for cotton brokers, who walked between and above the lower cotton warehouses. Cobblestone ramps lead pedestrians down to River Street. ■TIP→ **These are serious cobblestones, so wear comfortable shoes. Also be aware that pedicabs cannot ride over these cobblestones.** ✉*Bay St. to Factors Walk, Historic District.*

NEED A BREAK? The best place for an ice cream soda is at Leopold's (✉*212 E. Broughton St., Historic District* ☎*912/234–4442*), a Savannah institution since 1919. It's currently owned by Stratton Leopold, grandson of the original owner and a Hollywood producer whose films include *Mission Impossible 3*, *The General's Daughter*, and *The Sum of All Fears*. Movie posters and

Savannah
Historic District

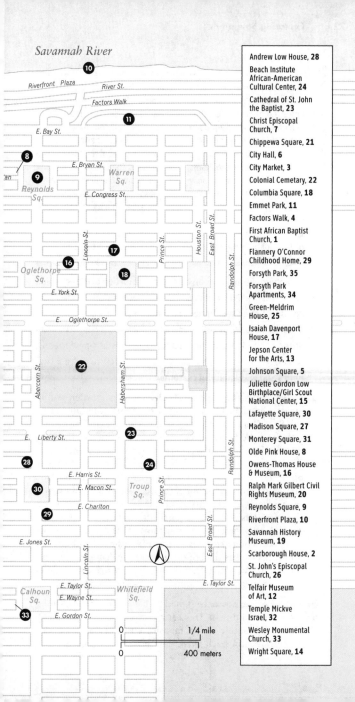

Savannah River

Riverfront Plaza

River St.

Factors Walk

E. Bay St.

E. Bryan St.

Warren Sq.

E. Congress St.

Reynolds Sq.

Lincoln St.

Prince St.

Houston St.

East Broad St.

Oglethorpe Sq.

E. York St.

E. Oglethorpe St.

Abercorn St.

Habersham St.

E. Liberty St.

Randolph St.

E. Harris St.

E. Macon St.

Troup Sq.

Prince St.

E. Charlton

East Broad St.

E. Jones St.

Lincoln St.

E. Taylor St.

E. Taylor St.

Calhoun Sq.

E. Wayne St.

Whitefield Sq.

E. Gordon St.

0   1/4 mile

0   400 meters

Andrew Low House, **28**

Beach Institute African-American Cultural Center, **24**

Cathedral of St. John the Baptist, **23**

Christ Episcopal Church, **7**

Chippewa Square, **21**

City Hall, **6**

City Market, **3**

Colonial Cemetery, **22**

Columbia Square, **18**

Emmet Park, **11**

Factors Walk, **4**

First African Baptist Church, **1**

Flannery O'Connor Childhood Home, **29**

Forsyth Park, **35**

Forsyth Park Apartments, **34**

Green-Meldrim House, **25**

Isaiah Davenport House, **17**

Jepson Center for the Arts, **13**

Johnson Square, **5**

Juliette Gordon Low Birthplace/Girl Scout National Center, **15**

Lafayette Square, **30**

Madison Square, **27**

Monterey Square, **31**

Olde Pink House, **8**

Owens-Thomas House & Museum, **16**

Ralph Mark Gilbert Civil Rights Museum, **20**

Reynolds Square, **9**

Riverfront Plaza, **10**

Savannah History Museum, **19**

Scarborough House, **2**

St. John's Episcopal Church, **26**

Telfair Museum of Art, **12**

Temple Mickve Israel, **32**

Wesley Monumental Church, **33**

Wright Square, **14**

CLOSE UP

Did You Know?

In Savannah, many of the houses are named, but sometimes the name reflects the person who built the property rather than the person for whom it was built. For example, the Stephen Williams House, now restored as an elegant B&B, was named for its builder, Stephen Williams, rather than the owner, William Thorn Williams, six-time mayor of Savannah. Some houses are named for the first owner and then a subsequent owner, like the Green-Meldrim House. The good news is that they didn't add the name Sherman—Gen. William T. Sherman, that is, who occupied the house during "The War" from 1864–1865—to the Green-Meldrim House's name. This extraordinary edifice, open for tours on certain days, is now the parish house for St. John's Episcopal Church.

paraphernalia make for an entertaining sideline to the selection of ice creams and sorbets, which taste wonderfully homemade. You might even see Stratton Leopold behind the counter; when he takes his leave of Hollywood, he is not above taking ice cream scoop in hand and serving his loyal patrons and new friends. Famed lyricist Johnny Mercer grew up a block away from Leopold's and was a faithful customer.

㉟ Forsyth Park. The park forms the southern border of Bull Street. On its 30 acres are a glorious white fountain dating to 1858, Confederate and Spanish-American War memorials, and the Fragrant Garden for the Blind, a project of Savannah garden clubs. There are tennis courts and a tree-shaded jogging path. Outdoor plays and concerts often take place here. At the northwest corner of the park, in **Hodgson Hall,** a 19th-century Italianate Greek–revival building, you can find the **Georgia Historical Society,** which exhibits selections from its collection of artifacts and manuscripts. The park's 1-mi perimeter is among the prettiest walks in the city and takes you past many beautifully restored and historic homes, as well as the boutique hotel The Mansion on Forsyth. ✉ *501 Whitaker St., Historic District* ☎ *912/651–2128* ⊕ *www.georgiahistory.com* ⊙ *Tues.–Sat. 10–5.*

㉕ Green-Meldrim House. Designed by New York architect John
★ Norris and built in 1850 for cotton merchant Charles Green, this Gothic-revival mansion cost $93,000 to build— a princely sum back then. The house was purchased in

1892 by Judge Peter Meldrim, whose heirs sold it to St. John's Episcopal Church in the 1940s to use as a parish house. General Sherman lived here after taking the city in 1864. Sitting on Madison Square, the house has Gothic features such as a crenellated roof, oriels, and an external gallery with filigree ironwork. Inside are mantels of Carrara marble, carved black-walnut woodwork, and doorknobs and hinges of either silver plate or porcelain. ■TIP→ **This remarkable house is open on Sundays, after the 10:30 church service at St. John's concludes. Not only is admission free, but there is an impressive "coffee," with everything from tomato sandwiches to nutty brownies and coffee punch served, all complimentary. Of course, it is politically correct to attend the atmospheric mass with a celestial choir and to place a donation in the silver receptacle at collection time.** ✉*1 W. Macon St., Historic District* ☎*912/233–3845* 💲*$8* ⊘*Tues., Thurs., and Fri. 10–4, Sat. 10–1. Closed last 2 wks of Jan. and 2 wks before Easter.*

⓱ Isaiah Davenport House. The proposed demolition of this historic Savannah structure galvanized the city's residents into action to save their treasured buildings. By 1955, this home had a history of dilapidation that lingered since the 1920s, when it was divided into tenements. One neighbor wanted to raze it to build a parking lot, so a group of women (later dubbed "The Magnificent Seven" for founding the Historic Savannah Foundation) raised $22,000 to buy and restore this property. This was but the first of many successful efforts to preserve the architectural treasure that is the city today. Semicircular stairs with some wrought iron lead to the recessed doorway of the redbrick Federal home that master builder Isaiah Davenport built for his family between 1815 and 1820. Three dormered windows poke through the sloping roof of the stately house, and the interior has polished hardwood floors and fine woodwork and plasterwork. Alas, neither the Davenports' furniture nor the furniture that was brought in to replicate it, bespeak of wealth. Venetian blinds were invented in 1820, and they replaced drapes—and not attractively. The real offense is the gray, mock-brick wallpaper that has been pasted in the foyer and up several walls. ✉*324 E. State St., at Columbia Sq., Historic District* ☎*912/236–8097* ⊕*www.davenport housemuseum.org* 💲*$8* ⊘*Mon.–Sat. 10–4, Sun. 1–4.*

★ FodorsChoice **Jepson Center for the Arts.** On Telfair Square is
⓭ Telfair's newest gallery (2006), an unexpectedly contemporary building amid so many 18th- and 19th-century

The Original Squares

Just as in Charleston, Savannah preservationists have wisely blocked developers from erecting burger joints and other contemporary eyesores in the Historic District, which is made up of the original squares planned by the town's founder, Gen. James Oglethorpe. Many argue that these squares are what make central Savannah one of the most attractive places in America.

Says writer John Jakes: "I also love the gorgeous fountain in Forsyth Park, south of the center of town. Is Savannah or Charleston the winner of the civic beauty prize? I've never been able to decide, perhaps because each in its own way weaves beauty and history inextricably together. Since the cities are little more than 100 miles apart, a visit to the Lowcountry should include both."

structures that are the city's hallmark. Within the steel-and-glass edifice, you can find permanent hangings of Southern art, African-American art, and photography. There's a sculpture gallery and an outdoor sculpture terrace, in addition to interactive, kid-friendly exhibits. ⊠*207 W. York St., Historic District* ☎*912/232–1177 or 912/790–8800* ⊕*www.telfair.org* ⊠*$10* ☉*Mon. noon–5, Tues.–Sat. 10–5, Sun. 1–5.*

NEED A BREAK? The **Jepson Center Café** (⊠ *Jepson Center for the Arts, 207 W. York St., Historic District* ☎ *912/790–8833*) is a delightful spot to stop for a coffee and fresh-baked pastry or even lunch while you take in the view of the square through all that glass. Let the minimalist decor, with the single flower in the vase, clear your cluttered mind. You do not have to pay the museum admission to visit the café; the receptionist will give you a special metal tab to wear. One Sunday every month, the Jepson Gospel Brunch is staged in the atrium from 12:30 to 2:30, a bountiful Southern buffet plus entertainment by a church gospel choir at 1:30.

❺ Johnson Square. The oldest of James Oglethorpe's original 24 squares was laid out in 1733 and named for South Carolina governor Robert Johnson. A monument marks the grave of Nathanael Greene, a hero of the Revolutionary War. The square was once a popular gathering place: Savannahians came here to welcome President Monroe in

1819, to greet the Marquis de Lafayette in 1825, and to cheer for Georgia's secession in 1861. ⊠*Bull St. between Bryan and Congress Sts., Historic District.*

⑮ Juliette Gordon Low Birthplace/Girl Scout National Center. This majestic Regency town house, attributed to William Jay (built 1818–21), was designated in 1965 as Savannah's first National Historic Landmark. "Daisy" Low, founder of the Girl Scouts, was born here in 1860, and the house is now owned and operated by the Girl Scouts of America. Mrs. Low's paintings and other artwork are on display in the house, restored to the style of 1886, the year of Mrs. Low's marriage. ■TIP→ **If you have ever wondered about the large number of Girl Scout troops you can see around town, they come to Savannah to see their founder's birthplace and to earn certain merit badges.** ⊠*142 Bull St., Historic District* ☎*912/233–4501* ⊕*www.girlscouts.org/birthplace* ☞*$8* ⊙*Mon.–Sat. 10–4, Sun. 11–4.*

★ **Fodor'sChoice Lafayette Square.** Named for the Marquis de **㉚** Lafayette, who aided the Americans during the Revolutionary War, the square contains a graceful three-tier fountain donated by the Georgia chapter of the Colonial Dames of America. The Cathedral of St. John the Baptist is located on this square, as is the Andrew Low House and the impressive Hamilton-Turner Inn. The childhood home of the celebrated Southern author Flannery O'Connor is also on this square (*see ☞Flannery O'Connor Childhood Home, below*). ⊠*Abercorn St. between E. Harris and E. Charlton Sts., Historic District.*

㉗ Madison Square. A statue on this square, which was laid out in 1839 and named for President James Madison, depicts Sgt. William Jasper hoisting a flag and is a tribute to his bravery during the Siege of Savannah. Though mortally wounded, Jasper rescued the colors of his regiment in the assault on the British lines. A granite marker denotes the southern line of the British defense during the 1779 battle. The Green-Meldrim House is here. ⊠*Bull St. between W. Harris and W. Charlton Sts., Historic District.*

★ **Fodor'sChoice Owens-Thomas House & Museum.** English architect **⑯** William Jay's first Regency mansion in Savannah is widely considered the country's finest example of that architectural style. Built in 1816–19, the English-style house was constructed mostly with local materials. Of particular note are the curving walls of the house, Greek-inspired ornamental molding, half-moon arches, stained-glass panels,

CLOSE UP

More Than You Need to Know

As you go on the various house tours, you may learn some "dirt" that you may wish you had never heard. For example, women from well-to-do-families in the mid-19th century would not cut their hair from birth to death. Nor would they wash it but every couple of months. Instead, they would put powder and even oatmeal in it, to absorb the oil. They would pile their hair on top of their head and had an assortment of small combs (often made from tortoise shells) to keep it up. Women from the lower classes might not wash their long hair for an entire year.

You may have heard the expression "Don't throw the baby out with the bath water!" This aphorism came about during this same time. Most families—even the prosperous ones—had the kind of demi-tubs you may have seen in Clint Eastwood westerns. Few houses had their own wells, so most Savannah citizens went to the public squares to fill their buckets from the communal wells. Others were lucky to have cisterns. Because water was hard to come by, submerged baths were infrequent, especially in cold weather. There might be a tub in the master bedroom or in the basement next to a fireplace. You can probably guess where this is going. The hierarchy of the bath ritual went like this: the father took his first, then any adult sons, then in went mom, followed by the other children, with the baby last. Thus the saying's origin. Now, mind you, hot water would be added gradually along the way, but by the time the baby was put in last, the water was filthy from the many bodies and used soap.

and Duncan Phyfe furniture and the hardwood "bridge" on the second floor. The carriage house includes a gift shop and rare urban slave quarters, which have retained the original furnishings and "haint-blue" paint made by the slave occupants. This house had indoor toilets before the White House and the Palace of Versailles. If you have to choose just one or two house-museums, let this be one. The history you will learn will better help you to understand Savannah. It is owned and administered by the Telfair Museum of Art. ✉ *124 Abercorn St., Historic District* ☎ *912/233–9743* ⊕ *www.telfair.org* ✆ *$10* ⊙ *Mon. noon–5, Tues.–Sat. 10–5, Sun. 1–5; last tour at 4:30.*

 Reynolds Square. John Wesley, who preached in Savannah and wrote the first English hymnal in the city in 1736, is remembered here. A monument to the founder of the Methodist Church is shaded by greenery and surrounded by park benches. The landmark Planters Inn is here, formerly the John Wesley Hotel. Ironically, though it was named after a man of the cloth, in the early 1900s it was considered the best brothel in town.

❽ The **Olde Pink House** (✉ *23 Abercorn St., Historic District*), built in 1771, is one of the oldest buildings in town. Now a restaurant, the portico pink-stucco Georgian mansion has also been a private home, a bank, and headquarters for a Yankee general during the Civil War. On its belowground level is the city's most beloved piano bar, Planters Tavern, and adjacent, the new bar and sidewalk café, Arches. ✉*Abercorn St. between E. Bryan and E. Congress Sts., Historic District.*

❿ **Riverfront Plaza.** Amid this nine-block brick concourse, you can watch a parade of freighters and pug-nosed tugs. Youngsters can play in the tugboat-shaped sandboxes. There is a steady stream of outlets for shopping and eating along the Savannah River. River Street is the main venue for many of the city's celebrations, including the First Saturday festivals, when flea marketers, artists, and artisans display their wares and musicians entertain the crowds. Savannah's Riverwalk is being extended 2,000 feet eastward from the Marriott hotel, with construction slated for completion in 2009. The city received a $1 million grant from the state's Department of Natural Resources for public docking facilities; the grant will pay for 1,000 linear feet of floating dock to be operated by the city for public use. ✉*River St., between Abercorn and Barnard Sts., Historic District.*

⓱ **Savannah History Museum.** This museum in a restored railway station is an excellent introduction to the city. Exhibits range from old locomotives to a tribute to Savannah-born songwriter Johnny Mercer. Built on the site of the Siege of Savannah, it marks the spot where in 1779 the colonial forces, led by Polish Count Casimir Pulaski, laid siege to Savannah in an attempt to retake the city from the redcoats. They were beaten back, and Pulaski was killed while leading a cavalry charge against the British. The dead lie underneath the building. ✉*303 Martin Luther King Jr. Blvd., Historic District* ☎*912/238–1779* ⊕*www.chsgeorgia.org* ✍*$4.25* ☼*Weekdays 8:30–5, weekends 9–5.*

❷ Scarborough House. This exuberant Greek-revival mansion,
★ built during the 1819 cotton boom for Savannah merchant prince William Scarborough, was designed by English
architect William Jay. Scarborough was a major investor
in the steamship *Savannah*. The house has a Doric portico
capped by one of Jay's characteristic half-moon windows.
Four massive Doric columns form a peristyle in the atrium
entrance hall. Inside is the Ships of the Sea Museum, with
displays of ship models, including steamships and a nuclear-
power ship. Young boys particularly are drawn to these
exhibits. You must arrive by 4:15 if you want to view the
house and museum. ✉*41 Martin Luther King Jr. Blvd.,
Historic District* ☎*912/232–1511* ⊕*www.shipsofthesea.
org* 🎫*$8* ⊙*Tues.–Sun. 10–5.*

⓬ Telfair Museum of Art. The oldest public art museum in the
★ Southeast was designed by William Jay in 1819 for Alex-
ander Telfair and sits across the street from Telfair Square.
Within its marble rooms are American, French, and Dutch
impressionist paintings; German tonalist paintings; a large
collection of works by Kahlil Gibran; plaster casts of the
Elgin Marbles, the Venus de Milo, and the Laocoön, among
other classical sculptures; and some of the Telfair family furnishings, including a Duncan Phyfe sideboard and
Savannah-made silver. During the Savannah Music Festival,
there are intimate, memorable classical music performances
here. ✉*121 Barnard St., Historic District* ☎*912/232–1177*
⊕*www.telfair.org* 🎫*$10* ⊙*Mon., Wed., Fri., and Sat. 10–5;
Thurs. 10–8; Sun. 12–5.*

THE WAVING GIRL. This charming statue at River Street and East
Board Ramp is a symbol of Savannah's Southern hospitality
and commemorates Florence Martus, the lighthouse keeper's
sister who waved to ships in Savannah's port for more than 44
years. She would wave a white towel and, when young, always
had her dog by her side. When she was in her last years, locals
threw her a huge birthday party at Fort Pulaski with more than
5,000 guests. Despite all of her waving to so many sailors, she
died without ever having been wed.

ALSO WORTH SEEING

㉔ Beach Institute African-American Cultural Center. Works by African-American artists from the Savannah area and around
the country are on display in this building, which once
housed the first school for African-American children in

Savannah, established in 1867. On permanent exhibit are more than 230 wood carvings by folk artist Ulysses Davis. ✉*502 E. Harris St., Historic District* ☎*912/234–8000* ⊕*www.kingtisdell.org* 🎟*$4* ⊙*Tues.–Sat. noon–5.*

2

NEED A BREAK? Near Congress Street, the rustic, brick-walled**Lulu's Chocolate Bar** (✉*42 Martin Luther King Jr. Blvd., Historic District* ☎*912/238–2012*) offers opportunities for a wonderful sugar rush by day or night. It's now open for Sunday brunch, too (11:30 AM to 4 PM). You can have a Bloody Mary with your eggs Benedict, or a champagne cocktail with your fruit custard tart. It's open until midnight from Sunday through Wednesday, until 1 AM Thursday through Saturday, and now has a happy hour from 5 to 7 with free cookie bites.

㉓ **Cathedral of St. John the Baptist.** Soaring over the city, this French Gothic–style cathedral, with pointed arches and free-flowing traceries, is the seat of the Catholic diocese of Savannah. It was founded in 1799 by the first French colonists to arrive in Savannah. Fire destroyed the early structures; the present cathedral dates from 1876. Its architecture, gold leaf adornments, and the entire edifice give testimony to the importance of the Catholic parishioners of the day, which included some dispossessed French planters from Haiti as well as a strong Irish contingent. ✉*222 E. Harris St., at Lafayette Sq., Historic District* ☎*912/233–4709* ⊕*www.savannahcathedral.org* ⊙ *Weekdays 9–5.*

❼ **Christ Episcopal Church.** This was the first church—then Anglican—established in the Georgia colony in 1733. It is often called "The Mother Church of Georgia." Located on Johnson Square, the centuries-old building with its tall spire and wrought-iron railings is a pure white sight indeed. The white banner that welcomes visitors to Christ Church's Gregorian Chant evenings reads: STEP OUT OF THE PRESENT AND ENTER THE DEEP STILLNESS OF ANOTHER AGE. Sung by candlelight by the Compline Choir from 9 to 9:30 every Sunday night, the concert is heavenly and reason enough to make the trip. ✉*28 Bull St., Historic District* ☎*912/232–4131* ⊕*www. christchurchsavannah.org.*

❻ **City Hall.** Built in 1906 on the site of the Old City Exchange (1799–1904), this imposing structure anchors Bay Street. Its landmark tower clock and bells once played a significant role in the day-to-day business of Savannah in those days before everyone had their own pocket watch. Today, residents may still look up instead of at their cell phones when they want to know the time. In 2006, in honor of its Centennial, this monumental municipal building had its granite facade repaired, while the gold leaf on the cupola and impressive dome were redone. Further interior cosmetic improvements have made this a must-see, and the public is welcome to come in and admire its dramatic four-story rotunda crowned with a stained-glass inner dome, mosaic tiles, marble wainscoting, mahogany and live oak pediments and banisters, and European sculptures. ✉*1 Bay St., Historic District* ☎*912/651–6410* ⊙*Weekdays 8:30–5.*

⓫ **Emmet Park.** Once an Indian burial ground, the lovely tree-shaded park is named for Robert Emmet, a late-18th-century Irish patriot and orator. The park contains monuments to German Hussars, Vietnam's fallen soldiers, and the Celtic Cross, among others. ✉*Borders E. Bay St., Historic District.*

❶ **First African Baptist Church.** This church was built by slaves at night by lamplight, after they worked the plantations during the day. The basement floor still shows signs of its time as a stop on the Underground Railroad. Designs drilled in the floor are thought to actually have been air holes for slaves hiding underneath, waiting to be transported to the Savannah River for their trip to freedom. ✉*23 Montgomery St., Historic District* ☎*912/233–6597* ⊕*www.firstafricanbc.org* ✍*Donations requested* ⊙*Tours: Tues.–Thurs. at 11, 1, and 3.*

㉙ **Flannery O'Connor Childhood Home.** The childhood home of the celebrated Southern author is open for regularly scheduled visits on weekends only; however, you may be able to make special arrangements for other viewing times by calling the museum in advance. O'Connor lived in this house from her birth in 1925 until 1938. The home reopened in October 2008 after a substantial renovation. ✉*207 E. Charlton St., at Lafayette Sq., Historic District* ☎*912/233–6014* ⊕*www.flanneryoconnorhome.org* ✍*$5* ⊙ *Sat.–Sun. 1–4.*

㉛ **Monterey Square.** Commemorating the victory of Gen. Zach-
★ ary Taylor's forces in Monterrey, Mexico, in 1846, this is the fifth and southernmost of Bull Street's squares. A monument honors Gen. Casimir Pulaski, the Polish nobleman who lost his life in the Siege of Savannah during the Revolutionary War. Also on the square is Temple Mickve Israel and some of the city's most beautiful mansions, including

CLOSE UP

Family-Friendly Savannah

Savannah does have its share of kid-appropriate activities. Juliette Gordon Low's Birthplace is the original home of the founder of the Girl Scouts, and girls of scouting age may find this house of interest. On the second floor is Juliette's childhood room with vintage toys and dolls and two dollhouses, one a Georgia Plains–style farmhouse.

Within the City Market are inexpensive shops where kids can find treasures they can afford. Horse carriage tours depart from here, and even if your child doesn't want to do a tour, it's always fun to pet the horses and have a picture with them.

Mrs. Wilkes Dining Room serves the kind of food that kids will eat, including real mashed potatoes and macaroni and cheese. Everything is served family-style at tables for 10.

The myriad ghost tours may appeal to older kids. Book a tour that includes dinner or lunch at The Pirates House. Older boys will adore the Hearse tours with their open-topped hearses.

Small pleasures are often the best. Children of all ages love to throw coins in the city's many fountains, particularly the one in Forsyth Park. You might want to have some peanuts in your arsenal to feed the friendly squirrels.

The Jepson Center for the Arts is a terrific venue for children and can instill the love of art; its ArtZeum is an interactive, two-story space especially designed for the kid in everyone.

Even little ones get a big kick out of the pedicabs. Belles Ferry, the free water taxi that goes back and forth to the Westin, can also be a kid-pleasing opportunity. One mother reports that her boys took it over and over again and then went for pralines at River St. Candies.

the (in)famous Mercer-Williams House. ⊠*Bull St. between Taylor and Gordon Sts., Historic District.*

❷⓿ **Ralph Mark Gilbert Civil Rights Museum.** In Savannah's Historic District, this history museum has a series of 15 exhibits on segregation, from emancipation through the civil rights movement. The role of black and white Savannahians in ending segregation in their city is detailed in these exhibits, largely derived from archival photographs. The museum also has touring exhibits. ⊠*460 Martin Luther King Jr. Blvd., Historic District* ☎*912/231–8900* ⊜*912/234–2577* ⊠*$4* ☉*Mon.–Sat. 9–5.*

Moss Mystique

Spanish moss—the silky gray, snakelike garlands that drape over the branches of live oaks—has come to symbolize the languorous sensibilities of the Deep South. A relative of the pineapple, the moisture-loving plant requires an average year-round humidity of 70%, and thus thrives in subtropical climates—including Georgia's coastal regions.

Contrary to popular belief, Spanish moss is not a parasite; it's an epiphyte, or "air plant,"

taking water and nutrients from the air and photosynthesizing in the same manner as soil-bound plants. It reproduces using tiny flowers. When water is scarce, it turns gray, and when the rains come it takes on a greenish hue. The old saying "Good night, sleep tight, don't let the bed bugs bite," is thought to come from the past practice of stuffing mattresses with Spanish moss, which often harbored the biting menaces commonly known as chiggers.

㉖ St. John's Episcopal Church. Built in 1852, this church is famous for its whimsical chimes and stained-glass windows. Its extraordinary parish house is the revered Green-Meldrim House. One interesting bit of trivia: on Christmas 1864, after General Sherman moved into the Green-Meldrim House, his army chaplain conducted the church's Christmas service. ✉*1 W. Macon St., at Madison Sq., Historic District* ☎*912/232–1251* ⊕*www.stjohnssav.org.*

㉜ Temple Mickve Israel. A Gothic-revival synagogue on Monterey Square houses the third-oldest Jewish congregation in the United States; its founding members settled in town five months after the establishment of Savannah in 1733. The synagogue's collection includes documents and letters (some from George Washington, James Madison, and Thomas Jefferson) pertaining to early Jewish life in Savannah and Georgia. ✉*20 E. Gordon St., Historic District* ☎*912/233–1547* ⊕*www.mickveisrael.org* ☞*Free; tour $3* ☉*Weekdays 10–noon and 2–4.*

㉝ Wesley Monumental Church. This Gothic-revival style church memorializing the founders of Methodism is patterned after Queen's Kerk in Amsterdam. It dates from 1868 and is particularly noted for its magnificent stained-glass windows. ✉*429 Abercorn St., Historic District* ☎*912/232–0191* ☉*By appointment only.*

⓮ Wright Square. Named for James Wright, Georgia's last colonial governor, this square has an elaborate monument in its center that honors William Washington Gordon, founder of the Central of Georgia Railroad. A slab of granite from Stone Mountain adorns the grave of Tomo-Chi-Chi, the Yamacraw chief who befriended General Oglethorpe and the colonists. ⊠*Bull St. between W. State and W. York Sts., Historic District.*

THE SAVANNAH AREA

Ebenezer. When the Salzburgers arrived in Savannah in 1734, Oglethorpe sent them up the Savannah River to establish a settlement. The first effort was assailed by disease, and they sought his permission to move to better ground. Denied, they moved anyway and established Ebenezer. Here, they engaged in silkworm production and, in 1769, built the Jerusalem Church, which still stands. After the revolution, the silkworm operation never resumed, and the town faded into history. Descendants of these Protestant religious refugees have preserved the church and assembled a few of the remaining buildings, moving them to this site from other locations. Be sure to follow Route 275 to its end and see Ebenezer Landing, where the Salzburgers came ashore. ⊠*Ebenezer Rd., Rte. 21–Rte. 275, 25 mi north of Savannah, Rincon.*

★ Fort Pulaski National Monument. Named for Casimir Pulaski, ☾ a Polish count and Revolutionary War hero, this must-see sight for Civil War buffs was designed by Napoléon's military engineer and built on Cockspur Island between 1829 and 1847. Robert E. Lee's first assignment after graduating from West Point was as an engineer here. During the Civil War the fort fell, on April 11, 1862, after a mere 30 hours of bombardment by newfangled rifled cannons. The restored fortification, operated by the National Park Service, has moats, drawbridges, massive ramparts, and towering walls. The park has trails and picnic areas. It's 14 mi east of downtown Savannah; you can see the entrance on your left just before U.S. 80 reaches Tybee Island. ⊠*U.S. 80, Fort Pulaski* ☎*912/786–5787* ⊕*www.nps.gov/fopu* ⊠*$3* ☺*Daily 9–7.*

Melon Bluff. On land obtained with a Kings Grant in 1745, this 9,500-acre plantation was in the same family for more than 300 years and is one of the few remaining stretches of pristine Georgia coastline. It is now owned by the Spring-

Famous Faces in Savannah

Here's a sampling of the figures who have etched themselves into Savannah's collective memory.

Actor **Robert Mitchum** (1917–1997) gave one of his finest performances as a psychotic ex-convict in 1961's *Cape Fear*, which was filmed in and around Savannah. In 1934, as a wayward 17-year-old, he roamed across America and was arrested on charges of vagrancy and begging while panhandling in Savannah. He was jailed but escaped. When he returned to Savannah as a Hollywood star, his earlier transgressions were never mentioned.

James L. Pierpont (1822–1893) probably wrote a classic Christmas carol in Savannah. A native of Medford, Massachusetts, Pierpont became music director of Savannah's Unitarian church in the 1850s. In 1857 he obtained a copyright for "The One Horse Open Sleigh," (more popularly known as "Jingle Bells"). In the 1980s, tempers boiled when Medford claimed that Pierpont had written the song there. This dispute was never resolved.

John Wesley (1703–1791), the founder of Methodism, arrived in 1735 and fell in love with Sophia Hopkey. But Wesley wasn't prepared to marry and Sophia found another suitor, William Williamson. The jealous Wesley charged Sophia with neglect of public church services and refused to let her participate in communion. Sophia's uncle, Thomas Causton, Savannah's chief magistrate, charged Wesley with defamation, claiming he was unfit to be a minister. Wesley, found guilty on some of the counts, fled to England. By the time he died, at 88, he had become one of the towering figures in religious history.

Names of note also include **Johnny Mercer** (1909–1976), a fourth-generation Savannah native and one of America's most popular and successful songwriters of the 20th century. He is buried in Bonaventure Cemetery.

Fiction writer **Flannery O'Connor** (1925–1964) spent the first 13 years of her life in Savannah. Known for her Southern–Gothic style, her greatest achievement is found in her short stories, published in the collections *A Good Man Is Hard to Find* and *Everything That Rises Must Converge*.

Savannah is also the proud hometown of Supreme Court Justice **Clarence Thomas**, America's second African-American Supreme Court Justice.

Greater Savannah

ATLANTIC OCEAN

Tybee Island Marine Science Center
Tybee Island
Little Tybee Island

Fort Pulaski Historical Monument
Fort Pulaski National Monument

Savannah River
South Channel

Wilmington Island

Oatland Island
Whitemarsh Island
Johnny Mercer Dr.

Skidaway Marine Science Complex

Skidaway Island
McWhorter Dr.
Skidaway Island State Park
Green Rd.

Old Fort Jackson
ALT 17

TO HILTON HEAD
The Eugene Talmadge Memorial Bridge

Hutchinson Island
Back River

THUNDERBOLT
Skidaway Rd.
Savannah State University
Laroche Av.

Wormsloe Plantation
Isle of Hope
Ferguson Av.
Diamond Cswy.

SAVANNAH
Liberty St.
Gwinnett St.
Victory Dr.
Derenne Av.
Skidaway Rd.
Harry S. Truman Pkwy.
Whitfield Av.

Bethesda Home for Boys
Vernon River

ALT 17
80

TO EBENEZER
21
17

Louisville Rd.
Mills B Lane Blvd (52nd St.)
516
17
White Bluff
Abercorn
Waters Av.
Montgomery Cross Rd.
204
White Bluff Rd.

Hunter Army Airfield
Middle Ground Rd.

Coffee Bluff

Little Ogeechee River

Amtrak Station
Chatham Pkwy.
16
17
307

GARDEN CITY
80

Savannah Int'l Airport
EXIT 102
95

POOLER
Quacco Rd.
80

SAVANNAH
Pooler Pkwy.
Quacco Rd.
16
17

EXIT 99B
17

Veterans Pkwy.
Atlantic Coast Hwy.

Armstrong Atlantic State University

Abercorn Pkwy.
204
EXIT 94
95
17

TO MIDWAY BLUFF
Ford Av.
Ogeechee River

0   3 miles
0   3 kilometers

field Legacy Foundation. ■TIP→ **Archaeological finds and historical records indicate that Melon Bluff is 37 years older than St. Augustine (long considered the oldest community in the United States).** You can find a nature center here and facilities for canoeing, kayaking, bird-watching, hiking, and other outdoor activities, as well as a campground. From Melon Bluff you can visit nearby **Seabrook Village,** a small but growing cluster of rural buildings from an African-American historic community; **Old Sunbury,** whose port made it a viable competitor to Savannah until the Revolutionary War ended its heyday; **Fort Morris,** which protected Savannah during the revolution; and **Midway,** an 18th-century village with a house museum and period cemetery. To reach Melon Bluff, take Interstate 95 south from Savannah (about 30 mi) to Exit 76 (Midway/Sunbury), turn left, and go east for 3 mi. ⊠*2999 Islands Hwy., Midway* ☎*912/884–5779 or 888/246–8188* ☎*912/884–3046* ⊕*www.melonbluff.com.*

Mighty Eighth Air Force Heritage Museum. The famous World War II squadron the Mighty Eighth Air Force was formed in Savannah in January 1942 and shipped out to the United Kingdom. Flying Royal Air Force aircraft, the Mighty Eighth became the largest air force of the period. Exhibits at this museum begin with the prelude to World War II and the rise of Adolf Hitler and continue through Desert Storm. You can see vintage aircraft, fly a simulated bombing mission with a B-17 crew, test your skills as a waist gunner, and view interviews with courageous World War II vets. The museum also has three theaters, an art gallery, a 1940s-era English pub, a 7,000-volume library, archives, memorial garden, chapel, and museum store. ⊠*175 Bourne Ave., I–95, Exit 102, to U.S. 80, 14 mi west of Savannah, Pooler* ☎*912/748–8888* ⊕*www.mightyeighth.org* ☜*$10* ⊗*Daily 9–5.*

Old Fort Jackson. About 2 mi east of Broad Street via President Street, you can see a sign for the fort, which is 3 mi from the city. Purchased in 1808 by the federal government, this is the oldest standing fort in Georgia. It was garrisoned in the War of 1812 and was the Confederate headquarters of the river batteries. The fort guards Five Fathom Hole, the 18th-century deep-water port in the Savannah River. The brick edifice is surrounded by a tidal moat, and there are 14 exhibit areas. Battle reenactments, blacksmithing demonstrations, and programs of 19th-century music are among the fort's activities for tour groups. ⊠*1 Fort Jackson*

Rd., Fort Jackson ☎*912/232–3945* ⊕*www.chsgeorgia.org/ jackson/home.htm* ☛*$4.25* ⊙*Daily 9–5.*

☺ **Skidaway Marine Science Complex.** On the grounds of the former Modena Plantation, Skidaway has a 14-panel, 12,000-gallon aquarium with marine and plant life of the continental shelf. Other exhibits highlight coastal archaeology and fossils of the Georgia coast. Nature trails overlook marsh and water. ⊠*30 Ocean Science Circle, 8 mi south of Savannah, Skidaway Island* ☎*912/598–2496* ☛*$2* ⊙ *Weekdays 9–4, Sat. noon–5.*

Tybee Island. *Tybee* is an Indian word meaning "salt." The Yamacraw Indians came to this island in the Atlantic Ocean to hunt and fish, and legend has it that pirates buried their treasure here. The island is about 5 mi long and 2 mi wide, with seafood restaurants, chain motels, condos, and shops—most of which sprang up during the 1950s and haven't changed much since. A few inns, each individually owned, have varying degrees of appeal. Each year, Tybee becomes more upscale and desirable. Well-heeled individuals have bought up many of the old shabby beach cottages and restore them or knock them down to build McMansions on the ocean. One 1920s beach house has been turned into the modern 17th Street Inn on the south end. A Savannah architect renovated a dilapidated 1950s beach shack, artistically transforming it into his primary residence. It is indicative of a trend for those who no longer need or want to live downtown. As there is no beach in the city, some parents like the idea of their children growing up near the water. As this all plays out, Tybee is losing its kitschy, tacky image, much like Myrtle Beach has, but that element definitely still exists and is what some perennial visitors love about it. Tybee Island's entire expanse of taupe sand is divided into a number of public beaches, where you can go shelling and crabbing, charter fishing boats, parasail, bike, jet-ski, kayak, and swim. Nearby, the misnamed Little Tybee Island, actually larger than Tybee Island, is entirely undeveloped.

Tybee Island Lighthouse & Museum (⊠*30 Meddin Dr.* ☎*912/786–5801* ⊕ *www.tybeelighthouse.org* has been well-restored and is considered one of North America's most beautifully renovated lighthouses. It was built on orders of General Oglethorpe in 1732. You can walk up 178 steps to the top for great views. The renovation on the second lighthouse keeper's cottage is just being completed;

the building will house a small theater showing a video about the lighthouse. The Head Keeper's Cottage is the oldest building on the island. The lighthouse opens daily at 9 AM, with the last tour at 4:30 PM; admission is $6. This should be on your list of must-sees if you visit Tybee.

Kids will enjoy the **Marine Science Center** (✉*1510 Strand Ave.* ☎*912/786–5917* ⊕ *www.tybeemarinescience.org*), which houses local marine life such as the Ogeechee corn snake, turtles, and American alligator. It is open daily from 10 to 5. Admission is $4. ✦*Tybee Island is 18 mi east of Savannah; take Victory Drive (U.S. 80)* ☎*800/868–2322 for Tybee Island Convention & Visitors Bureau* ⊕*www.tybeevisit.com.*

NEED A BREAK? Savannahians come to A-J's (✉*1315 Chatham Ave., Tybee Island* ☎*912/786–9533*) on Sundays, and Tybee residents (like Sandra Bullock) come here most anytime, especially when they want to chill. You sit at this dockside restaurant, have the fish from off the boats, drink your cocktails, and watch the sun do a spectacular set.

Where to Eat

WORD OF MOUTH

"[I eat at t]he [Olde] Pink House virtually every trip, whether it's "just dinner" or entertaining customers. Garibaldi [Café] is my backup for Pink House if I can't get a reservation. I LOVE the Pink House. [At] Paula Deen's [The] Lady & Sons, if it's too crowded for my timing I usually order a sandwich off the menu for lunch to go. All are good, but [the asparagus sandwich] is my favorite."

—starrs

By Eileen
Robinson
Smith

YOU WILL HEAR THAT SAVANNAH, the old Southern icon that she is, is on the cusp of a restaurant revolution. Frankly, the dining scene here—no longer just shrimp and grits and fried seafood plates—finds itself in a struggle to achieve consistency. Mainstay restaurants can no longer live off their laurels because the competition is simply too stiff. The beauty of this historic city, along with the availability of the freshest seafood and abundant produce, has attracted a legion of culinary talents from as far afield as France and Thailand. Some of the young chefs now setting culinary trends attended Johnson & Wales in Charleston (before its campus closed in 2006), and worked at the better restaurants there.

Since Lowcountry cuisine is indigenous to both cities, these chefs seized the opportunity to move farther south, where good chefs were not as readily available. With tourism booming, the market for good food was strong in Savannah, and now the city's restaurant inventory boasts many menus with genuine contemporary flair. The success of such mainstays as 700 Drayton Street and Sapphire Grill attest to this. Coming on strong are Cha Bella, Noble Fare, Local 1011, Bistro Savannah, and 45 Bistro.

Savannah has more distinctive and exceptional dining options than cities many times its size. It is the norm to find fresh, quality seafood, and locals also have a passion for smoked, barbecued meats. Most of the River Street restaurants are high-volume and touristy, but a good, high-end choice is Vic's on the River. Several of the city's landmark restaurants —such as Elizabeth on 37th and the Olde Pink House—are beacons that have drawn members of the culinary upper crust for decades. Other old Southern standards, such as Johnny Harris and Mrs. Wilkes' Dining Room, remain treasured mainstays. Paula Deen, the Southern Queen of the Food Network, has her place, The Lady & Sons, which still has lines out front.

Savoring the local flavors should not be limited just to the Historic District. You'll soon discover that good, even fine, dining can be found elsewhere in Savannah; nearby Tybee Island also has a handful of recommendable restaurants. If you go out to Tybee, make it early so you can enjoy the sunset on the island before settling in for your dinner.

BEST LOCAL SPECIALTIES

■ **Barbecue.** At Johnny Harris, you can watch as the meat is smoked on open pits. Blowin' Smoke serves quality meat smoked over Georgia pecan wood. At Barnes BBQ, the high-quality pork is the star. And at upscale Café 37, you can get a pulled pork sandwich with Gruyère on sourdough bread.

■ **Classic Lowcountry Cuisine.** Traditional specialties like shrimp and grits are still menu mainstays. So is fresh succotash (try it at Grace, on Tybee Island, or with the seared black grouper at Cha Bella). Variations on she-crab soup abound, including the version at Harris Baking Company. And crab cakes made from local blue crabs are ubiquitous; at Elizabeth on 37th they are served over southern fried grits.

■ **Reinvented Local Favorites.** B. Matthews puts a contemporary spin on black-eyed-pea cake with Cajun remoulade and fried green tomato sandwiches with oregano aioli. Olde Pink House serves an innovative shrimp 'n' grits with andouille sausage and sweet-potato biscuits. The creamy roasted Vidalia onion soup at Bistro Savannah is highly sought after. Garibaldi Café makes risotto with local crab and deftly fried, plump soft-shell crab.

■ **The Freshest Seafood.** Seafood is characteristically fresh off the Lowcountry boats. The chefs of the better restaurants all believe in sustainable seafood. Some of the better choices are Garibaldi's, Cha Bella, Vic's on the River, SoHo South Café, 45 Bistro, and Bistro Savannah.

■ **Sunday Brunch.** On Sundays, the landmark churches that visitors tour during the week are packed to the choir loft. After the service, parishioners head to such favorites as SoHo South Café, Firefly Café, Olde Pink House, and Belford's. Vic's on the River and The City Club even have live music. The Hyatt Regency and the Savannah Harbor Westin have admirable buffets and river views. On Tybee Island, Grace is the place.

HOURS, PRICES & DRESS

Most popular restaurants serve both lunch and dinner, usually until 9 or 10 PM, later on Friday and Saturday nights. Sunday brunch is a beloved institution; eat your fill because you will be hard pressed to find a top restaurant open on a Sunday night.

Prices, although on the rise, are less than in most major cities, especially on either coast.

Some locals and restaurant owners have a laid-back attitude about dressing for a night out. And if you are hitting a River Street tourist restaurant, a small neighborhood eatery, or a barbecue joint, jeans are just fine. However, if you are going to an upscale restaurant, dress in keeping with the environment, especially on weekend nights.

WHAT IT COSTS AT DINNER				
¢	$	$$	$$$	$$$$
under $10	$10–$14	$15–$19	$20–$24	over $24

Restaurant prices are for a main course at dinner and do not include tax.

HISTORIC DISTRICT

★ Fodor'sChoice ✕ **B. Matthews Eatery.** *Southern.* A change of
$$ ownership has not changed the homey, neighborhood feel of this unpretentious restaurant. If you have seen Paula Deen in a Food Network episode stop by for the 1,000-calorie sticky buns, you may miss the bakery because that's gone now. But this continues to be an in-spot for locals; tourists will appreciate that there is no hype. Three meals a day are served, with Sunday brunch (reservations essential) and its bottomless mimosas renowned all over Savannah. Lunch (until 3) and dinner share the same menu, which is still star-worthy. Certain faves like the black-eyed-pea cake with Cajun remoulade and fried-green-tomato sandwiches (with oregano aioli) have been retained. Dinner entrées are an excellent value, and the lamb shanks with white truffle risotto may make you moan. A good way to begin is with an exemplary wild mushroom strudel. On Tuesdays there are half-price bottles of select wines; the wines by the glass are exceptional every day. Smoking is allowed after 10 PM and anytime at the patio tables. ⊠ *325 E. Bay St., Historic District* ☎ *912/233–1319* ⊟ *AE, D, MC, V.*

¢–$ ✕ **Barnes BBQ Express.** *Southern.* At the sign of the pig, this
⟳ little barbecue joint may just be the city's best—and friendliest. It is an offshoot of the mama pig, Barnes Pit-Cooked Barbecue, which has been in business since 1975. It is a piglet in comparison, but this hole-in-the-wall is a personal

favorite. You sidle up to the counter, place your order, and pay. You then pick up your plastic ware and fill your cup at the soda machine or from the vats of tea. The ribs are lip-smacking but, of course, messy. For the many business-people stopping by for lunch, the barbecue sandwiches remain popular and less messy. Although many choose pulled pork on a bun, manager Frank advises that the chopped pork is the same good stuff and is substantially easier to eat. Have the red barbecue sauce on the side; the pork is so perfect, that you won't need much. The onion rings for about $2 are fried perfection. Kids will tell you that the chicken fingers (with requisite honey mustard) are the best ever. You can even get beer now. The only drawback is that closing time is 8 PM. ⊠*109 Whitaker St., Historic District* ☎*912/236–1557* ⌂*Reservations not accepted* ▭*MC, V* ⊘*Closed Sun.*

$$$–$$$$ ✕**Belford's Steak & Seafood.** *Southern.* In the heart of City Market, Belford's is good for brunch on Sunday, when so many of the downtown venues are closed. A complimentary glass of sparkling wine arrives at your table when you place your order, which might include egg dishes like smoked salmon Florentine, crab frittatas, or seafood crepes. The lunch and dinner menus focus on seafood, including Georgia pecan grouper. The building used to be a wholesale grocery company; modern tweaks include wooden floors, exposed brick walls, huge windows, and an expansive outdoor patio. The ambience is most appealing, and this is also a great spot for people-watching. Belford's mainly caters to the tourist trade now, and as a consequence, prices are not always a good value and the food quality can be inconsistent. ⊠*315 W. St. Julian St., Historic District* ☎*912/233–2626* ▭*AE, D, DC, MC, V.*

$$$ ✕**Bistro Savannah.** *Eclectic.* High ceilings, burnished heart-
★ pine floors, and gray-brick walls lined with local art—even undressed mannequins—contribute to the bistro qualities of this spot by City Market. The menu has specialties such as roasted Vidalia onion soup, which has a natural sweetness and is finished with cream and served with an herbed Parmesan crisp. Going international, Thai-spiced mussels with lemongrass, coconut, and red curry will heat you up after a nocturnal pedicab ride. The hanger steak is lean and flavorful, and the seared jumbo scallops are served over fresh crab succotash. Bistro is popular with local chefs, artsy types, and those who are concerned that the best of local, organic veggies, chemical-free meats, and fresh, certified wild shrimp are utilized. Like most everything, ice

Savannah River

Riverfront Plaza
River St.
Factors Walk

E. Bay St.

Reynolds Sq.
E. Bryan St.
Warren Sq.
E. Congress St.

Oglethorpe Sq.
Columbia Sq.
E. York St.

E. Oglethorpe St.

Colonial Park Cemetery

E. Liberty St.

Lafayette Sq.
E. Harris St.
E. Macon St.
Troup Sq.
E. Charlton

E. Jones St.

Calhoun Sq.
E. Taylor St.
E. Wayne St.
Whitefield Sq.
E. Gordon St.

Lincoln St.
Prince St.
Houston St.
East Broad St.
Randolph St.
Abercorn St.
Habersham St.

0   1/4 mile
0   400 meters

B. Matthew
Barnes Bar-
Express, 14
Belford's Stea
& Seafood, 1
Bella's Italian Cafe, 27
Bistro Savannah, 3
Blowin' Smoke BBQ, 20
Café 37, 24
Cha Bella, 10
Elizabeth on 37th, 23
Firefly Cafe, 19
45 Bistro, 12
Garibaldi Cafe, 2
Harris Baking Company, 16
Il Pasticcio, 11
Johnny Harris, 25
The Lady & Sons, 5
Local 11ten, 22
Mrs. Wilkes' Dining Room, 18
Noble Fare, 17
Olde Pink House, 7
Pirates House, 9
Sapphire Grill, 4
700 Drayton, 21
17 Hundred 90, 13
Soho South Café, 15
Toucan Café, 26
Vic's on the River, 6

creams, sorbets, and other desserts are made from scratch. Try Chef Scott Ostrander's twist on strawberry shortcake. The menu pairs it with one of the dessert wines, Chamber's Rosemount (a muscatel), and so can you. ✉ *309 W. Congress St., Historic District* ☎ *912/233–6266* ▭ *AE, MC, V* ⊙ *No lunch.*

$ ✕ **Blowin' Smoke BBQ.** *Southern.* The restaurant's name refers
🕙 to the serious smoking of the meats and chicken over Georgia pecan wood, before the housemade barbecue sauce is slathered on. This is a hip, contemporary barbecue shop but based on the same Southern premise as the down-home barbecue joints that are candidly shown in the artsy black-and-white photos hung on the deep-purple and yellow walls. Fellow diners are usually 70% locals, students, and families with kids (the latter usually choose the courtyard seating, where kids can play with chalk on the sidewalks). The specialties here are pork ribs and hand-pulled pork, as you might expect from a restaurant with a pig logo. Of the fried appetizers, the mushrooms with smoky ranch dressing are the ticket. A must is one of the local craft beers. It's open until 11 on Friday and Saturday nights, with live blues and jazz (and free parking). ✉ *514 Martin Luther King Jr. Blvd., Historic District* ☎ *912/231–2385* ▭ *AE, D, MC, V.*

SAVING MONEY ON DINING. **Order a Visitor VIP Dining Club Card for culinary savings during your stay in the Big S. It's plastic, just like a credit card, and costs $29.95 for six months ($39.95 for 12 months). Some of the top restaurants are included in the list of more than 100 that honor the card. You might get a free appetizer or dessert, a bottle of wine, or a half-price entrée. Order the card online at ⊕ savannahmenu.com, or stop by Destination Savannah to purchase one after you arrive.**

¢ ✕ **Café 37.** *Eclectic.* This small, unassuming spot is near the multifaceted 37th @ Abercorn antique complex. The artwork in the café is oversized, fun, and funky, a takeoff on Southern country landscapes. The breakfast/lunch menu is small and runs the gamut from Southern contemporary (a pork sandwich with Gruyère cheese, champagne vinaigrette, and Dijon mustard on herbed sourdough) to French classics (luscious duck mousse with cherry compote and crostini). Chef-owner Blake Elsinghorst is a Georgia boy but graduated from Le Cordon Bleu in Paris and worked there in a Michelin 3-star restaurant. This is one place in Savannah where you can find escargot. Blake has been granted his liquor license and is now serving dinner, though at this writing only on Friday and Saturday nights; his plans are to quickly expand to five nights. Expect to find such French bistro fare as cassoulet and duck confit and even housemade saucisson. At Sunday brunch you can now have a mimosa with your Belgian waffles. ⊠ *205 E. 37th St., corner of Abercorn, Historic District* ☎*912/236–8533* ▤*MC, V* ⊘*Closed Mon. No dinner Sun.–Thurs.*

★ Fodor'sChoice ✕ **Cha Bella.** *American.* "Organic is the only
$$$–$$$$ way," says chef/owner Matthew Roher and his partner Steve Howard, who do everything possible to conform their restaurant to this maxim as staunch supporters of the new farmer's market at Trustee Gardens at The Morris Center. Surrounding the outdoor seating, sheltered by a tin roof, you'll find an aromatic herb garden; the restaurant also has two plots of land nearby where they grow much of their produce. The menu includes some excellent, unusual salads including grilled eggplant with warm plum tomatoes flavored with sweet basil and topped with a goat cheese cake. Among the pastas, the wild porcini pappardelle has a distinctive flavor and mix of textures. A local, all-star black grouper, seared and served over fresh succotash with lump crab meat, takes center stage,. The decor is contemporary, with fresh local flowers, such as cala lilies. Lunch is now served as of this writing. ⊠ *10 E. Broad St., Historic District* ☎*912/790–7888* ▤*AE, D, MC, V* ⊘ *Closed Sun.*

$$$$ ✕ **Elizabeth on 37th.** *Southern.* Regional specialties are the
★ hallmark at this acclaimed restaurant that goes so far as to credit local produce suppliers on its menu. Although original chef and owner Elizabeth Terry retired in 1996, Kelly Yambor has helmed the kitchen ever since, and she replicates the blue crab cakes that sit comfortably beside Southern-fried grits and honey-roasted pork tenderloin with roasted shiitake and oyster mushrooms over dried tomatoes, black-eyed peas, and carrot ragout. The extravagant Savannah cream cake is the way to finish your meal in this elegant turn-of-the-20th-century mansion within the Victorian District. Splurge for the chef's seven-course tasting menu. Nightly or seasonal specialties are often the most creative. Tourists sometimes complain that more attention is paid to Old Guard locals; that may be true, but many of them have been regulars here for decades. Regardless, service is always professional, and the waitstaff works as a well-orchestrated team; all diners can expect to be taken care of well. ⊠ *105 E. 37th St., Historic District*

3

2/236–5547 🔔*Reservations essential* 🍽*AE, D, DC,* , V 🕐*No lunch.*

irefly Cafe. *American.* Chef and owner Sharon Stinogel fers a fresh twist on Southern fare at this upbeat neigh-borhood spot on the corner of Troup Square. The menu has something for everyone, including vegetarians and vegans, and offers a myriad of salads with intriguing dressings (the lemon chicken is especially good), as well as flavorful pork chops with garlic mashed potatoes. The outdoor tables are often taken by couples with their dogs in tow—perhaps that's because of the homemade dog biscuits. ✉*321 Hab-ersham St.,Historic District* 🕾*912/234–1971* 🍽*MC, V* 🕐*Closed Mon. No dinner Sun.–Thurs.*

$$$$ ✕**45 Bistro.** *Eclectic.* No one should mistake this for a non-★ descript hotel restaurant just because it is located within the Marshall House. The contemporary artwork and stel-lar bar with its ornate glass ceiling give you the first clues that this is a separate entity; the menu posted outside will beckon you to come in. Chef Patrick Best, whose middle name should be Perfection, is an artist as well. Watch him as he cooks; he is as intense as if he were finishing a paint-ing. His masterpieces include grilled hearts of romaine with homemade croutons and dressing that can go up against the world's best Caesar salads; duck with roasted parsnips, apples, cured bacon, and blackberry glacé that is a perfect cool-weather main course; and figgy bread pudding with coconut ice cream and marsala caramel, which is hard to top. ✉*123 E. Broughton St., Historic District* 🕾*912/655–3529* 🍽*AE, D, MC, V* 🕐*Closed Sun. No lunch.*

★ Fodor'sChoice ✕**Garibaldi Café.** *Eclectic.* With the same owners $$$–$$$$ of the Olde Pink House, Garabaldi might appear from the outside that it's just another tourist trap near the city mar-ket. Look closer and you'll see that the original tin ceilings are a burnished gold, the bar and its fixtures are opulent, and the circular maplewood tables have leather booth seats. This is a restaurant revered by the city's titans and Savannah's crème de la crème, who have their weddings and special events in the glamorous ballroom upstairs. Many remember Garibaldi for it's well-priced Italian classics, but the kitchen also sends out some much more ambitious offer-ings, albeit at higher prices. There are such unforgettable appetizers as lamb ribs, slow-cooked with a sweet ginger sauce and a fuchsia pear-cabbage relish, or a salad with poached pear, arugula, walnuts, and goat cheese fritters with a port-wine vinaigrette. Special salads are even more innovative (listen carefully to the specials recited by your waiter). Plump soft-shell crabs come with surprising glazes, and grouper and snapper with original treatments may be paired with house-made chutney and crab risotto. Have your knowledgeable and professional server offer wine pairings from the intelligent and global wine cart. ⊠*315 W. Congress, Historic District* ☎*912/232–7118* ⌂*Reservations essential* ☱*AE, D, MC, V* ⊘*No lunch.*

¢ ✕**Harris Baking Company.** *Café.* Owner Sam Harris is the ★ chief baker, and his raspberry-custard tarts and perfect éclairs will make your eyes roll back. This bakery-cum–breakfast/lunch spot is well worth the walk to the landmark Drayton Towers building. Facing Drayton, look for the outdoor market umbrellas and tables; inside, the café is a minimalist study in gray, taupe, and chrome, with symbolic stalks of wheat in bud vases. Order from the counter. Any of the baked goods are incredible, including the croissants and Euro-style artisan breads. But Sam also makes uncompromisingly good sandwiches, including a golden ciabatta panini with roast beef, aioli, sautéed onions, mushrooms, and provolone cheese. All salad dressings, the aioli, other condiments, and even the pickles are house-made. The lobster crab bisque, with homemade croutons, is particularly flavorful. And imagine banana bread pudding made with cinnamon buns and caramel sauce. ⊠*102 E. Liberty St., Historic District* ☎*912/233–6400* ⌂ ☱*AE, D, MC, V* ⊘*No dinner.*

$$$$ ✕**Il Pasticcio Restaurant & Wine Bar.** *Italian.* Sicilian Pino Venetico turned this former department store into his dream restaurant—a bistro-style place gleaming with steel, glass, and tile. The menu changes frequently, but fresh pasta dishes are a constant, and excellent desserts include a superior tiramisu. The signature filet mignon with melted Gorgonzola, pearl onions, and a port wine reduction is superb. Veal chops, at $40, are the top-priced entrée. As the evening progresses, live jazz ensembles start up around 9:30 PM on Tuesday through Saturday in the Luna Lounge, and the scene gets ever more lively and hip. The upper level, separate from the restaurant, is its sister restaurant, The Bull Street Chop House. ⊠*2 E. Broughton St., Historic District* ☎*912/231–8888* ☱*AE, D, DC, MC, V* ⊘*Closed Sun. No lunch.*

$$$ ✕**The Lady & Sons.** *Southern.* Put some South in your mouth! Expect to take your place in line simply to get reservations for either lunch or dinner. Everyone patiently waits to attack the buffet, which is stocked for both lunch and

dinner with moist, crispy fried chicken, mashed potatoes, collard greens, lima beans, and the like. Peach cobbler and banana pudding round off the offerings. These days, the quality can sometimes suffer because of the volume. Locals will tell you that in the early days, when Paula was doing her own cooking, it was decidedly better. The atmosphere is retro and will take you back to a small Southern town of decades past. Although most fans jump on the buffet when their name is called, you can order off the menu, and a crab-cake burger at lunch or chicken potpie or barbecue grouper at dinner can be a good choice. ⊠*102 W. Congress St., Historic District* ☎*912/233–2600* ⌂*Reservations essential* ▤*AE, D, MC, V* ⊘*No dinner Sun.*

$$$$ ✕ **Local 11ten.** *American.* New Wave, American cuisine is
★ served in what looks like an extension of the white-brick, American Legion post next door. A peek inside shows that it is light years away. The stark minimalist decor looks like something straight from the Pacific Rim, with bundles of tied reeds as decoration, Euro-style furniture, and outdoor seating, too. Upbeat and contemporary, this is where several of the top young chefs in Savannah come on their nights off. The menu is seasonally driven and is continually changing depending on the availability of produce and the new chef's vision on any given day. Chef Bradley Daniels came here from the prestigious Blackberry Farm in Tennessee, and his cuisine is as southern as the area's local favorites, including plump soft-shell crabs, but his menu also has definite Italian and French influences. At this writing, a new rooftop bar is in the works and should be open by spring 2009. ⊠*1110 Bull St., Historic District* ☎*912/790–9000* ⌂*Reservations essential* ▤*AE, D, MC, V* ⊘*Closed Sun. and Mon. No lunch.*

$$ ✕ **Mrs. Wilkes' Dining Room.** *Southern.* Folks line up out to the brick street for an orgy of fine Southern fare, served family style at big tables from 11 to 2. It's been family owned for decades, and the original Miz Wilkes really did run this historic home as a boarding house, serving three meals a day. On the ground floor, ceilings are low, but sharing one of the big tables with strangers is one way to make new friends. There might be fried or roasted chicken, beef stew, collard greens, okra, mashed potatoes, macaroni and cheese, sweet potato soufflé, and corn bread, with favorites like banana pudding for dessert. Locals can tell you that this is the city's best Southern buffet. Mrs. Wilkes made this place somewhat of a legend, and her granddaughter and great-grandson are keeping it a family affair in more

ways than one. Kids under age 12 eat for half price. No alcohol is served, but you can get a lot of sweet tea. ⊠*107 W. Jones St., Historic District* ☎*912/232–5997* ⚞*Reservations not accepted* ▭*No credit cards* ⊙*Closed weekends and Jan. No dinner.*

★ Fodor'sChoice ✕**Noble Fare.** *Eclectic.* This is one superior fine-
$$$–$$$$ dining experience, all the way from the amuse-bouche to dessert. In a gentrified neighborhood that now boasts high-end real estate, most of the clientele are well-heeled, older residents or thirtysomethings booking for a special occasion. The decor is "dressy," a study in opulent black, white, and red. The bread service includes honey butter, pistachio pesto, olive oil, and balsamic vinegar for your biscuits, flat breads, rolls, and foccacia, all of which are artistically presented on contemporary, white dishes. A choice appetizer is tuna tartare with avocado, American caviar, and mango, drizzled with curry oil; scoop it all up with the plantain chips. The scallops are laudable, and fish is so fresh it practically moves on your plate, but if you are a venison lover go for the tenderloin with carrot puree, potatoes, greens, and Pinotage syrup. A prix-fixe tasting menu is available as well. Red meat can produce a chemical need for chocolate, so the molten lava cake with raspberry sauce and custard ice cream may be a requirement, especially paired with a zinfandel port. The owners are Chef Patrick McNamara and his lovely bride Jenny, who runs the front of the house. ⊠*321 Jefferson St., Historic District* ☎*912/443–3210* ⚞*Reservations essential* ▭*AE, D, MC, V* ⊙*No Lunch. Closed Sun. and Mon.*

$$–$$$$ ✕**Olde Pink House.** *Southern.* This pink-brick Georgian man-
★ sion was built in 1771 for James Habersham, one of the wealthiest Americans of his time, and the historic atmosphere comes through in the original Georgia pine floors of the tavern, the Venetian chandeliers, and the 18th-century English antiques. Looking to contemporize a cherished landmark, the owners added a "new" dining room with vintage pine floors and walls. A stunning new bar, The Arches, is adjacent with curvaceous doors that can open on balmy nights for outdoor seating. Happily, lunch is now back on the menu, with a number of creative sandwiches and both cold and hot entrées like a shrimp 'n' grits and chilled shellfish sampler. New chef Timothy O'Neil, who apprenticed under French chefs and has both classical training and contemporary style, has been brought in to upgrade the menu and tweak what is already there. Though the offerings were still evolving at this writing, you can

expect Lowcountry classics and innovative specials with much local seafood and quality ingredients. How about a classic chicken potpie with roasted veggies, porcini cream sauce, and a sweet potato biscuit? ✉*23 Abercorn St., Historic District* ☎*912/232–4286* ⌖*Reservations essential* ▭*AE, MC, V* ⊘*No lunch Sun. and Mon.*

$$–$$$ ╳**Pirates House.** *Southern.* This Savannah landmark is as much a restaurant as it is an attraction on the tourist route (*See* ⇨*Exploring, above*), and many Savannah tours include the lunch buffet here. Kids love both the food and the pirates. There is a children's menu, too, but most kids are just biding their time to dessert: pecan pie, warm banana bread pudding, and Georgia peach ice cream cake. Adults may want to choose from the à la carte menu, which is always better than the buffet. The baby back ribs and the honey pecan chicken are especially good. There's no buffet for dinner, but the dining rooms do take on a more menacing atmosphere by night, and isn't that why you come here? Some of the nighttime ghost tours include dinner here. ▰TIP→ **If you don't come here with a tour group, try to reserve a window table in the Jolly Roger room, with its slanted floors and nice window seats facing E. Broad.** ✉*20 E. Broad St., at Bay St., Historic District* ☎*912/233–5757* ⌖*Reservations essential* ▭*AE, D, MC, V* ⊘*Closed Sun.*

$$$$ ╳**Sapphire Grill.** *American.* Savannah's young and restless ★ pack this trendy haunt with its loftlike style. Chef Chris Nason focuses his seasonal menus on local ingredients, such as Georgia white shrimp, crab, and fish. The Grill features succulent choices of steak, poultry, and fish, with a myriad of interesting à la carte accompaniments such as jalapeño tartar sauce, sweet soy-wasabi sauce, and lemongrass butter. Vegetarians will delight in the elegant vegetable presentations—perhaps including roasted sweet onions, spicy peppers, rice wine–marinated watercress, or fried green tomatoes with grilled ginger. An excellent value is the $21 three-course vegetarian tasting menu. The six-course chef's tasting menu, with fresh seafood and top-quality meats is $100. If you and, say, nine of your favorite people want to celebrate, reserve the private wine room on the third floor. Chocoholics Alert: you will find your bliss in the miniature cocoa gâteau with lavender almond ice cream. Downstairs, the decor is hip—think urban loft—with gray brick walls alongside those painted a deep sapphire and a stone bar; upstairs is quieter and more romantic. ✉*110 W. Congress St., Historic District* ☎*912/443–9962* ⌖*Reservations essential* ▭*AE, D, DC, MC, V* ⊘*No lunch.*

CLOSE UP

Learning to Cook at 700 Kitchen

Bring out your inner gourmet chef as you explore and create a unique culinary experience with a hands-on approach to food preparation, production, portioning, and appreciation at 700 Kitchen (⊠*Mansion on Forsyth Park,700 Drayton St., Historic District* ☏*912/2380–5158*)This educational and entertaining cooking school is within the Mansion on Forsyth complex and boasts a state-of-the-art kitchen. It offers daily and weekend interactive culinary courses for individuals, as well as team-building programs for groups, at all skill levels. These are participatory classes, and you do get to sample what you make. You will be given a little sparkling wine to smooth the palate, as well as a good-quality, long apron with the 700 kitchen logo. You do not have to be a guest at the hotel to be a student, but classes are held for a minimum of 10 persons. Depending on how many you are, you may have to buddy up with other people who register, just like in real college. Classes are normally three hours in length, $90 a person plus tax and gratuity.

$$$–$$$$ ✕**700 Drayton Restaurant.** *American.* This is a one-of-a-kind
★ Savannah experience that begins as you walk up the stairs of the former Keyton Mansion into a lounge that dazzles with eclectic furnishings like a Versace leopard-skin print chair, a suitable spot for a long power lunch or a romantic dinner. Enter the restaurant and marvel at the two Victorian credenzas painted orange—the same hue as the Italian, drop-crystal chandelier. You will have a delectable meal made from regionally inspired cuisine utilizing fresh local produce. As an appetizer, the scallops with asparagus and mushrooms with a vanilla sauce are sublime. The Moroccan-spiced rack of lamb is one of the best entrées, but the lime-and-whiskey–marinated snapper, pan-seared with herb grits and tomatillo-lime sauce, is also divine. Leopold's has made the restaurant its own luscious ice cream flavor, "Old Savannah." Breakfast is also served daily, and the Sunday brunch is a local favorite for special occasions. ⊠*700 Drayton St., Historic District* ☏*912/721–5002 or 912/238–5158* ⌂*Reservations essential* ▭*AE, D, DC, MC, V.*

$$$–$$$$ ✕**17 Hundred 90.** *French.* In a rustic structure dating to colonial days, tucked in among ancient oaks dripping with Spanish moss, you'll find a kitchen that is enmeshed in the classics, with some creative entrées. This isn't one of the revolutionary restaurants; you'll find traditional appetiz-

ers such as oysters Rockefeller and blue crab cakes, as well as steaks and potatoes. More exciting choices include Muscovy duck with a port-wine lingonberry sauce. Great desserts include Savannah mud pie. A new thing here is a classic Southern buffet at lunch, for $11.95 including a beverage, which pulls in the tourist crowd; you can still order à la carte, however. This restaurant is attached to a 14-room inn. ■TIP→ **There's a ghost to go with dinner, so make sure the waiter fills you in.** ✉*307 E. President St., Historic District* ☎*912/237–7122* ▬*AE, D, MC, V* ⊘*No lunch weekends.*

¢–$ ✕**SoHo South Cafe.** *Eclectic.* Chef/owner Bonnie Retsas lived
★   25 years in New York prior to "retiring" here and opening up this small restaurant. The long brick building had been an art gallery, though it still looks like the mechanic's garage that it once was, with an unfinished ceiling and exposed duct work. There is often a line for lunch and for Sunday brunch, though reservations are accepted now. The tables and chairs are a mismatch of Formica, wood, and enamel from the 1940s to '60s. The strength of Bonnie's food is that it is *consistent* and it tastes so homemade. Try the meat-loaf sandwich with Russian dressing or the flavorful quiches. Soups like the signature tomato-basil bisque are the perfect accompaniment for the grilled (three) cheese(es) on sourdough with pimento aioli. Some more contemporary choices are offered now like the sandwiches of grilled Portobello mushrooms or vegetables with roasted peppers and pesto mayo; a special might be organic chicken potpie. Only wine and beer are sold (only after noon on Sundays). ✉*12 W. Liberty St., Historic District* ☎*912/233–1633* ▬ *AE, MC, V* ⊘*No dinner.*

$$$–$$$$ ✕**Vic's on the River.** *Southern.* This upscale Southern charmer
★   is one of the hippest fine-dining rooms in town, where local residents congregate and tourists join in conversation at the bar as they listen to the talented pianists. The brick building was designed by the famous New York architect John Norris for John Stoddard in 1858 as a warehouse; the Civil War led to its desertion until the Union soldiers took it over for housing. Reserve a window table for the best views of the Savannah River. The young chef, Jay Cantrell, is becoming a local celebrity and is among those aggressively changing the dining scene for the better. Much of the menu is given over to classics like steaks and oysters Rockefeller. Pan-seared scallops are freshened up with crab and Andouille sausage risotto, wilted arugula, and lemon-herb truffle butter. Praline cheesecake is very decadent but

strongly recommended. Lunch is popular with local businesspeople and upscale tourists, and seafood po'boys and Angus burgers are sought after, as are the daily hot specials. ✉16 E. River St., Historic District ☎912/721–1000 ⌨Reservations essential ▤AE, D, MC, V.

ELSEWHERE IN SAVANNAH

$–$$ ✕**Bella's Italian Café.** *Italian.* From its unpretentious location in a Midtown shopping center, Bella's serves up simple, wildly popular fare, including scampi, ziti, pizza, and panini as well as a particularly good manicotti. Desserts are also standout versions of classics, such as Italian wedding cake, tiramisu, and cannoli. It is a good choice for family dining, and most come early. The genial, hospitable service makes this a perfect place to relax over a glass of wine, too. ✉4408 Habersham St., Midtown ☎912/354–4005 ⌨Reservations not accepted ▤AE, MC, V ⊘No lunch weekends.

$$ ✕**Johnny Harris.** *American.* What started as a small roadside stand in 1924, across from Grayson Stadium (10 minutes from downtown via the Truman Parkway) has grown into one of the city's beloved mainstays. Expect a 1950s ambience, and that's just how people like it. It's a trip down Memory Lane. The booths originally had doors for privacy (they catered to business cronies and romantic couples); while the doors are long gone, the seats are still the most comfortable in the house, and the old service bells are still there. The menu includes standbys like Brunswick stew, steaks, Southern fried chicken, seafood, and barbecued meats spiced with the restaurant's famous tomato-and-mustard sauces. The hickory-smoked pork (watch it slow-cooking out on the pits) is a particular treat. You can buy a bottle of sauce to take home with you. ✉1651 E. Victory Dr., Eastside ☎912/354–7810 ▤AE, D, DC, MC, V ⊘Closed Sun.

$$ ✕**Toucan Café.** *Eclectic.* This colorful café is well worth a trip a bit off the beaten path to Savannah's Southside. It's a favorite for Savannahians entertaining out-of-town visitors; no one, it seems, leaves unsatisfied. The menu defines the term *eclectic*, with plenty of appealing options for both vegetarians and meat eaters, including wasabi pea–encrusted tuna, tempura portobellos, black-bean burgers, spanakopita, Jamaican jerk chicken, and rib-eye steaks. Specialty salads, steaks and seafood, and international fusion food are how the menu goes. ✉531 Stephenson Ave., Southside ☎912/352–2233 ▤AE, D, MC, V ⊘ Closed Sun.

TYBEE ISLAND

$$ ✕**Charly's.** *Continental.* This upscale restaurant in a color-fully restored beach cottage (some rooms with pine floors) is a welcome alternative on an otherwise kitschy island. Throughout several dining rooms, the atmosphere is provided by local artwork, soft track lighting, and candles coupled with mellow jazz by Coltrane and Miles Davis. You will enjoy caring service, sometimes from the owner himself, Chuck Vonashek. Chef Ed Hornsby spends the quiet winter months honing a great new menu. The grilled lamb lollipops with a rosemary demi-glace are a study in well-executed simplicity. Such appetizers as potato-wrapped shrimp are surprisingly good and a great way to start your meal. The nightly specials are the most creative, and his lobster crab bisque is decadently rich. In shoulder seasons, there's an early dining menu with cheaper main courses, providing even more value for the dollar, as does everything offered. ✉*106 S. Campbell Ave., Tybee Island* ☎*912/786–0221, 912/398–4709 for limo reservations* ⊟*AE, D, MC, V* ⊘*Closed Mon. No lunch.*

$$ ✕**Grace.** *Southern.* A former turn-around barn for a long-gone trolley line, the dining room is warmed by a stone fireplace; wainscoting adds ambience in what continues to be one of the better restaurants on Tybee. Formerly George's of Tybee, the restaurant has changed a great deal in addition to its name; however, one of the Georges (Spriggs) remains at the restaurant and has partnered with the new chef, J.J. McFarland. He describes the cuisine as "upscale Southern bistro," and those who are familiar with the restaurant's previous incarnation will find the food more casual in style. Prices have been down-scaled accordingly. Of the many innovative appetizers, the blackened crawfish burrito with a chipotle cheese sauce is a standout. The chef is justifiably proud of his pan-sautéed grouper with Pernod butter and lemon confit, flanked by corn pudding and asparagus. Sunday brunch is well-priced and offers a good choice of entrées preceded by fruit and cheese. ✉*1105 E. U.S. 80, Tybee Island* ☎*912/786–9730* ⊟*AE, MC, V* ⊘*Closed Mon. No lunch.*

$$$ ✕**Hunter House.** *Southern.* Built in 1910 as a family beach house, this renovated brick home with its wraparound veranda offers an intimate dining experience with a dose of Victorian ambience. Owner John Hunter operates one of the island's most consistently good restaurants, and that consistency has continued for some 20 years. Seafood

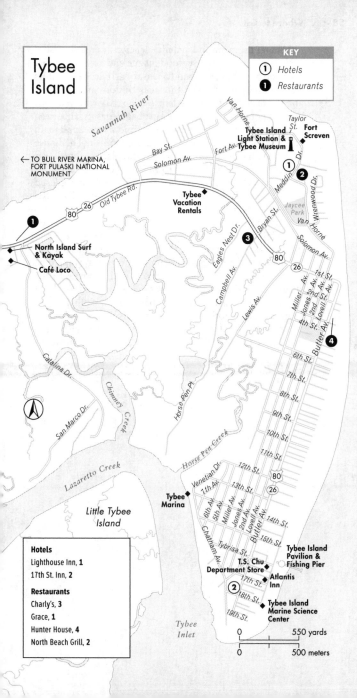

Tybee Island

KEY
① Hotels
❶ Restaurants

Savannah River

← TO BULL RIVER MARINA,
FORT PULASKI NATIONAL
MONUMENT

Van Horne

Taylor St.

Fort Screven

Tybee Island Light Station & Tybee Museum

Bay St.

Fort Av.

Solomon Av.

①

❷

Meddin Dr.

Jaycee Park

80 26 Old Tybee Rd.

Tybee Vacation Rentals

Bryan St.

Van Horne

Wrenwood Dr.

North Island Surf & Kayak

Café Loco

Eagles Nest Dr.

❸

80

Solomon Av.

26

1st St.

2nd St.

Miller Av.

Jones Av.

2nd Av.

Lowell Av.

Campbell Av.

Lewis Av.

4th St.

❹

Butler Av.

6th St.

Catalina Dr.

San Marco Dr.

Chimney Creek

Horse Pen Pt.

7th St.

8th St.

9th St.

10th St.

11th St.

Horse Pen Creek

Lazaretto Creek

12th St.

80

26

Venetian Dr.

13th St.

1th Av.

6th Av.

5th Av.

Millet Av.

Jones Av.

2nd Av.

Lowell Av.

Butler Av.

14th St.

Tybee Marina

Little Tybee Island

15th St.

Chatham Av.

Tybrisa St.

Tybee Island Pavilion & Fishing Pier

T.S. Chu Department Store

Atlantis Inn

❷

17th St.

18th St.

19th St.

Tybee Island Marine Science Center

Tybee Inlet

Hotels
Lighthouse Inn, **1**
17th St. Inn, **2**

Restaurants
Charly's, **3**
Grace, **1**
Hunter House, **4**
North Beach Grill, **2**

0   550 yards

0   500 meters

dominates the menu and includes deliciously creative dishes such as a cognac-laced seafood bisque and ahi tuna with a bourbon soy glaze, nori, and a wasabi drizzle. Meat eaters need not despair: chicken and steak options are available, and the restaurant offers a delicious pot roast, served with mashed potatoes and gravy, red cabbage, carrots, and green beans, as the perennial house special and the cheapest main course. The key lime tart is the perfect finish. The house offers two large suites (one with a fireplace) as well as a regular room for rent ($110 to $150). ✉*1701 Butler Ave., Tybee Island* ☎*912/786–7515* ▭*AE, D, MC, V* ☉*Closed mid-Dec.–mid-Jan. Closed Sun. Labor Day–mid-Dec. and mid-Jan.–Memorial Day.*

$$ ✕**North Beach Grill.** *Caribbean.* If you didn't know better, you might think you'd stepped into a Caribbean beach bar. Nestled in front of the dunes of Tybee Beach, this place is as mellow as the reggae playing in the background. The food offerings are island influenced as well. From under the shade of a market umbrella, order the fish taco—Caribbean style, made from fried tilapia, basil pesto, cabbage, and tomato salsa. Another lunchtime fave is the spicy ahi tuna salad over spinach with Thai dressing. By the light of the moon, try the jerk chicken or pork and the fresh-caught fish. ✉*41A Meddin Ave.,Tybee Island* ☎*912/786–9730* ▭*AE, D, MC, V.*

Where to Stay

4

WORD OF MOUTH

"[The Mansion on Forsyth Park.] Let's talk; the hotel is lovely. Yes there is art all over the place—walls, halls, even in the bathrooms—but you're in the city of SCAD. It ties together perfectly. Oh yeah, it's a little gaudy, but I think that is the personality of Savannah."

—johnb

Updated
by Eileen
Robinson
Smith

ALTHOUGH SAVANNAH HAS ITS SHARE OF CHAIN HOTELS
and motels, the city's most distinctive lodgings are in more
than two dozen historic inns, guesthouses, and B&Bs grac-
ing the Historic District. If the term *historic inn* brings to
mind images of roughing it in shabby-genteel mansions
with antiquated plumbing, you'll find that to be the case
in a few isolated instances. Such are the woes of older
buildings: the creaking staircase, the faucet that comes off
in your hand, even the rumors of ghosts.

However, many of these inns are beautifully restored mansions with the requisite high ceilings, spacious rooms, and
ornate carved millwork. Many do have canopy, four-poster,
and possibly even Victorian brass beds, but amid all the
antique surroundings you'll also find such luxuries as
enormous baths, film libraries for in-room DVD players,
excellent service, and perhaps even a discreet brandy on
your nightstand.

Continental or full Southern breakfasts are often included
in the rates, as are afternoon refreshments (usually wine
and cheese, sometimes elaborate hors d'oeuvres); these
extras definitely help to justify some of the escalated prices.
Some B&Bs offer a pass that will give you free on-street
parking; others have a few private parking spaces of their
own. Nearly all of the hotels and inns in the real downtown
sector have paid parking, which can range from $8 at the
riverfront inns to $18 a night for valet parking.

HOTEL PRICES

Savannah is not inexpensive because demand is high almost
year-round now. Although the number of hotel rooms
downtown has doubled since 2000, occupancy levels
remain high even in the formerly dead zone from September through December; October is especially busy. Holiday periods push prices up; St. Patrick's Day weekend is a
particularly busy period in Savannah.

You will sometimes save by booking online or by pur-
chasing a package. Look for good last-minute deals when
bookings are light. These are often available in late summer, when the heat and humidity are at their highest. The
hotel tax is now 13%.

WHAT IT COSTS FOR TWO PEOPLE				
¢	$	$$	$$$	$$$$
under $100	$100–$150	$151–$200	$201–$250	over $250

Hotel prices are for two people in a standard double room in high season and do not include 13% tax; most B&Bs (but not all) include breakfast in their rates.

HISTORIC DISTRICT

$$–$$$ ⊞**Azalea Inn & Gardens.** This personable inn is owned and operated by Teresa Jacobson and her husband Jake, who can be thanked for the subtropical gardens that surround the pool. They have an easygoing, live-and-let-live attitude and a connection with the Savannah College of Art & Design, and artwork by students lines some hallways. The slightly irreverent murals in the breakfast room depict the history of Savannah. The Forsyth Park neighborhood, near Gaston Street, offers quiet surroundings adored by the residents—and guests. This 1889 mansion built for a Cotton Exchange powerhouse has multiple fireplaces, private verandas with overhead fans and wicker furnishings, and handsome artisan craftsmanship. Expect a generous, hospitable ambience, a reinvented Southern breakfast, and house-baked desserts, not to mention afternoon wine service with attitude—a good one. **Pros:** The Gentlemen's Parlor and Magnolia Place, the two best rooms; baked goods are put out during the day. **Cons:** Typically Victorian, the decor is sometimes just too busy; the less-expensive rooms are small; the carriage house is not as distinctive. ⊠*217 Huntingdon St., Historic District* ☎*912/236–2707 or 800/582–3823* ⊕*www.azaleainn.com* ⤳*9 rooms, 2 suites* &*In-room: no phone, DVD, Wi-Fi. In-hotel: pool, Wi-Fi, parking (free), no kids under 12, no-smoking rooms* ⊟*AE, D, MC, V* ⊠*BP.*

BREAKFAST INCLUDED. When you are trying to decide on what kind of accommodation to reserve in Savannah, consider that B&Bs usually include breakfast (sometimes a lavish one), complimentary wine and cheese nightly, and even free bottled water; parking is sometimes free. Hotels, particularly the major ones, usually do not even give you a small bottle of water, and almost all charge substantially for parking.

SAVANNAH LODGING TIPS

■ **Do Your Research.** Read up on Savannah's many B&Bs and inns on blogs and in user-generated forums. Don't hesitate to call the innkeepers and chat; you'll quickly gauge their attitude and sense of hospitality. And know the parking situation; many of these B&Bs provide only on-street parking, though they usually pay for your parking pass (you still have to move the car on days when the streets need to be cleaned, however).

■ **Know What Historic Really Means.** Among the negatives can be antique beds, albeit beautifully canopied, that are short, not even as big as today's doubles. If you are a big guy or are used to a California King, that could be a definite issue. Rooms can be small, especially if they were originally backrooms meant for children or servants; rooms below street level—often called garden or courtyard

rooms—can be damp. Windows aren't usually sound-proof, and the squares can be noisy in the morning.

■ **Don't Neglect the Chains.** Mid-range chain hotels and motels that normally would not excite or even interest you can be surprisingly appealing. Those in the Historic District may be creatively renovated historic structures. If you can't afford to stay downtown, you'll find many mid-range chains in Midtown and the Southside (still less than 7 mi from downtown). The farther out you go, the less expensive your lodging will be.

■ **Savannah Has Hotels Too.** Full-service hotels such as Hyatt Regency, Marriott, Westin, and Hilton may be more appealing to visitors who actually prefer a larger, more anonymous property—or at least one with an elevator; swimming pool, or normal-sized bed.

$$$–$$$$ ⊤Ballastone Inn. On the National Register of Historic Places,
★ this sumptuous inn occupies an 1838 mansion that once served as a bordello. Rooms are handsomely furnished with antiques and fine reproductions; luxurious, scented linens and French down blankets on canopied beds; and a collection of original framed prints from *Harper's* scattered throughout. Garden (ground-floor) rooms are smaller but cozy, with exposed brick walls, beamed ceilings, and, in some cases, windows at eye level with the lush courtyard. Most rooms have working gas fireplaces, and three have whirlpool tubs. The aroma of fresh flowers permeates the air. Afternoon tea is served from a silver set and on fine

china; the evening social hour features hors d'oeuvres; and a full bar stocks boutique wines. **Pros:** Excellent location; romantic atmosphere; free passes to a downtown health club are included. **Cons:** Limited off-street parking; this busy downtown area can be noisy. ✉ *14 E. Oglethorpe Ave., Historic District* ☎ *912/236–1484 or 800/822–4553* ⊕ *www.ballastone.com* ⚐ *16 rooms, 3 suites* ♿ *In-room: Wi-Fi (some). In-hotel: bar, parking (free), no kids under 16, no-smoking rooms* ☐ *AE, MC, V* ⬤ *BP.*

$–$$ 🏠 **Bed & Breakfast Inn.** So called, the owner claims, because it was the first such property to open in Savannah almost 30 years ago, the inn is a restored 1853 Federal-style row house on historic Gordon Row near Chatham Square. The courtyard garden is a lovely cluster of potted tropical flowers surrounding an inviting koi pond. All rooms have private baths and retain many elements of the home's original charm, such as beamed ceilings and exposed-brick walls. There are four self-contained cottages, and some rooms also have kitchens. Breakfast is good and may include pecan corn bread, pancakes, and eggs to order. Afternoon pastries, lemonade, coffee, and tea are served. On weekends there is a wine-and-cheese reception. Guests who don't have a refrigerator in their room can use the one in the main kitchen's and the microwave. **Pros:** Children welcome; cable TV; cottages with kitchens are particularly well priced. **Cons:** Twenty-minute walk to the river; two-night minimum to get a free-parking pass; front desk not staffed after 9 PM. ✉ *117 W. Gordon St., Historic District* ☎ *912/238–0518* ⊕ *www.savannahbnb.com* ⚐ *15 rooms, 2 suites, 4 cottages* ♿ *In-room: kitchen (some), refrigerator (some), DVD (some), Wi-Fi (some). In-hotel: Internet terminal, Wi-Fi, parking (free), no-smoking rooms* ☐ *AE, D, MC, V* ⬤ *BP.*

$$–$$$ 🏠 **Catherine Ward House.** Built by a former sea captain for his
★ young wife in 1886, this Italianate home is within a block of Forsyth Park. When Leslie Larson, co-owner and innkeeper in residence, took over the existing B&B, she updated and totally redecorated it, adding her contemporary style while keeping it an exquisite period piece—not the dark and dowdy Victorian she bought. Her class shows through with the well-chosen gilt mirrors, antique pieces, fresh roses, and the communal dining table, set beautifully for a breakfast that gets raves. Most rooms have balconies that overlook the garden oasis with its koi pond and soothing fountain. **Pros:** All rooms are immaculate, with antique mantels and fireplaces, some of which work; some have two-person

Where to Stay in Savannah

River St.

Factors Walk

W. Bay St. **2** **3**

W. Bryan St.

Ellis Sq. W. Julian *Johnson Sq.* E. Julian **10**

W. Congress St.

W. Broughton St. E. Broughton St. **11**

W. State St. E. State St.

W. President *Telfair Sq.* *Wright Sq.* E. President

W. York St.

17 W. Oglethorpe Ave. **18**

Martin Luther King Jr. Blvd

Montgomery St.

Jefferson St.

Barnard St.

W. Hull **19**

Orleans Sq. W. Hull E. Hull

Chippewa Sq.

W. Perry E. Perry

Whitaker St.

20

Bull St.

21

W. Harris St.

Pulaski Sq. *Madison Sq.*

W. Charlton ◆ St. John's Episcopal Church

Jefferson St.

Tattnall St.

W. Jones St. **22** **23**

W. Taylor St.

Chatham Sq. W. Wayne St. *Monterey Sq.*

W. Gordon St. **26**

W. Gaston St. *Forsyth Park*

Drayton St.

29

W. Huntingdon St. **27** **31**

Azalea Inn & Gardens, **30**

Ballastone Inn, **18**

Bed & Breakfast Inn, **26**

Catherine Ward House, **32**

Courtyard Savannah Midtown, **34**

Dresser-Palmer House, **29**

East Bay Inn, **7**

Eliza Thompson House, **23**

Foley House Inn, **19**

Forsyth Park Inn, **27**

Gastonian, **28**

Green Palm Inn, **14**

Hamilton-Turner Inn, **24**

Hampton Inn & Suites, **17**

Hampton Inn Historic District, **5**

Holiday Inn Express Historic District, **6**

Hyatt Regency Savannah, **3**

Inn on Ellis Square, **2**

Kehoe House, **12**

Mansion on Forsyth Park, **31**

Marshall House, **11**

Mulberry Inn, **13**

Oglethorpe Inn & Suites, **23**

Olde Harbour Inn, **9**

Planters Inn, **10**

The President's Quarters, **16**

River Street Inn, **4**

Savannah Marriott Riverfront, **15**

Staybridge Suites, **8**

Stephen Williams House, **20**

Suites on Lafayette, **25**

Westin Savannah Harbor, **1**

Zeigler House Inn, **22**

whirlpool tubs, one a double-headed shower. **Cons:** The less expensive rooms are small, and some are on the garden level; the carriage-house rooms are not as atmospheric as the main house; this is a transitional neighborhood, and you don't want to wander farther south. ✉ *118 E. Waldburg St., Historic District* ☎*912/234–8564 or 800/327–4270* ⊕*www.catherinewardhouseinn.com* ⌕*9 rooms* ⌂*In-room: no phone, refrigerator, DVD (some), Wi-Fi. In-hotel: Internet terminal, Wi-Fi, parking (free), no children under 18, no-smoking rooms* ⊟*AE, D, MC, V* ⦿*BP.*

$$$–$$$$ **⛶The Dresser Palmer House.** This rambling Italianate town house (c. 1876) is a standout for its ornate exterior (painted mellow yellow and soft aqua), its front porch, its comfortable ambience, and its oversized rooms with high ceilings, fireplaces (some), and tasteful furnishings, such as canopied four-posters. Since this was once two separate houses, the room configurations can be unusual, but the inn exudes a historic, haunting atmosphere. Staff members are fun and make this a feel-good, homey place. Next to Forsyth Park, this quiet residential area offers a true slice of Savannah life. The Johnny Mercer room (the best accommodation) has a private bath across the hall; a major renovation is planned for 2009. **Pros:** The two back gardens with fountains are lovely; an evening "social" offers wine, cheese, and guest camaraderie; architectural details are beautiful. **Cons:** Decor is busy and ornate and may not be pleasing to a young or minimalist eye; although the building is 11,000 square feet, there's not the privacy of a large property; no in-room phones. ✉ *211 Gaston St., Historic District* ☎*912/238–3294 or 800/671–0716* ⊕*www.dresserpalmer house.com* ⌕*15 rooms* ⌂*In-room: no phone, Wi-Fi. In-hotel: Wi-Fi, parking (free), no kids under 14, no-smoking rooms* ⊟*AE, D, MC, V* ⦿*BP.*

★ Fodor'sChoice ⛶**East Bay Inn.** The charm of this tall, redbrick **$$** building with its hunter-green shutters and awnings, its first-floor facade fashioned from cast iron, and the half-dozen American flags, is not lost on passersby. Built in 1852, this inn was once a series of early cotton warehouses and factory offices. The cast-iron interior pillars were left and the brick walls exposed; the effect is handsome. The interior design is tasteful and professionally done with details that put it a step above what you will see in other similarly priced properties, notably the drapes, which are lavish and in a French toile pattern and look remarkable against the shellacked brick. Although the furnishings are reproductions, comfort has been emphasized, and all guest rooms are particularly inviting. Each has one or [...] a couch, and two comfy chairs, not to [...] ceilings. Breakfast is a good offering of [...] scrambled eggs, fresh fruit, and Danish. [...] ity and service get very high marks; the [...] tion goes further than the requisite wine a[nd cheese;] good restaurant. **Cons:** Not enough parking spaces (15) for the number of rooms; hallways, some art, and bathrooms are not as wonderful as the rooms; staff and clientele not as sophisticated as in pricier inns. ⊠ *225 E. Bay St., Historic District* ☎ *912/238–1225 or 800/500–1225* ⊕ *www.east bayinn.com* 🛏 *28 rooms* 🔒 *In-room: safe, Internet (some), Wi-Fi. In-hotel: restaurant, laundry service, Internet terminal, Wi-Fi, parking (free), some pets allowed, no-smoking rooms* ▭ *AE, D, MC, V* ⊚ *BP.*

$$$–$$$$ ▧ **Eliza Thompson House.** Eliza Thompson's loving husband
★ Joseph built this fine town house for her and their seven children in 1847, only to leave her a widow; albeit a socially prominent one. This gracious Victorian was transformed into a B&B by the first "new" owners in 1995, with furnishings and portraits in gold-leaf frames brought over from England. The rooms are handsomely appointed, some with antiques and vintage beds, fine linens, and other designer accents. The J. Stephen's room, with its aubergine walls, plaid chairs, and Victorian couch, looks out to the mossy branches of a live oak. Some of the back rooms are small. A full breakfast is taken in the tranquil brick courtyard with its soothing fountains. Adjacent is the New Orleans-esque carriage house, built in the 1980s; its 13 moderately priced rooms have just been completely upgraded, furnishings and all. Afternoon wine, cheese, and appetizers and, later, luscious evening desserts and sherry are served in the atmospheric main parlor. **Pros:** On one of Savannah's most beautiful, brick-lined streets in a lively, residential neighborhood; free parking passes are issued for street parking; flat-screen TV with cable in every room. **Cons:** No private parking lot; breakfast can be hit or miss; unattractive carpet in halls of main house. ⊠ *5 W. Jones St., Historic District* ☎ *912/236–3620 or 800/348–9378* ⊕ *www.elizathompson house.com* 🛏 *25 rooms* 🔒 *In-room: DVD, Wi-Fi. In-hotel: Internet terminal, parking (free), no kids under 12, no-smoking rooms* ▭ *AE, D, MC, V* ⊚ *BP.*

$$$–$$$$ ▧ **Foley House Inn.** Two town houses, built 50 years apart,
★ form this elegant inn. The architecture is stunning, the accommodations beautifully appointed. Most rooms have king-size beds, and all have fireplaces and reproduction

New Boutique Hotels Coming Online

CLOSE

Savannah awaits the opening of two new boutique hotels, which will target a high-end, sophisticated clientele.

The **AVIA Savannah** (⊠*14 Barnard St., Historic District* ⊕*www.aviahotels.com*), next to the *Savannah Morning News* building on Congress Street, will begin taking reservations in February 2009. Contemporary luxuries will include 42-inch flat-screen TVs, complimentary Wi-Fi, and laptop-size safes. Contemporary decor should still evoke Savannah.

The**Bohemian Hotel** (⊠*102 W. Bay St., Historic District*⊕*www. bohemiansavannah.com*) is slated to open in April 2009, on the river adjacent to the Hyatt Regency. It will work in tandem with its successful sister property, the Mansion on Forsyth Park. The hotel's design will be contemporary but will still have a vintage allure, including a brick facade, floor-to-ceiling windows, and a rooftop terrace. Centrally located, this boutique hotel will house 75 luxurious guest rooms and suites.

antique furnishings; four rooms have whirlpool tubs, three have balconies. There's also a carriage house to the rear of the property with less expensive rooms. For all its 1800s luxe touches, it does not lack for modern-day amenities like Wi-Fi and a fitness room. Ask for a room overlooking Chippewa Square, where Forrest Gump sat on a park bench giving a dissertation about a box of chocolates. **Pros:** Pets allowed for $50 cleaning fee; extremely central location within the Historic District. **Cons:** Not wheelchair accessible; four floors but no elevator. ⊠*14 W. Hull St., Historic District* ☎*912/232–6622 or 800/647–3708* ⊕*www.foleyinn.com* ➷*17 rooms, 2 suites* ♿*In-room: safe, Wi-Fi (some). In-hotel: Wi-Fi, gym, parking (free), some pets allowed, no kids under 12, no-smoking rooms* ⊟*AE, MC, V* ⃝*BP.*

$$$–$$$$ ⌧**Forsyth Park Inn.** First, do not make the mistake, as some do, and think that this is the Mansion on Forsyth Park, which is directly across the green. This is not even close to that luxury category. A yellow, wood-frame Queen Anne home (circa 1893), its exterior, gardens, and courtyard are its most appealing features. Indoors, the parlor is furnished with some proper Queen Anne pieces, but much is simply old. The parlor fireplace is a focal point, and it is fun to open the tall windows and step onto the veranda here; many guests take their breakfast out there among

the rockers and ferns. All rooms are exceptionally large, but the best are number 5 (with its black floral fabrics and fireplace) and number 9. Children and pets are allowed only in the cottage out back, but it's not in such good shape. **Pros:** Excellent Southern breakfast and good wine, hors d'oeuvres, and homemade, complimentary desserts; wedding groups can rent the entire property; on-street parking is free. **Cons:** Although spacious and with high ceilings, rooms are just adequate; bathrooms need an upgrade; prices seem high for the quality. ✉ *102 W. Hall St., Historic District* ☎ *912/233–6800* ⊕ *www.forsythparkinn. com* ➡ *11 rooms, 1 cottage* ⚷ *In-room: kitchen (some), refrigerator (some). In-hotel: Wi-Fi, parking (free), some pets allowed, no kids under 12 (some), no-smoking rooms* ⊟ *AE, D, MC, V* ⍟ *BP.*

$$$–$$$$ ⊠**Gastonian.** Many of the rooms in this atmospheric inn,
★ built in 1868, underwent an extensive remodeling in 2008. Fresh flowers throughout and the outdoor covered arbor are unexpected pleasures. Guest rooms are decorated with a mix of funky finds and antiques from the Georgian and Regency periods; all have fireplaces, and most have whirlpool tubs. In a second building, identical to the main house, where the dining and socializing go on, the Lafayette room has the most noteworthy fireplace; the Caracalla Suite is named for the oversize whirlpool tub built in front of its fireplace; the Low room has a private wrought-iron balcony looking out on the treetops. At breakfast you can have such hot entrées as omelets with creamed spinach and goat cheese. Afternoon tea, complimentary wine with cheese and hors d'oeuvres, and evening cordials are among the treats. **Pros:** Many rooms and suites are exceptionally spacious; the handsome and quiet Eli Whitney room is one of the least expensive; cordial and caring staff. **Cons:** Accommodations on the third floor are a hike; some of the furnishings are less than regal. ✉ *220 E. Gaston St., Historic District* ☎ *912/232–2869 or 800/322–6603* ⊕ *www. gastonian.com* ➡ *14 rooms, 3 suites* ⚷ *In-room: DVD, Wi-Fi. In-hotel: Wi-Fi, parking (free), no kids under 12, no-smoking rooms* ⊟ *AE, D, MC, V* ⍟ *BP.*

$$–$$$ ⊠**Green Palm Inn.** This inn is a pleasing little discovery. Originally built in 1897 but renovated top to bottom, it's now a delightful B&B. The elegant furnishings of the cottage-style rooms were inspired by Savannah's British-colonial heritage. All rooms have fireplaces, and a couple even have fireplaces in the bathrooms. Breakfasts are generous and served with style, and in the evening, you'll be

treated to homemade desserts. **Pros:** Spacious rooms with high ceilings; innkeeper is knowledgeable about Savannah's history; quiet location with a garden patio. **Cons:** Four blocks to the river, not as conveniently located as some. ⊠*548 E. President St., Historic District* ☎*912/447–8901 or 888/606–9510* ⊕*www.greenpalminn.com* ↪*4 suites* ⌂*In-room: refrigerator, Wi-Fi. In-hotel: parking (free), no kids under 14, no-smoking rooms* ⊟*AE, MC, V, D* ⊚|*BP.*

$$$–$$$$ 🖫**Hamilton-Turner Inn.** This French-Empire mansion is cel-
★ ebrated, if not in song, certainly in story. It was built ostentatiously in 1873 by Samuel Hamilton, Savannah's mayor (who made a *little* money as a blockade runner during the Civil War). By the 1990s, it was the crash pad for Joe Odom in *Midnight in the Garden of Good and Evil.* It was rescued from further ignominy in 1997 by a wealthy Savannah couple, who did the initial restoration. In 2006, new owners Gay and Jim Dunlop sank their money into a massive, two-year restoration. It certainly has a "wow" effect, especially the rooms that front Lafayette Square. The original arched doors are some 15 feet tall; the bathrooms are the size of a New York City apartment. The Dunlops strive for perfection, and the Southern mansion breakfast has baked items such as scones and hot entrées like perfect eggs Benedict. The afternoon reception features quality wine and both hot and cold hors d'oeuvres. **Pros:** CD players with CDs in rooms and free DVD library; the carriage house is the most private room, though not as atmospheric; pets are allowed in brick-walled, ground-level rooms ($50 deposit). **Cons:** Sedate and not for young kids or party types; no guest elevator (except for accessible room 201) and some rooms are on the fourth floor; no private parking (two-day street pass costs $8). ⊠*330 Abercorn St., Historic District* ☎*912/233–1833 or 888/448–8849* ⊕*www. hamilton-turnerinn.com* ↪*11 rooms, 6 suites* ⌂*In-room: refrigerator (some), DVD, Internet, Wi-Fi. In-hotel: Wi-Fi, some pets allowed, no kids under 12, no-smoking rooms* ⊟*AE, D, MC, V* ⊚|*BP.*

$$ 🖫**Hampton Inn & Suites.** This hotel was built in 2004, and it exceeds expectations for a mid-range chain. Everything still looks nearly new, and there's even a bank of public computers in the lobby near the concierge (which is also unusual for a limited-service hotel such as this). The rooms and particularly the suites (studios and one-bedrooms with fully equipped kitchenettes) are a good value. The beds have nice, soft linens. There is an adjacent parking lot and a small swimming pool but, alas, no restaurant or bar. **Pros:**

Much to choose from at the serve-yourself, hot breakfast bar; everything is still spiffy and clean; studio suites are only about $10 more than a regular room. **Cons:** Make sure not to get the suite next to the noisy boiler; parking is not free; Martin Luther King Boulevard location is not as good as others downtown. ⊠ *201 Martin Luther King Blvd., Historic District* ☎ *912/721–1600 or 800/426–7866* ⊕ *www.hamptoninn.com* 🛏 *124 rooms, 30 suites* ⚐ *In-room: kitchen (some), refrigerator (some), Internet (some), Wi-Fi (some). In-hotel: pool, laundry service, Internet terminal, Wi-Fi, parking (paid), no-smoking rooms* ☰ *AE, D, DC, MC, V* ☯ ❍ *BP.*

$$–$$$ 🏨 **Hampton Inn Historic District.** You may be amazed by this midpriced chain hotel, when you are immediately taken in by the antique heart pine floors that extend the length of the lobby of this former cotton warehouse. A long expanse of glass overlooks Bay Street, and there are strategically placed antiques, a vintage bar, front desk, *and* a concierge desk. Well located and directly across the street from its newer sister property, a Holiday Inn Express, the hotel was completely renovated in 2008 and early 2009. Rooms were upgraded, bathrooms gutted, and everything is just as contemporary as its sister. The hotel is very child-friendly, and you will often see troops of Girl Scouts headed to the former home of Juliette Low, the Girl Scouts' founder. **Pros:** Cushy bedding with nice duvet; a rooftop pool; friendly staff. **Cons:** Pool and deck are quite plain and not high enough for river views; public Wi-Fi but no public computers, though guests may use the ones at the nearby Holiday Inn Express. ⊠ *201 E. Bay St., Historic District* ☎ *912/231–9700 or 800/576–4945* ⊕ *www.hamptoninn. com* 🛏 *144 rooms* ⚐ *In-room: safe (some), refrigerator (some), DVD (some), Internet. In-hotel: bar, pool, gym, laundry service, Wi-Fi, parking (paid), no-smoking rooms* ☰ *AE, D, DC, MC, V* ❍ *CP.*

$–$$ 🏨 **Holiday Inn Express Historic District.** This hotel may change
★ your perception of what is generally thought of as a modest, limited-service chain, with no notable atmosphere. Since all buildings in the historic district must conform to the local charm, Holiday Inn went all out, creating a handsome interior design in the public spaces, with tasteful animal-print settees, leather club chairs, fireplaces, and classy chandeliers. Guest rooms, especially the deluxe ones on the concierge level, are particularly impressive. Done in a taupe palate with textured walls, they have wet bars, contemporary designer bathrooms, flat-screen TVs,

and microwaves. Along with luxury bedding, furnishings throughout the floors are tasteful with a minimalist appeal, not the prepackaged look you might expect. Plus, everything has a spiffy, new feeling, since the hotel just opened in 2008. The rooftop swimming pool has polka-dot market umbrellas, a shade gazebo, and fabulous river views. **Pros:** A bank of public computers; strong Wi-Fi throughout; exceptionally soundproof rooms. **Cons:** Not the more refined clientele you'd find in an upscale B&B; rates are higher than most Holiday Inn Express properties; some front-desk personnel are not polished professionals (though they are all hospitable). ✉ *199 E. Bay St., Historic District* ☎ *912/231–9000 or 888/231–9006* ⊕ *www.ichotelsgroup. com* ⤸ *143 rooms, 3 two-bedroom suites* ⚐ *In-room: safe (some), kitchen (some), refrigerator, DVD (some), Internet, Wi-Fi. In-hotel: bar, pool, gym, laundry service, Internet terminal, Wi-Fi, parking (fee), no-smoking rooms* ▤ *AE, D, DC, MC, V* ⦿ *BP.*

$$$–$$$$ ▧ **Hyatt Regency Savannah.** This is a study in modernity amid the history of Factors Walk: the seven-story structure, built in 1981, has marble floors as well as the Hyatt trademarks from that era, including glass elevators and a towering atrium. Rooms have balconies overlooking either the atrium or the Savannah River. Yes, there is a significant up-charge for river views, but, particularly by night, they're priceless. The contemporary decor, including large leather club chairs, working desk and ergonomic chair, and flat-screen TV, is attractive. The Vu Lounge is an appealing spot to have a drink and watch the river traffic drift by. Windows Restaurant serves breakfast and lunch—both a buffet and à la carte. The client mix is about 50% groups, the other half leisure and business travelers, particularly on weekends. **Pros:** The indoor heated pool has views of the river and Factors Walk; strong professional management and well-trained staff. **Cons:** Valet parking and Wi-Fi are both very expensive; bathrooms and popcorn ceilings were not redone when hotel was last renovated; many large groups. ✉ *2 W. Bay St., Historic District* ☎ *912/238–1234 or 800/233–1234* ⊕ *www.savannah. hyatt.com* ⤸ *325 rooms, 22 suites* ⚐ *In-room: safe, Wi-Fi. In-hotel: restaurant, room service, bar, pool, gym, Wi-Fi, no-smoking rooms* ▤ *AE, D, MC, V* ⦿ *EP.*

$$$$ ▧ **Kehoe House.** Originally the family manse of William
★   Kehoe, this house dating from the 1890s is now a handsomely appointed B&B, one of the better choices in Savannah. The Victorian charmer has brass-and-marble

chandeliers, a courtyard garden, and a music room with a baby grand piano. Guest rooms have a decidedly Victorian feel with a mix of antiques and gilt mirrors. The beds are dressed in contemporary, fine linens. On the main floor, a double parlor houses two fireplaces and sweeps the eye upward with its 14-foot ceilings, creating an elegant setting for a beautifully served, full gourmet breakfast. Guests enjoy afternoon tea and desserts, as well as a wine and hors d'oeuvres reception. Rates include access to the Downtown Athletic Club. **Pros:** Popular wedding and anniversary venue; the Mercer room (the best accommodation) has private verandas; B&B is wheelchair accessible, with two elevators. **Cons:** Only one king or queen bed per room; some details, including headboards and Victorian art, are not appealing; a few rooms have the sink and shower in the room, separated by drapes. ✉*123 Habersham St., Historic District* ☎*912/232–1020 or 800/820–1020* ⊕*www.kehoe house.com* ➪*13 rooms* ☆*In-room: DVD, Wi-Fi. In-hotel: Internet terminal, Wi-Fi, parking (free), no kids under 12, no-smoking rooms* ☰*AE, D, MC, V* ⊚|*BP.*

★ FodorsChoice ⊠**Mansion on Forsyth Park.** Sophisticated, chic, and
$$$$ artsy only begin to describe this Kessler property. The newer wings blend perfectly with its historic surroundings and the original, 18,000 square-foot Victorian-Romanesque, redbrick and terra cotta mansion. Sitting on the edge of Forsyth Park, its dramatic design, opulent interiors with a contemporary edge, and magnificently diverse collection of some 400 pieces of American and European art create a one-of-a-kind experience. Every turn delivers something unexpected—the antique hat collection; the pool with its creative water wall, and a canopied patio that looks like it's out of *Arabian Nights*; a Nordic-looking, full-service spa; back-lighted onyx panels and 100-year-old Italian Corona–marble pillars. The 700 Drayton Restaurant offers contemporary fine dining and professional, attentive service. Upstairs, Casimir's Lounge, with live piano and jazz, is one of the city's hot spots. **Pros:** No real breakfast, but Starbuck's coffee, pastries, and bagels are gratis in the Bosendorfer Lounge every morning; an exciting, stimulating environment that transports you from the workaday world; complimentary Lincoln Town Car and driver (limited). **Cons:** Very pricey, particularly for room service and phone calls; some of the art from the early 1970s is not appealing. ✉*700 Drayton St., Historic District* ☎*912/238–5158 or 888/711–5114* ⊕*www.mansiononforsythpark.com* ➪*126 rooms* ☆*In-room: safe, Internet, Wi-Fi. In-hotel: restaurant,*

room service, bars, spa, Internet terminal, Wi-Fi, parking (paid), no-smoking rooms ⊟*AE, D, DC, MC, V* ⃝*EP.*

$$$ 🖼**Marshall House.** This restored hotel, with original pine floors, woodwork, and exposed brick, caters to business travelers, as well as families, yet it provides the intimacy of a B&B. A second major renovation finished in winter 2008 has made a marked difference in the guest rooms, which are now nearly swank. Rooms with their own wrought-iron balconies, which overlook the street, are decidedly the best. Some bathrooms have a bear-claw tub and traditional shower, as well as a separate modern shower. Flat-screen cable TV is a welcome, contemporary touch; working desks are appreciated. The lobby segues into the bar and then into 45 Bistro—both are separate management but an integral part of the inn's experience. Different spaces reflect different parts of Savannah's history, from its founding to the Civil War. Artwork is mostly by local artists. A full breakfast is offered in the lovely atrium. **Pros:** Great location near stores and restaurants; exceptional restaurant on-site; guests get free passes to a downtown health club. **Cons:** No free parking; no room service; facade has somewhat of an urban motel appearance. ✉*123 E. Broughton St., Historic District* ☎*912/644–7896 or 800/589–6304* ⊕*www.marshallhouse. com* ➷*65 rooms, 3 suites* ⌂*In-room: safe, refrigerator, Internet. In-hotel: restaurant, bar, Wi-Fi, parking (paid), no-smoking rooms* ⊟ *AE, D, DC, MC, V* ⃝*BP.*

$$–$$$ 🖼**Mulberry Inn.** Everyone knows this 1860s landmark, with a white-painted brick facade and forest-green awnings, that was once a livery stable, then a cotton warehouse, and then a Coca-Cola bottling plant. Gleaming heart-pine floors and antiques, including a handsome English grandfather clock and an exquisitely carved Victorian mantel, make it unique. The pianist hitting the keyboard of a baby grand every afternoon adds to the elegant flair. The café is a notch nicer than most others of its class. An executive wing, at the back of the hotel is geared to business travelers. **Pros:** Room service; nice high tea; good, caring service translates to repeat clientele. **Cons:** No free parking; in a quiet but transitional neighborhood near some housing projects. ✉*601 E. Bay St., Historic District* ☎*912/238–1200 or 877/468–1200* ⊕*www.savannahhotel.com* ➷*145 rooms, 24 suites* ⌂*In-room: Internet. In-hotel: 2 restaurants, room service, bar, pool, gym, Wi-Fi* ⊟*AE, D, DC, MC, V* ⃝*EP.*

$–$$ 🖼**Olde Harbour Inn.** This inn, dating from 1892 and smack on the river, tries hard to please even if it doesn't always hit the heights. Nevertheless, it's a good option for longer stays, for families (even with pets), and for those who want to be near the action of River Street. Located between River Street and the cobblestone Factors Walk, this is an all-suites property. The two-bedroom loft suites are a definite thumbs-up. Bathrooms and kitchenettes are circa-1980s but recently spiffed up. Decor is big on florals and patterns with reproduction four-poster beds, giving it a homey, residential quality. Meet other guests at the nightly wine-and-cheese reception. **Pros:** Hearty breakfast with meats, quiches, and more; keen on security as far as locks and lights in parking lot; all suites have views of river. **Cons:** Not luxurious at all; location has some negatives, including nearby hard-party crowds. ✉508 E. Factors Walk, Historic District ☎912/234-4100 or 800/553-6533 ⊕www.oldeharbourinn.com ⌕24 rooms ⌂In-room: safe, kitchen, DVD (some), Wi-Fi. In-hotel: Internet terminal, Wi-Fi, parking (paid), some pets allowed, no-smoking rooms ⊟AE, D, MC, V ⌶◎BP.

$$-$$$ ⊠**Planters Inn.** Formerly the John Wesley Hotel, this inn is housed in a structure built in 1812; the lobby retains the regal tone of a bygone golden age with classical music adding to the ambience. This inn has the service and the charisma of a landmark Savannah property, yet with an elevator. Guest rooms are decorated with fine fabrics and Baker furnishings (a 1920s design named for the Dutch immigrant cabinetmaker). Breakfast is quite good, including eggs, yogurt, fresh fruit, and warm Danish. The evening reception with cheese, fruit, and good wine is a nightly house party, where the concierge introduces fellow guests, a good cross-section of leisure and business travelers, including many repeats. Either a mini-refrigerator or microwave can be rented for $15 a day. Guests are asked (with a wink) not to disturb the friendly ghost who reputedly inhabits the hotel. The best rooms overlook Reynolds Square. **Pros:** Management and key staffers truly make you feel at home; great architectural details in the lobby, notably the ceiling; convenient location near the Olde Pink House. **Cons:** Decor and bathrooms were last redone in 1984 and could benefit from an update; no public computers; no voice mail on room phones. ✉29 Abercorn St., Historic District ☎912/232-5678 ⊕www.plantersinnsavannah.com ⌕60 rooms ⌂In-room: safe, Wi-Fi (some). In-hotel: laundry service, Wi-Fi, parking (paid), no-smoking rooms ⊟AE, D, MC, V ◎CP.

$$$-$$$$ ⊠**The President's Quarters.** You'll be impressed even before you enter this lovely inn, which has an exterior courtyard

so beautiful and inviting it has become a popular wedding-reception spot. Each room in this classic Savannah inn, fashioned out of a pair of meticulously restored 1860s town houses, is named for an American president. Some have four-poster beds, working fireplaces, and private balconies. Expect to be greeted with wine and fruit and tempted by a complimentary afternoon tea with sweet cakes. Turndown service includes a glass of port or sherry. There are also rooms in an adjacent town house. **Pros:** Private parking and private entrances; romantic atmosphere; in-room Jacuzzis. **Cons:** Inn books up fast in spite of ghost rumors; location is not as good as some others. ✉225 E. President St., Historic District ☎912/233–1600 or 800/233–1776 ⊕www. presidentsquarters.com ➷11 rooms, 8 suites ⌂In-room: Wi-Fi. In-hotel: Wi-Fi, parking (free), no kids under 12, no-smoking rooms ▤D, DC, MC, V ⧄BP.

$$$–$$$$ ▣ **River Street Inn.** The interior of this 1817 converted warehouse has a harbor-from-yesteryear theme, with murals and model schooners; the five-story building once stood vacant in a state of disrepair. Formerly storerooms, the guest rooms are filled with antiques and reproductions from the era of King Cotton. French-style balconies overlook both River Street and Bay Street, and many rooms face the river itself. The elevator takes you directly down to the buzz and activity of the waterfront. There are two restaurants within the building, but they do not belong to the hotel. **Pros:** Packages available; hotel is wheelchair accessible; wine and cheese are laid out every evening. **Cons:** Hotel could use a major renovation to bring it from its original conversion to today's expectations; no breakfast included; no private parking (city garage across the street). ✉124 E. Bay St., Historic District ☎912/234–6400 or 800/253–4229 ⊕www.riverstreetinn. com ➷86 rooms ⌂In-room: safe, Wi-Fi. In-hotel: bar, gym, Wi-Fi ▤AE, D, MC, V ⧄EP.

$$–$$$ ▣ **Savannah Marriott Riverfront.** One of the few high-rise hotels in Savannah—and the major anchor of the Riverwalk—the Marriott delivers on all its trademark standards. The professional management and friendly staffers mean the hotel is geared for business, even if it still has some resort amenities. The views from riverfront rooms with balconies ($20 more) are truly magical at night. Service is elevated on the concierge level, which offers a complimentary breakfast and continuous coffee service but, alas, no wine or other alcohol. The handsome suites are among the recently renovated, but "suite" may be an embellishment since the bedroom is just separated by a partition. At this writing,

all rooms were expected to be renovated by spring 2009.
Pros: Marriott's River Walk with its wrought-iron railings
and outdoor seating is atmospheric; two pools (indoor and
outdoor); great spa. **Cons:** If there is a major convention
in-house, it dominates the main floor, limiting access to the
indoor pool; the hotel is a fair walk to the hot spots up
on River Street; pedicabs can't come here on the cobblestones. ✉ *100 General McIntosh Blvd., Historic District*
☎ *912/233–7722 or 800/285–0398* ⊕ *www.marriott.com*
🛏 *391 rooms, 46 suites* 🔸 *In-room: safe, kitchen (some),
refrigerator (some), DVD (some), Internet (some), Wi-Fi.
In-hotel: 2 restaurants, room service, bar, pools, gym, spa,
laundry service, Internet terminal, Wi-Fi, parking (paid),
no-smoking rooms* ☰ *AE, D, MC, V* ⊚ *EP.*

★ Fodor'sChoice ▦ **The Stephen Williams House.** Although named
$$ for its builder, this house was constructed for the honor-
able Mayor (six terms) William Thorn Williams in 1834.
This wonderful Federal-style mansion is now owned by
an equally exceptional, retired physician, Dr. Albert Wall.
Savannah-born, an inveterate storyteller, lover of history,
antique collector, and survivor of seven historic preserva-
tion projects, he was determined to save this house, which
had become one sad derelict. The sumptuous suite has an
entirely separate parlor and a draped bed. The less-expen-
sive garden rooms, which share a bath, are characterized
by beamed ceilings and exposed brick walls that open out
to the restored garden and walled courtyard with its lion's
head fountain. Dr. Wall has a deep affection for his city
and as he pours morning coffee for his guests, he suggests
his favorite things in Savannah for them to do and can
arrange for bicycles to be delivered. The hotel is a superb
wedding venue. **Pros:** Elegant furnishings (a 45-year col-
lection of period antiques, some museum quality, some
for sale); full Southern breakfast made from old Savannah
recipes; beds triple-sheeted with Frette linens and choice
of down pillows. **Cons:** Occasional plumbing problems as
befits an aged manse; no wine and hors d'oeuvres reception
in the evening; rooms facing Liberty Street catch the bus
and traffic noise. ✉ *128 W. Liberty St., Historic District*
☎ *912/495–0032* ⊕ *www.thestephenwilliamshouse.com* 🛏 *4
rooms, 1 suite* 🔸 *In-room: Wi-Fi. In-hotel: laundry service,
Wi-Fi, parking (free), no kids under 12, no-smoking rooms*
☰ *AE, D, MC, V* ⊚ *BP.*

$$$–$$$$ ▦ **The Zeigler House Inn.** This urban mansion on one of the
★ city's most desirable brick-paved streets will have you fan-
tasizing about living in such a place, just like the city's

upper crust. Owner Jackie Heinz came from Atlanta for a weekend and put in an offer to buy the house before she left. It is her home now, and her taste is admirable, from the hanging baskets of rare flowers to the chocolate brown ceilings in the main parlors that make the white ceiling medallions look like art. You can tap into Savannah's good life and have a romantic stay in a beautifully appointed room or, better yet, a suite with contemporary style juxtaposed with antiques, a custom-made king bed, and fine bedding. Jackie has a unique way of handling breakfast. Each room has a kitchenette or full kitchen with a coffeemaker; she stocks the fridge with juice and milk and bakes delectable pastries daily that she leaves for breakfast. A professional chef, she can prepare a gourmet, multicourse dinner for guests upon request. **Pros:** The privilege of being in such a lovable home; a stocked kitchen makes you feel like you really live here; lovely slate fireplaces and heart-pine floors and staircase. **Cons:** Garden-level rooms have a subterranean feel; not a full-service hotel; no full, hot breakfast. ⊠*121 W. Jones St., Historic District* ☎*912/233–5307 or 866/233–5307* ⊕*www.zieglerhouseinn.com* ⇨*4 rooms, 2 suites* ⚹*In-room: no phone, kitchen (some), refrigerator, DVD, Wi-Fi. In-hotel: Wi-Fi, parking (free), no kids under 12, no-smoking rooms* ☰*AE, MC, V* ⚏*CP.*

ELSEWHERE IN SAVANNAH

¢–$ ⛬**Oglethorpe Inn & Suites.** A nearly complete makeover in 2007 turned a nondescript motel into a new player, providing a viable midtown alternative for budget travelers, families, and business travelers. This modern white- and redbrick building has been gentrified with green awnings and shutters. It is easily reached I–95 and I–16. And as prices escalate in all the downtown properties, it can mean the difference between going to Savannah or not, especially for families. The benefits include free parking, a swimming pool, a fitness center, a Continental (plus) breakfast, free Wi-Fi, and an all-suites configuration. The six corner executive suites have doors (not just partitions) between the rooms and two TVs. Don't be surprised to see a small troop of Girl Scouts clad in green and carrying cookies; budget-minded properties in Savannah usually draw hordes of them. **Pros:** Trolley package includes trolley tour and free transportation to and from downtown for only $10 more; two lobby computers and a printer. **Cons:** For all the pluses, you still are not downtown; no in-house restaurant or bar (though there are dozens nearby), not the sophisticated clientele you get at the expensive B&Bs. ✉*7110 Hodgson Memorial Dr., Midtown* ☎*912/354–8560* ⊕*www.savannah suitehotel.com* ⇌*46 suites, 6 executive suites* ⌂*In-room: kitchen, refrigerator, Wi-Fi. In-hotel: pool, gym, laundry service, Internet terminal, Wi-Fi, parking (free), no-smoking rooms* ▭*AE, D, DC, MC, V* ⊙*CP.*

$$$$ 🏨**Westin Savannah Harbor Golf Resort & Spa.** Within its own fiefdom, this major high-rise property lords it over small Hutchinson Island, five minutes by water taxi from Factors Walk. It has more resort amenities than any other property in the area, including tennis courts, and most importantly, a golf course. Its professional, full-service spa is affiliated with the Greenbrier's in West Virginia. The island's adjacent Savannah International Convention Center is what keeps the hotel at high occupancy levels almost year-round, since many meeting attendees stay here; leisure guests predominate on the weekends. The lobby is swanky and upscale, but the hotel is undergoing a major renovation at this writing that should be complete by spring 2009. The Savannah Harbor Golf Course is open to the public and is the best bet for golfers staying in the Historic District. The island's ferries or water taxis dock at the Savannah Belles Ferry Dock in front of the Hyatt Regency. The first one departs from the hotel at 7 AM; scheduled runs are every 20 minutes, with the last one leaving downtown at midnight. If you miss the last ferry, you can still take a water taxi for about $7. **Pros:** Dreamy bedding; outdoor pool is heated; rooms can come with Pilates and fitness equipment for an extra charge. **Cons:** You are close, but still removed, from downtown; this is a major chain hotel, not an atmospheric, historic inn; hotel charges an expensive and annoying resort fee. ✉*1 Resort Dr., Hutchinson Island* ☎*912/201–2000* ⊕*www. westinsavannah.com* ⇌*390 rooms, 13 suites* ⌂*In-room: safe (some), kitchen (some), refrigerator, Wi-Fi. In-hotel: 2 restaurants, room service, bars, golf course, tennis courts, pool, gym, spa, children's programs (ages 4–12), laundry service, Internet terminal, Wi-Fi, parking (free), some pets allowed, no-smoking rooms* ▭*AE, D, MC, V* ⊙*EP.*

TYBEE ISLAND

If renting a 5-star beach house, a pastel island cottage, or a waterfront condo in a complex with a pool and tennis courts is more your Tybee dream, check out **Tybee Vacation Rentals** (✉*1010 Hwy. 80 E, Tybee Island* ☎*912/786–5853*

Additional Hotel Choices

There's simply not room to recommend all the good hotels, motels, inns, and B&Bs in Savannah. Below are a few more recommendations. And if you are just looking for a reliable chain hotel, consider the Hilton Garden Inn, Sheraton Four Points, Homewood Suites, Extended Stay, or Doubletree Suites.

Courtyard by Marriott Savannah Midtown (✉6703 Abercorn St., at Chatham Square, Historic District ☎912/354–7878 or 800/321–2211 ⊕www.marriott. com) has a good location. And for a mid-range chain, it has a good reputation for service. Pluses include an outdoor pool, free outdoor parking, and suites that include a wet bar, refrigerator, and microwave. You can get a package that includes breakfast. $–$$.

The **Hilton Savannah Desoto** (✉15 E. Liberty St., Historic District ☎912/232–9000 or 800/426–8483 ⊕www.desoto-hilton.com) is not the original grand hotel of the same name, which was a local landmark. Hilton constructed this 15-floor hotel in 1968 in the same desirable location. At this writing it is undergoing a complete reno-

vation of its public spaces and rooms, which is expected to be completed in early 2009. $$.

Inn at Ellis Square (✉201 W. Bay St., Historic District ☎912/236–4440 ⊕www.in-natellissquare.com) is a modest, moderately priced inn with an excellent location a whistlestop away from River Street. It is one of the best of the Days Hotel chain. A mid-rise property, its rooms are popular with Europeans and all have similar costs, so ask for a high-floor room with a view. Breakfast is included. $–$$.

Staybridge Suites (✉301 E. Bay St., Historic District ☎912/721–9000 ⊕www.staybridgesuites.com) has a great downtown location. Rates include Continental breakfast and a great gym. It's not cheap, but all rooms are suites. $$.

Suites on Lafayette (✉201 E. Charlton St., Lafayette Sq., Historic District ☎912/ 233–7815 or 866/578–4837 ⊕ www. suitesonlafayette.com) is ideally situated. Though intended for extended stays, you can stay a shorter period in the off-season for a reasonable price. Kitchens are large and fully equipped, though furnishings are not all wonderful. $–$$.

---

or 866/359–0297 ⊕*www.tybeevacationrentals.com*). This family-owned business has grown because the managers are so friendly and accommodating, and they now represent some 130 rentals. At the main rental office, you can use their computers or Wi-Fi to get online, and there's a machine that rents DVDs 24 hours a day. Expect to pay $600 for a three-night stay (minimum) for a one-bedroom condo.

A SIDE OF TYBEE ALMOST GONE. You may hear some wild stories about Tybee Island: that it is a hideout, a veritable Margaritaville, a kitschy resort area right out of the 1950s; the truth is that it is getting more upscale with each passing year. However, if you want to keep in the traditional Tybee spirit, check out the **Atlantis Inn** (⊕*www.atlantisinntybee.com*), which can be a big hoot if you are in the right mood.

$$-$$$ 🏠 **Lighthouse Inn.** This yellow-and-white frame house is a quiet getaway, a place to unplug and renew, to sit on the front porch and make the rocker creak while waiting for the sun to drop. There are absolutely no pretentions here, no airs, just the salt breeze. Tucked away on a lovely, residential street it is just minutes from a magnificent beach and the Tybee Lighthouse. Birders come with their binoculars and log books since it is so close to the national wildlife refuge. Each of the rooms is tastefully—not overly—decorated with appealing original art and overlooks the treetops. It is operated by the owners in residence, Susie and Stuart, who require a two-night minimum stay. **Pros:** Stuart's lovely breakfast entrées, which include spinach quiche, fresh fruit, and more; complimentary wine, beer, and sometimes cheese in the evenings. **Cons:** No water views; it is a relatively small, close environment; house rules are strictly enforced. ✉*16 Meddin Dr., Tybee Island* ☎*912/786–0901 or 866/786–0901* ⊕*www.tybeebb.com* 🛏*3 rooms* &In-room: no phone, refrigerator, DVD, Wi-Fi. In-hotel: Internet terminal, Wi-Fi, parking (free), no kids under 12, no-smoking rooms* ⊟ *MC, V* ⊚|*BP.*

$-$$ 🏠 **17th Street Inn.** You're steps from the beach at this Tybee Island inn dating from 1920. The front deck, adorned with plants, palms, and swings, is a gathering place where you can chat, sip wine, and enjoy breakfast. The inn's rooms each have a queen-size iron bed with designer comforters and quilts, efficiency kitchen, private bath, and private entrance. Unfortunately, there are no water views. **Pros: Cons:** ✉*12 17th St., Tybee Island* ☎*912/786–0607 or 888/909–0607* ⊕*www.tybeeinn.com* 🛏*8 rooms, 1 condo* &*In-room: no phone, kitchen. In-hotel: Wi-Fi* ⊟*AE, D, MC, V* ⊚|*EP.*

Nightlife & the Arts

WORD OF MOUTH

"[W]e went on the Haunted Pub Tour with our guide Greg and the experience was hilarious, entertaining & just the slightest bit scary. . . . After the Haunted Pub Crawl, we walked over to Jazz'd Tapas Bar in City Market to have dinner and enjoy some local music. We were really impressed with the quality of the jazz."

—Imoneylsauce

Updated
by Eileen
Robinson
Smith

SAVANNAH IS LIKE A MINI-NEW ORLEANS in its glory days. Appealing to a wide variety of ages and income levels, the nightlife in Savannah gives visitors an ideal way to get a feel for the Southern city on the move. Savannah's nightlife also reflects the city's laid-back personality. Some clubs have live reggae, hard rock, and other contemporary music, but most stick to traditional blues, jazz, and piano-bar vocalists. After-dark merrymakers usually head for watering holes on Riverfront Plaza or the Southside. Fine restaurants not only offer some superior culinary options, but their bars serve up the latest in creative martinis, cosmos, margaritas, and single-malt Scotches, and many offer live entertainment on weekend nights.

River Street may feel a bit like Bourbon Street, where you can walk with your drinks and where the bars stay open late. Smoking is still allowed at the bars, too. Savannah has a lively gay scene, but you may just as likely see straight people there dancing the night away. Make no mistake, this is a party town. After dark there's an abundance of fun. If you don't drink, you can simply stroll and people-watch along the touristy Factors Walk. Don't hesitate to venture off to the vast grid of squares and narrow streets of downtown to seek more local-oriented bars and clubs; it's hard to get lost here.

FREE FUN. Who said the best things in life aren't free? Certainly not the organizers of Savannah's many free summer concerts or the Savannah Jazz Festival in Forsyth Park each September. Why, even the downtown buses are free.

THE ARTS

FESTIVALS & SPECIAL EVENTS

Savannah is a festival kind of town, a party town that supports various festivals (in fact, many are free or nearly so).

The **Savannah Film Festival** (⊕*www.scad.edu*) is the creative brainchild of the Savannah School of Art & Design. Held annually in late October or early November, it is an independent film festival with nightly screenings showing flicks that the residents of a midsize Southern city would never see otherwise. Some 50 films are chosen from 600 entries from around the world. There are parties and gala affairs during the festival, even a black-tie block party for

NIGHTLIFE TIPS

■ **Stay in on Sunday Night.** Most bars and clubs are closed on Sunday. It's almost as if someone pulled the plug. And it's just as difficult to find a restaurant. If a place is open, know that it will almost for sure be closing at 10 o'clock. Monday is not much better.

■ **Smoking Alert.** Savannah is one of the last bastions of smoking, and you can smoke in almost all of the bars and restaurants, though some restrictions may apply in restaurants. Some don't allow smoking until after 10 PM. At restaurants that have outdoor seating, smoking is usually allowed outside at any time. The law is complicated, but no one under 18 is supposed to be in the bar area when smoking is allowed (including young employees). Some family-oriented chain restaurants don't allow smoking at all.

■ **Drinking on the Street is Allowed.** You can walk the streets and drink at the same time, just like in New Orleans. Barkeeps have a supply of plastic glasses on hand, and you can just tell them you want your cocktail "to go." However, you still cannot drink in your car; Georgia does have an open-container law.

■ **Don't Forget Restaurants.** Those restaurants that have live entertainment can be excellent places to go after dinner as well. And they often attract more high-end patrons than regular bars.

opening night, where you can meet the filmmakers. The restored Lucas Theater is just one of the many venues. In 2007, Michael Douglas attended, along with his wife Catherine Zeta-Jones, to accept that year's lifetime achievement award. The Redgrave sisters, Vanessa and Lynn, have also attended.

For three days in mid-October (usually the second weekend) the free **Savannah Folk Music Festival** (⊕*www.savannahfolk. org*) becomes the city's main musical attraction.

The **Savannah Jazz Festival** (⊕*www.savannahjazzfestival.org*) is a free event held each September in Forsyth Park featuring artists from around the region. The September weather is ideal, as is the ambience of the park setting.

★ Fodor'sChoice Georgia's largest and most acclaimed music festival, the **Savannah Music Festival** (⊕*www.savannahmusic festival.org*) begins on infamous St. Patrick's Day weekend and runs for 18 days, with four to six performances daily at some 20 downtown venues. The music ranges from foot-stomping gospel to mournful blues to frenetic Cajun zydeco. It is one of the most diverse festivals as venues range from honky-tonks to cavernous, beer-drinking dance halls—where you can listen to bluegrass, rock, funk, or contemporary jazz—on up to high-brow, modern classical and inspirational concerts in the elevated environments of the Telfair Museum. It is a fun, celebratory time to be in Savannah.

Savannah's **St. Patrick's Day Parade** (⊕*www.savannahsaint patricksday.com*) is Savannah's Mac Daddy of annual festivals. Savannah's large influx of Irish immigrants, some 180 years ago, means a lot of local Irish pride. This parade has evolved into one of the largest in the country. In 2008, some 700,000 parade participants and partygoers participated. As the revelers descend on River Street that March weekend, it is a sea of green—everything from the beer, the water in the fountains, the mashed potatoes, the grits, the hair, even the dog. Hotel rates during this period can be as much as three times the norm, that is if you can get a room (most are reserved a year in advance).

WATCH YOUR BACK. **Regrettably, street crime and muggings are on the rise in Savannah. While you can still enjoy yourself at night, it's important to exercise a certain amount of caution, as you would in any big city. When out and about at night, there is safety in numbers—make new friends and go around as a group. If you are a party of one, call a pedicab for transportation, especially after 10 PM. Don't carry excess cash, and put your money in several different places. Stay out of the alleys and even the squares late at night. Homeless people and drug-users frequent some of these lovely parks by night.**

VENUES

Johnny Mercer Theater/Savannah Civic Center (✉*301 W. Oglethorpe Ave., Orleans Sq., Historic District* ☎*912/ 651–6556 or 800/351–7469* ⊕*www.savannahcivic.com*) hosts many events and performances throughout the year, the Savannah Music Festival being a prime example. The Savannah Civic Orchestra performs here as well as giving free, city-sponsored concerts in Forsyth Park and on River Street for Fourth of July. This theater and center also features ballet, Broadway plays and musicals, and performances as disparate as the Harlem Globetrotters and the Lipizzaner Stallions. Tickets range from $20 to $100.

Lucas Theater (⊠*216 Broughton St., Historic District* ☎*912/ 525–5050* ⊕*www.lucastheater.com*) opened for the first time in 1921. After a long run, it closed its doors as a theater in 1976, becoming a comedy club and restaurant for the next 13 years, after which it was slated for demolition. After being purchased in 1986 by a local group, it underwent a long renovation process that lasted 13 years. In 2000 it reopened, and SCAD decided to assist and help support the theater. What is fascinating is that this historic landmark now features such cutting-edge performances as sci-fi documentaries, piano recitals, flamenco performances, and country music stars. It is a major venue for the Savannah Film Festival and the Savannah Music Festival.

The **Savannah Theater** (⊠*222 Bull St., at Chippewa Sq., Historic District* ☎*912/233–7764* ⊕*www.savannahtheater. com*) has been dubbed one of the most unique venues in America. At this writing, a musical entitled "The Beat Goes On" features music from the 1950s, '60s, '70s, and '80s. During the holiday season, the musical *A Christmas Tradition* delights families. Tickets for most events are about $35, with discounts for seniors and students.

NIGHTLIFE

BARS & NIGHTCLUBS

The **Bar Bar** (⊠*219 W. St. Julian St., Historic District* ☎*912/ 231–1910*), a neighborhood hangout, has pool tables, games, and a varied beer selection. It is open from Tuesday through Saturday, and on Friday and Saturday nights a DJ keeps 'em up and moving on the dance floor.

While strolling River Street, mosey into **Bernie's Restaurant & Bar** (⊠*115 E. River St., Historic District* ☎*912/236–1827* ⊕*www.berniesriverstreet.com*),in an old cotton warehouse, and try the Lowcountry boil as well as the house specialty, a Mason Jar Bloody Mary. This is a big karaoke venue, so you can sing your heart out just about every night.

★ A relatively new and certainly stellar nightspot **Casimir Lounge** (⊠ *Mansion on Forsyth Park, 700 Drayton St., Historic District* ☎*912/721–5061 or 912/238–5158*) is one of those magical Savannah experiences that you will

The CraftBrew Fest

Savannah's first annual Craft-Brew Fest held on Labor Day Weekend 2008 showcased breweries from the region, 125 brewers in all, including the city's own Moon River Brewery (the name adopted from that famous Johnny Mercer song). The festival was so successful that it is scheduled to become an annual event beginning in 2009.

Brewmasters come from around the region, including some from Atlanta, Athens, Terrapin, as well as from South and North Carolina. Each brewery has its own large white tent set up adjacent to the Savannah International Trade & Convention Center within the Westin Hotel complex on Hutchinson Island. Festival-goers meet the brewers and stay cool with tastings of their wares. Live entertainment keeps things festive. There's a gala dinner on Friday night. On Saturday, America's best craft beers are served at the grand tasting, followed by prix-fixe dinners at several area restaurants.

Clay Nordyke, manager of the local restaurant Blowin' Smoke, which has a separate menu for its craft beers, says: "I like to promote good-tasting craft beers versus the big-name American breweries." Clay adds: "Beer is one of the oldest alcoholic beverages recorded, dating back 9,000 years ago; interestingly, the Chinese are reputed to be the first to make it. It was a rice-based beer—The Dogfish Brewery in Delaware have [sic] obtained that early recipe and are re-creating it."

Check out the festival's Web site (⊕ *www.savannahcraft brewfest.com*) for the dates of the 2009 festival.

treasure. Casimir is not as formal as the lounge at the hotel's restaurant, 700 Drayton, which is downstairs. But its decor is gorgeous, too, with five hand-blown chandeliers in Mardi Gras colors, oversized mirrors, quality artwork, and a Bosendorfer piano. After 5, the bar menu is in effect, which allows you to order from the appetizer menu of the hotel's restaurant. The real draw is the live music that plays on Friday and Saturday nights (and sometimes Thursday or Sunday), beginning about 8:30. Jazz and blues are the norm, with jazz groups like The Chromatics (Sundays), singer Jeff Beasley (very bluesy), and Eat Mo Music, which is an upbeat band playing good dance music, with a vocalist and a man on trumpet.

A gay bar, **Club One Jefferson** (⊠*1 Jefferson St., Historic District* ☎*912/232–0200* ⊕*www.clubone-online.com*) has been dubbed one of the city's best dance clubs by the locals, and the notorious Lady Chablis still does cameo appearances here. She bumps and grinds her way down the catwalk, lip-synching disco tunes in a shimmer of sequins and satin gowns. Drag shows are a feature, but mostly it's a DJ keeping the dancers in motion. There's no cover.

You can catch the latest in athletic competition and racing at the lively and cheering **Coach's Corner Sports Bar** (⊠*3016 E. Victory Dr., Thunderbolt* ☎*912/352–2933*). Watch the action on one or more of the many screens surrounding this classic hang-out. You can order traditional American pub food like burgers, wings, and pizzas. Also, there's free Wi-Fi. This is far removed from the Historic District, some 10 miles from Reynold's Square. You follow Abercorn, take a left on Victory, cross Skidaway, and it is on the left.

Kevin Barry's Irish Pub (⊠*114 W. River St., Historic District* ☎*912/233–9626* ⊕*www.kevinbarrys.com*) has a friendly vibe, a full menu until 1 AM, and traditional Irish music seven days a week (the music generally begins at 8:30). The tiny stage is within the dining room, and you can still hear it in the bar, but from only a couple of stools will you see the Irish crooner. The place has a subterranean, dark feel but offers the promise of good times. It's *the* place to be on St. Patrick's Day, but the challenge is trying to get in. The rest of the year there's a mix of tourists and locals of all ages and the Guinness flows freely.

Molly MacPherson's Scottish Pub & Grill (⊠*311 W. Congress St., Historic District* ☎*912/239–9600*), near city market, is a must-stop destination for Scotch lovers who will find more than 100 single malts to choose from; you can also sample several whiskies in flights. Scottish and American specialties are well prepared; you'll find the typical bangers and mash, salmon, fish-and-chips, etc. During the day Scottish and Irish music is played, on CDs that is. Wednesday is open-mike night, and there are local bands on Friday and Saturday nights playing American rock and folk. Mostly, this is a tourist spot.

Across from the Hyatt Regency, **Moon River Brewing Co.** (⊠*21 W. Bay St., Historic District* ☎*912/447–0943* is one of the area's favorite and famous breweries of craft beer. Suds lovers check out the amazing variety of handcrafted lagers and ales in addition to the imported bottle selections.

You'll be able to choose from a good variety of pub food as well as spirits, and there's a definite fun quotient in the bar, which has a retro feel. There is a real brew master here who monitors the large steel vats of beer that are "working," and which you can see through the glass partition.

Do you like to get down and dirty? Then **Pinkie Masters** (⊠*318 Drayton St., Lafayette Sq., Historic District* ☎*912/238–0447*) may be the place for you. In fact, don't set your purse or coat down or even close to the floor (it can be wet with beer). This dive is a hoot and more so because it is just off swanky Lafayette Square, rather than in a bad neighborhood. But it has been here for decades, before the area was all so beautifully gentrified. Beer is served by the can, simple mixed drinks in plastic cups, and part of the draw is that you never know what you will see on a given night. To say that the bar crowd is diverse would be an understatement. You will see it all, from neighborhood residents dropping in after a black-tie affair to chicks dancing together to rednecks to lone dancers going round and round, spinning in their own little worlds.

★ Fodor'sChoice **Planters Tavern** (⊠*23 Abercorn St., Historic District* ☎*912/232–4286*), in the basement of the Olde Pink House, is one of Savannah's most romantic late-night spots for a nightcap. Intimacy notwithstanding, this is one fun time. Pianist and vocalist Gail Thurmond, who was a fixture here since 1993, has gone on down the road, but her replacements on the piano seat are crowd-pleasers, too. From Thursday through Monday, Downie Mosley, who both lived with and learned from Liberace during the 1970s, is a masterful talent and displays the hand flourishes that his old pal made famous. On Tuesday, Eddie Wilson is the man, and his repertoire includes favorites from Savannah's son Johnny Mercer, Billy Joel, the Beatles, and others. You name it, and he'll do his best to sing and play it. And finally on Wednesday, Diana Rogers can go from cabaret to classical. The decor hasn't changed, and that is part of what makes the scene, especially the stone fireplace and the fox hunt memorabilia.

Savannah Smiles (⊠*314 Williamson St., Historic District* ☎*912/527–6453*) is a dueling piano saloon in which the battles heat up the humor. Patrons are encouraged to participate, and the place promises good fun—though perhaps not for the prudish. Kitchen is open late. It's generally closed on Monday and Tuesday.

Particularly appealing on a chilly, rainy night, **Six Pence Pub** (⌂*245 Bull St., Historic District* ☎*912/233–3151*), feels as if it dates from Colonial times. This is where Julia Roberts caught husband Dennis Quaid cheating in the film *Something to Talk About*. The best of its food offerings is the Shepherd's Pie, washed down with some flavorful ale. Mostly patrons chose from the impressive beer selection and tell stories until the place closes around 1 AM; it is one place that is open Sunday nights. Props like a bobby's cap and a genuine red London phone booth give it British atmosphere. Now if only they could find barmen with a British accent, instead of the gals who ask: "Whadda y'all want to drink?"

Venus de Milo (⌂*38 Martin Luther King Blvd., Historic District* ☎*912/447–0901*) is a late-night club/wine bar as well as an upscale dive. It has a mixed bag of loyal clients, straight and gay, young and old, rich and not so rich. There are also statues of Venus de Milo, as you might have guessed, and little anterooms, one with a bank of couches. Expect anything and everything here, sometimes even a vocalist.

COFFEEHOUSES

Thanks to a substantial student population, the city has sprouted coffeehouses as if they were spring flowers. Tearooms also abound and seem fitting in a city with so many English influences. The **Express** (⌂*39 Barnard St., Historic District* ☎*912/233–4683*) is a warm, unassuming bakery and café that serves specialty coffees along with decadent desserts and tasty snacks.

Gallery Espresso (⌂*234 Bull St., Historic District* ☎*912/233–5348*) is a combined coffee haunt and art enclave, with gallery shows and free Internet access for customers. Plus, it stays open until 10 PM. This is quite a fascinating scene. You have to go to the counter and order, and staff can be curt, but it is a real neighborhood tableau, and a popular destination for students at SCAD.

For traditional afternoon high tea, you can't beat the lavishly outfitted **Gryphon Tea Room** (⌂*337 Bull St., Historic District* ☎*912/525–5880*) with its expansive range of teas, from English breakfast to Apricot Arabesque to Black Dragon Choicest Oolong. A former old-time pharmacy, with stained glass and apothecary motifs in tiles, this atmospheric tearoom also serves specialty coffees, alongside a full menu of scones, baklava, biscotti, and healthier salads and sandwiches. It does have afternoon tea service, complete with multilevel serving caddies for the finger sandwiches, the scones, the sweets. Though less expensive than its competitors, Gryphon does not serve any liquor, which may be matter to you if you also like a glass of sherry.

The **Tea Room** (⊠*7 E. Broughton St., Historic District* ☎*912/239–9690*) serves a formal afternoon tea, by reservation only, daily at 2:30. There are several tea service options, and this is a pretty expensive luxury, but you can get some alcohol add-ons. However, the cutsey decor, from antiques to oversized stuffed animals (all for sale) make for a darling ambience. The lunch menu has good-tasting fare like curried chicken salad.

LIVE MUSIC CLUBS

Bayou Café & Blues Bar (⊠*14 N. Abercorn St., at River St., Historic District* ☎*912/233–6411*) has acoustic music during the week and the Bayou Blues Band on the weekend. There's also Cajun food. You'll pay no cover, but there's a one-drink minimum.

Blowin' Smoke BBQ (⊠*514 Martin Luther King Jr. Blvd., Historic District* ☎*912/231–2385*), a family-friendly BBQ joint, has some good sounds on Friday and Saturday nights. The Roger Moss Jazz Quintet alternates between blues bands, bluegrass, and alternative country groups like the Train Wrecks. It's in the revitalized neighborhood along Martin Luther King Jr. Blvd., and there's free parking.

Outside Savannah, **Café Loco** (⊠*1 Old Hwy. 80, Tybee Island* ☎*912/786–7810* ⊕*www.cafelocotybee.com*) is on Tybee Island. Nestled under the Lazaretto Creek Bridge and overlooking the marshlands, Loco looks like a shack, but it showcases local blues and acoustic acts that make it well worth the trip. It's a laid-back, beach-bar format with an outdoor patio.

★ **Jazz'd Tapas Bar** (⊠*52 Barnard St., Historic District* ☎*912/236–7777*) is a chic basement venue. Gourmet grazing is the vogue, and a range of local artists are featured from Tuesday through Saturday. On Wednesday, Eddie Wilson, a singing solo pianist, plays a variety of styles from swing to classic rock and jazz. On Tuesday (sometimes Sunday, too), Jeff Beasley, an accomplished blues guitarist, entertains. Trae Gurley sings Sinatra over recorded instrumentals every Thursday. The tapas menu has healthy, contemporary small plates and is one of the city's best values; the place usually opens at 4. No one under 21 can enter once the kitchen closes (10 PM weekdays, midnight on weekends); there's never a cover.

Jen's and Friends (⊠7 E. Congress St., Historic District ☎912/238–5367), although dark even during the day, is popular among professionals after work, including bankers at the financial institutions that surround nearby Johnson Square. You will also see a lot of tattoos (as on Jen herself) and smell a lot of smoke, but this bar, although it looks like a dive, has a good spirit and offers some serious local fun. The small bar, often congested and abuzz with conversation, offers more than 100 martini selections, an appetizer and small-plate menu, and famous ciabatta bread sandwiches. Happy hour is daily from 3 to 7, when you'll pay just $2 for domestic beer, $3 for house liquors and wine, and $4 for cosmos. A simple joy is playing the juke box. Jen's is open late but closed on Sunday.

5

Local acts and nationally known performers take the stage at **JJ Cagney's** (⊠305 W. River St., Historic District ☎912/233–2444). You can listen to blues, jazz, Southern rock, R&B, and bluegrass while enjoying food from the light menu. There's also a gaming room.

Savannah's latest addition to the club scene is **Live Wire Music Hall** (⊠307 W. River St., Historic District ☎912/233–1192), where both up-and-coming and nationally known acts play. Most popular with the twenty- and thirtysomething crowd, the entertainment runs from R&B to jazz, funk, rock, and even comedy acts. There are drink specials, and happy hour lasts until 8 PM Monday to Saturday. Cover charges are low.

At **Mercury Lounge** (⊠125 W. Congress St., Historic District ☎912/447–6952) you can take a trip back in time and experience the furnishings and atmosphere of the swing era. Enjoy the pop, swing, and big band sounds. From Thursday through Saturday you'll find live jazz and blues. And it's open late (until 3 AM except on Sunday, when it's 2 AM).

Tantra Lounge (⊠8 E. Broughton St., Historic District ☎912/231–0888) offers Asian-oriented tapas including some spectacular sushi, and all manner of interesting creations served in martini glasses. This local meeting place has become a hub for thirst-quenching with new and inventive cocktails. Happy hour happens Monday through Friday from 5 to 8. Pick a night to be entertained. Theme nights range from swing and salsa to open-mike and remix DJs. Live bands perform Friday and Saturday from 9:30 PM to 1:30 AM. A Saturday night example is the funk band A Nickel Bag of Funk. As a general rule, the older crowd comes early; the young close the place.

Vic's on the River (✉ *26 E. Bay St. and 15 East Bay St., Historic District* ☎ *912/721–1000*) is one of Savannah's best restaurants, and also happens to have an excellent bar. The piano is manned by Jimmy Frushon from Sunday through Thursday; on Friday and Saturday nights there's usually a female vocalist. Every other weekend, Diana Rogers, after years in New York performing in cabarets, plays what she knows best and sings beautifully. A most interesting character, she usually wears a vintage hat and outfit.

Sports & the Outdoors

WORD OF MOUTH

"Tybee Island, near Savannah in Georgia, [is g]reat for walking and biking. Good shelling."

—mhc

By Eileen
Robinson
Smith

SAVANNAH RESIDENTS LOVE TO BE OUT ON THE WATER.
The area around Savannah and the barrier islands of the
Lowcountry is conducive to nearly all types of water sports,
whether you're partaking as an individual or in small
groups. Swimming, sailing, fishing, kayaking, jet skiing,
parasailing, and even surfing make up the most popular
core activities. The fresh water of the Savannah River that
flows alongside the city on its way to the Atlantic Ocean
is accessible by boat—even riverboat cruises. A multitude
of tidal creeks and marshlands intertwine the river to the
barrier islands like Wilmington and Tybee, where one can
enjoy the beaches and the Atlantic Ocean. The waters of
Savannah are generally warm enough for swimming from
May through September.

For those who would like to stay on land, bicycling, jogging,
golf, tennis, as well as arena sports dominate. Spas have
become increasingly popular, and many ladies and men have
made the spa visit their therapeutic sport of choice.

During the hot and humid months of summer, limit the
duration of strenuous activity, remember to drink lots of
water, and protect your skin from the sun.

SPORTS & ACTIVITIES

BASEBALL

Minor league baseball's Single-A **Savannah Sand Gnats**
(⊠*1401 E. Victory Dr., Midtown* ☎*912/351–9150* ⊕*www.
sandgnats.com*) play at Grayson Stadium. You may have
seen a Paula Deen segment on the Food Network that was
filmed there, with Paula throwing the first ball and fixing
her elaborate hot dogs. This is good old-fashioned family
fun, with traditional ballpark refreshments, beer, and even a
full bar. Goofy mascots entertain. For different events there
are even fireworks. Ticket prices begin at $7.

BIKING

Bicycle Link (⊠*408 Martin Luther King Jr. Blvd., near W.
Jones, Historic District* ☎*912/233–9401* ⊕*www.bicycle
linksav.com*) rents bicycles. Rates for the single-speed beach
cruisers are $15 for a half-day, $20 for a full day. The
shop provides helmets, locks, and trailers that will hold
one child. A deposit of $120 is required, and all credit
cards are accepted. The shop will sometimes pick up and

BEST BETS FOR ACTIVITIES

■ **Baseball.** A baseball game under a summer sky is an all-American pleasure. It is a family-bonding opportunity, and, more happily, ticket prices for the Savannah Sand Gnats start at just $7. Buy a hot dog and join in the fun.

■ **Golf.** The weather here, particularly in the spring and fall, is custom ordered for golf swings. Though the courses aren't as fine as those on Hilton Head, you'll still find some gems, including the Westin's Club at Savannah Harbor and the Wilmington Island Club, both of which are also much more moderately priced than most of the Hilton Head courses.

■ **Spas.** For those who are looking for something less strenuous and more relaxing, a soothing spa treatment may

fit the bill, whether it's at one of the big hotel spas, such as the Marriott's spa, or one of Savannah's independent day spas, such as Savannah Day Spa.

■ **Walking.** Walking is a perfect low-impact activity wherever you stay in Savannah. Forsyth Park is a favored venue for this casual workout. And locals love to hoof it. You will never see so many sneakers, tennis shoes, and other orthopedically correct walking shoes as you will in downtown Savannah.

■ **Watersports.** Watersports is the obvious choice for a city surrounded by rivers, creeks, marsh, and the Atlantic Ocean. Kayaking, fishing, sailing, and parasailing are all popular.

deliver to the inns, but they prefer that customers pick up bikes at the shop, which is open Monday through Saturday from 10 to 6.

Coastal Scooters (⊠65 E. Broughton St., Historic District ☎912/232–5513) rents scooters, offering a way to tour Savannah on your own. Expect to pay $35 for 2 hours. Electric bikes and three-wheels are available, too.

Island Bike (⊠14 W. State St., Historic District ⊠205 Johnny Mercer Blvd., Wilmington Island ☎912/236–8808 or 912/897–7474) rents single-speed adult bikes for $20 per day, kid's bikes for $15 per day, and multispeed bikes for $25 per day at both locations. Helmets and locks are available only at the downtown location (for an extra charge). A refundable deposit is based on the cost and age of the bike. All credit cards are accepted. The shops are

CLOSE UP

The No-Hills Workout

Savannah is table-flat—bad news indeed for any mountaineers who find themselves in coastal Georgia—but great for bicyclists. One favorite spot for local bikers is the 28,000-acre Savannah Wildlife Refuge, where alligators bask alongside the trail. Another possibility is Rails-to-Trails, a 3-mi route that starts 1 mi east of the Bull River Bridge on Highway 80 and ends at the entrance to Fort Pulaski. Tom Triplett Park, east of town on U.S. 80, offers three bike loops—3.5 mi, 5 mi, and 6.3 mi. Sunday is the best day for riding downtown, but be aware that throughout much of downtown there are restrictions for bikers. Riding through squares and on the sidewalks of Broughton Street is illegal

and carries a fine of more than $100. In general, cyclists should be careful to avoid the opening of car doors. Bikers should always ride with traffic, not against it, and obey the lights. Night riding requires bicycles to display a white light visible from 300 feet on the front and a red reflector on the back. Helmets are legally required for riders and passengers under the age of 16 and strongly recommended for adult riders. Several of the suburbs—Windsor Forest, Ardsley Park, the Isle of Hope—are fine for riding relatively free of traffic hassles, as are most of Wilmington and Tybee Islands. You can enjoy bike-friendly riding on Tybee's bike trails and rent a bike for half of what it costs downtown.

open Monday through Saturday from 10 to 7:30, sometimes on Sunday.

Although best known for its bicycle rickshaw service, **Savannah Pedi-Cabs** (⊠*711 Tattinell St., Historic District* ☎*912/232–7900*) also rents bikes by the day ($20) or week and will deliver them to your inn or B&B. Payment and deposits are usually worked out with the innkeepers.

On Tybee Island, you can enjoy a bike-friendly environment with ocean-view trails, at half the cost of biking downtown. **Tim's Beach Gear** (⊠*Tybee Island* ☎*912/786–8467* ⊕*www. timsbeachgear.com*) rents bikes for adults and kids as well as in-tow carriers. This is strictly a drop-off service, offering free delivery and pickup on Tybee Island—for just $10 a day ($8 per day for multiday rentals), and that includes helmets. Umbrellas, beach chairs, towels, games like boccie ball, and more are available, too. All manner of baby gear can be rented, from umbrella and jogging strollers to baby monitors.

BOATING & FISHING

At the **Bull River Yacht Club Marina** (⊠*8005 Old Tybee Rd., Tybee Island* ☎*912/897–7300* ⊕*www.bullriver.com*), you can arrange a dolphin tour, a deep-sea fishing expedition, or a jaunt through the coastal islands on an 18-foot Edgewater or a 26-foot catamaran. Up to three people will cost about $340 for four hours (add a fourth for $85); prices for fishing charters include bait and tackle. If you want to rent a boat, a 13-footer will run you $100 for two hours, plus $25 for each additional hour (not including the gas, of course).

Explore the natural beauty and wildlife on a narrated boat tour with **Dolphin Magic Tours** (⊠*101 River St., Historic District* ☎*800/721–1240* ⊕*www.dolphin-magic.com*). From River Street, you go out to the marshlands and tidal creeks near Tybee Island. The search for dolphin encounters lasts two hours and sightings are guaranteed. Departure times vary according to the tides and the weather; the cruise costs $30. Bring sunscreen and beverages.

Lake Mayer Park (⊠*Montgomery Crossroads Rd. and Sallie Mood Dr., Cresthill* ☎*912/652–6780*) contains a freshwater fishing pier, a 1.5-mi jogging/walking trail, and a softball field. A boat ramp is at the site. For a small sailboat rental, the price is $45 to $60 per hour. Paddleboats and canoes are also available, as well as an in-line skating and hockey facility.

Lowcountry River Excursions (⊠*Bull River Marina, 8005 Old Tybee Rd. [Hwy. 80 E], Tybee Island* ☎*912/898–9222*), which operates out of Bull River Marina, allows you to experience an encounter with friendly bottlenose dolphins and enjoy the scenery and wildlife during a 90-minute cruise down the Bull River aboard a 40-foot pontoon boat. Restrooms and beverages are on board. Call to confirm times and seasonal hours. Reservations are strongly advised.

Capt. Judy Helmley, a longtime and legendary guide of the region, heads up **Miss Judy Charters** (⊠*124 Palmetto Dr., Wilmington Island* ☎*912/897–4921 or 912/897–2478* ⊕*www.missjudycharters.com*) and provides packages ranging from two-hour sightseeing tours to 16-hour deep-sea fishing expeditions. Rates run about $500 for four hours and (up to) six people, and $650 for eight hours; a 16-hour adventure will cost you $1,800. Most major credit cards are accepted. Please don't forget to tip the mate 15% to 20%.

North Island Surf & Kayak (⊠*1C Old Tybee Rd., Tybee Island* ☎*912/786–4000* ⊕*www.northislandkayak.com*) is a young and versatile operation, but it will open up a whole new world of kayaking with the sit-on-top kayaks that are virtually unsinkable. Stable and safe on inland rivers, they allow you to navigate the shallowest of creeks where no other boats can go. You can put in at the company's floating dock, or launch wherever you want. All rentals include paddles, lifejackets, and seat backs. Prices are $40 per day for a single, $55 for a double; there are no hourly rentals. For $5 you can rent a "dry bag" to stow your important items while you kayak. Paddle to the beautiful uninhabited island of Little Tybee or to Cockspur Beacon, and climb to the dock (bring shoes) to see a wonderful watery panorama. The company also offers ecotours; although these tours require a minimum of six adults ($50), you can often join a scheduled group if you are a couple or a single. You can also rent paddleboards here for $50 a day, or a surfboard for $30. Lessons are an extra $10 an hour.

Savannah Islands Expressway (⊠*Adjacent to Frank W. Spencer Park, Skidaway Island*) provides boat ramps on the Wilmington River.

Savannah Marina (⊠*Thunderbolt*) provides boat ramps on the Wilmington River.

Reel 'Em N Deep Sea Fishing (⊠*Walsh's Dock, Tybee Island* ☎*800/721–1240 or 912/897–49900* ⊕*www.reelemn.com*) offers offshore fishing charters for one to 20 people; rates depend on the size of your group, the destination, and the length of the trip. A typical charter for six passengers for four hours to the Shell Banks costs $400.

GOLF

Bacon Park (⊠*1 Shorty Cooper Dr., Southside* ☎*912/354–2625*) is a public course with 27 holes of golf and a lighted driving range. The greens fee, including cart, runs $25–$38.

The Club at Savannah Harbor (⊠*2 Resort Dr., Hutchinson Island* ☎*912/201–2007* ⊕*www.theclubatsavannahharbor.com*) is an 18-hole course with a pro shop, spa, locker rooms, putting green, and driving range. This is the resort complex of the Westin Hotel, which is a free ferry ride

Georgia Football

Locals can't get over Georgia football. The guys eat it for breakfast. Bobby Deen, son of Paula, may take a couple of days off in September, but only to attend one of the first "Georgia White Bulldogs" weekends. If Sonny comes to, say, the Olde Pink House, the staff may brag as if they just saw a movie star. Don't be surprised if your waiter raises the sleeve of his T-shirt to show you his symbolic tattoo—"One big G! I got it at Superbowl 2003."

If you want to make friends fast, express an interest in the University of Georgia's football team. The mascot is a white bulldog, and there's always a pup ready to take on the team's elevated canine position. Sonny Siler, the keeper of the mascots, was a prominent attorney but is now retired and is a celebrity in his own right—he was even portrayed in Hollywood's *Midnight in the Garden of Good and Evil.*

Speaking of stars, Michael Douglas endeared himself to an already adoring crowd at a recent SCAD Film Festival when his first comment was to acknowledge a win that the University of Georgia had scored that Saturday. Cheers went up!

6

from Savannah's riverfront. The championship course has unparalleled views of the river and of historic downtown Savannah as it winds through wetlands. Greens fee, including cart, runs $60–$120.

Crosswinds Golf Club (⊠*232 James Blackburn Dr., Pooler* ☎*912/966–1909*), located north of town, has an 18-hole championship course as well as a 9-hole course that is lighted for night play. Greens fee, including cart, is $35–$60.

Henderson Golf Club (⊠*1 Al Henderson Dr., at I–95, Exit 94 to Rte. 204, Southside* ☎*912/920–4653*) is an 18-hole, par-71 course about 15 mi from downtown Savannah. Greens fee, including cart, is $28–$48.

The **Mary Calder Golf Course** (⊠*W. Lathrop Ave., West Chatham* ☎*912/238–7100*) is par-35 for its 9 holes. Greens fee is $28–$30.

Southbridge Golf Club (⊠*415 Southbridge Blvd., Southbridge* ☎*912/651–5455* ⊕*www.southbridgegc.com*), an 18- hole, par-72 course, has a driving range, putting green, practice bunker, chipping green, pro shop, restaurant, and bar. Greens fee, including cart, is $30 to $50.

Wilmington Island Club (⊠*501 Wilmington Island Rd., Wilmington Island* ☎*912/897–1612*) has an 18-hole, par-72 course with driving range, pro shop, practice green, and locker rooms. Greens fee for visitors, including cart, is $69.

JET-SKIING

If you want to enjoy the fast-paced and exciting rush of jet skiing on the waterways around Tybee Island or ride the swells of the beach, **Tybee Jet Ski & Watersports** (⊠*1 Hwy. 80 E, Tybee Island* ☎*912/786–8062* ⊕*www.tybeejetski. com*) rents Jet Skis for $75 per hour (not including gas). You must be 16 years or older with a valid driver's license to rent. The rental office is open from March through September, 9 AM to sunset.

PARASAILING

To get the big view from above, **Tybee Parasailing** (⊠*1C 45 Hwy. 80, Tybee Island* ☎*912/655–2316* ⊕*www.tybee-dolphin-tours.com*) can take you up 400 feet above the island's waterways and beaches from June through September. The cost is $85 for a 90-minute trip with 15 minutes of actual parasailing.

TENNIS

Bacon Park (⊠*6262 Skidaway Rd., Southside* ☎*912/351–3850*) has 16 lighted asphalt courts. Fees are $3 per person, and you can reserve courts in advance.

Daffin Park (⊠*1500 E. Victory Dr., Midtown* ☎*912/351–3851*) has tennis courts that you can use for free.

Forsyth Park (⊠*701 Drayton St., Historic District* ☎*912/351–3851*) contains four lighted courts available until about 10 PM; there's no charge to use them.

Lake Mayer Park (⊠*1850 Montgomery Crossroads, Southside* ☎*912/652–6780*) has eight asphalt lighted courts available at no charge and open 8 AM–10 PM; until 11 PM May through September.

SPAS

Spas are catching on in the city of Spanish moss, and the spa options in Savannah have now matured and expanded.

Magnolia Spa (✉*Marriott Savannah Riverfront, 100 General McIntosh Blvd., Historic District* ☎*912/373–2039* ⊕*www.marriott.com*) is a secret mother lode of pampering services that the occasional tourist may not stumble upon in his wanderings, tucked away as it is at the far end of the River Walk and located within the Marriott. Everything is new and fresh, and the service and quality of the treatments are laudable. There are massages par excellence, a litany of facials, body treatments, and even a teen spa for girls 16 and under. The spa will also cater to couples and, of course, gentlemen.

The very chic **Poseidon Spa** (✉ *The Mansion on Forsyth Park, 700 Drayton St., Historic District* ☎*912/721–5004* ⊕*www.mansiononforsythpark.com*) is a first-class European-style spa, with a number of rejuvenating treatments and refinement services. It offers manicures, pedicures, skin and body treatments, massages, and access to a 24-hour fitness center. One wet and three dry treatment rooms, women's and men's locker rooms, and a steam shower make up the facilities. This is the town's glamour spa, though in truth prices run just a little more than the rest. It's also a beautiful, calming place to be.

In addition to traditional spa services, **Savannah Day Spa** (✉*18 E. Oglethorpe St., Downtown* ☎*912/234–9100* ⊕*www. savannahdayspa.com*) offers a complete line of skin-care products, accessories for home, and a new line of vegan body products. This is a former urban mansion and a delightful place to take your treatments, be it one of the creative massages or a therapeutic facial for your particular skin issues.

Vanilla Day Spa (✉*1 E. Broughton St., Downtown* ☎*912/232–0040* ⊕*www.vanilladayspa.com*) is inside the Downtown Athletic Club (the health club for which many hotels and inns offer complimentary guest passes) and has access to steam rooms, saunas, and whirlpools. The spa offers a full menu of professional services for men and women such as manicures, pedicures, facials, waxing, and body treatments, with massage therapy a specialty. Inquire about spa packages.

6

Shopping

WORD OF MOUTH

"If you go nowhere else, stop into the SCAD store. They have loads of cool and unique things . . . [There are] individual and quirky shops along Bull Street or Broughton."

—SandyP

By Eileen
Robinson
Smith

FIND YOUR OWN LOWCOUNTRY TREASURES among a bevy of handcrafted wares—handmade quilts and baskets; wreaths made from Chinese tallow trees and Spanish moss; preserves, jams, and jellies. The favorite Savannah snack, and a popular gift item, is the benne wafer (from the African word for sesame seeds). These thin cookies are about the size of a quarter and come in different flavors. Handmade candies, specifically Southern pralines made with brown sugar and pecans, are a big draw with the little ones.

Savannah has a wide collection of colorful businesses— revitalization is no longer a goal but an accomplishment. Antiques malls and junk emporiums beckon you with their colorful storefronts and eclectic offerings, as do the many specialty shops and bookstores clustered along the moss-embossed streets.

On designated Friday nights throughout the year, the shops around certain squares stay open late and will offer patrons complimentary wine and cheese or other goodies. This is one fun way both to shop and to meet convivial locals. Stop by the Savannah Visitor Information Center (see ☞ Visitor Information *in* Travel Smart) to see if a walkabout is scheduled for your weekend.

SHOPPING DISTRICTS

For generations, **Broughton Street** (⊠*Between Congress and State Sts., Historic District*) was the main shopping street of the city. During the 1950s ladies would not think of going there without their white gloves and heels. Alas, the downtown decline that began in the late 1950s and continued through the '70s put that thought to rest. For-sale and for-lease signs were omnipresent, boarded-up storefronts the norm rather than the exception. All that sad past is behind us now, and Broughton is thriving, not only with shops but with restaurants and coffeehouses, too. West of Bull Street are more shops; east of Bull there are fewer stores, but you'll still find some high-end boutiques on both ends, as well as chain stores.

City Market (⊠ *W. St. Julian St. between Ellis and Franklin Sqs., Historic District*) takes its origins from a farmers' market back in 1755. Today it's a four-block emporium that has been involved in a renaissance program and constitutes an eclectic mix of artists' studios, sidewalk cafés, jazz haunts, shops, and art galleries.

BEST BETS FOR SHOPPING

■ **Art Galleries.** The Grand Bohemian Gallery (which is in the city's finest small hotel, the Mansion on Forsyth Park) is Savannah's best gallery, but other smaller venues give you the opportunity to buy well-priced local art, and you can always head over to the SCAD campus to buy the works of its emerging student artists from one of the campus galleries.

■ **Artsy Gifts.** If you want to find unique gifts to take back home, the quintessential place to stop is ShopSCAD, which sells the work of faculty, alumni, and students of the Savannah College of Art and Design, including everything from unique jewelry to handmade postcards.

■ **Chic Clothing.** Copper Penny, which started in Charleston, now has a branch here, and it offers one of the city's most eclectic arrays of chic, cutting-edge fashions, but it's worth strolling down Broughton Street to find other great local boutiques.

■ **Home Decor & Antiques.** The Paris Market & Brocante, which has two floors stuffed full of amazing finds, is one of your best options. But don't neglect 37th @ Abercorn Antique & Design, a full city block of stalls offering everything from vintage children's clothing to fabulous quilts and costume jewelry.

7

Madison Square (⊠*Bull St. bordered by Liberty and Charlton Sts., Historic District* , a tree-shaded residential/commercial neighborhood, offers an array of shops including the Christmas Shop and E. Shaver Booksellers. The Savannah College of Art and Design (SCAD) is in this area, too, and you can take afternoon tea at Gryphon Tea Room.

Riverfront Plaza/River Street (⊠*Historic District*) is nine blocks of renovated waterfront warehouses (once the city's cotton exchange) containing more than 75 boutiques, galleries, restaurants, and pubs; you can find everything from popcorn to pottery here, and even voodoo spells! Leave your stilettos at home, or you'll find the street's cobblestones hard and dangerous work.

The **Whitaker & Jones St. Market Area** (⊠*Between Whitaker and Jones Sts., Historic District*) is known for its antiques shops, interior design and home fashion stores, the Paris Market, and several art galleries. Several restaurants and outdoor cafés provide "take a break" time, including the landmark Mrs. Wilkes' Boarding House for family-style Southern food.

PARK & SAVE. Drivers be warned: Savannah parking officers are quick to dole out tickets. Tourists may purchase two-day parking passes ($8) at the Savannah Visitors Center and at some hotels and inns. Passes are valid in metered spots as well as in the city's lots and garages; they allow parkers to exceed the time in time-limit zones.

SPECIALTY SHOPS

ANTIQUES

Arthur Smith Antiques (⊠*402 Bull St., Historic District* ☎*912/236–9701*) has four floors showcasing 18th- and 19th-century European furniture, porcelain, rugs, and paintings. Near beautiful Monterey Square, the store is both a good destination shop and worth a detour while exploring the neighborhood.

★ **Fodor'sChoice 37th @ Abercorn Antique & Design** (⊠*37th St., at Abercorn St., Historic District* ☎*912/233–0064*) is a one-stop shop that encompasses a city block of antiques and collectibles spanning 200 years. Stroll with a cup of java from the property's European café, and peruse the area's largest collection of quilts, antique clocks, vintage costume jewelry, and museum-quality vintage children's clothes. Visit a primitive country kitchen displaying gadgets, enamelware, and 1950s-era linens. Original Persian rugs and antique sterling-silver jewelry are among other unique items available.

ART GALLERIES

Compass Prints, Inc./Ray Ellis Gallery (⊠*205 W. Congress St., Historic District* ☎*912/234–3537*) sells original artwork, prints, and books by internationally acclaimed artist Ray Ellis.

Gallery Espresso (⊠*6 E. Liberty St., Historic District* ☎*912/ 233–5348*) has a new show every two weeks focusing on work by local artists. A true coffeehouse, it stays open until the wee hours. Pastries, cheesecakes, muffins, scones, and luscious desserts are house-made and complement the heavy dose of caffeine and art.

Gallery 209 (✉*209 E. River St., Historic District* ☎*912/236–4583*) is a co-op gallery, with paintings, watercolors, pottery, jewelry, batik, stained glass, weavings, and sculptures by local artists.

★ Fodor'sChoice **Grand Bohemian Gallery**(✉*The Mansion at Forsyth Park, 700 Drayton St., Historic District* ☎*912/238–5158, ext. 5007*) is within the city's most luxurious hotel, and although it is a separate shop, the entire hotel showcases the Kessler Collection, which was acquired by the gallery's owner, Richard Kessler, a native Georgian. Much of his artwork can be purchased. Within the actual gallery you'll find the work of acclaimed artists, especially contemporary paintings, blown-glass art, ceramics, whimsical sculpture, and some incredibly innovative jewelry pieces. Check on the schedule of imaginative workshops and lectures conducted by some of the most respected artists worldwide.

Savannah Art Works (✉*250 Bull St., Historic District* ☎*912/443–9331*) is known for artsy creations of glass and metal that still have a purpose. For example, a martini glass wrapped with aluminum wire is a best-seller. Conversely, recycled and reclaimed metal and wood accessories are one of a kind. Functional ceramics, crafted from Georgia red clay, are popular. Work is mainly by local and Carolinian artists, mostly self-taught. Prices are inexpensive to moderate.

Savannah College of Art and Design (SCAD) (✉*516 Albercorn St., Historic District* ☎*912/527–4727*), a private art college, has restored at least 50 historic buildings often in mixed or marginal neighborhoods, the latest an imposing high school on Bull Street; these total rehabs include 12 galleries, one of which is in a former cafeteria. Touring exhibitions are frequently in the on-campus galleries. Stop by Exhibit A, Pinnacle Gallery, and the West Bank Gallery, and ask about other student galleries. Garden for the Arts has an amphitheater and shows performance art. The above number is for the exhibitions department, which has a recording giving the latest exhibits, and it is possible to speak to an informed representative.

2CarGarage Contemporary Art Gallery (✉*10 E. Broughton St., across from Starbucks, Historic District* ☎*912/236–0221* ⊕*www.2cargallery.com*) showcases the work of nationally exhibited as well as emerging artists to Savannah's fine-art scene. Alexandro Santana, a Spanish architect/artist and long-term Savannah resident, is one such talented example. The gallery's mission is to deliver engaging contemporary paintings and works on paper to discerning art collectors.

BOOKS

"The Book" Gift Shop and Midnight Museum (⊠*127 E. Gordon St., Historic District* ☏*912/233–3867*) sells all things related to *Midnight in the Garden of Good and Evil,* including souvenirs and author-autographed copies. It may not have a long life in that the keen interest in the subject is on the wane. In the meantime, if you have never read this Savannah classic, you can pick it up here. Seeing the decline, the shop is now wisely capitalizing on the various ghost tours and has a lot of haunt-y items.

E. Shaver Booksellers (⊠*326 Bull St., Historic District* ☏*912/234–7257*) is the source for 17th- and 18th-century maps and new books on regional subjects. It carries travel guides for Savannah and books on just about whatever you would want to know about the city, from its colonial beginnings to what there is for children to do. This shop occupies 12 rooms of a historic building, and it alone is something to see. The booksellers are knowledgeable about their wares.

V. & J. Duncan (⊠*12 E. Taylor St., Historic District* ☏*912/232–0338*) specializes in antique maps, prints, and books. Again, the shop itself is a historic home, and almost seems like an anachronism—from a past world.

CLOTHING FOR WOMEN

★ Fodor'sChoice **Copper Penny** (⊠*22 W. Broughton St., Historic District* ☏*912/629–6800*) was conceptualized by owner Penny Vaigneur in Charleston (there's a store there and in Myrtle Beach). Carrying Trina Turk, Nanette Lapore, and Hudson Jeans to name a few of the designers popular with young fashionistas, the more mature shopper comes to get some edgy pieces to contemporize her wardrobe. "Attached" is Copper Penny Shooz, where you'll find shoe fashion statements by BCB Girls, Kate Spade, Michael Kors, and the like. Great looking purses complement the shoes; you'll find names like Francesco Biasia, Hype Handbags, and Tano. Love those Lucchese boots.

Monkee's (⊠*5525 Abercorn St., Historic District* ☏*912/354–1212*) features the finest designer shoes and accessories from names like Kate Spade and Taryn Rose. Up-and-coming designers also display their trendy wares. There is something here for the "trendy chic" chick and the "fashion-forward" fem.

Red Clover (✉ *53 Montgomery St., Historic District* ☎ *912/236–4053*) is the place to be if you want fashionable and affordable apparel, shoes, and handbags. Steps from Broughton Street, the store offers the unusual and different. See the selection of unique gifts and jewelry, too.

FOODSTUFFS

Byrd Cookie Company & Gourmet Marketplace (✉ *6700 Waters Ave., Highland Park* ☎ *912/355–1716*), founded in 1924, sells picture tins of Savannah and gourmet foodstuffs such as condiments and dressings. It's the best place to get benne wafers ("the seed of good luck") and trademark Savannah cookies, notably key lime and other house-made crackers. Free samples of all are available. As this is a drive, look for their products in numerous gift shops around town.

The Lady and her sons have another hit to their credit. They have transformed what was the grungiest of bars into the fabulous **Paula Deen Store** (✉ *108 W. Congress St., Historic District* ☎ *912/232–1607*), which is filled with cookbooks by the Southern Queen of the Food Network. You can find some very Southern spices and sauces, such as a smokin' barbecue sauce and salad dressings, like peach pecan and blueberry walnut, that are so sweet they could double as dessert toppings. Two full floors of cooking goodies and gadgets are cleverly displayed against a backdrop of brick walls. Paula's husband, Capt. Michael Groover, sells a line of coffee beans from a Colombia fair-trade company. The shop is adjacent to Deen's famous Southern-style restaurant, so you may get lucky, for her son Jamie may be signing cookbooks on your day.

★ **Fodor'sChoice River Street Sweets** (✉ *13 E. River St., Historic District* ☎ *912/233–6220*) opened in 1973 and is Savannah's self-described "oldest and original" candy store. The aroma of creamy homemade fudge will draw you in, along with hot and fresh pralines, which are made all day long. The store is also known for milk chocolate bear claws. It's a great place to find a unique, edible gift. You'll always receive excellent customer service here.

Savannah Candy Kitchen (✉225 E. River St., Historic District
☎912/233–8411), the largest candy store in the South, is
right on Savannah's historic River Street. Come watch them
make yummy treats and Southern confections daily. You'll
find fudge, pralines, truffles, and candied apples, among
other scrumptious delights.

GIFTS

Baskets of Savannah (✉31 Island Creek La., Wilmington
Island ☎912/898–4731), which is owned by Melissa Car-
mody, has been in business since 1991. Call her to place
your custom order by phone. These baskets are about the
perfect gift. You can get gourmet food, corporate, and
personalized baskets, too. They make a wonderful "thank
you" for someone like your inn's concierge. Melissa takes
pride in impressing the recipient.

The Christmas Shop (✉307 Bull St., Historic District ☎912/234–
5343) features hand-smocked children's clothing, German pewter, and hard-to-find seasonal accessories and
collectibles. Even though it's hard to think sleigh bells in
the tropical heat of summer, these items are so special you
may not be able to resist a Savannah ornament.

Elegant Gifts (✉7400 Abercorn St., Suite 705–225, Historic
District ☎912/961–6778) makes elegant and affordable
gift baskets to your specifications. Just name the price and
the occasion and select from more than 30 theme baskets
for customization.

Elizabeth's Elegant Creations (✉317 W. Broughton St., Historic District ☎912/234–6414) is known for colorful plaid
and patchwork flip-flops with matching custom-designed
ribbon belts; you will also find purses and fashionable
tote bags. Sort through a selection of historical postcards,
books, and jewelry to find that perfect gift.

The Gray Horse Gift Shop (✉8413 Ferguson Ave., Suite A,
Midtown ☎912/691–4729) specializes in dog trinkets,
bed linens, and picture frames; you can also get Okab
shoes here.

Nourish (✉202 W. Broughton St., Historic District ☎912/232–
3213) is a scrumptious store, a must-do for those who
seek pure, natural bath products, skin creams and treatments, and soy-wax candles. Handmade and handcrafted
in downtown Savannah, the products contain no harsh
detergents. The wonderful line of natural bath products

includes soaps like glycerin by the slice and some made from hemp-seed oil. There are Dead Sea salt body scrubs, shea butter creams, badger lip balms, aromatherapy scents, essential oil inhalers, and more.

★ Fodor'sChoice **ShopSCAD** (✉ *340 Bull St., Historic District* ☎*912/525–5180* ⊕*www.shopscadonline.com*) sells amazing works by faculty, alumni, and students of SCAD, including handcrafted jewelry, clothing, furniture, glass work, and original postcards. You can also buy the coffee-table book *Savannah Sketch*, written by historian Jeff Eley and illustrated with watercolor impressions of the city by a chosen contingent of SCAD's most talented students. In most of the jewelry pieces, contemporary forms are integrated with antiques and unexpected finds. Handmade and hand-dyed silk accessories are cutting edge, as are the original fashion pieces and experimental purses by design students. Hand-painted and photographic note cards, retro aprons, finger puppets, and other small works of art are among the treasures you can easily walk with. Just remember that these originals do not come cheap.

HOME DECOR

One Fish Two Fish (✉ *401 Whitaker St., Historic District* ☎*912/447–4600*), whose whimsical name was taken from a Dr. Seuss book, is a creative, high-end, home-decor shop with quality contemporary furniture and art, fine linens, and bedroom and bathroom accessories. There are colorful, modern light fixtures and vintage-style and French decorative accessories.

★ Fodor'sChoice **The Paris Market & Brocante** (✉ *36 W. Broughton St., Historic District* ☎*912/232–1500*) is a Francophile's dream, from the time you open the antique front door and take in the intoxicating aroma of lavender. This two-story emporium with chandeliers and other lighting fixtures is a classy version of the Paris flea market, selling furniture, vintage art, garden planters and accessories, and Euro-home fashions like boudoir accessories and bedding. And although the store will ship, there are numerous treasures that can be easily carried away, like the soaps, candles, vintage jewelry, kitchen and barware, and dried lavender.

TOBACCO

Savannah Cigars (✉ *308 W. Congress St., Historic District* ☎*912/233–2643*), which is in the City Market, has a wide variety of handmade cigars. Add a carved Meerschaum pipe to your collection, or choose from an array of smoking accessories for gifts and souvenirs.

Ye Ole Tobacco Shop & Verdery's (✉*130 E. Bay St., Historic District* ☎*888/596–1425*) has been selling the finest hand-rolled cigars grown from Cuba seed since 1973; you can get all the major brands, including Arturo Fuente, Montecristo, and Cohiba, among others. Blended tobaccos are offered, as well as a large selection of pipes and accessories. It's a great place to buy a gift for your favorite smoker; you may just find that special lighter or humidor.

Hilton Head &
the Lowcountry

WORD OF MOUTH

"Fripp [Island], especially at south end, has a wide beach. During high tide north beach disappears. Fripp can be traversed on foot in about 30 minutes, if the marsh deer get out of your way. They're everywhere. Enjoy."

—Lex1

"[A] visit to Beaufort would . . . be a really nice addition to your stay. It's smaller and really manageable but quite lovely."

—cpdl

By Eileen
Robinson
Smith

THE ACTION-PACKED ISLAND OF HILTON HEAD anchors the southern tip of South Carolina's coastline and attracts 2.5 million visitors each year. Although historically it has drawn an upscale clientele, and it still does, you'll find that the crowd here is much more diverse than you might think. It has more than its fair share of millionaires (you might run into director Ron Howard at the Starbucks, for instance), but it also attracts families in search of a good beach.

This half-tame, half-wild island is home to more than 25 world-class golf courses and even more resorts, hotels, and top restaurants. Still, it's managed development thanks to building restrictions that aim to marry progress with environmental protection. North of Hilton Head, the coastal landscape is peppered with quiet small towns and flanked by rural sea islands. Beaufort is a cultural treasure, a graceful antebellum town with a compact historic district and waterfront promenade. Several of the 18th- and 19th-century mansions have been converted to bed-and-breakfasts.

The stretch of coastline between Hilton Head and Charleston is one of the most scenic parts of the state and is still a mostly rural blend of small towns, winding country roads, and semitropical wilderness that turns into pristine beachfront before ending at the Atlantic. Here, especially along U.S. 17, look for roadside stands that sell boiled peanuts and homemade jams, and small-time shrimpers selling their catch out of coolers. Listen, too, for Gullah-tinged accents among the African-American natives—the sound is musical.

Continuing north, midway between Beaufort and Charleston is Edisto Island, where you can comb the beach for shells and camp out on the mostly barren Edisto Beach State Park, or rent the modest waterfront cottages that have been in the same families for generations. Ocean Ridge, the one resort property there, formerly a Fairfield resort, is now a Wyndham.

ORIENTATION & PLANNING

GETTING ORIENTED

Hilton Head is just north of South Carolina's border with Georgia. It's so close to Savannah that they share an airport. This part of the state is best explored by car, as its points of interest spread over a flat coastal plain that is a

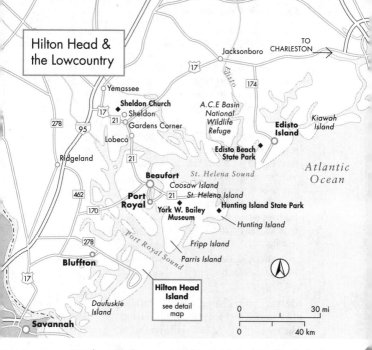

mix of wooded areas, marshes, and sea islands, the latter of which are sometimes accessible only by boat or ferry. Take U.S. 170 and 17 to get from one key spot (Hilton Head, Beaufort, and Edisto) to another. It's a pretty drive that winds through small towns and over old bridges. Charleston, the Queen Belle of the South, is at the northern end of the region.

WHEN TO GO

The high season follows typical beach-town cycles, with June through August and holidays year-round being the busiest and most costly. Mid-April, during the annual Verizon Heritage Golf Classic, is when rates tend to be highest. Thanks to the Lowcountry's mostly moderate year-round temperatures, tourists are ever present. Spring is the best time to visit, when the weather is ideal for tennis and golf. Autumn is almost as active for the same reason. Because the island is a popular destination for corporate meetings, business during the shoulder seasons and winter can still be brisk.

To get a good deal, it's imperative that you plan ahead. The choicest locations can be booked six months to a year in

LOWCOUNTRY BEST BETS

■ **Beaufort:** A small, antebellum town that offers large doses of heritage and culture; nearly everything you might want to see is within its downtown historic district.

■ **Beachcombing:** Hilton Head has 12 mi of beaches. You can swim, soak up the sun, or walk along the sand. The differential between the tides leaves a multitude of shells, sand dollars, and starfish.

■ **Challenging Golf:** Hilton Head's nickname is "Golf Island," and its many challenging courses have an international reputation.

■ **Serving up Tennis:** One of the nation's top tennis destinations, with academies run by legends like Stan Smith, former Wimbledon champion.

■ **Staying Put:** This semitropical island has been a resort destination for decades, and it has all of the desired amenities for visitors: a vast array of lodgings, an endless supply of restaurants, and excellent shopping.

advance, but booking agencies can help you make room reservations and get good deals during the winter season, when the crowds fall off. Villa rental companies often offer snowbird rates for monthly stays during the winter season. Parking is always free at the major hotels, but valet parking can cost from $10 to $15; the smaller properties have free parking, too, but no valet service.

GETTING HERE & AROUND

You can fly into Savannah's airport, which is about an hour from Hilton Head, but then you absolutely must have a car to get around.

BY AIR

Hilton Head Island Airport is served by US Airways Express. Most travelers use the Savannah/Hilton Head International Airport, less than an hour from Hilton Head, which is served by American Eagle, Continental Express, Delta, Northwest, United Express, and US Airways.

Contacts Hilton Head Island Airport (⊠ *120 Beach City Rd., Hilton Head, SC* ☎ *843/689–5400* ⊕ *www.hiltonheadairport.com*). **Savannah/Hilton Head International Airport** (⊠ *400 Airways Ave., Savannah, GA* ☎ *912/964–0514* ⊕ *www.savannahairport.com*).

BY BOAT & FERRY

Hilton Head is accessible via the intracoastal waterway, with docking available at Harbour Town Yacht Basin, Hilton Head Boathouse, and Shelter Cove Harbour.

Contacts **Harbour Yacht Basin** (☎ 843/671–2704). **Hilton Head Boathouse** (☎843/681–2628). **Shelter Cove Harbor** (☎843/842–7001).

BY BUS

Greyhound Bus connects Beaufort with other destinations in the area. The Lowcountry Regional Transportation Authority has a bus that leaves Beaufort in the morning for Hilton Head that costs $2.50. Exact change is required. This same company has a van that, with 24-hour notice, will pick you up at your hotel and drop you off at your destination for $3. You can request a ride weekdays 7 AM to 10 AM or 12:30 PM to 3 PM.

Contacts **Greyhound** (✉3659 Trask Pkwy., Beaufort ☎843/524–4646 or 800/231–2222 ⊕ www.greyhound.com). **The Lowcountry Regional Transportation Authority** (☎843/757–5782 ⊕www. gotohhi.com/bus).

BY TAXI

At Your Service and Gray Line Lowcountry Adventures are good options in Hilton Head.

Contacts **At Your Service** (☎843/837–3783). **Gray Line Lowcountry Adventures** (☎843/681–8212).

BY TRAIN

Amtrak gets you as close as Savannah or Yemassee. Gray Line Lowcountry Adventures will send a limo to pick you up at a cost of $66 per hour.

Contacts **Savannah Amtrak Station** (✉2611 Seaboard Coastline Dr., Savannah ☎912/234–2611 or 800/872–7245 ⊕www.amtrak. com). **Gray Line Lowcountry Adventures** (☎843/681–8212).

TOURS

Hilton Head's Adventure Cruises hosts dinner, sightseeing, and murder-mystery cruises. Several companies, including H20 Sports and Lowcountry Nature Tours in Hilton Head, run dolphin sightseeing, shark fishing, and delightful environmental trips. Carolina Buggy Tours show you Beaufort's historic district by horse-drawn carriage.

Gullah Heritage Trail Tours gives a wealth of history about slavery and the Union takeover of the island during the Civil War; tours leave from the Discovery Museum of Hilton Head and cost $35. Gullah 'n' Geechie Mahn Tours leads groups throughout Beaufort with a focus on African-American culture. Costumed guides sing and act out history during walking tours by the tour group, Spirit of Old Beaufort.

Contacts **Adventure Cruises** (✉ *Shelter Cove Marina, 9 Shelter Cove Lane, Mid-Island, Hilton Head Island* ☎ *843/785–4558* ⊕ *www.hiltonheadisland.com*). **Carolina Buggy Tours** (✉ *901 Port Republic St., Beaufort* ☎ *843/525–1300*). **Gullah Heritage Trail Tours** (✉ *Hilton Head* ☎ *843/681–7066* ⊕ *www.gullaheritage.com*). **Gullah 'n' Geechie Mahn Tours** (✉ *671 Sea Island Pkwy., Beaufort* ☎ *843/838–7516* ⊕ *www.gullahngeechietours.net*). **H2O Sports** (✉ *Harbour Town Marina, 149 Lighthouse Rd., South End, Hilton Head Island* ☎ *843/363–2628* ⊕ *www.h2osportsonline.com*). **Low Country Nature Tours** (✉ *Shelter Cover Marina, Shelter Cove Lane, Mid-Island, Hilton Head Island* ☎ *843/683–0187* ⊕ *www.lowcountry naturetours.com*). **Spirit of Old Beaufort** (✉ *103 West St., Beaufort* ☎ *843/525–0459* ⊕ *www.thespiritofoldbeaufort.com*).

ABOUT THE RESTAURANTS

Given the proximity to the Atlantic and small farms on the mainland, most locally owned restaurants are still heavily influenced by the catch of the day and seasonal field harvests. There are numerous national chain and fast-food restaurants within commercial complexes or malls. Although hard to fathom, relatively few restaurants on Hilton Head are on the water or even have a water view. Although you will find more high-end options, there are still holes-in-the-wall that serve good-tasting fare and are frequented by locals.

Most restaurants open at 11 and don't close until 9 or 10, but some take a break between 2:30 and 6. Most of the more expensive restaurants have an early dining menu aimed at seniors, and this is a popular time to dine. During the height of the summer season, reservations are essential at all times, though in the off-season you may need them only on weekends (still, more and more of the better restaurants require them).

ABOUT THE HOTELS

Hilton Head is known as one of the best vacation spots on the East Coast, and its hotels are a testimony to the reputation. The island is awash in regular hotels and resorts that are called plantations, not to mention beachfront or golf-course-view villas, cottages, and mansions. Here and on private islands you can expect the most modern conveniences and world-class service at the priciest places. Clean, updated rooms and friendly staff are everywhere, even at lower-cost hotels—this is the South, after all. Many international employees add a cosmopolitan atmosphere. Staying in cooler months, for extended periods of time, or commuting from nearby Bluffton, where there are some new limited-service properties, chains like Hampton Inn, can mean better deals.

WHAT IT COSTS				
¢	$	$$	$$$	$$$$
RESTAURANTS				
under $10	$10–$14	$15–$19	$20–$24	over $24
HOTELS				
under $100	$100–$150	$151–$200	$201–$250	over $250

Restaurant prices are for a main course at dinner. Hotel prices are for two people in a standard double room in high season. Tax of rooms is 12%; restaurant tax is 7.5% for food, and 8.5% for alcohol.

PLANNING YOUR TIME

Three days in the Hilton Head area will give you enough time to enjoy some outdoor fun, shopping, and a history lesson or two. No matter where you stay, spend your first day relaxing on the beach or hitting the links. After that, you'll have time to visit some of the area attractions, including the Coastal Discovery Museum or the Sea Pines Resort. Bluffton is a quaint 1850s town with many quirky, locally owned shops. You can also visit one of the many outlet malls. If you have a few more days, you should really visit Beaufort or even spend the night there. The ride along U.S. 17 or 170 from Hilton Head is a pretty one, so don't rush. The heart of this town is its historic district; if you have a week or more, spend a couple of nights here in an antebellum B&B. With a full week, you would also have time to visit Edisto or Daufuskie Island.

8

HILTON HEAD ISLAND

No matter how many golf courses pepper its landscape, Hilton Head will always be a semitropical barrier island. That means the 12 mi of beaches are lined with towering pines, palmetto trees, and wind-sculpted live oaks; the interior is a blend of oak and pine woodlands and meandering lagoons. Rental villas, lavish private houses, and luxury hotels line the coast as well.

Since the 1950s, resorts like Sea Pines, Palmetto Dunes, and Port Royal have sprung up all over. Although the gated resorts, called "plantations," are private residential communities, all have public restaurants, marinas, shopping areas, and recreational facilities. All are secured and cannot be toured unless arrangements are made at the visitor office near the main gate of each plantation. Hilton Head prides itself on strict laws that keep light pollution to a minimum. ■TIP→ **The lack of streetlights makes it difficult to find your way at night, so be sure to get good directions.**

EXPLORING HILTON HEAD & VICINITY

Driving Hilton Head by car or tour bus is the only way to get around. Off Interstate 95, take Exit 8 onto U.S. 278, which leads you through Bluffton and then onto Hilton Head proper. A 5¾-mi Cross Island Parkway toll bridge ($1) is just off 278, and makes it easy to bypass traffic and reach the south end of the island, where most of the resort areas and hotels are. Know that U.S. 278 can slow to a standstill at rush hour and during holiday weekends, and the signs are so discreet that it's easy to get lost without explicit directions. ⚠ **Be careful of putting the pedal to the metal, particularly on the Cross Island Parkway. The speed limits change dramatically.**

GETTING HERE & AROUND

Hilton Head Island is 19 mi east of I–95. Take Exit 8 off I–95 South and then Hwy. 278 directly to the bridge. If you're heading to the southern end of the island, your best bet to save time and avoid traffic is to take the Toll Expressway. The cost is $1 each way.

Visitor Information **Welcome Center of Hilton Head** (⊠*100 William Hilton Pkwy.* ☎*843/689–6302 or 800/523–3373* ⊕*www. hiltonheadisland.org.*

WHAT TO SEE

Audubon-Newhall Preserve, in the south, is 50 acres of pristine forest, where native plant life is tagged and identified. There are trails, a self-guided tour, and seasonal walks. ⊠*Palmetto Bay Rd., near southern base of Cross Island Pkwy., South End* ☎*843/842–9246* ⊕*www.hiltonhead audubon.org* ⊒*Free* ☉*Daily dawn–dusk.*

★ **Bluffton.** Tucked away from the resorts, charming Bluffton has several old homes and churches, a growing artists' colony, several good restaurants (including Truffles Cafe), and oak-lined streets dripping with Spanish moss. You could grab Southern-style picnic food and head to the boat dock at the end of Pritchard Street for great views. There are interesting little shops and galleries and some limited-service B&Bs that provide a nearby alternative to Hilton Head's higher prices. This town and surrounding area are experiencing some rapid growth since Hilton Head has little remaining undeveloped land. Much of the area's work force, especially its young, Latin, and international employees, live here. ⊠*Route 46, 8 mi northwest on U.S. 278.*

★ Fodor'sChoice **Coastal Discovery Museum.** The museum has relocated to what was the Horn Plantation, and it's an all-new and wonderful Lowcountry learning experience, especially for visitors with children. Although a small museum, its interpretive panels and exhibits have been done with a contemporary mind-set. Kids, for example, can dress up in the clothing of centuries past. The museum's mission is to develop an understanding and appreciation for the cultural heritage and natural history of the Lowcountry. Visitors will learn about the early development of Hilton Head as an island resort from the Civil War to the 1930s. Admission is free, and its litany of lectures and tours on subjects both historical and natural range from $3 and up. The terrace and grounds are such that it is simply a comfortable, stress-free green landscape just off the Cross Island Parkway entrance ramp, though it feels a century away. The gift shop remains in its original location, within the Visitors Center at 100 William Hilton Pkwy. ⊠*Hwy. 278 at Gumtree Rd., North End* ☎*843/689–6767* ⊕*www.coastaldiscovery.org* ⊒*Free* ☉*Mon.–Sat. 9–5, Sun. 10–3.*

Palmetto Dunes Resort. This complex is home to the renowned Rod Laver Tennis Center, a good stretch of beach, three golf courses, a golf academy and several oceanfront villa complexes. The oceanfront Hilton Head Marriott Beach

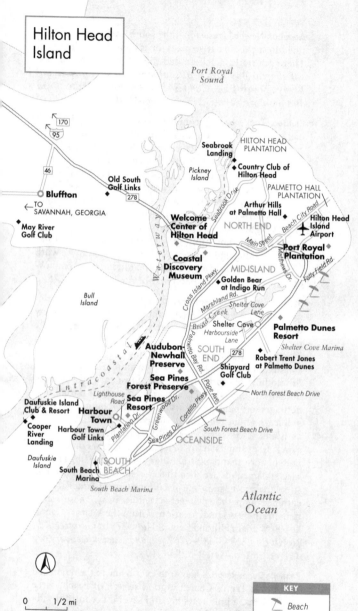

Hilton Head Island

Port Royal Sound

↖ 170
95

46

Bluffton
← TO
SAVANNAH, GEORGIA

May River
Golf Club

Old South
Golf Links
278

**Seabrook
Landing**

*Pickney
Island*

HILTON HEAD
PLANTATION

**Country Club of
Hilton Head**

PALMETTO HALL
PLANTATION

**Arthur Hills
at Palmetto Hall**

Beach City Road

**Hilton Head
Island
Airport**

**Welcome
Center of
Hilton Head**

Seabrook Drive

NORTH END

Main Street

Matthews Dr.

**Port Royal
Plantation**

**Coastal
Discovery
Museum**

Cross Island Pkwy.

MID-ISLAND

**Golden Bear
at Indigo Run**

Marshland Rd.

*Shelter Cove
Lane*

Folly Field Rd.

*Bull
Island*

Broad Creek

Shelter Cove
*Harbourside
Lane*

**Palmetto Dunes
Resort**

Shelter Cove Marina

Palmetto Bay Rd.

**SOUTH
END**
278

**Robert Trent Jones
at Palmetto Dunes**

**Audubon-
Newhall
Preserve**

**Sea Pines
Forest Preserve**

*Lighthouse
Road*

**Sea Pines
Resort**

Greenwood Dr.

**Shipyard
Golf Club**

Pope Ave.

Cordillo Pkwy.

North Forest Beach Drive

**Daufuskie Island
Club & Resort**

**Harbour
Town**

**Cooper
River
Landing**

**Harbour Town
Golf Links**

Plantation Dr.

Sea Pines Dr.

OCEANSIDE

South Forest Beach Drive

*Daufuskie
Island*

**SOUTH
BEACH**

**South Beach
Marina**

South Beach Marina

Intracoastal

Waterway

*Atlantic
Ocean*

N

0   1/2 mi
0   1/2 km

KEY
⛱ *Beach*
⛴ *Ferry*

CLOSE UP

Fodor's First Person: John Jakes, Writer, on Hilton Head

If you happened to be in Hilton Head in April 2008 and saw lines snaking out of Jump & Phil's Restaurant, it's probably because the famous historical novelist John Jakes was having a book signing for his latest novel, *The Gods of Newport*. Jakes and his wife, Rachel, will celebrate their 30th anniversary of living on Hilton Head in 2009.

He writes about his island: "Hilton Head is always good for a visit despite the clutter

of advancing 'development' between the island and I-95. Town organizers wisely kept the commercial buildings mostly low-rise—no towering oceanside condos here. Sugar-white beaches and Civil War ruins in Port Royal Plantation. In 1861, the island was captured by a Union fleet. A false-front town of some 15,000 civilians—cardsharps, floozies et al.—supplemented the military garrison until 1865. I'm told they even presented amateur theatricals."

& Golf Resort and the Hilton Oceanfront Resort are also within this plantation, as are villa-condo complexes with large inventories of rental units. ⊠*Queens Folly Rd. at U.S. 278, Mid-Island* ☎*800/845–8160* ⊕*www.palmetto dunesresort.com.*

Port Royal Plantation. The main draws here are the posh Westin Resort, which is on the beach, three PGA-championship golf courses, and the Port Royal racquet club, with 16 tennis courts. ⊠*2 Grasslawn Ave., Mid-Island* ☎*843/681–4000* ⊕*www.portroyalplantation.com.*

Sea Pines Forest Preserve. At this 605-acre public wilderness tract, walking trails take you past a stocked fishing pond, waterfowl pond, and a 3,400-year-old Indian shell ring. Pick up the extensive activity guide at the Sea Pines Welcome Center to take advantage of goings-on—moonlight hayrides, storytelling around campfires, and alligator- and bird-watching boat tours. The preserve is part of the grounds at Sea Pines Resort. ⊠*Off U.S. 278, Sea Pines Resort, South End* ☎*843/363–4530* ⊕*www.seapines.com* ⊠*$5 per car* ⊙*Daily dawn–dusk.*

★ **Fodor's**Choice **Sea Pines Resort.** The oldest and best known of Hilton Head's developments, this resort occupies 4,500 thickly wooded acres with three golf courses, tennis clubs, stables, a fine beach, and shopping plazas. The focus of

8

Sea Pines is **Harbour Town**, a charming marina with a luxury boutique hotel, shops, restaurants, condominiums and vacation rental homes, and the landmark, candy-striped Hilton Head Lighthouse. A free "trolley" shuttles visitors around the resort. There is a $5 charge per car for parking (nonguests only). ⊠*Off U.S. 278, South End* ☎*843/363–4530* ⊕*www.seapines.com* ⊠*$5 per car.*

WHERE TO EAT

$$$–$$$$ ✕**Aqua Grille & Lounge.** *Seafood.* A great deal of effort was expended to create the ambience here—a waterfall on the first level, a fireplace lounge adjacent to the second-story dining room. The food—particularly the shellfish—and portions are commendable, the wine list up with the latest trends, the servers savvy. Grazing is the way to go: the oysters with champagne mignonette or chili-lime remoulade; the delicious sashimi; the bibb and red-leaf salad with macadamias dressed with orange-miso vinaigrette. (Forget the spring rolls.) The more sought-after main courses are tuna, blackened mahimahi, and pecan-crusted sea bass, with the filet mignon the best steak. A late-night menu is served from 10 to midnight. Happy Hour is a must. ⊠*10 N. Forest Beach Dr., South End* ☎*843/341–3331* ⊟*AE, MC, V* ⊙*No lunch.*

$$$ ✕**Black Marlin Bayside Grill.** *Seafood.* If you want to dine in the marina with a view of the "blue," then head to this new player, the latest creation of a seasoned local restaurant group. Attracting local boat people and also business lunchers, there's a steady stream of customers most days, but Saturday and Sunday brunch are the highlights (check out the well-priced Bloody Marys) for eggs Benedict and live entertainment. For lunch, the best bets include one of the seafood sandwiches or Baja fish tacos; there are always two or three items under $10. Prices go up for dinner, and the buzz calms. The bar is fun and promulgates a gentrified Key West ambience, especially at happy hour from 4 to 7. There's an early dining menu, but the kitchen cranks out entrees until 10 every night. ⊠ *Palmetto Marina, 86 Helmsman Way, South End* ☎*843/785–4950* ⊟*AE, MC, V.*

$$$ ✕**Boathouse 11.** *Seafood.* Boathouse 11 is an actual waterfront restaurant; although hard to fathom, waterfront dining is difficult to find on this island. To soak in the salty atmosphere, reserve an outdoor table on the partially covered patio or grab a seat at the bar that looks out on the charter fishing pier. This is one fun place, and

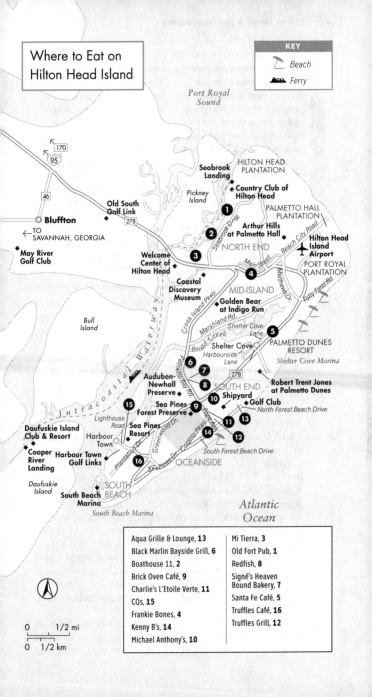

Where to Eat on Hilton Head Island

Port Royal Sound

Seabrook Landing

HILTON HEAD PLANTATION

Country Club of Hilton Head

Pickney Island

❶

❷

Arthur Hills at Palmetto Hall

PALMETTO HALL PLANTATION

Hilton Head Island Airport

Old South Golf Link

278

Seabrook Drive

NORTH END

Beach City Road

170

95

46

Bluffton

← TO SAVANNAH, GEORGIA

Welcome Center of Hilton Head

❸

Main Street

❹

Matthews Dr.

PORT ROYAL PLANTATION

May River Golf Club

Coastal Discovery Museum

MID-ISLAND

Golden Bear at Indigo Run

Cross Island Pkwy.

Marshland Rd.

Shelter Cove Lane

Fairy Field Rd.

Bull Island

Broad Creek

Shelter Cove

❺

PALMETTO DUNES RESORT

Shelter Cove Marina

Harbourside Lane

Palmetto Bay Rd.

❻

❼

❽

278

SOUTH END

❿

Robert Trent Jones at Palmetto Dunes

Audubon-Newhall Preserve

Shipyard Golf Club

North Forest Beach Drive

Intracoastal Waterway

Sea Pines Forest Preserve

❾

❶❶   ❶❸

❶❷

Lighthouse Road

⓯

Sea Pines Resort

❶❹

South Forest Beach Drive

Daufuskie Island Club & Resort

Harbour Town

Greenwood Dr.

Sea Pines Dr.—Cordillo Pkwy.

OCEANSIDE

Cooper River Landing

Harbour Town Golf Links

⓰

Plantation Dr.

Sea Pines Dr.

Daufuskie Island

SOUTH BEACH

Atlantic Ocean

South Beach Marina

South Beach Marina

Aqua Grille & Lounge, **13**	Mi Tierra, **3**
Black Marlin Bayside Grill, **6**	Old Fort Pub, **1**
Boathouse 11, **2**	Redfish, **8**
Brick Oven Café, **9**	Signé's Heaven Bound Bakery, **7**
Charlie's L'Etoile Verte, **11**	Santa Fe Café, **5**
CQs, **15**	Truffles Café, **16**
Frankie Bones, **4**	Truffles Grill, **12**
Kenny B's, **14**	
Michael Anthony's, **10**	

0   1/2 mi

0   1/2 km

CLOSE UP

Shrimp Boats Forever

The sunset sight of shrimp trawlers coming into home port, with mighty nets raised and an entourage of hungry seagulls, is a cherished Lowcountry tradition. The shrimping industry has been an integral staple of the South Carolina economy for nearly a century. (Remember Bubba Gump?) It was booming in the 1980s. But alas, cheap, farm-raised shrimp from foreign markets and now the cost of diesel fuel are decimating the shrimpers' numbers.

The season for fresh-caught shrimp is May to December. Lowcountry residents support the freelance fishermen by buying only certified, local wild shrimp in restaurants and in area fish markets and supermarkets. If you wish to follow this "when in Rome" mentality, visitors can follow suit by patronizing local restaurants and markets that display the logo that reads: CERTIFIED WILD AMERICAN SHRIMP. Or you can simply ask before you eat.

the simple fare is well-prepared. Fish and shellfish are the best choices here; for lunch you can order a perfect oyster po'boy. Yes, there are a few landlubber main courses, too. Want chicken instead? Ask for the teriyaki sandwich named after a local DJ. Distinguished by quality, fresh produce, this casual place also has a surprisingly admirable wine list with reasonably priced glasses and a number of bottles in the $30-something range. Brunch is a Sunday happening and quite popular. ⊠ *397 Squire Pope Rd., North End* ☎ *843/681–3663* ⚐ ▤ *AE, D, MC, V.*

$$–$$$ ✕**Brick Oven Café.** *American.* Velvet drapes, dramatic chandeliers, and 1940s-era lounge-style entertainment—on top of good, reasonably priced food served late—make this an *in* place. It's a refreshingly quirky joint on an island that is more 'luxe than funky, and the menu is equally eclectic. Appetizers include sweet-potato-and-lobster cakes, and shrimp-and-pork spring rolls; among the best entrées are wood-fired pizzas, roasted-veggie sandwiches, and veal meat loaf. Check out the new grazing menu called Tappatizers (appetizer-size small plates that can still make up a meal), as well as the pastas. The wine list has a good range and pricing. ⊠ *33 Park Plaza, Greenwood Dr., South End* ☎ *843/686–2233* ⚐ *Reservations essential* ▤ *AE, D, DC, MC, V* ⊘ *No lunch.*

$$$$ ✕**Charlie's L'Etoile Verte.** *French.* This family-owned culinary landmark has oozed personality for a quarter-century. Originally one tiny room, its popularity with locals and

repeat visitors sparked the move to these new spacious digs. As you first step in the door, you'll be wowed by the eclectic, country-French decor and the homey ambience. Unusual for Hilton Head, the blackboard menu is hand-written daily according to market availability. The menu is just as homespun and cozy, primarily French classics. Certain items are constants, like the perfectly perfect curried shrimp salad at lunch. Come nightfall, out comes the *pâté maison* and veal tenderloin with wild mushroom sauce. The wine list is distinguished. ✉*8 Orleans Rd., Mid-Island* ☎*843/785–9277* ⌂*Reservations essential* ▭*AE, MC, V* ⊘*Closed Sun. No lunch Mon.*

★ FodorśChoice✕**CQs.** *Eclectic.* If you heard that all island res-
$$$$ taurants are in shopping centers and lack atmosphere, then you need to experience CQs. Its rustic ambience— heart-pine floors, sepia-toned island photos, and a lovely second-story dining room—coupled with stellar cuisine, a personable staff, live piano music, and a feel-good spirit put most of the island's other restaurants to shame. Chef Eric Sayer's imaginative, original creations are divine. Imagine a lobster triumvirate as an appetizer, with an incredible lobster cheesecake the standout. Imagine a golden brown Alaskan halibut afloat in a crab cream sauce. Manager Drew can pair your wine perfectly from an impeccable list. You will awake next morning thinking about it all. The gate pass for Sea Pines ($5) will be reimbursed with purchase of one main course or more. ✉*Harbour Town, 140 Lighthouse La., South End* ☎*843/671–2779* ⌂*Reservations essential* ▭*AE, MC, V* ⊘*No lunch.*

$$–$$$ ✕**Frankie Bones.** *Italian.* Since this restaurant is dedicated to the loving memory of Frank Sinatra, you might assume that its name is also one of the handles of "ole blue eyes." But no, "Bones" was a Chicago gangster before Prohibition. This place has a strong appeal to an older set of regulars who like the traditional parmegianas and marsalas on the early-dining menu. But during happy hour, the bar and tall cocktail tables are populated with younger patrons who order flat-bread pizzas and small portions of pasta. It's especially popular with guys who prefer the substantial and familiar, but some dishes have more innovative twists, including a 16-ounce rib eye with a sweetened coffee rub. Be an honorary Italian and just drink your dessert, something Amaretto-based such as a Godfather or a Burnt Almond. ✉*1301 Main St., North End* ☎*843/682–4455* ⌂*Reservations essential* ▭*AE, D, MC, V* ⊘*Closed Sun. No lunch.*

8

Cooking Italian Style in Hilton Head

You can "get naked" in a hands-on cooking class with Chef Michael Cirafesi, the talented chef of Michael Anthony's, one of the island's best restaurant experiences. Held on the restaurant's second floor, where he has his chef's table, too, you can also attend demonstration classes, wine tastings, and spouse programs for visiting corporate groups. You get to sample what is cooked with wine that will complement it and add to the camaraderie. Since there is a high demand for these classes, not to mention limited availability, check the schedule and reserve your place as far in advance as possible on the Michael Anthony Web site (⊕ *www.michael-anthonys.com*).

WORD OF MOUTH. "Not the 'country club' you might expect, Harold's Country Club & Grill is a sprawling, remodeled gas station in the little town of Yemassee, a short way east of I-95, south of Charleston. Cheerful ladies slap a steak on your plate (or whatever the featured entrée is that evening), then you proceed past an array of sides and find a place in one of the large, kitschy dining rooms. Karaoke begins in the bar at 8 pm on weekends; good-natured local people throng in to sing or watch." —John Jakes

¢–$ ✕ **Kenny B's French Quarter Café.** *Cajun-Creole.* Surrounded by Mardi Gras memorabilia, Kenny himself cooks up jambalaya, gumbo, and muffaletta sandwiches. His wife runs the dining room, serving hungry working folks golden-fried oyster po'boys topped with real remoulade sauce. Go for the Sunday buffet brunch: there's chicory coffee, perfect beignets, spicy omelets, and various eggs Benedicts. A local haunt for nearly 10 years, this place in a shopping center is open from morning until 9 PM. ⊠ *Bi-Lo Circle, 70 Pope Ave., Mid-Island* ☎ *843/785–3315* ⊟ *AE, D, MC, V* ⊘ *No dinner Sun.*

★ Fodor'sChoice ✕ **Michael Anthony's.** *Italian.* This throwback goes
$$$–$$$$ back to the days when the most exotic ethnic restaurant in a town was a family-owned Italian spot, where professional waiters would receive your rapt attention as they described the nightly specials. This is that kind of place, but contemporized and more upscale, with fresh, top-quality ingredients, simple yet elegant sauces, and waiters

who know and care about the food they serve. Owned by a talented, charismatic Philadelphia family, the restaurant has a convivial spirit, and its innovative pairings and plate presentations are au courant. Locals file in for the early-dining menu, which includes three courses and a glass of wine; this is a superior value for about $20. But you can order from the à la carte menu, and after homemade gnocchi or a succulent veal chop with wild mushroom sauce, you can finish happily with a sambuca and panna cotta. Then sing "Volare"! ⊠ *Orleans Plaza, 37 New Orleans Rd., Ste. L, South End* ☎ *843/785–6272* ⌫ *Reservations essential* ⊟ *AE, D, MC, V* ⊗ *Closed Sun. No lunch.*

$ ✕ **Mi Tierra.** *Tex-Mex.* At this friendly Mexican restaurant, freshness is the key to tasty fare like fried-fish tacos. You can also grab takeout from Baja Tacos—next door, run by the same people—a simple taco stand with counter service, café tables, and a condiments bar with fresh salsas and relishes. Down a *cerveza* (beer) as you watch Mexican *telenovelas* (soap operas). ⊠ *160 Fairfield Sq., North End* ☎ *843/342–3409* ⊟ *MC, V.*

$$$–$$$$ ✕ **Old Fort Pub.** *Continental.* Overlooking the sweeping
★ marshlands of Skull Creek, this romantic restaurant has almost panoramic views. It offers one of the island's best overall dining experiences: the building is old enough to have some personality, and the professional waiters do their duty. More important, the kitchen serves flavorful food, including a great appetizer of roasted calamari with sun-dried tomatoes and olives. Entrées like duck confit in rhubarb sauce and filet mignon with shiitake mushrooms hit the spot. The wine list is extensive, and there's outdoor seating plus a third-floor porch for toasting the sunset. Sunday brunch is celebratory and includes a mimosa. "Pub Hour" downstairs from Monday through Friday offers discounted drinks and an interesting crowd to drink with (it lasts from 5 to 6:30). ⊠ *65 Skull Creek Dr., North End* ☎ *843/681–2386* ⊟ *AE, D, DC, MC, V* ⊗ *No lunch.*

✕ **Redfish.** *Caribbean.* The "naked" catch of the day—seafood grilled with olive oil, lime, and garlic—is a low-cal, heart-healthy specialty that many diners opt for; it's a welcome change from the fried fare at many other local spots. Caribbean and Cuban flavors pervade the rest of the menu in dishes such as red trout with Boursin-cheese grits; spicy tasso ham in a cream sauce spiked with Amaretto, Tabasco, and Worcestershire; and Dominican braised pork, roasted with bananas, chilies, and coconut. The restaurant's wine cellar is full with some 1,000 bottles, and there's also a retail

8

wine shop. Although this commercial strip location isn't inspired, the lively crowd sitting amid candlelight, subdued artwork, dark furniture, and white linens more than makes up for this typical island shortcoming. The increasingly innovative cooking is a draw for chic tourists; locals don't frequent as they once did since menu prices have gone up. ⊠ *8 Archer Rd., corner Palmetto Bay Rd., South End* ☎ *843/686–3388* ⊟ *AE, D, MC, V* ⊘ *No lunch Sun.*

¢ ✕ **Signe's Heaven Bound Bakery & Café.** *American.* Every morn-
★ ing locals roll in for the deep-dish French toast, crispy polenta, and whole-wheat waffles. Since 1974, European-born Signe has been feeding islanders her delicious soups (the chilled cucumber has pureed watermelon, green apples, and mint), curried chicken salad, and loaded hot and cold sandwiches. The beach bag ($10 for a cold sandwich, pasta or fresh fruit, chips, a beverage, and cookie) is a great deal. The key-lime bread pudding is amazing, as are the melt-in-your mouth cakes and the rave-worthy breads, especially the Italian ciabatta. Wedding cakes are a specialty—Signe decorates more than 300 a year, and she'll provide other special-occasion cakes, too. If you want to become part of the Hilton Head scene, you need to know Signe. ⊠ *93 Arrow Rd., South End* ☎ *843/785–9118* ⊟ *AE, D, MC, V* ⊘ *Closed Sun. No dinner.*

$$$–$$$$ ✕ **Santa Fe Café.** *Southwestern.* The Southwest has been convincingly recreated here in South Carolina. Guests are greeted by the sights, sounds, and aromas of New Mexico: native American rugs, Mexican ballads, steer skulls and horns, and the pungent smells of chilies and mesquite on the grill. The restaurant is perhaps best experienced on a rainy, chilly night when the adobe fireplaces are cranked up. Go for the rush of spicy food chased with an icy Mexican cerveza or one of the island's best margaritas (order one up, with top-shelf tequila, and let the fiesta begin). A party for the senses, after the fiery and artistic Painted Desert soup (a thick puree of red pepper and chilies in chicken stock), you can chill with the Yucatan *ceviche* made from a mix of fish and shellfish. Forgo the Tex-Mex standards like burritos or the appetizer sampler and experience instead the better Southwestern dishes like mesquite lamb with cranberry-chipotle sauce. Plan on listening to *guitarra* music in the rooftop cantina on Wednesday through Saturday nights. ⊠ *700 Plantation Center, Mid-Island* ☎ *843/785–3838* ⊲ *Reservations essentials* ⊟ *AE, MC, V* ⊘ *No lunch Sat. and Sun.*

$$–$$$ ×**Truffles Cafe.** *American.* When a restaurant survives here for more than 20 years, there's a reason. This place has personable, hands-on owners, prices low enough to keep the islanders coming all year, and food that is fresh and flavorful. There are none of the namesake truffles, but there's grilled salmon with a mango-barbecue glaze and—if you're gonna be bad—barbecued baby back ribs. This is a favorite for families because of its kid-friendly environment. Check out the wildly creative gift shop. ⊠*Sea Pines Center, 71 Lighthouse Rd.* ☎*843/671–6136* ⊟*AE, D, MC, V.*

$$$–$$$$ ×**Truffles Grill.** *American.* The latest entrant in the island's Truffles trilogy is also the best for those who like contemporary takes on American food. The decor, including giant-size black-and-white, island-themed photos, is striking; the lighting is also trendy. All five appetizers are outstanding, with the famous Tee-time cheese ring a great item to share. The Oriental Napa salad with tuna is big enough to be a main course. If you're on a budget, choose a specialty like the Kobe burger with pimento cheese. If you're not, then venture to pricey-yet-juicy center-cut steaks. You will need to order sides, too. As always with Price Beall's restaurants, the ingredients are super fresh and wholesome, so you can devour a scrumptious blondie for dessert without guilt. Speaking of naughty, martinis are full-sized, with a creative twist or straight-on up, for a moderate price; you can also get excellent wines by the glass. ⊠*8 Executive Park Rd., off Pope Ave., South End* ☎*843/785-3663* ⌂*Reservations essential* ⊟*AE, D, MC, V* ⊘*Closed Sun. No lunch.*

WHERE TO STAY

$$$–$$$$ ☖**Crowne Plaza Hilton Head Island Beach Resort.** Decorated in a classy nautical theme and set in a luxuriant garden, the Crowne Plaza is appropriately resplendent. It's the centerpiece of Shipyard Plantation, which means guests have access to all its amenities. It also has one of the more elegant lobbies and public spaces; however, this resort has the fewest oceanfront rooms of the majors and is the farthest from the water. Its latticed bridge and beach pavilion have seen many an island wedding. **Pros:** It is the closest hotel to all the restaurants and nightlife in Coligny Plaza and Park Plaza; parking is free, although valet parking costs $10. **Cons:** Wi-Fi and cell service are problematic due to low-rise, older concrete structures; large and sometimes impersonal. ⊠ *Shipyard Plantation, 130 Shipyard Dr., Mid-Island* ☎*843/842–2400 or 800/334–1881* ⊕*www.ichotels*

The International Connection

When guests pull up to the grand entrance of a Hilton Head resort and a dark-skinned bellman greets them with a smile, extending a welcome in a lilting accent, visitors assume he is of local African-American decent, known in the Lowcountry as a "Gullah."

Although that is possible—some of the Gullahs have been employed in the hotel industry here for more than 25 years—chances are that the man is Jamaican. Since 2002, the island's resorts have been importing thousands of Jamaicans during peak season to fill service openings that they have trouble staffing locally. These willing workers come on annual visas that can be renewed after a return trip to Jamaica for several months. All went well until 2008, when South Carolina politicians voted to stop issuing these visas. Those who

had already obtained green cards were able to stay on, and repeat guests to Hilton Head are pleased to see them.

Another plan had to be implemented, especially for the outlying resorts like the Daufuskie Island Club. These resorts tapped into agencies that handle staffing for ski resorts and were able to fill their quotas. The Marriott, for example, has an extensive international intern program, with trainees eventually being able to transfer to other Marriott properties and to move into management positions. Under a staffer's name badge you will see his country of origin: Turkey, the Philippines, Australia, Brazil, etc. At the Inn at Harbour Town, where the bellmen traditionally wear Scottish kilts, the young man parking your car may have a Russian accent!

---

group.com *331 rooms, 9 suites ↺In-room: refrigerator, Internet. In-hotel: 3 restaurants, golf courses, pools, gym, bicycles, Wi-Fi, children's programs (ages 3–12), parking (free), no-smoking rooms.* =AE, D, DC, MC, V ⚏EP.

$$$$ ⛱Disney's Hilton Head Island Resort. Disney's typical cheery
⟳ colors and whimsical designs create a look that's part South-
★ ern beach resort, part Adirondack hideaway. The villas here
have fully furnished dining, living, and sleeping areas, as
well as porches with rocking chairs and picnic tables. It's
on a little islet in Broad Creek; many units have marsh or
marina views. The smallest villa is a studio; the largest has
three bedrooms, four baths, and space to sleep a dozen.
The resort has a fishing pier and a lively beach club a
mile from the accommodations (shuttle service provided).

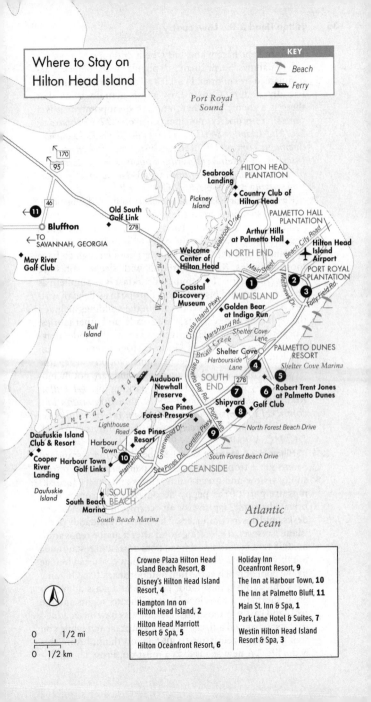

Where to Stay on Hilton Head Island

KEY
Beach
Ferry

Port Royal Sound

170
95
46
11 Bluffton

TO SAVANNAH, GEORGIA

Old South Golf Link
278

May River Golf Club

Welcome Center of Hilton Head

Coastal Discovery Museum

Bull Island

Seabrook Landing

Pickney Island

HILTON HEAD PLANTATION

Country Club of Hilton Head

PALMETTO HALL PLANTATION

Arthur Hills at Palmetto Hall

Beach City Road

Hilton Head Island Airport

Main Street

NORTH END

Matthews Dr.

PORT ROYAL PLANTATION

Folly Field Rd.

MID-ISLAND

Golden Bear at Indigo Run

Marshland Rd.

Shelter Cove Lane

Shelter Cove

Harbourside Lane

SOUTH END

PALMETTO DUNES RESORT

Shelter Cove Marina

Robert Trent Jones at Palmetto Dunes

Audubon-Newhall Preserve

Sea Pines Forest Preserve

Shipyard Golf Club

North Forest Beach Drive

Daufuskie Island Club & Resort

Cooper River Landing

Harbour Town Golf Links

Harbour Town

Sea Pines Resort

Lighthouse Road

Daufuskie Island

South Beach Marina

SOUTH BEACH

South Beach Marina

OCEANSIDE

South Forest Beach Drive

Atlantic Ocean

Intracoastal Waterway

Cross Island Pkwy.

Palmetto Bay Rd.

Pope Ave.

Greenwood Dr.

Cordillo Pkwy.

Sea Pines Dr.

Plantation Dr.

Broad Creek

0   1/2 mi
0   1/2 km

Crowne Plaza Hilton Head Island Beach Resort, 8

Disney's Hilton Head Island Resort, 4

Hampton Inn on Hilton Head Island, 2

Hilton Head Marriott Resort & Spa, 5

Hilton Oceanfront Resort, 6

Holiday Inn Oceanfront Resort, 9

The Inn at Harbour Town, 10

The Inn at Palmetto Bluff, 11

Main St. Inn & Spa, 1

Park Lane Hotel & Suites, 7

Westin Hilton Head Island Resort & Spa, 3

Kids are kept happy and busy, be it crabbing or roasting marshmallows. Surprisingly, it's popular with couples unaccompanied by children. **Pros:** It's all about kids; young and friendly staffers. **Cons:** Many guests actually think that there is a theme park here and are disappointed; it is a time-share property; not inexpensive. ✉ *22 Harbourside La., Mid-Island* ☎*843/341–4100 or 407/939–7540* ⊕*www. dvcmagic.com* ⊶*102 units* ⚿*In-room: kitchen (some), Internet. In-hotel: 2 restaurants, pools, gym, watersports, bicycles, children's programs (ages 3–16), laundry service, no-smoking rooms* ⊟*AE, MC, V* ⦿*EP.*

$ 🖫**Hampton Inn on Hilton Head Island.** Tree-shaded, this hotel, which is sheltered from the noise and traffic, is a good choice if you have kids. The two-bedroom family suites are surprisingly upscale; the parents' rooms are tastefully appointed, and the kids' rooms are cool enough to have foosball tables. King-size studios with sleeper sofas are another alternative for families. Breakfast is as Southern as country gravy and biscuits or as European as Belgian waffles. Major renovations throughout the buildings included the replacement of carpets, bedspreads, and other fabrics. Corporate and business travelers favor this moderately-priced option, too. **Pros:** Good customer service; clean; eight different breakfast menus. **Cons:** Not on a beach (the closest is Folly Field, 2 mi away); grounds are not memorable, and your view is often the parking lot. ✉ *1 Dillon Rd., Mid-Island* ☎*843/681–7900* ⊕*www.hampton-inn. com* ⊶*115 rooms, 7 suites* ⚿*In-room: Internet. In-hotel: pool, Wi-Fi, parking (free), no-smoking rooms* ⊟*AE, D, DC, MC, V* ⦿*BP.*

$$$$ 🖫**Hilton Head Marriott Resort & Spa.** Marriott's standard
Ⓒ rooms get a tropical twist at this palm-enveloped resort:
★ sunny yellow-and-green floral fabrics and cheery furnishings are part of the peppy decor. All guest rooms have private balconies (spring for an oceanfront room), writing desks, and down comforters. The tallest granddaddy of the island's resorts, it's looking good after a major renovation in 2008 that includes revamped pool areas and restaurants, notably Conroy's. To take in the sea views, you can lounge by the pool or lunch at the fun, outdoor snack bar. On rainy days and at dusk, the indoor pool under a glass dome is a great alternative. Kids love Dive-in Theater nights and the real sand castle in the lobby. Hammocks have been added to the sandy knoll adjacent to the pool area, and while you swing yourself gently into a siesta, you think, "Ahh, this is the life." A new spa is also a must-do. **Pros:** The multi-

cultural staff has a great spirit; a full-service Marriott, it is one of the best-run operations on the island. **Cons:** Rooms could be larger; in the summer kids are everywhere; in-room Wi-Fi costs $9.95 a day. ⊠*1 Hotel Circle, Palmetto Dunes, Mid-Island* ☎*843/686–8400 or 888/511–5086* ☐*843/686–8450* ⊕*www.hiltonheadmarriott.com* ⬎*476 rooms, 36 suites* ⌂*In-room: safe, kitchen (some), Wi-Fi. In-hotel: restaurant, bar, golf courses, tennis courts, pools, gym, spa, beachfront, watersports, bicycles, Wi-Fi, children's programs (ages 3–12), no-smoking rooms* ⊟*AE, D, DC, MC, V* ⊚*EP.*

$$–$$$ ▦ **Hilton Oceanfront Resort.** Unquestionably, there's a Caribbean sensibility to this five-story chain hotel; the grounds are beautifully landscaped with deciduous and evergreen bushes, and palms run along the beach. This is not what you think of when you think Hilton, which usually denotes a high-rise property; rather, this resort is far more casual, laid back, and more family-friendly than business-friendly. The smallest accommodations are large, commodious studios with a kitchenette; they go on up to two-bedroom suites. Many rooms face the ocean, and all are decorated with elegant wood furnishings, such as hand-carved armoires. A new, urbane lounge called the XO is a happening nightspot. HH Prime is the steak house, and the excellent deli/breakfast restaurant is being expanded at this writing. The resort has three pools, one strictly for little children, another for families, and an adults-only pool overlooking the ocean. Prices span a long range; online deals can be the best, with outdoor cabana massages, breakfast, and a bottle of wine included in some packages. **Pros:** Competes more with condos than hotels because of the size of its accommodations; lots of outdoor dining options. **Cons:** Boisterous wedding parties can be too noisy; problems with cell reception; minimum stay is two nights during summer. ⊠*23 Ocean La., Palmetto Dunes, Mid-Island* ⌂*Box 6165, 29938* ☎*843/842–8000 or 800/845–8001* ⊕*www.hiltonheadhilton.com* ⬎*303 studios, 20 suites* ⌂*In-room: kitchen, Internet. In-hotel: restaurants, golf courses, pools, gym, watersports, bicycles, Wi-Fi, children's programs (ages 5–12), no-smoking rooms* ⊟*AE, D, DC, MC, V* ⊚*EP.*

▦ **Holiday Inn Oceanfront Resort.** This high-rise on one of the island's busiest beaches is within walking distance of major South End shops and restaurants. Standard rooms are spacious and furnished in a contemporary style, recently renovated in bright and bold color schemes. It attracts a

8

diverse crowd: budget-minded vacationers, mainly families, corporate travelers and meeting groups, and those who like the fun social aspects of the beach scene. Golf and tennis packages are available, and rates with breakfast included are the better deal. A resort fee is charged, $8.95 a day that includes Wi-Fi and parking. The two-bedroom suites with ocean views usually have to be booked a month in advance, particularly in summer. The outdoor Tiki Hut lounge, a poolside bar, is hugely popular at one of the island's most populated beaches. Pets are allowed, but not during peak season. **Pros:** The price is a good value for Hilton Head, particularly for families; strong professional management and corporate standards; microwaves in rooms. **Cons:** If you are looking for posh, it is not; in summer, the number of kids raises the noise volume; small front desk can back up. ✉ *S. Forest Beach Dr., South End* ☐ *Box 5728, 29938* ☎ *843/785–5126 or 800/423–9897* 🖷 *843/785–6678* ⊕ *www.hihiltonhead.com* ☞ *201 rooms* ⚷ *In-room: refrigerator, Internet, Wi-Fi. In-hotel: restaurant, bar, pool, gym, bicycles, Wi-Fi, children's programs (ages 3–12), no-smoking rooms* ▭ *AE, D, DC, MC, V* ⬡ *EP.*

$$$ 🏨 **The Inn at Harbour Town.** The most buzz-worthy of Hilton
★ Head's properties is this European-style boutique hotel. A proper staff, clad in kilts, pampers you with British service and a dose of Southern charm. Butlers are on hand any time of the day or night, and the kitchen delivers around the clock. The spacious guest rooms, decorated with neutral palettes, have luxurious touches like Frette bed linens, which are turned down for you each night. The back patio with its upscale furnishings, landscaping, and brickwork is enviable and runs right up to the greens of the fairways of the Harbour Town course. The lobby isn't a lobby per se; it just has a concierge desk for check-in. There are three additional seating areas, each with a different high-end decor. The Harbour Town Grill serves some of the best steaks on the island. Parking is free and easy, and valet service costs only $10. **Pros:** A service-oriented property, it is a centrally located Sea Pines address; unique, it is one of the finest hotel operations on island; complimentary parking. **Cons:** Some concierges give you too much information to digest; no water views; golf-view rooms are $20 extra. ✉ *Lighthouse La., off U.S. 278, Sea Pines, South End* ☎ *843/363–8100 or 888/807–6873* ⊕ *www.seapines. com* ☞ *60 rooms* ⚷ *In-room: refrigerator, Wi-Fi. In-hotel: restaurant, golf courses, tennis courts, bicycles, laundry*

service, Wi-Fi, parking (free), no-smoking rooms ⊟*AE, D, DC, MC, V* ⌷⌷*EP.*

★ FodorsChoice ⛫**The Inn at Palmetto Bluff.** Fifteen minutes from
$$$$ Hilton Head and a member of the Leading Small Hotels of
the World, this is the Lowcountry's most luxurious resort.
This 22,000-acre property has been transformed into a perfect replica of a small island town, complete with its own
clapboard church. As a chauffeured golf cart takes you to
your cottages, you'll pass the clubhouse, which resembles
a mighty antebellum great house. All of the cottages are
generously sized—even the one-bedrooms have more than
1,100 square feet of space. The decor is coastal chic, with
sumptuous bedding, gas fireplaces, surround-sound home
theaters, and marvelous bathroom suites with steam show-
ers. Your screened-in porch puts you immediately in touch
with nature. Rental homes (four bedrooms) with chic interiors are also available. New is the Canoe Club with its
restaurant, family pool, and bar. The spa puts you close to
heaven with its pampering treatments. Dinner at its River
House Restaurant is definitely worth an excursion from
Hilton Head even if you do not stay here. **Pros:** The ten-
nis/boccie/croquet complex has an atmospheric, impressive
retail shop; the river adds both ambience and boat excursions; pillared ruins dotting the grounds are like sculpture.
Cons: The mock Southern town is not the real thing; not
that close to the amenities of Hilton Head. ⊠*476 Mount
Pelia Rd., Bluffton* ☎*843/706–6500 or 866/706–6565*
⊕*www.palmettobluffresort.com* ⋗*50 cottages* ⚿*In-room:
safe, refrigerator, Wi-Fi. In-hotel: 4 restaurants, bars, golf
course, pools, watersports, bicycles, Internet terminal,
Wi-Fi, no-smoking rooms* ⊟*AE, MC, V* ⌷⌷*EP.*

★ FodorsChoice ⛫**Main Street Inn & Spa.** This Italianate villa has
$$–$$$ stucco facades ornamented with lions' heads, elaborate
ironwork, and shuttered doors. Staying here is like being
a guest at a rich friend's estate. Guest rooms have velvet and silk brocade linens, feather duvets, and porcelain
and brass sinks. An ample breakfast buffet is served in a
petite, sunny dining room. In the afternoon there's complimentary wine at cocktail hour; before that, you can
get gourmet coffee and homemade cookies, which can be
taken into the formal garden. Wi-Fi is free. The spa offers
treatments ranging from traditional Swedish massages to
Indian Kyria massages. Four king-size junior suites overlook the pool and gardens and are the inn's largest rooms.
Some rooms have balconies and fireplaces. **Pros:** When
someone plays the piano while you are having your wine,

it's super-atmospheric; the lion's head fountains and other Euro-architectural details. **Cons:** Weddings can overwhelm the resort, especially on weekends and throughout June; regular rooms are small. ✉*2200 Main St., North End* ☎*843/681–3001 or 800/471–3001* ⊕*www.mainstreetinn. com* ⌨*29 room, 4 jr. suites* ⚭*In-room: refrigerator, Wi-Fi. In-hotel: pool, spa, Internet terminal, Wi-Fi, no-smoking rooms* ▤*AE, D, MC, V* ⎍*BP.*

\$\$ 🍽 **Park Lane Hotel & Suites.** The island's only all-suites property has a friendly feel, since many guests stay for weeks. Each suite has a full kitchen, so there's no need to eat out for every meal. Pet-friendly, the hotel is definitely geared to families, though retirees also favor it and represent most of the long-term guests. You can cool off in the pool after heating up on the tennis courts, but the public beach is 2 mi away. You will be close to Sea Pines Resort and its facilities in Harbour Town. A free shuttle runs hourly to Caligny Beach. Both parking and Wi-Fi are free. **Pros:** This is one of the island's most reasonably priced lodgings; the bigger the unit, the nicer the condition and decor; flat-screen TVs. **Cons:** Not high-end; more kids mean more noise, especially around the pool area; rooms need to be renovated (a total renovation was just beginning at this writing and was expected to finish by March 2009). ✉*12 Park Lane, South End* ☎*843/686–5700* ⊕*www.hiltonheadparklanehotel.com* ⌨*156 suites* ⚭*In-room: kitchen, Wi-Fi. In-hotel: tennis court, pool, bicycles, Internet terminal, Wi-Fi, no-smoking rooms* ▤*AE, D, MC, V* ⎍*BP.*

★ Fodor$Choice 🍽 **Westin Hilton Head Island Resort & Spa.** A circular
\$\$\$\$ drive winds around a metal sculpture of long-legged marsh
☺ birds as you approach this luxury resort. The lush landscape lies on the island's quietest, least inhabited stretch of sand. Guest rooms, most with ocean views from the balconies, have homey touches, crown molding, and contemporary furnishings. If you need space to spread out, there are two- and three-bedroom villas. The service is generally efficient and caring. A new spa opened in 2007 and has become the big buzz on the island. This continues to be one of the top resorts on Hilton Head, particularly for honeymooners. **Pros:** The number and diversity of children's activities is amazing; a good destination wedding hotel, ceremonies are performed on the beach and at other atmospheric outdoor venues; the beach here is absolutely gorgeous. **Cons:** In the off-seasons, the majority of its clientele are large groups; the hotel's phone service can bog down; difficult to get cell phone reception indoors. ✉*2 Grass Lawn Ave., North*

End ☎843/681–4000 or 800/228–3000 ⊕www.westin. com ⚲412 rooms, 29 suites ♿In-room: Internet, Wi-Fi. In-hotel: 3 restaurants, golf courses, tennis courts, pools, gym, beachfront, bicycles, children's programs (ages 4–12), no-smoking rooms ⊟AE, D, DC, MC, V ❙⭘❙EP.

PRIVATE VILLA RENTALS

Hilton Head has some 6,000 villas, condos, and private homes for rent, almost double the island's available hotel rooms. Villas and condos seem to work particularly well for families with children, especially if they want to avoid the extra costs of staying in a resort. Often these vacation homes cost less per diem than hotels of the same quality. Guests on a budget can further economize by cooking some meals at the house, and most villas have laundry facilities; some even have private pools. Villas and condos are primarily rented by the week, Saturday to Saturday.

RENTAL AGENTS

ResortQuest (☎843/686–8144 or 800/448–3408 ⊕www. resortquesthiltonhead.com) boasts that it has the most comprehensive selection of accommodations (500-plus) on Hilton Head, from oceanfront to golf views, all in premier locations. A quality rating helps prospective guests know the type of decor their accommodation will have. Guests receive an exclusive ResortQuest Recommends card that gives discounts to shops, restaurants, and island activities. Generally, guests renting from this company can play tennis for free and get preferred golf rates at the most prestigious courses. Departure cleaning is not included in the quoted rates, but ResortQuest does offer optional cleaning services from a daily towel-and-trash service to a mid-week "full clean."

Resort Rentals of Hilton Head Island (☎843/686–6008 or 800/845–7017 ⊕www.hhivacations.com) represents some 300 homes and villas island-wide from the gated communities of Sea Pines, Palmetto Dunes, and Shipyard to some of the older nongated areas that have the newest homes such as North and South Forest Beach and the Folly Field, Singleton Beach area. Stays are generally Saturday to Saturday during the peak summer season; three- or four-night stays may be possible off-season. Most of the properties are privately owned, so decor and amenities can vary. In addition to the rental fee, you'll pay 11% tax, a $60 reservation fee, and a 4% administration fee. Linens and departure cleaning are included in the quoted rates, but daily maid service or additional cleaning is not.

Sea Pines Resort (☎ *843/842–1496* ⊕ *www.seapines.com*) operates in its own little world, a microcosm on the far south end of the island. The vast majority of the overnight guests rent one of the 500 suites, villas, and beach houses. In addition to quoted rates, expect to pay an additional 19.5% to cover the combined taxes and resort fees. Minimum rental periods are one-week in summer, three nights otherwise. All houses have landlines and most have Wi-Fi. In general, housekeeping throughout the week is additional, and price depends on the size of the villa, but departure cleaning is included. A special racquet club privilege is two hours a day of free tennis per rental unit. Sea Pines has its own security force that patrols the community.

$$$$ 🖺**Hot Tin Roof.** Now this is a beach house! Smack on North
★ Forest Beach with sweeping views of the Atlantic Ocean, this elevated, two-story home (circa 2001) is breathtaking. From the time you enter the spacious, open living area, the ocean commands your attention. The kitchen brings out the gourmet in guests, and cooks can watch the view while they work. There are two master suites, one downstairs and one up. Upstairs a large living area functions as a media room with a wet bar, commodious sofas, and a game table. This is a great choice for double families, *Big Chill* reunions, and incentive groups. **Pros:** Handsomely furnished with several plasma and flat-screen TVs and upscale contemporary furnishings; oceanfront pool deck is outfitted with a whirlpool tub, bar, shower, gas grill, and high-end outdoor furniture. **Cons:** Pool is small and half under the deck; house does not have a traditional warm and fuzzy feeling; the elevator is off-limits to renters. ✉ *North Forest Beach, 129 Dune Lane, South End* ☎ *843/686–6008 or 800/845–7017* ⊕ *www.hhivacations. com* ⌖ *7 bedrooms, 7.5 bathrooms* ⚬ *Dishwasher, DVD, Internet, Wi-Fi, pool, beachfront, laundry facilities, no smoking* ▭ *AE, D, MC, V.*

$$$$ 🖺**Hunt Club Three.** This remarkable home is a great value
★ for the money. Tall, coffered ceilings, an open layout with wide arches, and exquisite details like a downstairs powder room with black floral wallpaper and an oversized leather mirror make it special. An African motif takes in tiger wallpaper and various leopard-skin prints, yet it is not overdone; the whole feel is elegant yet tropical. In the den, a white life preserver emblazoned with WELCOME TO

THE BEACH hangs on a fieldstone fireplace, but guests aren't allowed to light a fire. An oversized gas grill overlooks the atmospheric pool area with tiered palms and a mature live oak. **Pros:** Real Euro tiles, even in the pool, which is surrounded by lush tropical vegetation; the jazz/media room with its 50-inch plasma TV; an eat-in gourmet kitchen is great for vacationing families. **Cons:** Some older TVs; not very close to the beach; no water views. ⊠ *Palmetto Dunes, 3 Hunt Club Dr., Mid-Island* ☎ *843/785–2248* ⊕ *www. resortquesthiltonhead.com* ⌑ 6 bedrooms, 6.5 bathrooms ⚬ *Dishwasher, DVD, VCR, Wi-Fi, pool, laundry facilities, no smoking* ⊟ *AE, E, MC, V.*

★ Fodor's Choice 🏠 **The Manor.** A modern-day mansion, with
$$$$ shades of *The Great Gatsby,* this very large home was built in 2007 with top-of-the-line materials. From the front entrance you admire the interior pillars in the living room, the high ceilings and ornate fireplace, and the Brazilian cherry and maple hardwood floors. A chef's dream kitchen has exquisite marble countertops. (Most guests hire the chef and butler.) There's a wine-storage room as well as a formal dining room. Take the elevator up to the media room, which has a phenomenal sound system and leather recliners. The billiards room has its own bar and balcony. Commodious bedrooms are carpeted; some have French doors, espresso machines, and mini-refrigerators. It's a perfect wedding venue or a place for a corporate retreat. **Pros:** All fireplaces are working; beautiful saltwater infinity pool and waterfall with a hot tub and even a screened, outdoor living area with fireplace; separate guest house with two bedrooms and two baths. **Cons:** No ocean view; a walk or bike ride to the beach. ⊠ *Sea Pines Resort, 206 N. Sea Pines Dr., South End* ⊕ *www.seapines.com* ⌑ 7 *bedrooms, 8.5 bathrooms* ⚬ *Dishwasher, DVD, Wi-Fi, daily maid service, hot tub, pool, gym, laundry facilities, no smoking* ⊟ *AE, MC, V.*

$$$$ 🏠 **Saint Andrews Place 1.** This is one of Hilton Head's early contemporary homes, which has been painstakingly remodeled. It has strong appeal to multigenerational families. The upscale but traditional decor and one-level design suit seniors. Located within a swing of the second tee of the Harbour Town Golf Links, the house has a strong draw for golfers; it is in demand for the Heritage Golf Tourney. Another major enticement is a private pool, the deck equipped with a giant gas grill, and stylish outdoor furnishings. Prep can be done in the gourmet kitchen, while dinner is served in the formal dining room. **Pros:**

8

Screened-in porch and large windows bring the outdoors in; preferred golf rates to guests; an office/media room has a plasma TV and premier channels. **Cons:** No water views; you have to bike or drive to a beach. ⊠ *Sea Pines Resort, Saint Andrews Place 1, South End* ☎843/363–2115 ⊕*www. resortquesthiltonhead.com* ⊅4 *bedrooms, 4.5 bathrooms* ⚭*Dishwasher, DVD, VCR, Wi-Fi, pool, laundry facilities, no-smoking* ⊟ *AE, D, MC, V.*

$$$$ ⊡ **Sound Villa 1458.** Sound Villas is the oldest condominium cluster on the island (some 25 years old) and was developed by founder Charles Fraser, yet these villas are not inexpensive. Smack on South Beach Marina, this is a prime location. You can just sit on the deck and watch the boats go by. The well-appointed, tri-level town house is also very special inside, with an urbane sophistication and excellent details: gorgeous ochre-and-brown granite countertops; a wine cooler; wainscoting on doors; an aged pine dining-room table; hardwood floors; leather furniture; plasma TVs; a fieldstone fireplace; an outdoor shower; a large BBQ grill; and expensive outdoor furniture. **Pros:** The water view is of Calibogue Sound meeting the Atlantic; small but exquisite garden and landscaping with impressive interior/exterior design. **Cons:** The 1970s faux-stucco facade could be on a downscale apartment complex; the tiny front porch, with two wicker chairs, looks down on two a/c units; it's only 100 yards to the beach, but you may need transportation if you have kids or a lot of stuff to carry. ⊠*Sea Pines, 253 South Sea Pines Drive, South End* ☎843/785–1171 ⊕*www. resortquesthiltonhead.com* ⊅5 *bedrooms, 5 bathrooms* ⚭*Dishwasher, DVD, Wi-Fi, laundry facilities, no smoking* ⊟*AE, D, MC, V.*

$$$$ ⊡ **10 Singleton Shores.** New and unblemished (the home was built in 2008), this three-story 5,000 square-foot home is an exceptional value for the price. It's not within one of the established plantations; instead, it's in one of the newer, upscale residential enclaves with views across the wetlands to the ocean, notably from the balcony of the third-floor master suite but also from the back porch. There are 1,800 square-feet of verandas; one has a large barbecue grill. With a gourmet kitchen and a butler's pantry on the second and third floors, it is ideal for a family reunion, a wedding group, or a two-family vacation. There are even two laundry rooms. No worries about stair climbing for senior members; the hardwood-paneled elevator is just a push-button away. **Pros:** Gorgeous Brazilian hardwood floors and granite countertops; oversized bathrooms and closets; stereo system throughout and media room great for kids. **Cons:** Not in a plantation; it's a long trip to the beach; although the furnishings are handsome, the decor doesn't quite gel. ⊠*10 Singleton Shores, Mid-Island* ☎*843/686–2361* ⊕*www.resortquesthiltonhead.com* ⇆*7 bedrooms, 7.5 bathrooms ⚒Dishwasher, DVD, Wi-Fi, pool, laundry facilities, no smoking* ⊟*AE, MC, V.*

$$$–$$$$ ⊡ **1024 Caravel Court.** This villa is smack on Harbour Town Marina. Like many of the Sea Pines condo complexes built on choice waterfront property, this one dates from the early 1970s. And like most of them, this unit has been well-maintained and nicely updated. Golfers like the location and price, and corporate groups book during shoulder season, as the conference centers are a quick walk away. Seniors like the compact size and first-floor location, as well as the homey, traditional furnishings. Everyone likes the price. The kitchen is adequate for the limited cooking that you might do. Guests happily enjoy their cocktails on the spacious balcony overlooking the action of the yacht basin as colorful parasailers float by. **Pros:** Handsome granite countertops; it's a short walk to Harbour Town Golf Links and the resort's amenities. **Cons:** Public areas are reminiscent of a mediocre apartment complex; a bike ride or drive to the beach; not terribly spacious. ⊠*Sea Pines Resort, 1024 Caravel Court, South End* ⊕*www.seapines. com* ⇆*2 bedrooms, 2 bathrooms ⚒DVD, Wi-Fi, laundry facilities, no smoking* ⊟*AE, MC, V.*

$$$$ ⊡ **13 Mizzenmast Court.** A view of the 18th hole of the Harbour Town Golf Links is a great tease for golfers. A view of the lagoon and even Calibogue Sound are more eye candy. This well-appointed home has a special quality with such details as a first-floor kitchen with two skylights, Charles Fraser-style. Constructed during Fraser's heyday, it has been considerably updated. It's a great retreat during big island golf events, especially because it has another kitchen and bar on the second floor, with the adjacent deck a good vantage point for watching the play. During the spring this charmer can be had for as little as $300 a night. Come peak wedding season, this is one of the most popular villas. **Pros:** The contemporary spiral staircase; the coziness will appeal to those who like traditional interiors; several fireplaces, a small plunge pool, and a hot tub. **Cons:** Some undersized TVs with wires too obvious; master bedroom is three flights up; it's one mile from the beach club. ⊠*Sea Pines Resort, 13 Mizzenmast Court, South End* ⊕*www. seapines.com* ⇆*3 bedrooms, 2.5 bathrooms ⚒Dishwasher,*

8

DVD, Wi-Fi, pool, hot tub, laundry facilities, no smoking ➡ AE, MC, V.

$–$$ ▦**Turnberry 251.** This is a perennial favorite condo for golf and tennis retreats, and the price is certainly right. Alas, it is not in a waterfront complex. However, golfers will appreciate that both the George Fazio and Robert Trent Jones courses are within walking distance. It's popular for girls' getaways and family trips, too, perhaps because of the complex's playground, oversized pool, children's wading pool, and open-air pavilion. The condo is quite spacious, simple in its furnishings, but attractive and with a private deck. The kitchen opens into the dining area. The beach is close, but you'll still need to take a bike or golf cart. **Pros:** Free daily tennis and preferred golf rates; in sports-oriented shoulder seasons, it is a real value; not as large as a home but substantially larger than a good hotel room and less expensive. **Cons:** The exterior is not so attractive; as a condo, it lacks the privacy of a villa. < ✉ *Palmetto Dunes, 59 Carnoustie, Mid-Island* ☎ *843/842–2093* ⊕ *www.resort questhiltonhead.com* ➬ *2 bedrooms, 2 bathrooms* ⚭ *Dishwasher, DVD, Internet, laundry facilities, no smoking* ➡ *AE, D, MC, V.*

$$$$ ▦**Villamare 1402.** This condo is in a complex near the Marriott, and its oceanfront location and extensive beachfront, with many family-oriented amenities, is why it is priced higher than the typical two-bedroom. Moms love the fully-equipped kitchen and indoor and outdoor pools, the elevator, and the convenience of it all. Active guests will love the fitness center and outdoor grilling area; plus, these condos offer free tennis and golf discounts for ResortQuest guests. This fourth-floor unit has a unique decor, which you will either love or not. The tiled bar is boldly creative; the sofa has red seat pillows and head pillows with a dramatic print. The furniture is mostly blond, Scandinavian design. The master bathroom has a whirlpool tub and two freestanding, black bowl sinks. **Pros:** Beachfront location with its own beach walk; next door to the Marriott. **Cons:** Concrete building and facades look like a modest apartment complex; although Villamare has always been one of the most requested complexes in Palmetto Dunes, it may not be worth the high-end price tag; not so spacious, especially for the price. ✉ *Palmetto Dunes, 1 Ocean Lane, Mid-Island* ☎ *843/785–1316* ⊕ *www.resortquesthiltonhead.com* ➬ *2 bedrooms, 2 bathrooms* ⚭ *Dishwasher, DVD, Wi-Fi, beachfront, laundry facilities, no smoking* ➡ *AE, D, MC, V.*

$$$ ☒**Windsor 2219.** Windsor is in a secluded, villa condo complex that is oceanfront in Palmetto Dunes. This unit is on the second floor and has water views from the living/dining area and two of the bedrooms. With a spacious kitchen (for a condo), it lends itself to families. The master and second bedrooms have ocean views; the third bedroom is simplistic, with twin beds (better suited for kids). The building is elevated, offering a covered, complimentary parking area. Amenities in the complex include an oceanfront swimming pool, children's play pool, hot tub, a large deck, and covered gazebo with a grill. A private boardwalk leads directly to the ocean. **Pros:** Excellent location; with an elevator and communal amenities, it is convenient for parents with small children; a library offers several DVDs to watch. **Cons:** The building is getting old and is not memorable; not as commodious and appealing as a private home; decor has that packaged look. ☒*Palmetto Dunes, 2219 Windsor 11, Mid-Island* ☎*843/686–6008 or 800/845–7017* ⊕*www. hhivacations.com* ↪*3 bedrooms, 3 bathrooms* ⌂*Dishwasher, DVD, Wi-Fi, pools, beachfront, laundry facilities, no smoking* ⊟*AE, D, MC, V.*

SPORTS & THE OUTDOORS

BEACHES

Although resort beach access is reserved for guests and residents, there are four public entrances to Hilton Head's 12 mi of ocean beach. The two main parking spots are off U.S. 278 at Coligny Circle in the South End, near the Holiday Inn, and on Folly Field Road, Mid-Island. Both have changing facilities. South of Folly Field Road, Mid-Island along U.S. 278, Bradley Beach Road and Singleton Road lead to beaches where parking is limited. ■TIP→**A delightful stroll on the beach can end with an unpleasant surprise if you don't put your towels, shoes, and other earthly possessions way up on the sand. Tides here can fluctuate as much as 7 feet. Check the tide chart at your hotel.**

BIKING

There are more than 40 mi of public paths that crisscross Hilton Head Island, and pedaling is popular along the firmly packed beach. The island keeps adding more to the "boardwalk" network as visitors are utilizing it and it is such a safe alternative for kids. Keep in mind when crossing streets that in South Carolina, vehicles have the right-of-way. ■TIP→**Bikes with wide tires are a must if you**

8

want to ride on the beach. They can save you a spill should you hit loose sand on the trails.

Bicycles can be rented at most hotels and resorts. You can also rent bicycles from the **Hilton Head Bicycle Company** (✉112 Arrow Rd., South End ☎843/686–6888 ⊕www. hiltonheadbicycle.com).

Pedals Bicycles (✉71 Pope Ave., South End ☎843/842–5522).

South Beach Cycles (✉Sea Pines Resort, off U.S. 278, South End ☎843/671–2453 ⊕www.southbeachracquetclub.com) rents bikes, helmets, tandems, and adult tricycles.

HOT WHEELS. An amazing array of bicycles can be hired, from beach cruisers to mountain bikes to bicycles built for two. Many can be delivered to your hotel, along with helmets, baskets, locks, child carriers, and whatever else you might need. There are 40 mi of trails, as well as 12 mi of hard-packed beach, so the possibilities are endless.

CANOEING & KAYAKING

This is one of the most delightful ways to commune with nature on this commercial but physically beautiful island. You paddle through the creeks and estuaries and try to keep up with the dolphins!

★ **Outside Hilton Head** (✉Sea Pines Resort, off U.S. 278, South End ✉Shelter Cove Lane at U.S. 278, Mid-Island ☎843/686–6996 or 800/686–6996 ⊕www.outsidehilton head.com) is an ecologically sensitive company that rents canoes and kayaks; it also runs nature tours and dolphin-watching excursions.

FISHING

Captain Jim of **The Stray Cat** (✉The Docks at Charlie's Crab, 3 Hudson La., North End ☎843/683–5427 ⊕www. straycatcharter.com) will help you decide whether you want to fish "in-shore" or go offshore into the deep blue. You can go for four, six, or eight hours, and the price is $120 an hour; bait and tackle are provided, but you must bring your own lunch. If his 27-foot power catamaran is booked for the day, Jim will set you up with one of the other seven boats that call this pier home. All of the charter boats here enjoy a good reputation and maintain it. Equipped with a head and a T-top shade, all these boats have a good catch record and offer great fun.

GOLF

Hilton Head is nicknamed "Golf Island" for good reason: the island itself has 25 championship courses (most semi-private), and the outlying area has 16 more. Each offers its own packages, some of which are great deals. Almost all charge the highest greens fees in the morning and lower the rates as the day goes on. Some offer lower rates in the hot summer months. It's essential to book tee times in advance, especially in the busy summer season; resort guests and club members get first choices. *Most courses can be described as casual-classy, so you will have to adhere to certain rules of the greens.* ■TIP→ **The dress code on island golf courses does not permit blue jeans, gym shorts, or jogging shorts. Men's shirts must have collars.**

The most internationally famed golf event in Hilton Head is The Heritage, now named the annual **Verizon Heritage PGA Golf Tournament** *(⊕www.seapines.com/golf), which is held mid-April.*

GOLF SCHOOLS

The Academy at Robert Trent Jones (⊠*Palmetto Dunes Resort, 7 Trent Jones La., Mid-Island* ☎*843/785–1138* ⊕*www. palmettodunes.com*) offers one-hour lessons, daily clinics, one- to three-day schools, family clinics, ladies programs, instructional videos, and free demonstrations at 4 PM each Monday from Doug Weaver, former PGA tour pro and director of instruction for the academy.

The TOUR Academy of Palmetto Hall Plantation (⊠ *Palmetto Hall Plantation, 108 Fort Hollow Dr., North End* ☎*843/681–1516* ⊕*www.palmettohallgolf.com*) is the only golf school on the island affiliated with the PGA and is one of only six in the country. This academy is known for its teaching technologies that include video analysis, which compares one's swing on a split-screen with the best golfers in the world. Students can choose from a one-hour private lesson to up to five days of golf instruction to include a round of golf with an instructor. There are two pristine 18-hole courses at the school, one designed by Arthur Hills and the other, Robert Cupp.

GOLF COURSES

Arthur Hills at Palmetto Hall (⊠ *Palmetto Hall, 108 Fort Howell Dr., North End* ☎*843/689–9205* ⊕*www.palmetto hallgolf.com* ⚑*18 holes. 6,918 yds. Par 72. Greens fee: $60–$104* is a player favorite from the renowned designer

8

CLOSE UP

Susan Yeager, Writer, on Golf Schools

It was a mildly windy Tuesday afternoon in May when Doug Weaver, a top instructor (according to *Golf Digest*), and Lindsey Letzig, an LPGA golf instructor, gave me an hour lesson at the Arthur Hills Golf Course in Leamington (a subdivision of Palmetto Dunes). They are part of a team of professional instructors for the Academy at Robert Trent Jones, another golf course located in Palmetto Dunes Resort.

Doug noticed my problems from the very first swing and jumped in with enthusiasm. I improved immediately with his instructions. He has a unique way of teaching golf. His artful approach is from a personal as well as a scientific perspective: while he identifies what type of personality one has by his golf swing, he sees his attitude towards the game, and applies the science of the swing. Doug's golf science included how to lighten one's grip on the club and how to use less effort in the swing. I also liked that he videotaped my swing, because when do we ever get to see our own selves swinging a club? There are no vanity mirrors out there!

After much improvement from a private lesson with these two professionals, it was suggested that I come out the next morning for Lindsey's group, a ladies clinic. And that I awaited with anticipatory delight.

I found that the ladies clinic (my first) was the best way to learn how to hit the ball from every lie on the course. In 3½ hours, Lindsey covered the most important shots of the game, with individual attention and such professionalism and gentleness. I now feel confident enough to play golf with my colleagues and look as respectable as they do. The golf course is a great place to network. Now I have one less worry: I can keep up!

I have never walked away from lessons feeling so learned and fulfilled. These pros know their game and now I am more confident with mine.

Arthur Hills; this course has his trademark: undulating fairways. The course, punctuated with lakes, gently flows across the island's rolling hills, winding around moss-draped oaks and towering pines. The clubhouse is a replica of an antebellum great house. This course is managed by Heritage Golf Group.

Although it's part of a country club, the course at **Country Club of Hilton Head** (⊠*70 Skull Creek Dr., North End* ☎*843/681–4653 or 888/465–3475* ⊛*www.golfisland.com*

⚓*Reservations essential* ⚑*18 holes. 6,919 yds. Par 72. Greens fee: $50–$119)* is open for public play. A well-kept secret, it's never overcrowded. This 18-hole Rees Jones–designed course is a more casual environment than many of the others.

On an island renowned for its exceptional golf, Jack Nicklaus, the golf legend and course designer, has created **Golden Bear Golf Club at Indigo Run** (⊠*Indigo Run, 72 Golden Bear Way, North End* ☎*843/689–2200* ⊕*www.golden bear-indigorun.com* ⚑*18 holes. 6,643 yds. Par 72. Greens fee: $85–$109)*, another must-play course for Hilton Head. Located in the upscale Indigo Run community, it's in a natural woodlands setting and offers easygoing rounds. It is a course that requires more thought than muscle, yet you will have to earn every par you make. Though fairways are generous, you may end up with a lagoon looming smack ahead of the green on the approach shot. And there are the fine points—the color GPS monitor on every cart and women-friendly tees. After an honest, traditional test of golf, most golfers finish up at the plush clubhouse, with some food and drink at Just Jack's Grille.

★ **Fodor'sChoice** **Harbour Town Golf Links** (⊠*Sea Pines Resort, 11 Lighthouse La., South End* ☎*843/842–8484 or 800/ 955–8337* ⊕*www.golfisland.com* ⚑*18 holes. 6,973 yds. Par 71. Greens fee: $153–$295)* is considered by many golfers to be one of those must-play-before-you-die courses. It's extremely well known because it has hosted The Heritage every spring for the last three decades. Designed by Pete Dye, the layout is reminiscent of Scottish courses of old. The Golf Academy is ranked among the top 10 in the country.

The May River Golf Club (⊠*Palmetto Bluffs, 476 Mt. Pelia Rd., Bluffton* ☎*843/706–6500* ⊕*www.palmettobluff resort.com/golf* ⚑*18 holes. 7,171 yds. Par 72. Greens fee: $90–$260)*, an 18-hole Jack Nicklaus course, has several holes along the banks of the scenic May River and will challenge all skill levels. The greens are covered by Paspalum, the latest eco-friendly turf. A distinction of this classy operation is that caddy service is always required, even if you choose to rent a golf cart, and then no carts are allowed earlier than 9 AM. This is to encourage walking so golfers will enjoy the beauty of the course.

Old South Golf Links (⊠*50 Buckingham Plant Dr., Bluffton* ☎*843/785–5353* ⊕*www.golfisland.com* ⚑*18 holes. 6,772 yds. Par 72. Greens fee: $75–$85)* has scenic holes with marshland and views of the intracoastal waterway. A recent Internet poll had golfers preferring it over the famous Harbour Town Golf Links and Robert Trent Jones.

Robert Trent Jones at Palmetto Dunes (⊠ *7 Robert Trent Jones Way, North End* ☎ *843/785–1138* ⊕ *www.palmettodunes. com* ↖ *18 holes. 7,005 yds. Par 72. Greens fee: $125–$165*) is one of the island's most popular layouts. Its beauty and character are accentuated by the par-5, 10th hole, which offers a panoramic view of the ocean. It's one of only two oceanfront holes on Hilton Head.

HORSEBACK RIDING

☾ **Lawton Stables** (⊠ *Sea Pines Resort, Plantation, off U.S.*
★ *278, South End* ☎ *843/671–2586*) gives riding lessons and pony rides, in addition to having horseback tours through the Sea Pines Forest Preserve. The latter can be troop movements, with many participants. It is a safe ride, if not adrenaline-racing.

SPAS

Spa visits have become a recognized activity on the island, and for some people they are as popular as golf and tennis. In fact, spas have become one of the top leisure-time destinations, particularly for golf "widows." And this popularity extends to the men as well; previously spa-shy guys have come around, enticed by couples massage, deep-tissue sports massage, and even the pleasures of the manicure and pedicure. One landmark spa, Faces, has a men's night.

There are East Indian–influenced therapies, hot-stone massage, Hungarian organic facials—the treatments span the globe. Do your research, go online, and call or stop by the various spas and ask the locals their favorites. The quality of therapists island-wide is noteworthy—their training, certifications, and expertise. In the words of Jack Barakitis, premier therapist at Main Street Inn & Spa and one of the island's most respected instructors: "Body therapies strengthen more positive perceptions on your daily outlook of life. Spa services are intended to simply have you feeling better when you finish than when you started."

The low-key **Faces** (⊠ *The Village at Wexford, 1000 William Hilton Pkwy., North End* ☎ *843/785–3075* ⊕ *www. facesdayspa.com*) has been pampering loyal clients for 20 years, with body therapists and cosmetologists who do what they do well. It has a fine line of cosmetics and does

CLOSE UP

The World of Gullah

In the Lowcountry, Gullah refers to several things: a language, a people, and a culture. Gullah (the word itself is believed to be derived from *Angola*), an English-based dialect rooted in African languages, is the unique language of the African-Americans of the Sea Islands of South Carolina and Georgia, more than 300 years old. Most locally born African-Americans of the area can understand, if not speak, Gullah.

Descended from thousands of slaves who were imported by planters in the Carolinas during the 18th century, the Gullah people have maintained not only their dialect but also their heritage. Much of Gullah culture traces back to the African rice-coast culture and survives today in the art forms and skills, including sweetgrass basket-making, of Sea Island-ers. During the colonial period, when rice was king, Africans from the West African rice kingdoms drew high premiums as slaves. Those with basket-making skills were extremely valuable because baskets were needed for agricultural and household use. Made by hand, sweetgrass baskets are intricate coils of marsh grass with a sweet, haylike aroma.

Nowhere is Gullah culture more evident than in the foods of the region. Rice appears at

nearly every meal—Africans taught planters how to grow rice and how to cook and serve it as well. Lowcountry dishes use okra, peanuts, *benne* (the African word for sesame seeds), field peas, and hot peppers. Gul-lah food reflects the bounty of the islands: shrimp, crabs, oys-ters, fish, and such vegetables as greens, tomatoes, and corn. Many dishes are prepared in one pot, a method similar to the stew-pot cooking of West Africa.

On St. Helena Island, near Beaufort, Penn Center is the unofficial Gullah headquarters, preserving the culture and developing opportunities for Gullahs. In 1852 the first school for freed slaves was established at Penn Center. You can delve into the culture further at the York W. Bailey Museum.

On St. Helena, many Gullahs still go shrimping with hand-tied nets, harvest oysters, and tend their own vegetables. Nearby on Daufuskie Island, as well as on Edisto, Wadmalaw, and Johns islands near Charleston, you can find Gullah communities. A famous Gullah proverb says: *If oonuh ent kno weh oonuh dah gwine, oonuh should kno weh oonuh come f'um.* Translation: If you don't know where you're going, you should know where you come from.

8

makeovers or evening makeups. Open seven days a week, Monday night is for the guys.

★ FodorsChoice **Heavenly Spa by Westin** (✉ *Westin Resort Hilton Head Island, Port Royal Plantation, 2 Grasslawn Ave., North End* ☎*843/681–4000, ext. 7519*) is a new facility at the Westin resort offering the quintessential sensorial spa experience. Known internationally for its innovation and latest in therapies and decor, Westin's Heavenly spa brand also brings the treatments home. Prior to a treatment, clients are told to put their worries in a Gullah (a sweetgrass burden basket); de-stressing is a major component here. Unique is a collection of treatments based on the energy from the color indigo, once a cash crop in the Lowcountry. The full-service salon, the relax room with its teas and healthy snacks, and the adjacent retail area with products like sweetgrass scents are heavenly, too.

The **Spa at Main Street Inn** (✉*2200 Main St., North End* ☎*843/681–3001* ⊕*www.mainstreetinn.com*) has holistic massages that will put you in another zone. A petite facility, it offers deep muscle therapy, couples massage, hydrotherapy soaks and outdoor courtyard massages. Jack Barakitis instructs both his students and his own clients in the art of de-stressing, with a significant dose of spirituality.

The **Spa at Palmetto Bluffs** (✉*476 Mount Pelia Rd., Bluffton* ☎*843/706–6500* ⊕*www.palmettobluffresort.com*) has been dubbed the "celebrity spa" by locals, for this two-story facility is the ultimate pamper palace. It is as creative in its names, which often have a Southern accent, as it is in its treatments. There are Amazing Grace and High Cotton bodyworks and massages, sensual soaks and couples massage, special treatments for gentlemen/golfers, and Belles and Brides packages as this is a premier wedding destination. Nonguests are welcome.

Spa Soleil (✉*Marriott Hilton Head Resort & Spa, Palmetto Dunes, 1 Hotel Circle, Mid-Island* ☎*843/686–8400* ⊕*www. csspagroup.com*) is one of the newest spas on island; this $7-million facility has the atmosphere and professionalism, the therapies, and litany of massages found in the country's finest spas. Since the facility is all new, everything is still quite pristine. The colors, aromas, teas, and snacks make your treatment a soothing, therapeutic experience.

TENNIS

There are more than 300 courts on Hilton Head. Tennis comes in at a close second as the island's premier sport after golf. It is recognized as one of the nation's best tennis destinations. Hilton Head has a large international organization of coaches. Spring and fall are the peak seasons for cooler play with numerous tennis packages available at the resorts and through the schools.

Palmetto Dunes Tennis Center (⊠*6 Trent Jones La., Mid-Island* ☎*843/785–1152* ⊕*www.palmettodunes.com*) welcomes nonguests.

Port Royal (⊠*15 Wimbledon Ct., North End* ☎*843/686–8803* ⊕*www.heritagegolfgroup.com*) has 16 courts, including two grass.

★ **Sea Pines Racquet Club** (⊠*Sea Pines Resort, off U.S. 278, 32 Greenwood Dr., South End* ☎*843/363–4495*) has 23 courts, instructional programs, and a pro shop.

★ Fodor'sChoice Highly rated **Van der Meer Tennis Center/Shipyard Racquet Club** (⊠*Shipyard Plantation, 19 de Allyon Rd., Mid-Island* ☎*843/686–8804* ⊕*www.vandermeertennis. com*) is recognized for tennis instruction. Four of its 28 courts are covered.

NIGHTLIFE & THE ARTS

THE ARTS

In warm weather, free outdoor concerts are held at Harbour Town and Shelter Cove Harbour; at the latter, fireworks light up the night every Tuesday from June to August. Guitarist Gregg Russell has been playing for children under Harbour Town's mighty Liberty Oak tree for decades. He begins strumming nightly at 8, except on Saturday.

The **Arts Center of Coastal Carolina** (⊠*Shelter Cove La., Mid-Island* ☎*843/686–3945* ⊕*www.artscenter-hhi.org*) has a gallery and a theater with programs for young people. The Hallelujah Singers, Gullah performers, appear regularly.

The **Native Islander Gullah Celebration** (☎*843/689–9314* ⊕*www.gullahcelebration.com*) takes place in February and showcases Gullah life through arts, music, and theater.

Hilton Head has always been a party place, and that's true now more than ever. Bars, like everything else in Hilton Head, are often in strip malls. A fair number of clubs (often restaurants that crank up the music after dinner) cater to younger visitors, others to an older crowd, and still others that are "ageless" and are patronized by all generations. Some places are hangouts frequented by locals, and others get a good mix of both locals and tourists. As a general rule, the local haunts tend to be on the north end of the island. Why? There is more affordable housing there, and it is where the large contingent of young people live—there and over the bridge in Bluffton.

BARS

Reggae bands play at **Big Bamboo** (⊠*Coligny Plaza, N. Forest Beach Dr., South End* ☎*843/686–3443*), a bar with a South Pacific theme.

Boathouse 11 (⊠*397 Squire Pope Rd., North End* ☎*843/681–3663*), a popular waterfront restaurant, has two buzzing bars; in season, there's nightly entertainment (mainly vocalist/guitarists) seven nights a week. This is one of those restaurants where a lot of the locals "hang," boating types in particular.

The **Hilton Head Brewing Co.** (⊠*Hilton Head Plaza, Greenwood Dr., South End* ☎*843/785–2739*) lets you shake your groove thing to 1970s-era disco on Wednesday. There's live music on Friday and karaoke on Saturday.

Jazz Corner (⊠*The Village at Wexford, C-1, South End* ☎*843/842–8620*) will always be known and remembered for its live music and fun New Orleans–style atmosphere. Each Friday and Saturday night, entertainers are brought in who are quite well known for their jazz, swing, Broadway, blues, or Motown performances. On Sunday through Thursday, co-owner and horn player Bob "Jazz" Masteller is the leader of his band, and he has a strong following, mainly an older crowd. The restaurant has a newly updated menu, so to assure yourself of a seat on busy nights, make reservations for dinner.

Jump & Phil's Bar & Grill (⊠*3 Hilton Head Plaza, South End* ☎*843/785–9070*) is a happening scene, especially for locals, and you could pass this nondescript building by if you didn't know. "Jump," whose real name is John Griffin, is an author of thriller novels under the pen name

John R. Maxim, and this place is a magnet for area writers and football fans during the season.

The Metropolitan Lounge (⊠*Park Plaza, Greenwood Dr., South End* ☎*843/785–8466*) is the most sophisticated of several fun places on Park Plaza. With a Euro-style that appeals to all ages, it is known for its martini menu. On weekends, there is dancing in an anteroom separated by a wrought-iron gate. Here you will see all ages, from golf guys to the island's sassy, young, beautiful people.

Monkey Business (⊠*Park Plaza, Greenwood Dr., South End* ☎*843/686–3545*) is a dance club popular with young professionals. On Friday there's live beach music.

One of the island's latest hot spots, **Santa Fe Cafe** (⊠*Plantation Center in Palmetto Dunes, 700 Plantation Center, North End* ☎*843/785–3838*) is where you can lounge about in front of the adobe fireplace or sip top-shelf margaritas on the rooftop. The restaurant's clientele is predominately local residents and tends to be older than those who frequent the Boathouse because of its Southwestern atmosphere, unique on the island, and its guitarist(s).

Turtle's (⊠*The Westin Hilton Head Resort & Spa, 2 Grass Lawn Ave., North End* ☎*843/681–4000*) appeals to anyone who still likes to hold their partner when they dance.

SHOPPING

8

Shopping is starting to become a key component of the Hilton Head experience. While husbands play golf, the stores fill up with their wives. There are no megamalls on the island; rather, Hilton Head's shopping areas are tasteful enclaves. The mid-island Mall at Shelter Cove is the largest; farther north, the village of Wexford has an interesting collection of stylish shops. Sea Pines Center is also memorable, not only for its shops but also its park benches, landscaping, and outdoor alligator sculpture. There are some 700 stores on the island, and they run the gamut, including fine jewelry boutiques, upscale men's shops, sporting goods stores, art galleries, designer consignment shops, and charity-based thrift shops. Nearly half a dozen consignment shops featuring gently used clothing, furniture, sports equipment, and art; because Hilton Head Islanders are characteristically well heeled and well turned-out, many shed their clothes each season like molting birds. There's also an outlet mall over the bridge in Bluffton, while Old Town Bluffton has its own eclectic and artsy mix of shops selling mainly crafts, gifts, and art.

ART GALLERIES

Linda Hartough Gallery (⊠*Harbour Town, 140 Lighthouse Rd., South End* ☎843/671–6500) is all about golf. There's everything from landscapes of courses to golden golf balls to pillows embroidered with sayings like "Queen of the Green."

The **Red Piano Art Gallery** (⊠*220 Cordillo Pkwy., Mid-Island* ☎843/785–2318) showcases 19th- and 20th-century works by regional and national artists.

GIFTS

The **Audubon Nature Store** (⊠*The Village at Wexford, U.S. 278, Mid-Island* ☎843/785–4311) has gifts with a wild-life theme.

Outside Hilton Head (⊠*The Plaza at Shelter Cove, U.S. 278, Mid-Island* ☎843/686–6996 or 800/686–6996) sells Pawleys Island hammocks (first made in the late 1800s) and other items that let you enjoy the great outdoors.

JEWELRY

The **Bird's Nest** (⊠*Coligny Plaza, Coligny Circle and N. Forest Beach Dr., South End* ☎843/785–3737) sells locally made shell and sand-dollar jewelry, as well as island-theme charms.

The **Goldsmith Shop** (⊠*3 Lagoon Rd., Mid-Island* ☎843/785–2538) carries classic jewelry and island charms.

Forsythe Jewelers (⊠*71 Lighthouse Rd., South End* ☎843/342–3663) is the island's leading jewelry store.

BEAUFORT

38 mi north of Hilton Head via U.S. 278 and Rte. 170; 70 mi southwest of Charleston via U.S. 17 and U.S. 21.

Charming homes and churches grace this old town on Port Royal Island. Come here on a day-trip from Hilton Head, Savannah, or Charleston, or to spend a quiet weekend at a B&B while you shop and stroll through the historic district. Tourists are drawn equally to the town's artsy scene (art walks are regularly scheduled) as well as the area's water sports possibilities. Actually, more and more transplants have decided to spend the rest of their lives here, drawn to Beaufort's small-town charms, and the area is burgeoning.

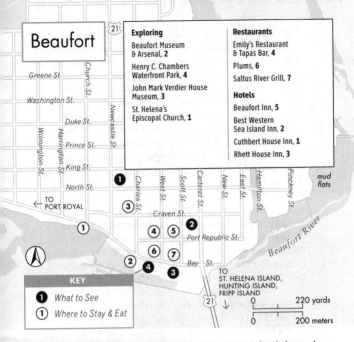

Beaufort

Exploring	Restaurants
Beaufort Museum & Arsenal, **2**	Emily's Restaurant & Tapas Bar, **4**
Henry C. Chambers Waterfront Park, **4**	Plums, **6**
John Mark Verdier House Museum, **3**	Saltus River Grill, **7**
St. Helena's Episcopal Church, **1**	**Hotels**
	Beaufort Inn, **5**
	Best Western Sea Island Inn, **2**
	Cuthbert House Inn, **1**
	Rhett House Inn, **3**

KEY

1 *What to See*

① *Where to Stay & Eat*

A truly Southern town, its picturesque backdrops have lured filmmakers here to film *The Big Chill*, *The Prince of Tides*, and *The Great* Santini, the last two being Hollywood adaptations of best-selling books by author Pat Conroy. Conroy has waxed poetic about the Lowcountry and calls the Beaufort area home. The city closest to the Marine base on Parris Island, Beaufort also has a naval hospital.

GETTING HERE & AROUND

Beaufort is 25 mi east of Interstate 95, on U.S. 21. The only way here is by private car.

Visitor Information Beaufort Visitors Center (✉ *2001 Boundaray St. Beaufort 29901* ☎ *843/525–8523*).

Regional Beaufort Chamber of Commerce (✉ *1106 Carteret St., Box 910, Beaufort* ☎ *843/986–5400* ⊕ *www.beaufortsc.org*).

EXPLORING BEAUFORT

Built in 1795 and remodeled in 1852, the Gothic-style building that was the home of the Beaufort Volunteer Artillery now houses the **Beaufort Museum & Arsenal**. Prehistoric relics, Native American pottery, and Revolutionary War and Civil War exhibits are on display. At present it

Pat Conroy, Writer, on Beaufort

While ambling down Bay Street, you can't help but notice the life-size, paper cut-out of author Pat Conroy in the window of Bay Street Traders. It is their way of saying that they stock his work. Conroy has had signings for all seven of his books at this landmark bookstore, and adds laughingly: "They say I am their cottage industry!"

Many Conroy fans consider Beaufort *his* town because of his autobiographical novel, *The Great Santini*, which was set here. He, too, considers it home base: "We moved to Beaufort when I was 15. We had moved 23 times. (My father was in the Marines.) I told my mother, 'I need a home.' Her wise reply was: 'Well, maybe it will be Beaufort.' And so it has been. I have stuck to this poor town like an old barnacle. I moved away, but I came running back in 1993."

A number of Hollywood films have been shot here, not just Conroy's: "The beautiful white house on The Point was called the 'Big Santini House' until the next movie was shot and now it is known as 'The Big Chill House.' If a third movie was made there, it would have a new name."

"One of the great glories of Beaufort is found on St. Helena Island," he says. "You get on Martin Luther King Jr. Blvd. and take a right at the Red Piano 11 Gallery to the Penn Center. Before making the right turn, on the left, in what was the Bishop family's general store, is Gullah Grub, one of the few restaurants that serve legitimate Gullah food."

He continues: "At the end of St. Helena, toward the beach, take Seaside Road. You will be in the midst of the Gullah culture. You end up driving down a dirt road and then an extraordinary avenue of oaks that leads to the Coffin Point Plantation, which was the house where Sally Field raised Forrest Gump as a boy."

---

is undergoing a major renovation and is slated to open in spring 2009 with exciting new exhibits. The admission price may go up. ✉*713 Craven St.* ☎*843/379–3331* 🖂*$3* ⏱*Mon.–Sat. 11–4.*

John Mark Verdier House Museum, built in the Federal style, has been restored and furnished as it would have been between its construction in 1805 and the visit of Lafayette in 1825. It was the headquarters for Union forces during the Civil War. A combination ticket that gets you into the Beaufort Museum & Arsenal (under renovation until spring 2009) and the John Mark Verdier House Museum saves you $1. ✉ *801 Bay St.* ☎ *843/379–6335* 🖅 *$5* 🕑 *Mon.–Sat. 10–3:30.*

The 1724 **St. Helena's Episcopal Church** was turned into a hospital during the Civil War, and gravestones were brought inside to serve as operating tables. ✉ *505 Church St.* ☎ *843/522–1712* 🕑 *Tues.–Fri. 10–4, Sat. 10–1.*

Henry C. Chambers Waterfront Park, off Bay Street, is a great place to survey the scene. Trendy restaurants and bars overlook these seven landscaped acres along the Beaufort River. There's a farmers' market here on Saturday, April through August, 8 to noon.

St. Helena Island, 9 mi southeast of Beaufort via U.S. 21, is the site of the Penn Center Historic District. Established in the middle of the Civil War, Penn Center was the South's first school for freed slaves; now open to the public, the center provides community services, too. This island is both residential and commercial, with nice beaches, cooling ocean breezes, and a great deal of natural beauty.

The **York W. Bailey Museum** has displays on the Penn Center, and on the heritage of Sea Island African-Americans; it also has pleasant grounds shaded by live oaks. The Penn Center (1862) was one of the first schools for the newly emancipated slaves. These islands are where Gullah, a musical language that combines English and African languages, developed. This is a major stop for anyone interested in the Gullah history and culture of the Lowcountry. ✉ *16 Martin Luther King Jr. Blvd., St. Helena Island* ☎ *843/838–2432* ⊕ *www.penncenter.com* 🖅 *$5* 🕑 *Mon.–Sat. 11–4.*

★ Secluded **Hunting Island State Park** has nature trails and about 3 mi of public beaches—some dramatically and beautifully eroding. Founded in 1993 to preserve and promote its natural existence, it harbors 5,000 acres of rare maritime forests. Nonetheless, the light sands decorated with driftwood and the raw, subtropical vegetation is breathtaking. Stroll the 1,300-foot-long fishing pier, among the longest on the East Coast, or you can go fishing or crabbing. You will be at one with nature. The fit can climb the 181 steps of the **Hunting Island Lighthouse** (built in 1859 and abandoned in 1933) for sweeping views. The nature center has exhibits, an aquarium, and lots of turtles. The park is 18 mi southeast of Beaufort via U.S. 21; if you want to stay on the island, be sure to call for reservations. From April 1 to October 31, there is a one-week minimum stay; November 1 to

CLOSE UP

Pat Conroy, Writer, on Fripp Island

"What has Fripp Island meant to me?" Pat Conroy, one of the Lowcountry's famous writers, answered: "The year was 1964. I was living in Beaufort. And when the bridge to Fripp Island was built, I was a senior in high school. My English teacher *and* my chemistry teacher moonlighted as the island's first security guards. It was a pristine island; there were no houses on it yet, and it was as beautiful as any desert island.

"In 1978, my mother moved over there, and all our summers were spent on the island. It was to be her last home. That sealed the island in our family history. In 1989, I bought a house there, both because it is a private island and [because it] is good for a writer, but also so that our family—my brothers and sisters—could always have a home on Fripp to come to."

March 31, the minimum is two nights. Cabins that sleep up to six or eight ($–$$) must be reserved far in advance for summer weekends (there are only 12). Expect to pay about $25 for campsites with electricity, $17 without. ✉*1775 Sea Island Pkwy., off St. Helena Island, Hunting Island* ☎*843/838–2011* ⊕*www.southcarolinaparks.com* 🎫*$4* ⊙*Park: Apr.–Oct., daily 6 AM–9 PM; Nov.–Mar., daily 6–6. Lighthouse daily 11–4.*

WHERE TO EAT

★ Fodor'sChoice ✕**Bateaux.** *Eclectic.* This contemporary restaurant, which was formerly on Lady's Island, has a new home in a historical brick building in Port Royal, 6 mi southwest of Beaufort. The location affords waterfront views, which are best from the second story, although some downstairs tables also offer a glimpse of the blue. The move has brought major changes: lunch is no longer served, and "Chip" Ulbrich is no longer a partner. For now, owner Richard Wilson is in the kitchen. He continues creating imaginative Southern cuisine, and the menu keeps evolving. The food is fresh, elegant, and artistically presented. Foodies love that they can get foie gras in crepes and other dishes. Seafood is the obvious specialty; try the shrimp and scallops over red-pepper risotto with fried prosciutto and spinach. The staff is well-trained and knowledgeable. ✉*610 Paris Ave., Port Royal* 📮*Box 2179, Port Royal, 29935* ☎*843/379–0777* ⊟*AE, MC, V* ⊙*Closed Sun. No lunch.*

$$$$

$$$ ×**11th Street Dockside.** *Seafood.* The succulent fried oysters, shrimp, and fish are some of the best around. In addition to Lowcountry fried seafood, more healthful options are available, including a steamed seafood hot pot filled with crab legs, oysters, shrimp, and lobster; by request only you can get Frogmore stew (with shrimp, potatoes, sausage, and corn). Everything is served in a classic wharfside environment, where you can eat on a screened porch and have water views from nearly every table. The restaurant is open from 4:30 to 10 every day. ⊠ *1699 11th St. W, 6 mi southwest of Beaufort, Port Royal* ☎ *843/524–7433* ⊟ *AE, D, DC, MC, V* ⊘ *No lunch.*

$$$ ×**Emily's Restaurant & Tapas Bar.** *American.* Long, narrow, and wood-paneled, Emily's is a lively restaurant, definitely a haunt where the cool locals hang out. It has full dining service, mainly simple fare—heavy on steaks, which come with a generous salad. Crowds linger over the tapas, including spring rolls, garlic beef, and even baby lamb chops. This is a great place to come early or late, since the kitchen serves from 4 PM to 10 PM. (and on weekends, the bar may be open later). At this writing, the restaurant was considering whether to start opening at lunch, and the piano bar had gone quiet but was still hoping for a comeback. ⊠ *906 Port Republic St.* ☎ *843/522–1866* ⊟ *AE, MC, V* ⊘ *Closed Sun. No lunch.*

$–$$ ×**Plums.** *American.* Down the alley behind Shipman's Gallery is this homey frame house with plum-colored awnings shading the front porch. Plums still uses old family recipes for its crab-cake sandwiches and curried chicken salad, but now it also offers a blue-cheese-and-portobello-mushroom sandwich. Dinner has creative and affordable pasta and seafood dishes. The crowd is a mix of locals and tourists, often with children. Its downtown riverfront location, fun atmosphere, and reasonable prices are the draw. There's live music on weekends, starting at around 10 PM and geared to the younger crowd. ⊠ *904½ Bay St.* ☎ *843/525–1946* ⊟ *AE, MC, V.*

★ Fodor'sChoice ×**Saltus River Grill.** *Eclectic.* Owner Lantz Price
$$$$ has given this 19th-century loft a classy sailing motif, with portals and oversized photos of sailboats. The hippest eatery in Beaufort wins over epicureans with its cool design (subdued lighting, mod booths, dark-wood bar), waterfront patio, and modern Southern menu. Come early (the kitchen opens at 4 PM) and sit outdoors on the river with your cocktails. There are separate menus for sushi and oysters. A flawless dinner might start off with the skillet

crab cakes with corn relish and beurre blanc sauce, then segue to the skewered, grilled quail with Oriental glaze. The wine list is admirable, and the staff is adept at pairings. Desserts change nightly; if offered, the pineapple upside-down cake can be the perfect end to your meal. ⊠*802 Bay St.* ☎*843/379–3474* ⊟*AE, D, MC, V.*

$–$$ ✕**Shrimp Shack.** *Seafood.* On the way to Fripp and Hunting islands, follow the cue of locals and stop at this endearing little place where Ms. Hilda, the owner, will take good care of you. All seating is outdoors, and once seated, you can't see the water. The menu includes all of the typical Lowcountry fried plates, as well as South Carolina crab cakes, boiled shrimp, and gumbo, but it is best known for its shrimp burgers, sweet-potato fries, and sweet tea. Dinner is served only until 8 PM. Doors open at 11 AM. ⊠*1929 Sea Island Pkwy., 18 mi southeast of Beaufort, St. Helena* ☎*843/838–2962* ⊟*No credit cards* ⊘*Closed Sun.*

WHERE TO STAY

$$–$$$ ✕⬚**Beaufort Inn.** This peach-painted 1890s Victorian inn charms you with its gables and wraparound porches. Pine-floor guest rooms have period reproductions, striped wallpaper, and comfy chairs. Several have fireplaces and four-poster beds. This is a homey place right in the heart of the historic district, and most rooms have views of the surrounding buildings. Room options in the main inn range from a standard queen-size room to suites, which are the most popular. Deluxe suites have living rooms and are in separate cottages. There's also one two-bedroom, two-bathroom apartment in a separate, historic building overlooking Bay Street. Garden Cottages are modern buildings and don't have the same traditional feel, but they do have garden or courtyard views; decor here is more contemporary with heavier, darker woods, and replica claw-foot tubs. Regrettably, the restaurant has closed, which is a loss to Beaufort's culinary scene. **Pros:** Located in the heart of the historic district; Continental breakfast has a chef-attended omelet station; the evening social hour includes snacks, refreshments, and wine. **Cons:** Atmosphere may feel too dated for those seeking a more contemporary hotel; no more restaurant; deluxe suites have the worst views of all—the parking lot. ⊠*809 Port Republic St.* ☎*843/521–9000* ⊕*www.beaufortinn.com* ⇌*28 rooms* ⬚*In-room: DVD. In-hotel: bicycles, no kids under 8, parking (free), no-smoking rooms* ⊟*AE, D, MC, V* ⍟◎*BP.*

$ 📺**Best Western Sea Island Inn.** At this well-maintained motel in the downtown historic district, you are within walking distance of shops and restaurants. Guests can see the bay from the front terrace. Ample rooms have two queen or king beds. Cookies and coffee are always available in the lobby. **Pros:** Only accommodation in historic district that is not a B&B; directly across from marina and an easy walk to art galleries and restaurants; Continental breakfast (early) and hot breakfast included. **Cons:** Complaints about dim lighting in rooms; not an upscale property. ✉*1015 Bay St.* ☎*843/522–2090 or 800/528–1234* ⊕*www.sea-island-inn. com* ⏎*43 rooms* ⌂*In-room: refrigerator, Internet. In-hotel: pool, gym, Internet terminal, no-smoking rooms* ▤*AE, D, DC, MC, V* ⏍*BP.*

$$$–$$$$ 📺**Cuthbert House Inn.** Named after the original Scottish
★ owners, who made their money in cotton and indigo, this 1790 home is filled with 18th- and 19th-century heirlooms. It retains the original Federal fireplaces and crown and rope molding. When Beaufort was occupied by the Union army during the Civil War, this home was used as the generals' headquarters. Guest rooms and oversized suites have endearing architectural details, with hand-knotted rugs on the pine floors and commanding beds piled high with quilts. Choose one that looks out on the bay and the glorious sunset. The Mariner's Suite has a veranda, too. Beautifully lit at night, this antebellum house, with white pillars and dual verandas, typifies the Old South. Wedding parties can rent out the whole inn, and many couples spend their honeymoon nights here, but it appeals foremost to an older generation. A renovation of all rooms was in progress at this writing and was expected to be finished by mid-2009. **Pros:** Owners are accommodating; other guests provide good company during the complimentary wine service. **Cons:** Some furnishings are a bit busy; some artificial flower arrangements; stairs creak. ✉*1203 Bay St.* ☎*843/521–1315 or 800/327–9275* ⊕*www.cuthbert-houseinn.com* ⏎*6 rooms, 2 suites* ⌂*In-room: refrigerator, DVD, Wi-Fi. In-hotel: bicycles, no kids under 12, no-smoking rooms* ▤*AE, D, MC, V* ⏍*BP.*

$$$ 📺**Fripp Island Resort.** This resort sits on the island made
☾ famous in *Prince of Tides*, with 3½ miles of broad, white
★ beach and unspoiled sea island scenery. It has long been known as one of the more affordable and casual of the island resorts. It is private and gated, a safe haven, where kids are allowed to be free, to go crabbing at low tide, bike the trails, and swim, swim, swim. Families love the narrated

Sea Monkeys

There is a colony of monkeys living on a little isle near Fripp Island. If you are in a boat cruising or on a fishing charter and think you might be seeing monkeys running on the beach, it may not be your imagination. The state of South Carolina leases one of these tiny islands to raise monkeys, both those that are used for medical research and also rare golden rhesus monkeys that are put up for sale as exotic pets. This deserted island and the sub-tropical climate and vegetation have proved ideal for their breeding. But you can't land on the island or feed the monkeys, so bring binoculars.

nature cruise and love Camp Fripp, the nature center, not to mention all the teen activities. Most residents are retired and happily tool around in golf carts. Golf carts, mopeds, and bikes can be rented. This is no swinging-singles destination, but it is a good getaway for sporty couples who like to kayak and canoe. Of course, you can play highly rated golf or tennis and go fishing out of the marina as well. There are more than 200 individual villas here instead of a hotel, though there is a variety of small efficiencies. There's a pavilion with shops and a choice of restaurants, often with live entertainment, from the rollicking Bonito Boathouse to the sophisticated Beach Club. ⊠*1 Tarpon Blvd., 19 mi south of Beaufort, Fripp Island* ☎*843/838–3535 or 877/374–7748* ⊕*www.frippislandresort.com* ⤳*210 units* ♿*In-room: kitchen, DVD (some). In-hotel: 5 restaurants, golf courses, tennis courts, pools, bicycles, children's programs (ages 3–12), laundry facilities, parking (free), no-smoking rooms* ☰*AE, D, DC, MC, V* ⏀*EP.*

★ Fodor'sChoice ☆ **Rhett House Inn.** Art and antiques abound in a
$$$–$$$$ circa-1820 home turned storybook inn. Look for the little luxuries—down pillows and duvets, a CD player in each room, and fresh flowers. The best rooms open out onto the veranda (No. 2) or the courtyard garden (No. 7). The interior decor is Beaufort traditional coupled with Manhattan panache. Breakfast, afternoon tea, evening hors d'oeuvres, and dessert are included in the rate. Visiting celebrities have included Barbra Streisand, Jeff Bridges, and Dennis Quaid. The remodeled (not so historic) house across the street has eight more rooms, each of which has

a gas fireplace, a whirlpool bath, a private entrance, and a porch. **Pros:** All guests come together for breakfast and other social hours; more private in annex. **Cons:** Annex does not have the charisma of the main inn; in the main house you can hear footsteps on stairs and in hallways. ✉*1009 Craven St.* ☎*843/524–9030* ⊕*www.rhetthouseinn. com* ⚲*16 rooms, 1 suite* ♿*In-hotel: restaurant, bicycles, no kids under 5, parking (free), no-smoking rooms* ▤*AE, D, MC, V* ⏍*BP.*

NO ROOM AT THE INN. The military has a commanding presence in Beaufort, and throughout the year there are various graduation ceremonies on Wednesday and Thursday. Lodgings can fill up fast, so make sure to call ahead.

PRIVATE VILLAS ON FRIPP ISLAND

$–$$ ▦**Beach Club Villa 172.** Since its development in the 1960s, Fripp Island has been known as one of the more moderately priced, private resort islands. Yes, like everything, prices have risen, but this condo/villa is an example of how to keep costs down. A couple of decades old, this building is well maintained, the roof recently replaced, and the view is of marshland and a canal with an access to a private crabbing dock. Individually owned, like most of the units on Fripp, the unit has been renovated with an updated furniture package, flat-screen TVs, stainless-steel appliances, and a granite countertop. Condos like this one are well-suited to small families, golf buddies, and corporate groups. Daily maid service is an option. **Pros:** Price is right; conveniently located to main facilities; on the first floor, so there are no stairs to climb. **Cons:** The better views are on the second and third floors; not as commodious as a house; not on the ocean; no barbecue grills are allowed. ✉*172 Beach Club, Fripp Island* ⊕*www.frippislandresort. com* ⚲*2 bedrooms, 2 baths* ♿*Dishwasher, DVD, VCR, Wi-Fi, daily maid service, on-site security, laundry facilities* ▤*AE, D, M, V.*

$$$$ ▦**424 Ocean Point Lane.** A view of the indigo ocean is a straight shot across the 18th hole of the Ocean Point Golf Course from this villa. Watch sons learn how to play golf from their fathers and spy dolphins cruising in close. Light streams in through the front wall of glass that extends from the open living/dining room to the cozy loft on the second floor. A sunny, happy home, it is contemporary and individualistic. The two master suites, one on each floor, make sharing democratic, with privacy a plus. It's just

footsteps from the pool complex, and along the way you can talk to the docile marsh deer. Daily maid service is an option. **Pros:** Spacious; captivating views and sea breezes on the second-floor deck; wonderfully quiet yet with a superior media system. **Cons:** Interior decor somewhat dated; kitchen isn't large; not on the beach. ✉424 Ocean Point La., Fripp Island ☎843/838–1696 ⊕www.fripp islandresort.com ☞3 bedrooms, 3.5 baths ♿Dishwasher, DVD, VCR, Wi-Fi, daily maid service, on-site security, laundry facilities, no smoking ⊟AE, D, MC, V ☞2-night min. (1-week Jun.–Aug.).

SPORTS & THE OUTDOORS

BIKING

Beaufort is great for biking. In town, traffic is moderate, and you can cruise along the waterfront and through the historic district. However, if you ride on the sidewalks or after dark without a headlight, you run the risk of a city fine of nearly $150. If you stopped for happy hour, say at Emily's, and come out as the light is fading, walk your bike back "home." Some inns rent them to guests, but alas, they may not be in great shape and usually were not the best even when new.

If you want to have decent tires, call **Lowcountry Bicycles** (✉102 Sea Island Pkwy. ☎843/524–9585).For just $5 you can rent bike headlights on your rental wheels that will cost just $15 for a half day, $30 a full day, $80 a week. Adult bicycles only are available, either a 3-speed or 8-speed.

CANOE & BOAT TOURS

★ Beaufort is where the Ashepoo, Combahee, and Edisto rivers form the A.C.E. Basin, a vast wilderness of marshes and tidal estuaries loaded with history. For sea kayaking, tourists meet at the designated launching areas for fully guided, two-hour tours.

Adults pay $40 at **Beaufort Kayak Tours** (✉600 Linton La. ☎843/525–0810 ⊕www.beaufortkayaktours.com).

A.C.E. Basin Tours (✉1 Coosaw River Dr., Coosaw Island ☎843/521–3099 ⊕www.acebasintours.com) might be the best bet for the very young, or anyone with limited mobility, as it operates a 38-foot pontoon boat tour. A tour costs $35.

GOLF

Most golf courses are about a 10- to 20-minute scenic drive from Beaufort.

In a gated community, **Dataw Island** (⊠*Dataw Club Rd., off U.S. 21, 6 mi east of Beaufort, Dataw Island* ☎*843/ 838–8250* ⊕*www.dataw.org* ⚑*Cotton Dike: 18 holes. 6,799 yds. Par 72. Morgan River: 18 holes. 6,646 yds. Par 72. Greens fee: $69–$120*) has Tom Fazio's Cotton Dike Course, with spectacular marsh views, and Arthur Hill's Morgan River Course, with ponds, marshes, and wide, open fairways. The lovely 14th hole of the Morgan River Course overlooks the river. You must be accompanied by a member or belong to another private club. To tap into the reciprocal system, one's home-club pro has to call Dataw's golf pro to make arrangements.

Fripp Island Golf & Beach Resort (⊠*201 Tarpon Blvd., Fripp Island* ☎*843/838–2131 or 843/838–1576* ⊕*www.fripp islandresort.com* ⚑*Ocean Creek: 18 holes. 6,643 yds. Par 71. Ocean Point: 18 holes. 6,556 yds. Par 72. Greens fee: $89–$99*) has a pair of championship courses. Ocean Creek Golf Course, designed by Davis Love, has sweeping views of saltwater marshes. Designed by George Cobb, Ocean Point Golf Links runs along the ocean the entire way. This is a wildlife refuge, so you'll see plenty of it, particularly marsh deer. In fact, the wildlife and ocean views may make it difficult for you to keep your eyes on the ball. Nonguests should call the golf pro to make arrangements to play.

8

Sanctuary Golf Club at Cat Island (⊠*8 Waveland Ave., Cat Island, Beaufort* ☎*843/524–0300* ⚑*18 holes. 6,625 yds. Par 71. Greens fee $60–$90*) is a semiprivate club, so members get priority. Its scenic course is considered tight with plenty of water hazards. The course reopened after a major renovation in fall 2008 of greens, tees, bunkers, and even the driving range.

NIGHTLIFE & THE ARTS

The **Hallelujah Singers** (⊠*806 Elizabeth St.* ☎*843/379–3594*), Gullah performers, perform at Lowcountry venues. They foot-stomp and clap hands and sing spirituals.

The late-night hangout **Luther's** (⊠*910 Bay St.* ☎*843/521– 1888*) rocks on weekends.

SHOPPING

ART GALLERIES

At **Bay Street Gallery** (✉*719 Bay St.* ☎*843/525–1024 or 843/522–9210*), Laura Hefner's oils of coastal wetlands magically convey the mood of the Lowcountry.

At **Four Winds Gallery** (✉*709 Bay St.29901* ☎*843/838–3295*) Marianne Norton imports folk art, antiques, sculpture, photography, furniture, rugs, textiles, and weavings, connecting cultures and artists and artisans around the world. Southern art, both Gullah and New Orleans artwork, is new. (Ask about her four rooms to let at 1103 Craven Street, for about $100 a night.)

The colorful designs of Suzanne and Eric Longo decorate the **Longo Gallery** (✉*103 Charles St.* ☎*843/522–8933*).

The **Rhett Gallery** (✉*901 Bay St.* ☎*843/524–3339*) sells Lowcountry art by four generations of the Rhett family, as well as antique maps and Audubon prints.

DAUFUSKIE ISLAND

13 mi (approx. 45 minutes) from Hilton Head via ferry.

From Hilton Head you can take a 45-minute ferry ride to nearby Daufuskie Island, the setting for Pat Conroy's novel *The Water Is Wide,* which was made into the movie *Conrack*. The boat ride may very well be one of the highlights of your vacation. The Lowcountry beauty enfolds before you, as pristine and unspoiled as you can imagine. Since the island is in the Atlantic, nestled between Hilton Head and Savannah, you can also pick up a launch from Savannah, and that's another delightful ride. Many visitors do come just for the day, to play golf and have lunch or dinner; you might indulge your senses in the New Age Breathe Spa, or kids might enjoy biking or horseback riding.

Most of the island's development is at the Daufuskie Island Club & Resort and Melrose, which is now a private club, but the island also has acres of unspoiled beauty. On a bike, in a golf cart, on horseback, or in a horse-drawn carriage you can easily explore the island. You will find remnants of churches, homes, and schools—all reminders of antebellum times. Guided tours include sights such as an 18th-century cemetery, former slave quarters, a local winery, and the Haig Point Lighthouse. The scenic boat ride and the physically beautiful island itself will become etched in your memories.

GETTING HERE & AROUND

The only way to Daufuskie is a ferry from Hilton Head or Savannah. It's possible to come on a day trip. On arrival you can rent a golf cart or bicycle or take a tour. If you are coming to Daufuskie Island for a multiday stay with luggage and/or groceries, and perhaps a dog, be absolutely certain that you allow a full hour to park and check in for the ferry, particularly on a busy summer weekend. Whether you are staying on island or just day-tripping, the ferry costs $40 round-trip from Hilton Head ($45 from Savannah).

WHERE TO STAY

$$$$ ⊠**Daufuskie Island Resort & Breathe Spa.** Overnight visitors can stay at the Inn at Melrose, in rooms that are twice as large as most of the hotels on the main island. Rooms are traditional but contemporary in style and have a separate sitting area. Families might be tempted to opt for the even larger space of the cottages, with the two-bedroom options the most popular. (It is a pet-friendly resort, too, though pets are allowed only in some cottages.) Corporate groups usually take both inn rooms and cottages. Note that those run high-occupancy in the summer, especially on the weekends and for holidays such as Thanksgiving. In June, especially, it is a destination resort for weddings. Sophisticated dining at Jack's Grill (named after J. Nicklaus) and its golf motif is the adult choice, whereas families enjoy the Beach Club Restaurant. ⊠*Embarkation Center, 421 Squire Pope Rd., North End* ☎*843/341–4820 or 800/648–6778* ⊕*www.daufuskieresort.com* ⏎*52 rooms* ⏶*In-room: kitchen (some), refrigerator, Internet. In-hotel: 4 restaurants, room service, bars, golf courses, tennis courts, pools, gym, spa, beachfront, watersports, bicycles, laundry facilities, parking (free), some pets allowed, no-smoking rooms* ▭*AE, D, MC, V* ⊚ *EP.*

SPORTS & THE OUTDOORS

Calibogue Cruises (⊠*Broad Creek Marina, 164B Palmetto Bay Rd., Mid-Island* ☎*843/342–8687* ⊕*www.freeport-marina. com*) has several Daufuskie tour options, including guided tours with lunch and gospel-music performances starting at $40.

Vagabond Cruises (✉*Harbour Town Marina, South End* ☎*843/785–2662* ⊕*www.vagabondcruise.com*) conducts daytime boat rides, from dolphin tours to runs to Savannah, sails on the *Stars & Stripes* of America's Cup fame, and dinner cruises.

EDISTO ISLAND

62 mi northeast of Beaufort via U.S. 17 and Rte 174; 44 mi southwest of Charleston via U.S. 17 and Rte. 174.

On rural Edisto (pronounced *ed*-is-toh) Island, find magnificent stands of age-old oaks festooned with Spanish-moss border, quiet streams, and side roads; wild turkeys may still be spotted on open grasslands and amid palmetto palms. Twisting tidal creeks, populated with egrets and herons, wind around golden marsh grass. A big day on the island may include shelling and shark-tooth hunting.

Edisto is one of the less costly, more down-home of the Carolina sea islands. Adults sing their hearts out on karaoke nights while their kids sip rocking root beer floats. And now bingo is big, and not just for seniors.

The small "downtown" beachfront is a mix of public beach-access spots, restaurants, and old, shabby-chic beach homes that are a far cry from the palatial villas rented out on the resort islands. The outlying Edisto Beach State Park is a pristine wilderness and camper's delight. The one actual resort was bought by Wyndham and, although it houses time-share units, it also has a number of rental accommodations.

GETTING HERE & AROUND

Edisto is connected to the mainland by a causeway. The only way here is by private car.

Visitor Information **Edisto Island Chamber of Commerce** (✉*430 Rte. 174, Box 206, Edisto Island* ☎*843/869–3867 or 888/333–2781* ⊕*www.edistochamber.com*).

★ Fodor'sChoice **Edisto Beach State Park** covers 1,255 acres and
☺ includes marshland and tidal rivers, a 1½-mi-long beachfront, towering palmettos, and a lush maritime forest with a 3½-mi trail running through it. The park has the best shelling beach on public property in the Lowcountry. Overnight options include rustic furnished cabins (with basic, no frills decor) by the marsh and campsites by the ocean (although severe erosion is limiting availability). Sites are $23 with

electricity, $17 without. This park stays extremely busy, so with only seven cabins (the park system struggles to maintain their livability), you have to reserve far in advance. They are so sought after that reservations sometimes go on the lottery system. The campsites are another story: reservations are on a first come, first serve basis. Deluxe resort development has begun to encroach around the edges of the park. ⊠*Route 174, off U.S. 17* ☎*843/869–2156* ⊕*www. southcarolinaparks.com* ⊠*$4* ⊙*Early Apr.–late Oct., daily 8 AM–10 PM; Late Oct.–early Apr., daily 8–6.*

The ruins of **Sheldon Church,** built in 1753, make an interesting stop if you're driving from Beaufort or Charleston to Edisto Island. The church burned down in 1779 and again in 1865. Only the brick walls and columns remain. With its moss-draped live oaks, it has an eerie Lowcountry beauty about it. At dusk it takes on a preternatural cast, the kind of atmosphere that gives rise to the ghost stories that Southern children are raised on. On the weekends in and around June, you can almost always witness a wedding. No matter, it is a good spot to get off the highway and stretch a spell. You can pick up a snack or some fixin's at the filling station nearby at Gardens Corner. It was modernized about 10 years back, but this highway landmark is still shades of decades past. ⊠*18 mi northwest of Beaufort; Hwy. 17 S .*

WHERE TO EAT

8

¢–$ ×**Po' Pigs Bo-B-Q.** *Southern.* Step inside the super-casual
★ restaurant for pork barbecue that has South Carolinians raving. Sample the different sauces (sweet mustard, tomato, or vinegar) and wash it all down with a tall glass of sweet tea. Don't miss down-home sides like squash casserole, pork skins, lima beans and ham, and red rice. The blink-and-you-miss-it location is on the tail end of an undeveloped road. ⊠*2410 Rte. 174* ☎*843/869–9003* ⊟*No credit cards* ⊙*Closed Sun.–Tues.*

WHERE TO STAY

¢ ⊞**Atwood Vacations.** For complete privacy, rent out a family-owned cottage on Edisto, which will be much more comfortable than the bare-bones options that the park maintains. The list of properties includes everything from one-bedroom condos to six-bedroom homes. All kitchens are stocked with appliances and dishes, but you need to bring your own bed linens. Two-day minimum stays are required. ✉*495 Rte. 174* ☎*843/869–2151* ⊕*www.atwood vacations.com* ⌂*In-room: kitchen* ⊟*AE, MC, V* ⋈*EP.*

$ 🖥**Wyndham Ocean Ridge Resort.** Looking for resort ame-
☾ nities in a get-away-from-it-all escape? You've found it here, at the only resort on the island. This is the former Fairfield Ocean Ridge, which was taken over by Wyndham in 2006. It is a time share, so all of the attractive units are individually owned and decorated according to the owner's taste. Nonowners can still rent these units, but, alas, there are fewer available than in the past, so reserve as far in advance as possible. There is a two-day minimum stay in-season (April 1–August 30), and you will pay a $25 reservation fee. Summers are solidly booked, especially the weekends; in the off-season, the major holidays find few available units. Although few of the accommodations (efficiencies to five-bedroom villas and houses) are on the beach, most are just a short walk away from it. Be sure to ask if this is important to you. There is no daily maid service, nor can you pay extra for it, although towels can be switched out. The family-oriented staff knows how to keep kids amused. A shuttle transports guests to the resort's beach cabana, which is delightful, with plenty of chaises. Wyndham has done an admirable renova- tion on The Plantation Golf Course. ✉*1 King Cotton Rd. Box 27, 29438* ☎*843/869–2561; 843/869–4527 or 877/296–6335 for reservations* ☎*843/869–2384* ⊕*www. wyndhamoceanridge.com* ↝*38 units* ⌂*In-hotel: restaurant, bar, golf course, tennis courts, pool, children's programs (ages 6–14), beachfront, bicycles, no-smoking rooms* ⊟*AE, D, MC, V* ⋈*EP.*

Travel Smart
Savannah

GETTING HERE & AROUND

Fodors.com is a great place to begin any journey. Scan Travel Wire for suggested itineraries, travel deals, restaurant and hotel openings, and other up-to-the-minute info. Check out Booking to research prices and book plane tickets, hotel rooms, rental cars, and vacation packages. Head to Talk for on-the-ground pointers from travelers who frequent our message boards.

▌ BY AIR

Savannah and Hilton Head share an airport, which is not really in either place. There are flights, though you may find more options into either Charleston or Atlanta.
■TIP→ **If you have an afternoon flight, check in your bags early in the morning (keep a change of clothes in a carry-on), then go back to the beach for one last lunch, returning to the airport an hour before your flight departs. It makes for much easier traveling, saves time, and you get your last beach fix.**

Airlines & Airports **Airline and Airport Links.com** (⊕www.airline andairportlinks.com) has links to many of the world's airlines and airports.

Airline-Security Issues **Transportation Security Administration** (⊕www.tsa.gov) has answers for almost every question that might come up.

AIRPORTS
Savannah/Hilton Head International Airport (SAV) is 18 mi west of downtown. Despite the name, there are no international flights from here; the foreign trade zone, a site for importing, constitutes the "international" aspect. Despite the distance, the airport is only 20 minutes from the Historic District. Allow a little extra time if you arrive at midday during the week.

Airport Information **Savannah/ Hilton Head International Airport** (⊠400 Airways Ave., West Chatham ☎912/964-0514 ⊕www.savannah airport.com).

GROUND TRANSPORTATION

Airport Transfers **First City Limousine** (☎912/484-0455). **Old Savannah Tours** (☎912/234-8128 ⊕ www.oldsavannahtours.com).

FLIGHTS
Savannah is served by Continental Express, Northwest Airlink, Delta, United Express, and US Airways/Express.

Airline Contacts **Continental Airlines** (☎800/523-3273 for U.S. reservations, 800/231-0856 for international reservations ⊕www.continental.com). **Delta Airlines** (☎800/221-1212 for U.S. reservations, 800/241-4141 for international reservations ⊕www. delta.com). **Northwest Airlines** (☎800/225-2525 ⊕www.nwa.com). **United Airlines** (☎800/864-8331 for U.S. reservations, 800/538–2929 for international reservations ⊕www.united.com). **USAirways** (☎800/428–4322 for U.S. and Canada reservations, 800/622–1015 for international reservations ⊕www.usairways.com).

BY BOAT & FERRY

On the Savannah River, the Port of Savannah is the busiest port from New Orleans to New York. Belles Ferry provides a regular service from the City Hall dock in the Historic District to the Westin Savannah Harbor Golf Resort & Spa at the International Convention Center, on Hutchinson Island. Ferries are part of the transit system and run daily 7 AM to 11 PM with departures every 15 minutes. The complimentary crossing takes two minutes. The Belles Ferry fleet includes three vessels, each named after a notable Savannah woman.

Contact **Savannah Belles Ferry** (✉900 E. Gwinnett St. ☎912/233–5767 ⊕www.catchacat.org).

▌ BY BUS

Savannah and Brunswick are the coastal stops for Greyhound.

Contacts **Greyhound/Trailways** (✉610 W. Oglethorpe Ave., Downtown ☎912/232–2135 or 800/231–2222 ⊕www.greyhound.com).

▌ BY CAR

Interstate 95 slices north–south along the eastern seaboard, intersecting 10 mi west of town with east–west Interstate 16, which dead-ends in downtown Savannah. U.S. 17, the Coastal Highway, also runs north–south through town. U.S. 80, which connects the Atlantic to the Pacific, is another east–west route through Savannah.

This is one city where it is to your advantage not to rent a car unless and until you plan on leaving the immediate area. You'll find an abundance of transportation options downtown and to the surrounding areas: buses (two downtown lines are free), taxis, pedicabs (up to two persons can be pedaled in a cart attached to a bicyclist), horse carriages, trolley tours (which allow you to get on and off), free ferries, rental bikes, and rental scooters. This is a walking city, primarily, so you must remember to bring at least one pair of comfortable walking shoes.

GASOLINE

At this writing, gas prices have begun to drop after reaching historic highs. In general, gas is less expensive here than in central Florida but slightly more than Charleston. Gas stations are not difficult to find; there are several on Martin Luther King Jr. Boulevard.

PARKING

Downtown, parking can be a challenge, but it is easier in the residential neighborhoods. Tourists may purchase a two-day parking pass for $8 from the Savannah Visitors Center, the Parking Services Department, and various hotels and inns (many places give you this pass for free). Rates vary at local parking garages, but you should expect to pay at least $1 for the first hour and 75¢ for each additional hour. Metered parking costs vary depending on the location of the meter, from a low of 25¢ up to a maximum of about $1 per hour. Some meters do not charge on Saturday and Sunday. Most downtown hotels have paid parking, and some B&Bs and inns have their own parking lots or advise guests on how to park on the street. Few restaurants have parking.

RENTAL CARS

The major rental agencies can be found both in town, on the south side, and at the airport. They include Avis, Budget, Hertz, and Enterprise, which provide pickup and delivery service (within limits); Thrifty is just at the airport. Almost all car-rental offices are closed on Sunday.

Contacts **Avis Rent a Car** (☎912/354–4718 or 912/354–4718 ⊕ www.avis.com). **Budget Car Rental** (☎912/964–4600 ⊕www. budget.com). **Enterprise Rent-A-Car** (☎912/964–0171 ⊕www. enterprise.com). **Hertz Rent A Car** (☎912/921–0423 or 912/964–9595 ⊕wwww.hertz.com). **Thrifty** (☎912/964–0300 or 912/966–2277 ⊕www.thrifty.com).

RENTAL CAR INSURANCE

Everyone who rents a car wonders whether the insurance that the rental companies offer is worth the expense. No one—including us—has a simple answer. If you own a car, your personal auto insurance may cover a rental to some degree; always read your policy's fine print. If you don't have auto insurance, then seriously consider buying the collision- or loss-damage waiver (CDW or LDW) from the car-rental company, which eliminates your liability for damage to the car. Some credit cards offer CDW coverage, but it's usually supplemental to your own insurance and rarely covers SUVs, minivans, luxury models, and the like.

If your coverage is secondary, you may still be liable for loss-of-use costs from the car-rental company. But no credit-card insurance is valid unless you use that card for *all* transactions, from reserving to paying the final bill. All companies exclude car rental in some countries, so be sure to find out about the destination to which you are traveling. It's sometimes cheaper to buy insurance as part of your general travel insurance policy.

ROADSIDE EMERGENCIES

Discuss with the rental car agency what to do in the case of an emergency, as this sometimes differs between companies. Make sure you understand what your insurance covers and what it doesn't, and it's a good rule of thumb to let someone at your accommodation know where you are heading and when you plan to return. Keep emergency numbers (car rental agency and your accommodation) with you, just in case.

ROAD CONDITIONS

Savannah streets are not only clean and litter-free but in fine to excellent condition. The same good conditions exist on the major highways. There is heavy truck traffic on I–95, where the speed limit is 70 mph. Within the Historic District, you may encounter slow-moving horse carriages, but please don't honk your horn at the horses.

BY PUBLIC TRANSPORTATION

Chatham Area Transit (CAT) operates buses in Savannah and Chatham County Monday through Saturday from 6 AM to 11 PM, Sunday from 9 to 7. Some lines may stop running earlier or may not run on Sunday. The CAT Shuttle operates throughout the Historic District, running on a north–south route once an hour, but is free. For other CONNECT Savannah buses, the fare is $1.

The Dot is Savannah's free downtown transportation system. In addition to the Savannah Belles Ferry, the Dot operates an Express Shuttle around downtown and historic 1930s River Street Streetcars, which began service in late 2008.

Contacts **Chatham Area Transit (CAT)** (☎912/233–5767 ⊕www.catchacat.org). **CONNECT Savannah** (✉1800 E. Victory Dr. ☎912/721–4350. **The Dot** (☎912/447–4026 ⊕connectonthedot.com).

BY TAXI

AAA Adam Cab Co. is a reliable 24-hour taxi service. Calling ahead for reservations could yield a flat rate. Otherwise, it's $1.82 per mile. Yellow Cab Company is another dependable taxi service. Standard taxi fare is $1.92 per mile. The flat rate between Savannah's Historic District and the airport can be as high as $42 if you're staying in Savannah's South Side.

MC Transportation is a taxi and shuttle service that operates 24 hours a day and will go anywhere, anytime. To Tybee Island, for example, the metered fare is $1.92 per mile, with a surcharge for slow-moving traffic; expect the fare to be in the range of $25 to $35 for one person, $1 for each additional passenger. These white cabs with blue lettering have a flat rate from the downtown Historic District to the airport of $25 for the first person, $5 each additional passenger. You can hail these cabs on the street, if they do not have riders and if they are not "on a mission."

Savannah Pedicab is a bicycle rickshaw that costs $45 per hour or $25 per half-hour (you can also rent a pedicab for the day for $150). They operate from 11 AM to midnight (2 AM on weekends). They also rent cruiser-style bikes for $20 per day and will deliver to your inn.

Contacts **AAA Adam Cab Incorporated** (☎912/927–7466). **MC Transportation** ☎912/786–9191. **Savannah Pedicab** (☎912/232–7900 ⊕www.savannah pedicab.com).**Yellow Cab** (☎912/236–1133).

BY TRAIN

Amtrak runs its Silver Service/Palmetto route down the East Coast from New York to Miami, stopping in Savannah. The station is about 6 mi from downtown.

Contacts **Amtrak** (☎800/872–7245 ⊕www.amtrak. com).

ESSENTIALS

▊ COMMUNICATIONS

INTERNET

Savannah offers free Wi-Fi services, and most hotels and inns offer complimentary access to the Internet. Consequently, although some cafés and coffeehouses such as Gallery Espresso provide customers with free Wi-Fi, you usually have to bring your own laptop. The Live Oak Public Library offers free Internet access on a first-come, first-served basis. The main branch is open 9 to 9 weekdays, 9 to 6 Saturday, and 2 to 6 Sunday.

Contacts **Gallery Espresso** (✉234 Bull St., Historic District ☎912/233–5348). **Live Oak Public Library** (✉2002 Bull St., Savannah ☎912/652-3600). **Panera Bread** (✉1 W. Broughton St., Historic District ☎912/236–0275) **Starbucks** (✉1 E. Broughton St. [Corner Bull St.], Historic District ☎912/447–6742)

PHONES

The area code in Charleston is 912. You can still find a few phone booths, but as in most American cities, they are becoming anachronisms as cell-phone use spreads.

▊ EMERGENCIES

Candler Hospital and Memorial Health University Medical Center are the area hospitals with 24-hour emergency rooms.

Emergency Services **Ambulance, police** (☎911).

Hospitals **Candler Hospital** (✉5353 Reynolds St., Kensington Park ☎912/692–6000). **Memorial Health University Medical Center** (✉4700 Waters Ave., Fairfield ☎912/350–8000).

Late-Night Pharmacy **CVS Pharmacy** (✉Medical Arts Shopping Center, 4725 Waters Ave., Fairfield ☎912/355–7111).

▊ HOURS OF OPERATION

Most businesses operate on a 9 to 5 basis, although some offices open at 8:30. Shops that are geared to tourists usually open daily at 10 and close at 6, including Sundays.

▊ MAIL

Postal services in the Historic District include an outlet at Telfair Square. There's also a handy UPS Store in the heart of downtown at W. Bryan and Bull streets.

Post Offices **UPS Store** (✉22 W. Bryan St., Savannah ☎912/233–7807). **U.S. Post Office** (✉118 Barnard St., Savannah ☎912/232–2952).

▊ MONEY

Bank of America, Wacovia, BB&T, and other major financial outlets have branches in Savannah; most operate normal office hours weekdays, with half days on Saturday. ATM machines are numerous. Savannah is not inexpensive as far as its accommodations, although there is good value to be had, as with its fine-dining establishments. There are a number of reasonably priced and even inexpensive places to eat, however.

Contacts **Bank of America** (✉22 Bull St., Historic District ☎912/651–8250).

CREDIT CARDS

Throughout this guide, the following abbreviations are used: **AE,** American Express; **D,** Discover; **DC,** Diners Club; **MC,** MasterCard; and **V,** Visa.

Reporting Lost Cards **American Express** (☎800/528–4800 ⊕www. americanexpress.com). **MasterCard** (☎800/627–8372 ⊕www.master card.com). **Visa** (☎800/847–2911 ⊕www.visa.com).

▌ SAFETY

Savannah officials take safety seriously, and you will see both city police cars and SCAD security patrol cars throughout the downtown area. By day, you do not need to fear walking downtown streets, but you should always lock your car and utilize your hotel's safe for your cash and valuables. By night, exercise reasonable caution, especially in darker areas such as along River Street. Squares that are not surrounded by residences can also be problematic late at night. Ask your hotel or inn concierge about issues in your immediate surroundings, and don't walk alone downtown after 9 PM. Instead, carry the number for the Pedi-Cabs; a simple call on your cell phone will summon one quickly. If you are a morn-

ing jogger, it is best to run at a time that people are going to work.

▌ TAXES

The sales tax is 7%; hotel tax is 13%.

▌ TIPPING

Tip as you would in any other U.S. city; waiters in restaurants expect to receive 10% to 20% (the larger amount in more upscale establishments); 15% is still the norm here. Tip hotel maids about $1 or $2 per day (leave this each morning since the person who cleans your room may change over the course of a multiday stay).

▌ TOURS

BOAT TOURS

Riverboat cruises go up the river from Factors Walk and cost about $20. The causeway is mainly commercial, with many deserted warehouses, so it's not a terribly scenic ride, but it is narrated, has a bar, plays Jimmy Buffet, and is most relaxing. It's a particularly good activity in the dog days of summer, when the breeze will cool you. The gospel dinner cruise ($35) has a Southern buffet and gospel singers to entertain. The river with its night lights on is a joy.

Contacts **Riverboat Cruises** (☎912/232–6404 ⊕www.savannah riverboat.com).

HISTORIC DISTRICT TOURS

Carriage Tours of Savannah, whose tours depart from the City Market or the Visitor Center (seasonally), takes you through the Historic

District by day or by night at a 19th-century clip-clop pace, with coachmen spinning tales and telling ghost stories along the way. A romantic evening tour in a private carriage costs $85 (add $20 per person over two); regular tours are a modest $20 per person.

The Freedom Trail Tour is a black history tour that takes in the Beach Institute African Cultural Center, the First African Baptist Church, the Ralph Mark Gilbert Civil Rights Museum, and the Laurel Grove Cemetery, along with its slave burial grounds. Two daily tours leave from the Savannah Welcome Center, and tickets cost $20 per person.

Historic Savannah Carriage Tours concentrates on private tours aboard a European vis-à-vis carriage. Romantic, to be sure, the Champagne Tour includes a bottle, the Rose Tour, a dozen roses, and both cost $120. It goes up from there with the Proposal Tour topping out at $175.

Old Savannah Tours is the city's award-winning company with years of experience and the widest variety of tours, including the following popular options: the hop-on/hop-off trolley tour; the 90-minute Historic District tour in a van with air-conditioning; the Paula Deen Tour; the ghost tour with dinner at Pirates House; the walking ghost tour; Civil War tours; riverboat cruise; ecotour; and more.

Old Town Trolley Tours has narrated 90-minute tours traversing the Historic District. Trolleys stop at 13 designated stops every half hour daily from 9 to 4:30; you can hop on and off as you please. The cost is $23.

Savannah Movie Tours shows you the locations where the many Hollywood films were shot, with a running commentary giving the inside scoop ($25). This same company gives the popular Foody Tours, where you tour, eat, drink, and be merry ($48).

The Hearse Ghost Tours may be like nothing you have ever done before. As they say, for 15 years these hearses did the job they were intended for. When retired, their roofs were cut open, and now these black hulks can carry eight live bodies for ghost tours, cruising the cemetery and haunted inns and pubs, for just $15 a head.

Contacts Carriage Tours of Savannah (☎912/236–6756 ⊕www.carriagetoursofsavannah.com). **Freedom Trail Tours** (☎912/398–2785 ✉freedomtrailtours@bellsouth.net). **Hearse Tours** (☎912/695–1578 ⊕www.hearseghosttours.com). **Historic Savannah Carriage Tours** (☎912/443–9333 ⊕www.savannahcarriage.com). **Old Savannah Tours** (☎912/234–8128 or 800/517–9007 ⊕www.oldsavannahtours.com). **Old Town Trolley Tours** (☎912/233–0083). **Savannah Movie Tours** (☎912/234–3440 ⊕www.savannahmovietours.com). **Savannah Area Welcome Center** (✉301 Martin Luther King Jr. Blvd., ☎912/944–0455 ⊕www.savannahvisit.com).

SPECIAL-INTEREST TOURS

Historic Savannah Foundation, a preservation organization, leads tours of the Historic District and the Lowcountry. *Midnight in the Garden of Good and Evil* ($65), the Golden Isles, group, and private tours are also available. In addition, the foundation leads specialty excursions to the fishing village of Thunderbolt; the Isle of Hope, with its stately mansions lining Bluff Drive; the much-photographed Bonaventure Cemetery, on the banks of the Wilmington River; and Wormsloe Plantation Site, with its mile-long avenue of arching oaks. Fees for the specialty tours start at $75 per hour, with a two-hour minimum for a private group of up to five people.

Personalized Tours of Savannah is a small company offering upscale and intimate tours of the city, with customized themes covering movies filmed in Savannah, the city's extraordinary architecture, history, and a very good Jewish heritage tour. The owner is a longtime Savannah resident, and tours are peppered with history, anecdotes, and insider knowledge. Each has a two-hour minimum, is highly individualized, and starts at $65 per hour.

Contacts Historic Savannah Foundation (☎912/234-4088 or 800/627-5030).

Personalized Tours of Savannah (☎912/234-0014 or 800/627-5030 ⊕www.savannahsites.com).

WALKING TOURS

Much of the downtown Historic District can easily be explored on foot. Its grid shape makes getting around a breeze, and you can find any number of places to stop and rest.

A Ghost Talk Ghost Walk tour should send chills down your spine during an easy 1-mi jaunt through the old colonial city. Tours, lasting 1½ hours, leave from the middle of Reynolds Square, at the John Wesley Memorial at 7:30 PM and 9:30 PM, weather permitting. The cost is $10. The Saturday night tours include entry and a tour of the William Washington Gordon House.

Savannah-by-Foot's Creepy Crawl Haunted Pub Tour is a favorite. According to the true believers there are so many ghosts in Savannah they're actually divided into subcategories. On this tour, charismatic guide and storyteller Greg Proffit specializes in those ghosts that haunt taverns only, regaling you with tales from secret sub-basements discovered to house skeletal remains, possessed gumball machines, and animated water faucets. Tours traditionally depart from the Six Pence Pub at 8 PM. Since this is a cocktail tour, children are not permitted. Routes can vary, so call for departure times and locations; the cost is $15 and lasts for 2½ hours.

Sixth Sense Savannah offers the city's most sophisticated, specialized ghost tours. With all the ghostly story opportunities in the Savannah area, they have multiple tours, such as Bonaventure

Cemetery, Historic District, and Haunted Oatland Island. For the latter, groups will be equipped with digital therms, dousing rods, etc. Prices range from $18 to $56.

Savannah Fun Tours is a unique way to explore Savannah at your own pace with a "to-go cup" if you like. It is a self-guided, scavenger hunt put together by a lifelong Savannahian. Solve the puzzle and collect a prize at the end. The tour book with clues for the hunt costs $25 and was designed to be used by two to four people. Do everything at your own pace. Check the company's Web site for locations where you can buy the book.

Contacts **A Ghost Talk Ghost Walk Tour** (⊠Reynolds Sq., Congress and Abercorn Sts., Historic District ☎912/233–3896). **Savannah-By-Foot's Creepy Crawl Haunted Pub Tour** (☎912/238–3843). **Savannah Fun Tours** (☎912/667–9760 ⊕www. savannahfuntours.com). **Sixth Sense Savannah** (☎912/501–9788 or 866/666–3323 ⊕www.sixthsense savannah.com).

▌ TRIP INSURANCE

Comprehensive travel policies typically cover trip cancellation and interruption, letting you cancel or cut your trip short because of a personal emergency, illness, or, in some cases, acts of terrorism in your destination. Such policies also cover evacuation and medical care. Some also cover you for trip delays because of bad weather or mechanical problems as well as for lost or delayed baggage. Another type of coverage to look for is financial default—that is, when your trip is disrupted because a tour operator, airline, or cruise line goes out of business. Generally you must buy this when you book your trip or shortly thereafter, and it's only available to you if your operator isn't on a list of excluded companies.

Expect comprehensive travel insurance policies to cost about 4% to 7% or 8% of the total price of your trip (it's more like 8%–12% if you're over age 70). Always read the fine print of your policy to make sure that you are covered for the risks that are of most concern to you. Compare several policies to make sure you're getting the best price and range of coverage available.

▐TIP➔ **OK. You know you can save a bundle on trips to warm-weather destinations by traveling in rainy season. But there's also a chance that a severe storm will disrupt your plans. The solution? Look for hotels and resorts that offer storm/hurricane guarantees. Although they rarely allow refunds, most guarantees do let you rebook later if a storm strikes.**

Insurance Comparison Sites **Insure My Trip.com** (☎800/487–4722 ⊕www.insuremytrip.com). **Square Mouth.com** (☎800/240–0369 or 727/490–5803 ⊕www.squaremouth. com).

Comprehensive Travel Insurers **Access America** (☎866/729–6021 ⊕www.accessamerica.com) **AIG Travel Guard** (☎800/826–4919 ⊕www.travelguard.com) **CSA Travel**

Protection (☎800/873-9855 ⊕www.csatravelprotection.com) **HTH Worldwide** (☎610/254-8700 ⊕www.hthworldwide.com) **Travelex Insurance** (☎888/228-9792 ⊕www.travelex-insurance.com) **Travel Insured International** (☎800/243-3174 ⊕www.travel insured.com)

▌ VISITOR INFORMATION

The Savannah Area Convention & Visitors Bureau does a grand job in providing quality information. The welcome center is easily accessed from U.S. 17 and Highway 80. It's open daily weekdays 8:30 to 5 and weekends 9 to 5. The center has a useful audiovisual overview of the city and is the starting point for a number of guided tours. For detailed information about Tybee Island, drop by the island's visitor center, just off Highway 80. It's open daily 10 to 6.

Contacts Savannah Area Convention & Visitors Bureau (✉101 E. Bay St., Historic District, ☎912/644-6401 or 877/728-2662 ⊕www.savannahvisit.com). **Savannah Visitor Information Center** (✉301 Martin Luther King Jr. Blvd., ☎912/944-0455 ⊕www.savannahvisit.com). **Tybee Island Visitor Information Center** (✉Campbell Ave. and Hwy. 80, Tybee Island, ☎912/786-5444 or 800/868-2322 ⊕www.tybeevisit.com).

INDEX

A

A.C.E. Basin Tours, *168*
A-J's✕, *38*
African-American history sites, *11–12, 28–29, 30, 31, 33, 36, 119–120, 161, 170–171, 182*
Air travel
Hilton Head, 118
Savannah, 176–177
Andrew Low House, *18*
Antiques, *107, 108*
Aqua Grille & Lounge✕, *126*
Aquarium, *37, 161*
Architecture, *17*
Art galleries
Beaufort, 170
Hilton Head Island, 158
Savannah, 23–24, 25, 28–29, 36, 107, 108–110
Arthur Hills at Palmetto Hall (golf course), *149–150*
Arthur Smith Antiques, *108*
Atlantis Inn 🛏, *81*
Atwood Vacations 🛏, *173–174*
Audubon Nature Store, *158*
Audubon-Newhall Preserve, *123*
AVIA Savannah 🛏, *68*
Azalea Inn & Gardens 🛏, *61*

B

B. Matthews Eatery✕, *42*
Bacon Park, *100, 102*
Ballastone Inn 🛏, *62–63*
Banks, *180–181*
Barnes BBQ Express✕, *42–43*
Bars, *87–91, 156–157*
Baseball, *96, 97*

Bateaux✕, *162*
Beach Club Villa 172 🛏, *167*
Beach Institute African-American Cultural Center, *28–29*
Beachcombing, *118*
Beaches, *118, 147*
Beaufort, *118, 158–170*
dining, 162–164
exploring, 159–162
lodging, 164–168
nightlife & the arts, 169
shopping, 170
sports & the outdoors, 168–169
transportation, 159
Beaufort Inn 🛏, *164*
Beaufort Kayak Tours, *168*
Beaufort Museum & Arsenal, *159–160*
Bed & Breakfast Inn 🛏, *63*
Bed & Breakfasts, *17*
Belford's Steak and Seafood✕, *43*
Bella's Italian Café✕, *55*
Berendt, John, *17*
Best Western Sea Island Inn 🛏, *165*
Biking, *96–98, 147–148, 168*
Bistro Savannah✕, *43, 46*
Black Marlin Bayside Grill✕, *126*
Blowin' Smoke BBQ✕, *46, 92*
Bluffton, *123*
Boat and ferry travel
Hilton Head, 119
Savannah, 177
Boat tours, *119–120, 171–172, 181*
Boathouse 11✕, *126, 128*
Boating and kayaking, *99–100, 148, 168*

Bohemian Hotel 🛏, *68*
Book shops, *110*
Brick Oven Café✕, *128*
Bus travel
Hilton Head, 119
Savannah, 177, 179
Business hours, *180*

C

Café 37✕, *46–47*
Camping, *161–162, 172–173*
Canoeing & kayaking, *36, 148, 168*
Car rental, *178*
Car travel
Hilton Head, 118
Savannah, 177–178
Carriage tours, *181–182*
Casimir Lounge, *87–88*
Cathedral of St. John the Baptist, *29*
Catherine Ward House 🛏, *63, 66*
Cemeteries, *19*
Cha Bella✕, *47*
Charlie's L'Etoile Verte✕, *128–129*
Charly's✕, *56*
Children
Hilton Head, 134, 136–137, 140–141, 152, 165–166, 172–173, 174
Savannah, 31, 33, 37, 42, 46, 52
Chippewa Square, *18*
Christ Episcopal Church, *29*
Churches, *13, 29, 30, 32, 173*
City Hall (Savannah), *29–30*
City Market, *19*
Civil War sites, *33, 36–37*
Climate, *6*
Clothing, *107, 110–111*

Club at Savannah Harbor, The✕, 100–101
Coastal Discovery Museum, 123
Coffeehouses, 91–92
Colonial Park Cemetery, 19
Columbia Square, 19
Communications, 180
Cooking school, 53, 130
Copper Penny (shop), 110
Country Club of Hilton Head, 150–151
Courtyard by Marriot Savannah Midtown ⌂, 80
CQs✕, 129
Crabbing, 161
CraftBrew Fest, 88
Credit cards, 5, 181
Crosswinds Golf Club, 101
Crowne Plaza Hilton Head Island Beach Resort ⌂, 133–134
Cruises, 120, 171–172, 181
Cuisine, 12, 41, 130
Cuthbert House Inn ⌂, 165

D
Daffin Park, 102
Dataw Island, 169
Daufuskie Island, 170–172
Daufuskie Island Resort & Breathe Spa ⌂, 171
Davenport, Isaiah, 23
Dining, 5, 12, 17 ⇨ See also Restaurants
Beaufort, 162–164
Edisto Island, 173
Hilton Head, 126, 128–133
price categories, 42, 121
Savannah, 5, 12, 17, 19, 22, 27, 40–55
Tybee Island, 56, 58
Dinner cruises, 119–120, 172, 181

Disney's Hilton Head Island Resort ⌂, 134, 136
Dresser Palmer House ⌂, 66

E
East Bay Inn ⌂, 66
Ebenezer, 33
Edisto Beach State Park, 172–173
Edisto Island, 172–174
11th Street Dockside✕, 163
Eliza Thompson House ⌂, 67
Elizabeth on 37th✕, 47–48
Emergencies, 180
Emily's Restaurant & Tapas Bar✕, 42
Emmet Park, 30

F
Faces (spa), 152, 154
Factors Walk, 19
Festivals and special events, 84–86
Firefly Cafe✕, 48
First African Baptist Church, 30
Fishing, 99–100, 148, 161
Flannery O'Conner Childhood Home, 30
Foley House Inn ⌂, 67–68
Foodstuffs, 111–112
Football, 101
Forsyth Jewelers (shop), 158
Forsyth Park, 22, 102
Forsyth Park Inn ⌂, 68–69
Fort Morris, 36
Fort Pulaski National Monument, 33
424 Ocean Point Lane ⌂, 167–168
45 Bistro✕, 48
Frankie Bones✕, 129

Fripp Island Golf & Beach Resort ⌂, 169
Fripp Island Resort ⌂, 165–166

G
Gardens, 22
Garibaldi Café✕, 48–49
Gasoline, 177
Gastonian ⌂, 69
Georgia Historical Society, 22
Ghost tours, 182–184
Gifts
Hilton Head, 158
Savannah, 107, 112–113
Girl Scout National Center, 25
Golden Bear Club at Indigo Run, 151
Golf
Beaufort, 169
Hilton Head, 118, 149–152
Savannah, 97, 100–102
Grace✕, 56
Grand Bohemian Gallery, 109
Green-Meldrim House, 22–23
Green Palm Inn ⌂, 69–70
Gullah, 134, 153, 155, 161, 169

H
Hamilton-Turner Inn ⌂, 70
Hampton Inn & Suites ⌂, 70–71
Hampton Inn-Historic District ⌂, 71
Hampton Inn on Hilton Head Island ⌂, 136
Harbour Town, 126
Harbour Town Golf Links, 151
Harold's Country Club & Grill✕, 130
Harris Baking Company✕, 49

Heavenly Spa by Westin, *154*
Henderson Golf Club, *101*
Henry C. Chambers Waterfront Park, *151*
Hilton Head & the Low Country, *122–158*
Beaufort, *158–170*
dining, *120*
Daufuskie Island, *170–172*
Edisto Island, *172–174*
Hilton Head Island, *122–158*
lodging, *120–121*
price categories, *121*
tours, *119–120*
transportation, *118–119*
when to go, *116*
Hilton Head Island, *122–158*
dining, *126, 128–133*
lodging, *133–134, 136–146*
nightlife & the arts, *155–157*
shopping, *157–158*
sightseeing, *123, 125–126*
sports & the outdoors, *147–152, 154*
transportation, *122*
Hilton Head Marriott Resort & Spa 🖫, *136–137*
Hilton Oceanfront Resort 🖫, *137*
Hilton Savannah Desoto 🖫, *80*
Historic district, *18–19, 22–33, 42–43, 46–55, 61–63, 66–78*
Historic district tours, *181–183*
Historic Inns, *17*
History, *9–10*
Hodgson Hall, *22*
Holiday Inn Historic District 🖫, *71–72*
Holiday Inn Oceanfront Resort 🖫, *137–138*
Home decor, *107, 113*

Homes, historic
Beaufort, *160–161*
Savannah, *17, 18, 19, 22–23, 25–26, 27, 28, 30*
Horseback riding, *152*
Hot Tin Roof 🖫, *142*
Hunt Club Three 🖫, *142–143*
Hunter House ✕, *56, 58*
Hunting Island Lighthouse, *161*
Hunting Island State Park, *161–162*
Hyatt Regency Savannah 🖫, *72*

I
Il Pasticcio Restaurant & Wine Bar ✕, *49*
Inn at Ellis Square 🖫, *80*
Inn at Harbour Town 🖫, *138–139*
Inn at Palmetto Bluff 🖫, *139*
Insurance, *178, 184–185*
Internet, *180*
Isaiah Davenport House, *23*

J
Jakes, John, *125*
Jazz'd Tapas Bar, *92–93*
Jepson Center Café ✕, *24*
Jepson Center for the Arts, *23–24*
Jet-skiing, *102*
Jewelry, *158*
John Mark Verdier House Museum, *160–161*
Johnny Harris ✕, *55*
Johnny Mercer Theater/ Savannah Civic Center, *86–87*
Johnson Square, *24–25*
Juliette Gordon Low Birthplace/Girls Scout National Center, *25*

K
Kehoe House 🖫, *72–73*
Kenny B's French Quarter Café ✕, *130*

L
Lady & Sons ✕, *49–50*
Lafayette, Marquis de, *25*
Lafayette Square, *25*
Lake Mayer Park, *102*
Lawton Stables, *152*
Leopold's ✕, *19, 22*
Lighthouse Inn 🖫, *81*
Lighthouses, *37–38, 126, 161*
Local 11ten ✕, *50*
Lodging, *5*
Beaufort, *164–168*
Daufuskie Island, *171*
Edisto Island, *173–174*
Hilton Head, *133–147*
price categories, *61, 121*
Savannah, *5, 17, 60–79*
Tybee Island, *79–81*
Low, Andrew, *18*
Low, Juliette Gordon, *25*
Lucas Theater, *87*
Lulu's Chocolate Bar ✕, *29*

M
Madison Square, *25*
Magnolia Spa, *103*
Mail, *180*
Main Street Inn & Spa 🖫, *139–140*
Manor, The 🖫, *143*
Mansion on Forsyth Park 🖫, *73–74*
Marine Science Center, *38*
Marshall House 🖫, *74*
Mary Calder Golf Course, *101*
May River Golf Club, *151*
Melon Bluff, *33, 36*
Mercer, Johnny, *34*
Mi Terra ✕, *131*

Michael Anthony's ✕, 130–131
Midnight in the Garden of Good and Evil, 17
Midway, 36
Mighty Eighth Air Force Heritage Museum, 36
Mitchum, Robert, 34
Money, 180–181
Monkeys, 166
Monterey Square, 30–31
Movie tours, 182
Mrs. Wilkes Dining Room ✕, 50–51
Mulberry Inn 🗊, 74
Museums
Beaufort, 159–161
Hilton Head, 123
Savannah, 22, 23–24, 25–26, 27, 28–29, 30, 31, 36, 37–38
Music clubs, 92–94

N
Nightclubs, 87–91
Nightlife and the arts
Beaufort, 169
Hilton Head, 155–157
Savannah, 17, 84–94
Noble Fare ✕, 51
North Beach Grill ✕, 58

O
O'Connor, Flannery, 30, 34
Oglethorpe Inn & Suites 🗊, 78–79
Old Fort Jackson, 36–37
Old Fort Pub ✕, 131
Old South Golf Links, 151–152
Old Sunbury, 36
Olde Harbour Inn 🗊, 74–75
Olde Pink House ✕, 27, 51–52
Outside Hilton Head (tours), 148, 158
Owens-Thomas House and Museum, 25–26

P
Palmetto Dunes Resort, 123, 125
Palmetto Dunes Tennis Center, 155
Parasailing, 102
Paris Market & Brocante, The (shop), 113
Park Lane Hotel & Suites 🗊, 140
Parking, 108, 177–178
Parks, 22, 30, 99, 102, 161–162, 172–173
Paula Deen Store, 111
Pierpont, James L., 34
Pirates House ✕, 52
Plantations, 33, 36
Planters Inn 🗊, 75
Planters Tavern, 90
Plums ✕, 163
Po' Pigs Bo-B-Q ✕, 173
Port Royal (tennis courts), 155
Port Royal Plantation, 125
Poseidon Spa, 103
Preserves, 123, 125
President's Quarters 🗊, 75–76
Price categories, 42, 61, 121
Public transportation, 179

R
Ralph Mark Gilbert Civil Rights Museum, 31
Redfish ✕, 131–132
Resort Rentals of Hilton Head Island, 141–142
ResortQuest, 141
Restaurants
American, 19, 22, 47, 48, 50, 52–53, 55, 128, 132, 133, 163
barbeque, 41
brunch, 41
Cajun-Creole, 41, 130
Caribbean, 58, 131–132
continental, 56, 131
eclectic, 43, 46–47, 48–49, 51, 54, 55, 129, 162, 163–164
French, 53–54, 128–129
Italian, 17, 41, 49, 55, 129, 130–131
lowcountry, 41
seafood, 41, 126, 128, 163, 164
southern, 12, 17, 24, 42–43, 46, 47–48, 49–50, 51–52, 54–55, 56, 58, 173
southwestern, 132
Tex-Mex, 131
Revolutionary War sites, 19, 25, 27, 30–31, 36–37
Reynolds Square, 26–27
Rhett House Inn 🗊, 166–167
River Street Inn 🗊, 76
River Street Sweets (shop), 111
Riverfront Plaza, 27
Robert Trent Jones at Palmetto Dunes, 49

S
Safety, 181
Saint Andrews Place 1 🗊, 143–144
St. Helena's Episcopal Church, 161
St. Helena's Island, 161
St. John's Episcopal Church, 32
St. Patrick's Day Parade, 86
Saltus River Grill ✕, 163–164
Sanctuary Golf Club at Cat Island, 169
Santa Fe Café ✕, 132
Sapphire Grill ✕, 52
Savannah College of Art and Design (SCAD), 10–11, 109
Savannah Day Spa, 103
Savannah Film Festival, 84–85
Savannah Folk Music Festival, 85

Savannah Historic District, *18–19, 22–33*
Savannah History Museum, *27*
Savannah Jazz Festival, *85*
Savannah Marriot Riverfront 🏨, *76–77*
Savannah Music Festival, *85–86*
Savannah Theatre, *18, 87*
Scarborough House, *28*
Sea Monkeys, *166*
Sea Pines Forest Preserve, *125*
Sea Pines Racquet Club, *155*
Sea Pines Resort, *125–126, 142*
Seabrook Village, *36*
Second African Baptist Church, *11*
700 Drayton Restaurant✕, *53*
17 Hundred 90✕, *53–64*
17th Street Inn 🏨, *81*
Sheldon Church, *173*
Sherman, William T., *9–10, 11*
Shopping
Beaufort, 170
Hilton Head, 157–158, 170
Savannah, 13, 106–114
ShopSCAD (shop), *113*
Shrimp boats, *128*
Shrimp Shack✕, *164*
Siege of Savannah site, *27*
Signe's Heaven Bound Bakery & Café✕, *132*
Skidaway Marine Science Complex, *37*
Smoking, *85*
Soho South Cafe✕, *54*
Sound Villa 1458 🏨, *144*
Southbridge Golf Club, *101–102*
Spa at Main Street Inn, *154*

Spa at Palmetto Bluffs, *154*
Spa Soleil, *154*
Spanish moss, *32*
Spas, *79, 97, 103, 136–137, 139–140, 141, 152, 154, 171*
Sports and the outdoors
Beaufort, 168–169
Daufuskie Island, 171–172
Hilton Head, 147–152
Savannah, 96–102
Squares, *12–13, 18, 19, 24–25, 26–27, 30–31, 33, 107*
Staybridge Suites 🏨, *80*
Stephen Williams House, The 🏨, *77*
Suites on Lafayette 🏨, *80*
Symbols, *5*
Synagogues, *32*

T
Taxes, *181*
Taxi travel
Hilton Head, 119
Savannah, 179
Telephones, *180*
Telfair Museum of Art, *28*
Telfair Square, *13, 28*
Temple Mickve Israel, *32*
Ten Singleton Shores 🏨, *144–145*
Tennis, *102, 118, 155*
1024 Caravel Court 🏨, *145*
Theaters, *18, 86–87*
13 Mizzenmast Court 🏨, *145–146*
37th @ Abercorn Antique & Design (shops), *108*
Thomas, *Clarence, 34*
Tipping, *181*
Tobacco shops, *114*
Toucan Café✕, *55*
Tours
Daufuskie Island, 171–172

Hilton Head, 119–120, 168
Savannah, 31, 181–184
Train travel
Hilton Head, 119
Savannah, 179
Transportation
Daufuskie Island, 171
Hilton Head, 118–119
Savannah, 176–179
Trolley tours, *182*
Truffles Cafe✕, *133*
Truffles Grill✕, *133*
Turnberry 251 🏨, *146*
Tybee Island, *37–38, 56, 58, 79–81*
dining, 56, 58
lodging, 79–81
nightlife, 92
sports and the outdoors, 98, 99, 100, 102
Tybee Island Lighthouse and Museum, *37–38*

V
Van der Meer Tennis Center/Shipyard Racquet Club, *155*
Vanilla Day Spa, *103*
Venues, *86–87*
Verizon Heritage PGA Golf Tournament, *149*
Vic's on the River✕, *54–55, 94*
Villa rentals, *141–147, 167–168*
Villamare 1402 🏨, *146*
VIP Dining Club Card, *46*
Visitor information, *116–121, 185*

W
Walking tours, *97, 183–184*
Watersports, *97*
Waving Girl Statue, *28*
Weather, *6*
Wesley, John, *26–27, 34*
Wesley Monumental Church, *32*

Westin Hilton Head Island Resort & Spa ☒, *140–141*
Westin Savannah Harbor Golf Resort & Spa ☒, *79*
When to go, *6, 117–118*

Wilmington Island Club, *102*
Windsor 2219 ☒, *147*
World War II exhibits, *36*
Wright Square, *33*
Wyndham Ocean Ridge Resort ☒, *174*

Y
York W. Bailey Museum, *161*

Z
Zeigler House Inn, The ☒, *77–78*

ABOUT OUR WRITER

Eileen Robinson Smith, a veteran Fodor's writer for more than 15 years, spent part of her childhood in South Carolina and chose to return and live there as an adult. Though Yankee born, she has always had strong Southern leanings, and her love for the Lowcountry of the Coastal South has grown with time. After living in the Caribbean for years, a hurricane blew her back to her lakeside home in Charleston in the early 1990s, where she remains. Although she still spends several months a year in the islands writing for our Caribbean and Dominican Republic guides, her home base is Charleston. Specializing in food and travel, she has contributed to such magazines as *Condé Nast Traveler*, *Caribbean Travel & Life*, *American Eagle's Latitudes*, Delta's *Sky*, and many more magazines. She is a former editor of *Charleston* magazine.